THE

Last Letter

FROM YOUR

Lover

I am going to take the job. I'll be at Platform 4 Paddington at 7:15 on Monday evening, and there is nothing in the world that would make me happier than if you would find the courage to come with me.

If you don't come, I know that whatever we might feel for each other, it isn't quite enough. I won't blame you, my darling. I know the past weeks have put an intolerable strain on you, and I feel the weight of that keenly. I hate the thought that I could cause you unhappiness.

I'll be waiting on the platform from a quarter to seven. You hold my heart, my hopes in your hands.

Your
B.

PAMELA DORMAN BOOKS
VIKING

THE

Last Letter

FROM YOUR

Lover

JOJO MOYES

VIKING
Published by the Penguin Group
Penguin Group (USA) Inc., 375 Hudson Street, New York, New York 10014, U.S.A.
Penguin Group (Canada), 90 Eglinton Avenue East, Suite 700, Toronto, Ontario, Canada M4P 2Y3
(a division of Pearson Penguin Canada Inc.)
Penguin Books Ltd, 80 Strand, London WC2R 0RL, England
Penguin Ireland, 25 St. Stephen's Green, Dublin 2, Ireland (a division of Penguin Books Ltd)
Penguin Books Australia Ltd, 250 Camberwell Road, Camberwell, Victoria 3124, Australia
(a division of Pearson Australia Group Pty Ltd)
Penguin Books India Pvt Ltd, 11 Community Centre, Panchsheel Park, New Delhi – 110 017, India
Penguin Group (NZ), 67 Apollo Drive, Rosedale, Auckland 0632, New Zealand
(a division of Pearson New Zealand Ltd)
Penguin Books (South Africa) (Pty) Ltd, 24 Sturdee Avenue, Rosebank, Johannesburg 2196,
South Africa

Penguin Books Ltd, Registered Offices: 80 Strand, London WC2R 0RL, England

First American edition
Published in 2011 by Viking Penguin, a member of Penguin Group (USA) Inc.

10 9 8 7 6 5 4 3 2 1

Copyright © Jojo Moyes, 2010
All rights reserved

A Pamela Dorman Book / Viking

LIBRARY OF CONGRESS CATALOGING IN PUBLICATION DATA
Moyes, Jojo, date.
    The last letter from your lover : a novel / Jojo Moyes.
        p. cm.
    ISBN 978-0-670-02280-9
    I. Title.
    PR6113.O94L37 2011
    823'.92—dc22   2011002023

Printed in the United States of America
Designed by Nancy Resnick

To Charles, who started it all with a paper message

Acknowledgments

Thank you to the truly excellent team at Pamela Dorman Books/ Viking, especially Pamela Dorman and Julie Miesionczek. Thanks as always to the wonderful team at Hachette in the UK: my editor, Carolyn Mays, as well as Francesca Best, Eleni Fostiropoulos, Lucy Hale, the sales team, and the fearsome copyediting skills of Hazel Orme. Thanks also all at Curtis Brown, especially my agent, Sheila Crowley, Sarah Lewis, and Tally Garner. My gratitude goes to the British Newspaper Library at Colindale, a wonderful resource for writers seeking to immerse themselves in another world.

I would like to acknowledge Jeanette Winterson, the Estate of F. Scott Fitzgerald, and the University Press of New England for allowing me to reproduce the literary correspondence used in some versions of this book.

Thank you, in no particular order, to Brigid Coady, Suzanne Parry, Kate Lord Brown, Danuta Kean, Louise McKee, Suzanne Hirsh, and Fiona Veacock. Other thanks are due to my parents, Jim Moyes and Lizzie Sanders, and Brian Sanders, and to the Writers-block board, a constant source of support, encouragement, and time-wasting.

Greatest thanks—and love—go to my family, Charles, Saskia, Harry, and Lockie.

Part 1

Chapter 1

OCTOBER 1960

"She's waking up."

There was a swishing sound, a chair was dragged, then the brisk click of curtain rings meeting. Two voices murmuring.

"I'll fetch Dr. Hargreaves."

A brief silence followed, during which she slowly became aware of a different layer of sound—voices, muffled by distance, a car passing: it seemed, oddly, as if it were some way below her. She lay absorbing it, letting it crystallize, letting her mind play catch-up, as she recognized each for what it was.

It was at this point that she became aware of the pain. It forced its way upward in exquisite stages: first her arm, a sharp, burning sensation from elbow to shoulder, then her head: dull, relentless. The rest of her body ached, as it had done when she . . .

When she . . . ?

"He'll be along in two ticks. He says to close the blinds."

Her mouth was so dry. She closed her lips and swallowed painfully. She wanted to ask for some water, but the words wouldn't come. She opened her eyes a little. Two indistinct shapes moved around her. Every time she thought she had worked out what they were, they moved again. Blue. They were blue.

"You know who's just come in downstairs, don't you?"

One of the voices dropped. "That singer. The one who looks like Paul Newman."

"I thought I heard something on the wireless about it. Lend me your thermometer, will you, Vi, mine's acting up again."

"I'm going to try and have a peek at him at lunchtime. Matron's had newspapermen outside all morning. I'll wager she's at her wits' end."

She couldn't understand what they were saying. The pain in her head had become a thumping, rushing sound, building in volume and intensity until all she could do was close her eyes again and wait for it, or her, to go away. Then the white came in, like a tide, to envelop her. With some gratitude she let out a silent breath and allowed herself to sink back into its embrace.

"Are you awake, dear? You have a visitor."

There was a flickering reflection above her, a phantasm that moved briskly, first one way and then another. She had a sudden recollection of her first wristwatch, the way she had reflected sunlight through its glass casing onto the ceiling of the playroom, sending it backward and forward, making her little dog bark.

The blue was there again. She saw it move, accompanied by the swishing. And then there was a hand on her wrist, a brief spark of pain so that she yelped.

"A little more carefully with that side, Nurse," the voice chided. "She felt that."

"I'm terribly sorry, Dr. Hargreaves."

"The arm will require further surgery. We've pinned it in several places, but it's not there yet."

A dark shape hovered near her feet. She willed it to solidify, but, like the blue shapes, it refused to do so, and she let her eyes close.

"You can sit with her, if you like. Talk to her. She'll be able to hear you."

"How are her . . . other injuries?"

"There'll be some scarring, I'm afraid. Especially on that arm. And she took quite a blow to the head, so it may be a while before she's herself again. But given the severity of the accident, I think we can say she's had a rather lucky escape."

There was a brief silence.

"Yes."

Someone had placed a bowl of fruit beside her. She had opened her eyes again, her gaze settling on it, letting the shape, the color, solidify until she grasped, with a stab of satisfaction, that she could identify what was there. *Grapes*, she said. And again, rolling the silent word around the inside of her head: *grapes*. It felt important, as if it were anchoring her in this new reality.

And then, as quickly as they had come, they were gone, obliterated by the dark blue mass that had settled beside her. As it moved closer, she could just make out the faint scent of tobacco. The voice, when it came, was tentative, perhaps a little embarrassed, even. "Jennifer? Jennifer? Can you hear me?" The words were so loud; strangely intrusive.

"Jenny, dear, it's me."

She wondered if they would let her see the grapes again. It seemed necessary that she did; blooming, purple, solid. Familiar.

"Are you sure she can hear me?"

"Quite sure, but she may find communicating rather exhausting to begin with."

There was some murmuring that she couldn't make out. Or perhaps she just stopped trying.

Nothing seemed clear. "Can . . . you . . . ," she whispered.

"But her mind wasn't damaged? In the crash? You know that there will be no . . . lasting . . . ?"

"As I said, she took a good bump to the head, but there were no medical signs for alarm." The sound of shuffled papers. "No fracture. No swelling to the brain. But these things are always a little unpredictable, and patients are affected quite differently. So, you'll just need to be a little—"

"Please . . ." Her voice was a murmur, barely audible.

"Dr. Hargreaves! I do believe she's trying to speak."

". . . want to see . . ."

A face swam down to her. "Yes?"

". . . want to see . . ." *The grapes,* she was begging. *I just want to see those grapes again.*

"She wants to see her husband!" The nurse sprang upward as she announced this triumphantly. "I think she wants to see her husband."

There was a pause, then someone stooped toward her. "I'm here, dear. Everything is . . . everything's fine."

The body retreated, and she heard the pat of a hand on a back. "There, you see? She's getting back to herself already. All in good time, eh?" A man's voice again. "Nurse? Go and ask Sister to organize some food for tonight. Nothing too substantial. Something light and easy to swallow. . . . Perhaps you could fetch us a cup of tea while you're there." She heard footsteps, low voices, as they continued to talk beside her. Her last thought as the light closed in again was, Husband?

Later, when they told her how long she had been in the hospital, she could barely believe it. Time had become fragmented, unmanageable, arriving and departing in chaotic clumps of hours. It was Tuesday breakfast. Now it was Wednesday lunchtime. She had apparently slept for eighteen hours—this was said with some disapproval, as if there were an implied rudeness in being absent for so long. And then it was Friday. Again.

Sometimes when she woke it was dark, and she would push her head up a little against the starched white pillow and watch the soothing movements of the ward at night; the soft-shoe shuffle of the nurses moving up and down the corridors, the occasional murmur of conversation between nurse and patient. She could watch television in the evenings if she liked, the nurses told her. Her husband was paying for private care—she could have almost anything she liked. She always said, No, thank you: she was confused enough by the unsettling torrent of information without the endless chatter of the box in the corner.

As the periods of wakefulness stretched and grew in number, she became familiar with the faces of the other women on the little ward. The older woman in the room to her right, whose jet-black hair was pinned immaculately in a rigid, sprayed sculpture upon her head, her features fixed in an expression of mild, surprised disappointment. She had apparently been in a moving picture when she was young, and would deign to tell any new nurse about it. She had a commanding voice, and few visitors. There was the plump young woman in the room opposite, who cried quietly in the early hours of the morning. A brisk, older woman—a nanny perhaps?—brought young children in to see her for an hour every evening. The two boys would climb onto the bed, clutching at her, until the nanny told them to get down for fear they would "do your mother an injury."

The nurses told her the other women's names, and occasionally their own, but she couldn't remember them. They were disappointed in her, she suspected.

Your Husband, as everyone referred to him, came most evenings. He wore a well-cut suit, dark blue or gray serge, gave her a perfunctory kiss on the cheek, and usually sat at the foot of her bed. He would make small talk solicitously, asking how she was finding the food, whether she would like him to have anything else sent along. Occasionally he would simply read a newspaper.

He was a handsome man, perhaps ten years older than she was, with a high, noble forehead and serious, hooded eyes. She knew, at some deep level, that he must be who he said he was, that she was married to him, but it was perplexing to feel nothing when everyone so obviously expected a different reaction. Sometimes she would stare at him when he wasn't looking, waiting for some jolt of familiarity to kick in. Sometimes, when she woke, she would find him sitting there, newspaper lowered, gazing at her as if he felt something similar.

Dr. Hargreaves, the attending physician, came daily, checking her charts, asking if she could tell him the day, the time, her name. She always got those right now. She even managed to tell him the prime minister was Mr. Macmillan and her age, twenty-seven. But she struggled with newspaper headlines, with events that had taken place before she arrived here. "It will come," he would say, patting her hand. "Don't try to force it, there's a good girl."

And then there was her mother, who brought little gifts—soap, nice shampoo, magazines—as if they would nudge her into a semblance of who she apparently used to be. "We've all been so worried, Jenny darling," she said, laying a cool hand on her head. It felt nice. Not familiar, but nice. Occasionally her mother would begin to say something, then mutter, "I mustn't tire you out with questions. Everything will come back. That's what the doctors say. So you mustn't worry."

She wasn't worried, Jenny wanted to tell her. It was quite peaceful in her little bubble. She just felt a vague sadness that she couldn't be the person everyone evidently expected her to be. It was at this point, when the thoughts got too confusing, that she would invariably fall asleep again.

They finally told her she was going home on a morning so crisp that the trails of smoke broke into the blue sky above the capital like a spindly forest. By then she could walk around the ward occasionally, swapping magazines with the other patients, who would be chatting to the nurses, sometimes listening to the wireless, if they felt so inclined. She had had a second operation on her arm and it was healing well, they told her, although the long red scar where the plate had been inserted made her wince, and she tried to keep it hidden under a long sleeve. Her eyes had been tested, her hearing checked; her skin had healed after the myriad scratches caused by fragments of glass. The bruises had faded, and her broken rib and collarbone had knitted well enough for her to lie in a variety of positions without pain.

To all intents and purposes, she looked, they claimed, like "her old self," as if saying it enough times might make her remember who that was. Her mother, meanwhile, spent hours rummaging through piles of black-and-white photographs so that she could reflect Jennifer's life back at her.

She learned that she had been married for four years. There were no children—from her mother's lowered voice, she guessed this was a source of some disappointment to everyone. She lived in a very smart house in a very good part of London, with a housekeeper and a driver, and plenty of young ladies would apparently give their eyeteeth to have half of what she had. Her husband was something big in mining and was often away, although his devotion was such that he had put off several very important trips since the accident. From the deference with which the medical staff spoke to him, she guessed he was indeed quite important and, by extension, that she might expect a degree of respect, too, even if it felt nonsensical to her.

Nobody had said much about how she had got there, although she had once sneaked a look at the doctor's notes and knew that she had been in a car accident. On the one occasion she had pressed her mother about what had happened, she had gone quite pink and, placing her plump little hand on Jennifer's, had urged her "not to dwell on it, dear. It's all been . . . terribly upsetting." Her eyes had filled with tears, and not wanting to upset her, Jennifer had moved on.

A chatty girl with a bright orange helmet of hair came from another part of the hospital to trim and set Jennifer's hair. This, the young woman told her, would make her feel a lot better. Jennifer had lost a little hair at the back of her head—it had been shaved off for a wound to be stitched—and the girl announced that she was a wonder at hiding such injuries.

A little more than an hour later she held up a mirror with a flourish. Jennifer stared at the girl who stared back at her. Quite pretty, she thought, with a kind of distant satisfaction. Bruised, a little pale, but an agreeable face. My face, she corrected herself.

"Do you have your cosmetics on hand?" the hairdresser said. "I could do your face for you, if your arm's still sore. Bit of lipstick will brighten any face, madam. That and some Pan-Cake."

Jennifer kept staring at the mirror. "Do you think I should?"

"Oh, yes. A pretty girl like you. I can make it very subtle . . . but it'll put a glow into your cheeks. Hold on, I'll pop downstairs and get my kit. I've got some lovely colors from Paris, and a Charles of the Ritz lipstick that'll be perfect on you."

"Well, don't you look fetching? It's good to see a lady with her makeup on. Shows us that you're a little more on top of things," Dr. Hargreaves said on his rounds, some time later. "Looking forward to going home, are we?"

"Yes, thank you," she said politely. She had no idea how to convey to him that she didn't know what that home was.

He studied her face for a moment, perhaps gauging her uncertainty. Then he sat on the side of her bed and laid a hand on her shoulder. "I understand it must all seem a little disconcerting, that you might not feel quite yourself yet, but don't be too concerned if lots of things are unclear. It's quite common to get amnesia after a head injury.

"You have a very supportive family, and I'm sure once you're surrounded by familiar things, your old routines, friends, shopping trips, and the like, you'll find that it's all popping back into place."

She nodded obediently. She had worked out pretty quickly that everyone seemed happier if she did so.

"Now, I'd like you to come back in a week so that I can check the progress of that arm. You'll need some physiotherapy to recover the full use of it. But the main thing is simply for you to rest and not worry too much about anything. Do you understand?"

He was already preparing to leave. What else could she say?

Her husband picked her up shortly before teatime. The nurses had lined up in the downstairs reception area to say good-bye to her, bright as pins in their starched pinafores. She still felt curiously weak and unsteady on her feet, and was grateful for the arm that he held out to her.

"Thank you for the care you've shown my wife. Send the bill to my office, if you would," he said to the Sister.

"Our pleasure," she said, shaking his hand and beaming at Jennifer. "It's lovely seeing her up and about again. You look wonderful, Mrs. Stirling."

"I feel . . . much better. Thank you." She was wearing a long cashmere coat and a matching pillbox hat. He had arranged for three outfits to be sent over for her. She had chosen the most muted; she didn't want to draw attention to herself.

They glanced up as Dr. Hargreaves put his head out of an office. "My secretary says there are some newspapermen outside. You might wish to leave by the back entrance if you want to avoid any fuss."

"That would be preferable. Would you mind sending my driver round?"

After weeks in the warmth of the ward the air was shockingly cold. She struggled to keep up with him, her breath coming in short bursts, and then she was in the back of a large black car, engulfed by the huge leather seats, and the doors closed with an expensive clunk. The car moved off into the London traffic with a low purr.

She peered out of the window, watching the newspapermen, just visible on the front steps, and muffled photographers comparing lenses. Beyond, the central London streets were thick with people hurrying past, their collars turned up against the wind, men with trilbies pulled low over their brows.

"Who was the singer?" she said, turning to face him.

He was muttering something to the driver. "Who?"

"A singer. Apparently he'd been in some kind of accident."

"I have no idea who you are talking about."

"They were all talking about him. The nurses, at the hospital."

"Oh. Yes. I think I read something." He appeared to have lost interest. "I'll be dropping Mrs. Stirling back at the house, and once she's settled I'll be going on to the office," he was saying to the driver.

"What happened to him?" she said.

"Who?"

"The singer."

Her husband looked at her, as if he was weighing something up. "He died," he said. Then he turned back to his driver.

She walked slowly up the steps to the white stucco house and the door opened, as if by magic, as she reached the top. The driver placed her valise carefully in the hallway and retreated. Her husband, behind her, nodded to a woman who was standing in the hallway, apparently to greet them. She was in late middle age; her dark hair was pulled back into a tight chignon, and she was dressed in a navy two-piece. "Welcome home, madam," she said, reaching out a hand. Her smile was genuine, and she spoke in heavily accented English. "We are so very glad to have you well again."

"Thank you," she said. She wanted to use the woman's name, but felt uncomfortable asking it.

The woman waited to take their coats, and disappeared along the hall with them.

"Are you feeling tired?" He dipped his head to study her face.

"No. No, I'm fine." She gazed around her at the house, wishing she could disguise her dismay that she might as well have never seen it before.

"I must go back to the office now. Will you be all right with Mrs. Cordoza?"

Cordoza. It wasn't entirely unfamiliar. She felt a little surge of gratitude. *Mrs. Cordoza.* "I'll be quite all right, thank you. Please don't worry about me."

"I'll be back at seven . . . if you're sure you're fine . . ." He was clearly keen to leave. He stooped, kissed her cheek, and, after a brief hesitation, was gone.

She stood in the hallway, hearing his footsteps fade down the steps outside, the soft hum of the engine as his great car pulled away. The house seemed suddenly cavernous.

She touched the silk-lined wallpaper, took in the polished parquet flooring, the vertiginously high ceilings. She removed her gloves, with precise, deliberate motions. Then she leaned forward for a closer look at the photographs on the hall table. The largest was a wedding picture, framed in ornate, highly polished silver. And there she was, wearing a fitted white dress, her face half masked by a white lace veil, her husband smiling broadly at her side. *I really did marry him,* she thought. And then: *I look so happy.*

She jumped. Mrs. Cordoza had come up behind her and was standing there, her hands clasped in front of her. "I was wondering if you would like me to bring you some tea. I thought you might like to take it in the drawing room. I've laid a fire in there for you."

"That would be . . ." Jennifer peered down the hallway at the various doors. Then she looked back at the photograph. A moment passed before she spoke again. "Mrs. Cordoza . . . would you mind letting me take your arm? Just till I sit down. I'm feeling a little unsteady on my feet."

Afterward she wasn't sure why she didn't want the woman to know quite how little she remembered about the layout of her own house. It just seemed to her that if she could pretend, and everyone else believed it, what was an act might end up being true.

The housekeeper had prepared supper: a casserole, with potatoes and fine French beans. She had left it in the bottom oven, she told Jennifer. Jennifer had had to wait for her husband to return before she could put anything on the table: her right arm was still weak, and she was afraid of dropping the heavy cast-iron pot.

She had spent the hour when she was alone walking around the vast house, familiarizing herself with it, opening drawers and studying photographs. My house, she told herself over and over. My things. My husband. Once or twice she let her mind go blank and her feet carry her to where she thought a bathroom or study might be, and was gratified to discover that some part of her still knew this place. She gazed at the books in the drawing room, noting, with a kind of mild satisfaction, that while so much was strange she could mentally recite the plots of many.

She lingered longest in her bedroom. Mrs. Cordoza had unpacked her suitcase and put everything away. Two built-in cupboards opened to reveal great quantities of immaculately stored clothes. Everything fitted her perfectly, even the most well-worn shoes. Her hairbrush, perfumes, and powders were lined up on a dressing table. The scents met her skin with a pleasant familiarity. The colors of the cosmetics suited her: Coty, Chanel, Elizabeth Arden, Dorothy Gray—her mirror was surrounded by a small battalion of expensive creams and unguents.

She pulled open a drawer, held up layers of chiffon, brassieres, and other foundation garments made of silk and lace. I am a woman to whom appearances matter, she observed. She sat and stared at herself in the three-sided mirror, then began to brush her hair with long, steady strokes. *This is what I do*, she said to herself, several times.

In the few moments when she felt overwhelmed by strangeness, she busied herself with small tasks: rearranging the towels in the downstairs cloakroom, putting out plates and glasses.

He arrived back shortly before seven. She was waiting for him in the hall, her makeup fresh and a light spray of scent over her neck and shoulders. She could see it pleased him, this semblance of normality. She took his coat, hung it in the cupboard, and asked if he would like a drink.

"That would be lovely. Thank you," he said.

She hesitated, one hand poised on a decanter.

Turning, he saw her indecision. "Yes, that's it, darling. Whiskey. Two fingers, with ice. Thank you."

At supper, he sat on her right at the large, polished mahogany table, a great expanse of which was empty and unadorned. She ladled the steaming food onto plates, and he placed them at each setting. *This is my life*, she found herself thinking, as she watched his hands move. *This is what we do in the evenings.*

"I thought we might have the Moncrieffs to dinner on Friday. Might you be up to it?"

She took a little bite from her fork. "I think so."

"Good." He nodded. "Our friends have been asking after you. They would like to see that you're . . . back to your old self."

She raised a smile. "That will be . . . nice."

"I thought we probably wouldn't do too much for a week or two. Just till you're up to it."

"Yes."

"This is very good. Did you make it?"

"No. It was Mrs. Cordoza."

"Ah."

They ate in silence. She drank water—Dr. Hargreaves had advised against anything stronger—but she envied her husband the glass in front of him. She would have liked to blur the disconcerting strangeness, to take the edge off it.

"And how are things at . . . your office?"

His head was down. "All fine. I'll have to visit the mines in the next couple of weeks, but I'll want to be sure that you can manage before I go. You'll have Mrs. Cordoza to help, of course."

She felt faint relief at the thought of being alone. "I'm sure I'll be all right."

"And afterward I thought we might go to the Riviera for a couple of weeks. I have some business there, and the sun might do you good. Dr. Hargreaves said it might help your . . . the scarring . . ." His voice faded.

"The Riviera," she echoed. A sudden vision of a moonlit seafront. Laughter. The clinking of glasses. She closed her eyes, willing the fleeting image to become clear.

"I thought we might drive down, this time, just the two of us."

It was gone. She could hear her pulse in her ears. *Stay calm*, she told herself. *It will all come. Dr. Hargreaves said it would.*

"You always seem happy there. Perhaps a little happier there than in London." He glanced up at her and then away.

There it was again, the feeling that she was being tested. She forced herself to chew and swallow. "Whatever you think best," she said quietly.

The room fell silent but for the slow scraping of his cutlery on his plate, an oppressive sound. Her food suddenly appeared insurmountable. "Actually, I'm more tired than I thought. Would you mind terribly if I went upstairs?"

He stood as she got to her feet. "I should have told Mrs. Cordoza a kitchen supper would suffice. Would you like me to help you up?"

"Please, don't fuss." She waved away the offer of his arm. "I'm just a little tired. I'm sure I'll be much better in the morning."

At a quarter to ten she heard him enter the room. She had lain in the bed, acutely aware of the sheets around her, the moonlight that sliced through the long curtains, the distant sounds of traffic in the square, of taxis slowing to disgorge their occupants, a polite greeting from someone walking a dog. She had kept very still, waiting for something to click into place, for the ease with which she had fitted back into her physical environment to seep into her mind.

And then the door had opened.

He did not turn on the light. She heard the soft clash of wooden hangers as he hung up his jacket, the soft vacuum *thuck* of his shoes being pulled from his feet. And suddenly she was rigid. Her husband— this man, this stranger—was going to climb into her bed. She had been so focused on getting through each moment that she hadn't considered it. She had half expected him to sleep in the spare room.

She bit down on her lip, her eyes shut tight, forcing her breathing to stay slow, in semblance of sleep. She heard him disappear into the bathroom, the sluice of the tap, vigorous brushing of teeth and a brief gargle. His feet padded back across the carpeted floor, and then he was sliding between the covers, causing the mattress to dip and the bedstead to creak in protest. For a minute he lay there, and she fought to maintain her even breaths. *Oh, please, not yet,* she willed him. *I hardly know you.*

"Jenny?" he said.

She felt his hand on her hip, forced herself not to flinch.

He moved it tentatively. "Jenny?"

She made herself let out a long breath, conveying the blameless oblivion of deep sleep. She felt him pause, his hand still, and then, with a sigh of his own, he lay back heavily on his pillows.

Chapter 2

Moira Parker regarded the grim set of her boss's jawline, the determined way in which he strode through her office to his own, and thought it was probably a good thing that Mr. Arbuthnot, his two-thirty, was late. Clearly the last meeting had not gone well.

She stood up, smoothing her skirt, and took his coat, which was speckled with rain from the short walk between his car and the office. She placed his umbrella in the stand, then took a moment longer than usual to hang the coat carefully on the hook. She had worked for him long enough now to judge when he needed a little time alone.

She poured him a cup of tea—he always had a cup of tea in the afternoons, two cups of coffee in the mornings—collected up her papers with an economy born of years' practice, then knocked on his door and walked in. "I suspect Mr. Arbuthnot has been held up in traffic. Apparently there's a big jam on the Marylebone Road."

He was reading the letters she had left on his desk earlier for his signature. Evidently satisfied, he took his pen from his breast pocket and signed with short, abrupt strokes. She placed his tea on his desk and folded the letters into her pile of papers. "I've picked up the tickets for your flight to South Africa, and arranged for you to be collected at the airport."

"That's the fifteenth."

"Yes. I'll bring them through if you'd like to check the paperwork. Here are the sales figures for last week. The latest wage totals are in this folder here. And as I wasn't sure you would have had time for lunch after the car manufacturers' meeting, I've taken the liberty of ordering you some sandwiches. I hope that's acceptable."

"Very kind, Moira. Thank you."

"Would you like them now? With your tea?"

He nodded and smiled at her briefly. She did her best not to color. She knew the other secretaries mocked her for what they considered her overattentive manner with her boss, not to mention her prim clothes and slightly stiff way of doing things. But he was a man who liked things done properly, and she had always understood that. Those silly girls, with their heads always stuck in a magazine, their endless gossiping in the ladies' cloakroom, they didn't understand the inherent pleasure in a job well done. They didn't understand the satisfaction of being indispensable.

She hesitated briefly, then pulled the last letter from her folder. "The second post has arrived. I thought you should probably see this. It's another of those letters about the men at Rochdale."

His eyebrows lowered, which killed the small smile that had illuminated his face. He read the letter twice. "Has anyone else seen this?"

"No, sir."

"File it with the others." He thrust it at her. "It's all troublemaking stuff. The unions are behind it. I won't have any truck with them."

She took it wordlessly. She made as if to leave, then turned back. "And may I ask . . . how is your wife? Glad to be back at home, I should say."

"She's fine, thank you. Much—much more her old self," he said. "It's been a great help for her to be at home."

She swallowed. "I'm very pleased to hear it."

His attention was already elsewhere—he was flicking through the sales figures she had left for him. Her smile still painted on her face, Moira Parker clasped her paperwork to her chest and marched back out to her desk.

Old friends, he had said. Nothing too challenging. Two of those friends were familiar now, having visited Jennifer in the hospital and again once she had returned home. Yvonne Moncrieff, an elongated, dark-haired woman in her early thirties, had been her friend since they had become close neighbors in Medway Square. She had a dry, sardonic manner, which stood in direct contrast to that of the other friend, Violet, whom Yvonne had known at school and who seemed to accept the other's cutting humor and droll put-downs as her due.

Jennifer had struggled initially to catch the shared references, to gauge any significance from the names they bandied between them, but she had felt at ease in their company. She was learning to trust her gut reactions to people: memories could be lodged in places other than the mind.

"I wish I could lose my memory," Yvonne had said, when Jennifer confessed how strange she had felt on waking up in the hospital. "I'd walk off into the sunset. Forget I ever married Francis in the first place." She had popped over to reassure Jennifer that all was in order. It was to be a "quiet" dinner party, but as the afternoon had worn on, Jennifer had become almost paralyzed with nerves.

"I don't know why you're flapping, darling. Your parties are legendary." She perched on the bed, as Jennifer wriggled in and out of a succession of dresses.

"Yes. But for what?" She tried to rearrange her bust inside a dress. She seemed to have lost a little weight in the hospital, and the front puckered unattractively.

Yvonne laughed. "Oh, relax. You don't have to do a thing, Jenny. The marvelous Mrs. C will have done you proud. The house looks beautiful. You look stunning. Or, at least, you will if you put some damned clothes on." She kicked off her shoes and lifted her long, elegant legs onto the bed. "I've never understood your enthusiasm for entertaining. Don't get me wrong, I do love going to parties, but all that organizing." She was examining her nails. "Parties are for going to, not for having. That's what my mother said, and frankly, it still stands. I'll buy myself a new dress or two, but canapés and seating plans? Ugh."

Jennifer wrestled the neckline into shape and stared at herself in the mirror, turning to the left, then the right. She held out her arm. The scar was raised and still angrily pink. "Do you think I should wear long sleeves?"

Yvonne sat up and peered at her. "Does it hurt?"

"My whole arm aches, and the doctor gave me some pills. I just wondered whether the scar would be a bit . . ."

"Distracting?" Yvonne's nose wrinkled. "You probably would do better in long sleeves, darling. Just until it fades a little. And it's so cold."

Jennifer was startled by her friend's blunt assessment but not offended. It was the first straightforward thing anyone had said to her since she had come home.

She stepped out of the dress, went to her wardrobe, and rifled through it until she found a sheath in raw silk. She pulled it off the rail and gazed at it. It was so flashy. Since she had been at home she had wanted to hide in tweed, subtle grays and brown, yet these jeweled dresses kept leaping out at her. "Is this the kind of thing?" she said.

"What kind of thing?"

Jennifer took a deep breath. "That I used to wear? Is this how I used to look?" She held the dress against herself.

Yvonne pulled a cigarette from her bag and lit it, studying Jennifer's face. "Are you telling me you really don't remember anything?"

Jennifer sat on the stool in front of her dressing table. "Pretty much," she admitted. "I know I know you. Just like I know him. I can feel it here." She tapped her chest. "But it's . . . there are huge gaps. I don't remember how I felt about my life. I don't know how I'm meant to behave with anyone. I don't . . ." She chewed the side of her lip. "I don't know who I am." Unexpectedly her eyes filled with tears. She pulled open one drawer, then another, searching for a handkerchief.

Yvonne waited a moment. Then she stood up, walked over, and sat down with her on the narrow stool. "All right, darling, I'll fill you in. You're lovely and funny and full of joie de vivre. You have the perfect life, the rich, handsome husband who adores you, and a wardrobe any woman would die for. Your hair is always perfect. Your waist is the span of a man's hand. You're always the center of any social gathering, and all our husbands are secretly in love with you."

"Oh, don't be ridiculous."

"I'm not. Francis adores you. Whenever he sees your minxy little smile, those blond tresses of yours, I can see him wondering why on earth he married this lanky, cranky old Jewess. As for Bill . . ."

"Bill?"

"Violet's husband. Before you were married, he virtually followed you around like a lapdog. It's a good job he's so terrified of your husband, or he would have made off with you under his arm years ago."

Jennifer wiped at her eyes with a handkerchief. "You're being very kind."

"Not at all. If you weren't so nice, I'd have to have you bumped off. But you're lucky. I like you."

They sat together for a few minutes. Jennifer rubbed at a spot on the carpet with her toe. "Why don't I have children?"

Yvonne took a long drag on her cigarette. She glanced at Jennifer and arched her eyebrows. "The last time we spoke about it, you remarked that to have children it's usually advisable for husband and wife to be on the same continent for a while. He's away an awful lot, your husband." She smirked, exhaled a perfect smoke ring. "It's one of the other reasons I've always been horribly envious of you." As Jennifer gave a reluctant chuckle, she continued, "Oh, you'll be fine, darling. You should do what that ridiculously expensive doctor said and stop fretting. You'll probably have some eureka moment in a couple of weeks and remember everything—disgusting snoring husband, the state of the economy, the awful size of your account in Harvey Nichols. In the meantime, enjoy your innocence while it lasts."

"I suppose you're right."

"And having said that, I think you should wear the rose pink thing. You have a quartz necklace that goes fabulously with it. The emerald doesn't do you any favors. It makes your bust look like two deflated balloons."

"Oh, you are a friend!" Jennifer said, and the two began to laugh.

The door had slammed, and he had dropped his briefcase on the hall floor, the chill air of outside on his overcoat and skin. He took off his scarf, kissed Yvonne, and apologized for his lateness. "Accountants' meeting. You know how these money men go on."

"Oh, you should see them when they get together, Larry. Bores me to tears. We've been married five years, and I still couldn't tell you the difference between a debit and a credit." Yvonne checked her watch. "He should be here soon. No doubt some unmissable column of figures to wave his magic wand over."

He faced his wife. "You look very fetching, Jenny."

"Doesn't she? Your wife always scrubs up rather well."

"Yes. Yes, indeed. Right." He ran a hand across his jawline. "If you'll both excuse me, I'll go and freshen up before our other guests arrive. I don't suppose one of you ladies could pour me a whiskey? Two fingers, no ice?"

"We'll have a drink waiting for you," Yvonne called.

By the time the door opened a second time, Jennifer's nerves had been dulled by a potent cocktail. *It will be fine*, she kept telling herself. Yvonne would step in with prompts if she was about to make a fool of herself. These were her friends. They wouldn't be waiting for her to trip up. They were another step to bringing her back to herself.

"Jenny. Thank you so much for asking us." Violet Fairclough gave her a hug, her plump face almost submerged in a turban. She unpinned it from her head and handed it over with her coat. She was wearing a scoop-necked silk dress, which strained like a wind-filled parachute around her ample contours. Violet's waist, as Yvonne would later remark, would require the hands of a small infantry company to span it.

"Jennifer. A picture of loveliness, as always." A tall, redheaded man stooped to kiss her.

Jennifer was astonished by the unlikeliness of this coupling. She didn't remember the man at all, and found it almost funny that he should be little Violet's husband. "Do come through," she said, tearing her eyes off him and recovering her composure. "My husband will be down in a few minutes. Let me get you a drink in the meantime."

"'My husband,' eh? Are we terribly formal this evening?" Bill laughed.

"Well . . ." Jennifer faltered. ". . . as it's been so long since I've seen you all . . ."

"Beast. You've got to be kind to Jenny." Yvonne kissed him. "She's still terribly fragile. She should be reclining upstairs consumptively while we select one man at a time to peel her a grape. But she would insist on martinis."

"Now that's the Jenny we know and love." Bill's smile of appreciation was so lingering that Jennifer glanced twice at Violet to make sure she wasn't offended. She didn't seem to mind: she was rummaging in her handbag. "I've left your number with the new nanny, Jenny," she said, glancing up. "I hope you don't mind. She really is the most useless woman. I fully expect her to be calling here at any minute to say she can't get Frederick's pajama bottoms on or some such."

Jennifer caught Bill rolling his eyes and, with a flash of dismay, realized that the gesture was familiar to her.

There were eight around the table, her husband and Francis at either end. Yvonne, Dominic, who was quite high up in the Horse Guards, and Jennifer sat along the window side, with Violet, Bill, and Anne, Dominic's wife, opposite. Anne was a cheerful sort, guffawing at the men's jokes with a benign twinkle in her eye that spoke of a woman comfortable in her skin.

Jennifer found herself watching them as they ate, analyzing and examining with forensic detail the things they said to each other, seeking out the clues to their past life. Bill, she noted, rarely looked at his wife, let alone addressed her. Violet seemed oblivious to this, and Jennifer wondered whether she was unaware of his indifference or just stoic in hiding her embarrassment.

Yvonne, for all her joking complaints about Francis, watched him constantly. She delivered her jokes at his expense while directing at him a smile of challenge. This is how they are together, Jennifer thought. She won't show him how much he means to her.

"I wish I'd put my money in refrigerators," Francis was saying. "The newspaper said this morning that there should be a million of the things sold in Britain this year. A million! Five years ago that was . . . a hundred and seventy thousand."

"In America it must be ten times that. I hear people exchange them every couple of years." Violet speared a piece of fish. "And they're huge—double the size of ours. Can you imagine?"

"Everything in America is bigger. Or so they love to tell us."

"Including the egos, judging by the ones I've come up against." Dominic's voice lifted. "You have not met an insufferable know-all until you've met a Yank general."

Anne was laughing. "Poor old Dom was a bit put out when one tried to tell him how to drive his own car."

" 'Say, your quarters are pretty small. These vehicles are pretty small. Your rations are pretty small . . .' " Dominic mimicked. "They should have seen what it was like with rationing. Of course, they have no idea—"

"Dom thought he'd have some fun with him and borrowed my mother's Morris Minor. Picked him up in it. You should have seen his face."

" 'Standard issue over here, chum,' I told him. 'For visiting dignitaries we use the Vauxhall Velox. Gives you that extra three inches of leg room.' He virtually had to fold himself in two to fit inside."

"I was howling with laughter," said Anne. "I don't know how Dom didn't end up in the most awful trouble."

"How's business, Larry? I hear you're off to Africa again in a week or so."

Jennifer watched her husband settle back in his seat.

"Good. Very good, in fact. I've just signed a deal with a certain motor company to manufacture brake linings." He placed his knife and fork together on his plate.

"What exactly is it you do? I'm never quite sure what this new-fangled mineral you're using is."

"Don't pretend to be interested, Violet," Bill said, from the other side of the table. "Violet's rarely interested in anything that isn't pink or blue or starts a sentence with 'Mama.' "

"Perhaps, Bill, darling, that simply means there isn't enough stimulation for her at home," Yvonne parried, and the men whistled exuberantly.

Laurence Stirling had turned toward Violet. "It's not actually a new mineral at all," he was saying. "It's been around since the days of the Romans. Did you study the Romans at school?"

"I certainly did. I can't remember anything about them now, of course." Her laugh was shrill.

Laurence's voice dropped, and the table hushed, the better to hear him. "Well, Pliny the Elder wrote about how he had seen a piece of cloth thrown into a banqueting-hall fire and brought out again minutes later without a scrap of damage. Some people thought it was witchcraft, but he knew this was something extraordinary." He pulled a pen from his pocket, leaned forward, and scribbled on his damask napkin. He pushed it round for her to see better. "The name chrysotile, the most common form, is derived from the Greek words *chrysos*, which means 'gold,' and *tilos*, 'fiber.' Even then they knew it had terrific value. All I do—my company, I mean—is mine it and mold it into a variety of uses."

"You put out fires."

"Yes." He looked thoughtfully at his hands. "Or I make sure they don't start in the first place." In the brief silence that followed, an atmosphere fell over the table. He glanced at Jennifer, then away.

"So where's the big money, old chap? Not flameproof tablecloths."

"Car parts." He sat back in his chair, and the room seemed to relax with him. "They say that within ten years most households in Britain will have a car. That's an awful lot of brake linings. And we're in talks with the railways and the airlines. But the uses of white asbestos are pretty limitless. We've branched out into guttering, farm buildings, sheeting, insulation. Soon it'll be everywhere."

"The wonder mineral indeed."

He was at ease as he discussed his business with his friends in a way that he had not been when the two of them were alone, Jennifer thought. It must have been strange for him, too, to have her so badly injured, and even now not quite herself. She thought of Yvonne's description of her that afternoon: gorgeous, poised, *minxy*. Was he missing that woman? Perhaps conscious that she was watching him, he turned his head and caught her eye. She smiled, and after a moment, he smiled back.

"I saw that. C'mon, Larry. You're not allowed to moon at your wife." Bill began to refill their glasses.

"He certainly is allowed to moon at his wife," Francis protested, "after everything that happened to her. How are you feeling now, Jenny? You look wonderful."

"I'm fine. Thank you."

"I should think she's doing terribly well holding a dinner party not—what?—not a week after getting out of hospital."

"If Jenny wasn't giving a dinner party I should think there was something terribly wrong—and not just with her but the whole damned world." Bill took a long swig of his wine.

"Awful business. It's lovely to see you looking like your old self."

"We were terribly worried. I hope you got my flowers," Anne put in.

Dominic laid his napkin on the table. "Do you remember anything about the accident itself, Jenny?"

"She'd probably prefer not to dwell on it, if you don't mind." Laurence stood up to fetch another bottle of wine from the sideboard.

"Of course not." Dominic lifted a hand in apology. "Thoughtless of me."

Jennifer began to collect the plates. "I'm fine. Really. It's just that there isn't much I could tell you. I don't remember very much at all."

"Just as well," Dominic observed.

Yvonne was lighting a cigarette. "Well, the sooner you're responsible for everyone's brake linings, Larry darling, the safer we'll all be."

"And the richer he'll be." Francis laughed.

"Oh, Francis, darling, must we really bring every single conversation back to money?"

"Yes," he and Bill answered in unison.

Jennifer heard them laughing as she picked up the pile of dirty china and headed toward the kitchen.

"Well, that went well, didn't it?"

She was seated at her dressing table, carefully removing her earrings. She saw his reflection in the mirror as he came into the bedroom, loosening his tie. He kicked off his shoes and went into the bathroom, leaving the door open. "Yes," she said. "I think it did."

"The food was wonderful."

"Oh, I can't take any credit for that," she said. "Mrs. Cordoza organized it all."

"But you planned the menu."

It was easier not to disagree with him. She placed the earrings carefully inside their box. She could hear the washbasin filling with water. "I'm glad you liked it." She stood up and wrestled herself out of her dress, hung it up, and began to peel off her stockings.

She had removed one when she looked up to see him standing in the doorway. He was gazing at her legs. "You looked very beautiful tonight," he said quietly.

She blinked hard, rolling off the second stocking. She reached behind her to undo her girdle, now acutely self-conscious. Her left arm was still useless—too weak to reach round to her back. She kept her head down, hearing him moving toward her. He was bare-chested now, but still in his suit trousers. He stood behind her, moved her hands away, and took over. He was so close that she could feel his breath on her back as he parted each hook from its eye.

"Very beautiful," he repeated.

She closed her eyes. *This is my husband,* she told herself. *He adores me. Everyone says so. We're happy.* She felt his fingers running lightly along her right shoulder, the touch of his lips at the back of her neck. "Are you very tired?" he murmured.

She knew this was her chance. He was a gentleman. If she said she was, he would step back, leave her alone. But they were married. *Married*. She had to face this some time. And who knew? Perhaps if he seemed less alien, she would find that a little more of herself was restored to her.

She turned in his arms. She couldn't look at his face, couldn't kiss him. "Not if . . . not if you're not," she whispered into his chest.

She felt his skin against hers and clamped her eyes shut, waiting to feel a sense of familiarity, perhaps even desire. Four years, they had been married. How many times must they have done this? And since her return he had been so patient.

She felt his hands moving over her, bolder now, unclipping her brassiere. She kept her eyes closed, conscious of her appearance. "May we turn out the light?" she said. "I don't want . . . to be thinking about my arm. How it looks."

"Of course. I should have thought."

She heard the click of the bedroom light. But it wasn't her arm that bothered her: she didn't want to look at him. Didn't want to be so exposed, vulnerable, under his gaze. And then they were on the bed, and he was kissing her neck, his hands, his breath, urgent. He lay on top of her, pinning her down, and she linked her arms around his neck, unsure what she should be doing in the absence of any feelings she might have expected. What has happened to me? she thought. What did I used to do?

"Are you all right?" he murmured into her ear. "I'm not hurting you?"

"No," she said, "no, not at all."

He kissed her breasts, a low moan of pleasure escaping him. "Take them off," he said, pulling at her knickers. He shifted his weight off her so that she could tug them down to her knees, then kick them away. And she was exposed. *Perhaps if we . . .* , she wanted to say, but he was already nudging her legs apart, trying clumsily to guide himself into her. *I'm not ready*—but she couldn't say that: it would be wrong now. He was lost somewhere else, desperate, wanting.

She grimaced, drawing up her knees, trying not to tense. And then he was inside her, and she was biting her cheek in the dark, trying to ignore the pain and that she felt nothing except a desperate desire for it to be over and him out of her. His movements built in speed and urgency, his weight squashing her, his face hot and damp against her shoulder. And then, with a little cry, a hint of vulnerability he did not show in any other part of his life, it was over, and the thing was gone, replaced by a sticky wetness between her thighs.

She had bitten the inside of her cheek so hard that she could taste blood.

He rolled off her, still breathing hard. "Thank you," he said, into the darkness.

She was glad he couldn't see her lying there, gazing at nothing, the covers pulled up to her chin. "That's quite all right," she said quietly.

She had discovered that memories could indeed be lodged in places other than the mind.

Chapter 3

AUGUST 1960

"A profile. Of an industrialist." Don Franklin's stomach threatened to burst over the top of his trousers. The buttons strained, revealing, above his belt, a triangle of pale, pelted skin. He leaned back in his chair and tilted his glasses to the top of his head. "It's the editor's 'must,' O'Hare. He wants a four-page spread on the wonder mineral for the advertising."

"What the hell do I know about mines and factories? I'm a foreign correspondent, for Christ's sake."

"You were," Don corrected. "We can't send you out again, Anthony, you know that, and I need someone who can do a nice job. You can't just sit around here making the place look untidy."

Anthony slumped in the chair on the other side of the desk and drew out a cigarette.

Behind the news editor, who was just visible through the glass wall of his office, Phipps, the junior reporter, ripped three sheets of paper from his typewriter and, face screwed up in frustration, replaced them, with two sheets of carbon between.

"I've seen you do this stuff. You can turn on the charm."

"So, not even a profile. A puff piece. Glorified advertising."

"He's partly based in Congo. You know about the country."

"I know about the kind of man who owns mines in Congo."

Don held out his hand for a cigarette. Anthony gave him one and lit it. "It's not all bad."

"No?"

"You get to interview this guy at his summer residence in the south of France. The Riviera. A few days in the sun, a lobster or two on expenses, maybe a glimpse of Brigitte Bardot . . . You should be thanking me."

"Send Peterson. He loves all that stuff."

"Peterson's covering the Norwich child killer."

"Murfett. He's a crawler."

"Murfett's off to Ghana to cover the trouble in Ashanti."

"Him?" Anthony was incredulous. "He couldn't cover two school-boys fighting in a telephone box. How the hell is he doing Ghana?" He lowered his voice. "Send me back, Don."

"No."

"I could be half insane, alcoholic, and in a ruddy asylum, but I'd still do a better job than Murfett, and you know it."

"Your problem, O'Hare, is that you don't know when you're well off." Don leaned forward and dropped his voice. "Listen—just stop crabbing and listen. When you came back from Africa, there was a lot of talk upstairs"—he motioned to the editor's suite—"about whether you should be let go. The whole incident . . . They were worried about you, man. Anyway, God only knows how but you've made a lot of friends here, and some fairly important ones. They took everything you've been through into account and kept you on the payroll. Even while you were in"—he gestured awkwardly behind him—"you know."

Anthony's gaze was level.

"Anyhow. They don't want you doing anything too . . . pressured. So get a grip on yourself, get over to France, and be grateful that you've got the kind of job that occasionally involves dining in the foothills at ruddy Monte Carlo. Who knows? You might bag a starlet while you're there."

A long silence followed.

When Anthony failed to look suitably impressed, Don stubbed out his cigarette. "You really don't want to do it."

"No, Don. You know I don't. I start doing this stuff, it's just a few small steps to Births, Marriages, and Deaths."

"Jesus. You're a contrary bugger, O'Hare." He reached for a piece of typewritten paper that he ripped from the spike on his desk. "Okay, then, take this. Vivien Leigh is headed across the Atlantic. She's going to be camping outside the theater where Olivier's playing. Apparently he won't talk to her, and she's telling the gossip columnists she doesn't know why. How about you find out whether they're going to divorce? Maybe get a nice description of what she's wearing while you're there."

There was another lengthy pause. Outside the room, Phipps ripped out another three pages, smacked his forehead, and mouthed expletives.

Anthony stubbed out his cigarette and shot his boss a black look. "I'll go and pack," he said.

There was something about seriously rich people, Anthony thought as he dressed for dinner, that always made him want to dig at them a little. Perhaps it was the inbuilt certainty of men who were rarely contradicted; the pomposity of those whose most prosaic views everyone took so damned seriously.

At first he had found Laurence Stirling less offensive than he had expected; the man had been courteous, his answers considered, his views on his workers pretty enlightened. But as the day had worn on, Anthony saw he was the kind of man to whom control was paramount. He spoke at people, rather than soliciting information from them. He had little interest in anything outside his own circle. He was a bore, rich and successful enough not to try to be anything else.

Anthony brushed down his jacket, wondering why he had agreed to go to the dinner. Stirling had invited him at the end of the interview and, caught off guard, he had been forced to admit that he didn't know anyone in Antibes and had no plans, other than for a quick bite at the hotel. He suspected afterward that Stirling had invited him to make it more likely that he would write something flattering. Even as he accepted reluctantly, Stirling was instructing his driver to pick him up from the Hôtel du Cap at seven thirty. "You won't find the house," he said. "It's quite well hidden from the road."

I'll bet, Anthony had thought. Stirling didn't seem the kind of man who would welcome casual human interaction.

The concierge woke up visibly when he saw the limousine waiting outside. Suddenly he was rushing to open the doors, the smile that had been absent on Anthony's arrival now plastered across his face.

Anthony ignored him. He greeted the driver and climbed into the front passenger seat—a little, he realized afterward, to the driver's discomfort, but in the rear he would have felt like an impostor. He wound down his window to let the warm Mediterranean breeze stroke his skin as the long, low vehicle negotiated its way along coastal roads scented with rosemary and thyme. His gaze traveled up to the purple hills beyond. He had become accustomed to the more exotic landscape of Africa and had forgotten how beautiful parts of Europe were.

He made casual conversation—asked the driver about the area, who else he had driven for, what life was like for an ordinary man in this part of the country. He couldn't help it: knowledge was everything. Some of his best leads had come from the drivers and other servants of powerful men.

"Is Mr. Stirling a good boss?" he asked.

The driver's eyes darted toward him, his demeanor less relaxed. "He is," he said, in a way that suggested the conversation was closed.

"Glad to hear it," Anthony replied, and made sure to tip the man generously when they arrived at the vast white house. As he watched the car disappear to the back and what must have been the garage, he felt vaguely wistful. Taciturn as he was, he would have preferred to share a sandwich and a game of cards with the driver than make polite conversation with the bored rich of the Riviera.

The eighteenth-century house was like that of any wealthy man, oversize and immaculate, its facade suggesting the endless attention of staff. The graveled driveway was wide and manicured, flanked by raised flagstone paths from which no weed would dare to emerge. Elegant windows gleamed between painted shutters. A sweeping stone staircase led visitors into a hallway that already echoed with the conversation of the other diners and was dotted with pedestals containing huge arrangements of flowers. He walked up the steps slowly, feeling the stone still warm from the fierce heat of the day's sun.

There were seven other guests at dinner: the Moncrieffs, friends of the Stirlings from London—the wife's gaze was frankly assessing; the local mayor, M. Lafayette, with his wife and their daughter, a lithe brunette with heavily made-up eyes and a definite air of mischief; and the elderly M. and Mme Demarcier. Stirling's wife was a clean-cut, pretty blonde in the Grace Kelly mold; such women tended to have little to say of interest, having been admired for their looks all their lives. He hoped to be placed next to Mrs. Moncrieff. He hadn't minded her summing him up. She would be a challenge.

"And you work for a newspaper, Mr. O'Hare?" The elderly Frenchwoman peered up at him.

"Yes. In England." A manservant appeared at his elbow with a tray of drinks. "Do you have anything soft? Tonic water, perhaps?" The man nodded and disappeared.

"What is it called?" she asked.

"The *Nation*."

"The *Nation*," she repeated, with apparent dismay. "I haven't heard of it. I have heard of the *Times*. That is the best newspaper, isn't it?"

"I've heard that people think so." Oh, Lord, he thought. Please let the food be good.

The silver tray appeared at his elbow with a tall glass of iced tonic water. Anthony kept his gaze away from the sparkling kir the others were drinking. Instead he tried out a little of his schoolboy French on the mayor's daughter, who replied in perfect English, with a charming French lilt. Too young, he thought, registering the mayor's sideways glance.

He was gratified to find himself seated beside Yvonne Moncrieff when they finally sat down. She was polite, entertaining—and completely immune to him. *Damn the happily married.* Jennifer Stirling was on his left, turned away in conversation.

"Do you spend much time here, Mr. O'Hare?" Francis Moncrieff was a tall, thin man, the physical equivalent of his wife.

"No."

"You're more usually tied to the City of London?"

"No. I don't cover it at all."

"You're not a financial journalist?"

"I'm a foreign correspondent. I cover . . . trouble abroad."

"While Larry causes it." Moncrieff laughed. "What sort of things do you write about?"

"Oh, war, famine, disease. The cheerful stuff."

"I don't think there is much cheerful about those." The elderly Frenchwoman sipped her wine.

"For the last year I've been covering the crisis in Congo."

"Lumumba's a troublemaker," Stirling interjected, "and the Belgians are cowardly fools if they think the place will do anything but sink without them."

"You believe the Africans can't be trusted to manage their own affairs?"

"Lumumba was a barefoot jungle postman not five minutes ago. There isn't a colored with a professional education in the whole of Congo." He lit a cigar and blew out a plume of smoke. "How are they meant to run the banks once the Belgians have gone, or the hospitals? The place will become a war zone. My mines are on the Rhodesian-Congolese border, and I've already had to draft in extra security. Rhodesian security—the Congolese can no longer be trusted."

There was a brief silence. A muscle had begun to tick insistently in Anthony's jaw.

Stirling tapped his cigar. "So, Mr. O'Hare, where were you in Congo?"

"Léopoldville, mainly. Brazzaville."

"Then you know that the Congolese army cannot be controlled."

"I know that independence is a testing time for any country. And that had Lieutenant General Janssens been more diplomatic, many lives might have been saved."

Stirling stared at him over the cigar smoke. Anthony felt he was being reassessed. "So, you've been sucked into the cult of Lumumba too." His smile was icy.

"It's hard to believe that the conditions for many Africans could become any worse."

"Then you and I must differ," Stirling retorted. "I think that there are people for whom freedom can be a dangerous gift."

The room fell silent. In the distance, a motorbike whined up a hillside. Madame Lafayette reached up anxiously to smooth her hair.

"Well, I can't say I know anything about it," Jennifer Stirling observed, laying her napkin neatly on her lap.

"Too depressing," Yvonne Moncrieff agreed. "I simply can't look at the newspapers some mornings. Francis reads the sport and City pages, and I stick to my magazines. Often the news goes completely unread."

"My wife considers anything not in the pages of *Vogue* to not be proper news at all," Moncrieff said.

The tension eased. Conversation flowed again, and the waiters refilled the glasses. The men discussed the stock market and developments on the Riviera—the influx of campers, which led the elderly couple to complain of a "lowering in tone," and which awful newcomers had joined the British Bridge Club.

"I shouldn't worry too much," said Moncrieff. "The beach huts at Monte Carlo cost fifty pounds a week this year. I shouldn't think too many Butlins types are going to pay that."

"I heard that Elsa Maxwell proposed covering the pebbles with foam rubber so the beach wouldn't be uncomfortable for one's feet."

"Terrible hardships one faces in this place," Anthony remarked quietly. He wanted to leave, but that was impossible at this stage of the meal. He felt too far from where he had been—as if he had been dropped into a parallel universe. How could they be so inured to the mess, the horror, of Africa, when their lives were so plainly built upon it?

He hesitated for a moment, then motioned to a waiter for some wine. Nobody at the table seemed to notice.

"So . . . you're going to write marvelous things about my husband, are you?" Mrs. Stirling was peering at his cuff. The second course, a platter of fresh seafood, had been laid in front of him, and she had turned toward him.

He adjusted his napkin. "I don't know. Should I? Is he marvelous?"

"He's a beacon of sound commercial practice, according to our dear friend Mr. Moncrieff. His factories are built to the highest standards. His turnover increases year after year."

"That's not what I asked you."

"No?"

"I asked you if he was marvelous." He knew he was being spiky, but the alcohol had woken him up, made his skin prickle.

"I don't think you should ask me, Mr. O'Hare. A wife can hardly be impartial in such matters."

"Oh, in my experience there is no one more brutally impartial than a wife."

"Do go on."

"Who else knows all her husband's faults within weeks of marrying him, and can pinpoint them—regularly and from memory—with forensic accuracy?"

"Your wife sounds terribly cruel. I rather like the sound of her."

"Actually, she's an immensely clever woman." He watched Jennifer Stirling pop a prawn into her mouth.

"Really?"

"Yes. Clever enough to have left me years ago."

She passed him the mayonnaise. Then, when he didn't take it from her, she spooned a dollop onto the side of his plate. "Does this mean you were not very marvelous, Mr. O'Hare?"

"At being married? No. I don't suppose I was. In all other respects, I am, of course, peerless. And please call me Anthony." It was as if he had picked up their mannerisms, their carelessly arrogant way of speaking.

"Then, Anthony, I'm sure you and my husband will get along terribly well. I believe he has a similar view of himself." Her eyes settled on Stirling, then returned to him, and lingered just long enough for him to decide she might not be as wearisome as he'd thought.

During the main course—rolled beef, with cream and wild mushrooms—he discovered that Jennifer Stirling, née Verrinder, had been married for four years. She lived mostly in London, and her husband made numerous trips abroad to his mines. They came to the Riviera for the winter months, part of the summer, and odd holidays when London society proved dull. It was a tight crowd here, she said, eyeing the mayor's wife opposite. You wouldn't want to live here full-time, in the goldfish bowl.

These were the things she told him, things that should have marked her out as just another rich man's overindulged wife. But he observed other things too: that Jennifer Stirling was probably a little neglected, more clever than her position required her to be, and that she had not realized what the combination might do to her within a year or two. For now, only the hint of sadness in her eyes suggested such self-awareness. She was caught up in a never-ending but meaningless social whirl.

There were no children. "I've heard it said that two people must be in the same country for a while to have one." As she said this, he wondered if she was sending him a message. But she appeared guileless, amused by her situation rather than disappointed. "Do you have children, Anthony?" she inquired.

"I—I seem to have mislaid one. He lives with my ex-wife, who does her best to make sure that I don't corrupt him." He knew as soon as he'd said it that he was drunk. Sober, he would never have mentioned Phillip.

This time he saw something serious behind her smile, as if she was wondering whether to commiserate. *Don't*, he willed her silently. To hide his embarrassment, he poured himself another glass of wine. "It's fine. He—"

"In what way might you be considered a corrupting influence, Mr. O'Hare?" Mariette, the mayor's daughter, asked from across the table.

"I suspect, mademoiselle, that I'm more likely to be corrupted," he said. "Had I not already decided to write a most flattering profile of Mr. Stirling, I should imagine I would be won over by the food and company at his table." He paused. "What would it take to corrupt you, Mrs. Moncrieff?" he asked—she seemed the safest person to whom he could direct this question.

"Oh, I'd be as cheap as anything. Nobody ever tried hard enough," she said.

"What rot," said her husband, fondly. "It took me months to corrupt you."

"Well, you had to buy me, darling. Unlike Mr. O'Hare here, you were entirely lacking in looks and charm." She blew him a kiss. "Whereas Jenny is entirely incorruptible. Don't you think she gives off the most terrifying air of goodness?"

"No soul on earth is incorruptible if the price is right," said Moncrieff. "Even sweet little Jenny."

"No, Francis. M. Lafayette is our true beacon of integrity," said Jennifer, her lips twitching mischievously at the corners. She had begun to look a little giddy. "After all, there's no such thing as corruption in French politics."

"Darling, I don't think you're equipped to discuss French politics," Laurence Stirling interjected.

Anthony saw the faint color that rose to her cheeks.

"I was just saying—"

"Well, don't," he said lightly. She blinked and gazed at her plate.

There was a brief hush.

"I believe you are right, madame," M. Lafayette said gallantly to Jennifer, as he put down his glass. "However, I can tell you what a dishonest scoundrel my rival at the town hall is . . . at the right price, of course."

A ripple of laughter passed around the table. Mariette's foot pressed against Anthony's under the table. On his other side, Jennifer Stirling was quietly instructing staff to clear the plates. The Moncrieffs were engaged in conversation on each side of M. Demarcier.

Jesus, he thought. What am I doing with these people? This is not my world. Laurence Stirling was talking emphatically to his neighbor.

A fool, thought Anthony, aware even as he said it that he, with his lost family, his disappearing career, his lack of riches, might more accurately fit that description. The reference to his son, Jennifer Stirling's humiliation, and the drink had conspired to darken his mood. There was only one thing for it: he motioned to the waiter for more wine.

The Demarciers left shortly after eleven, the Lafayettes a few minutes later—council business in the morning, the mayor explained. He shook hands around the huge veranda to which they had retreated for coffee and brandy. "I will be very interested to read your article, M. O'Hare. It has been a pleasure."

"All mine. Believe me"—Anthony swayed as he stood—"I have never been more fascinated by council politics." He was now very drunk. The words emerged from his mouth almost before he knew what he wanted to say, and he blinked hard, conscious that he had little control over how they might be received. He had almost no idea of what he had discussed over the past hour. The mayor's eyes met Anthony's for a moment. Then he relinquished his hand and turned away.

"Papa, I will stay, if you don't mind. I'm sure one of these kind gentlemen will walk me home in a little while." Mariette stared meaningfully at Anthony, who gave an exaggerated nod.

"I may need your help, mademoiselle. I haven't the faintest idea where I am," he said.

Jennifer Stirling was kissing the Lafayettes. "I'll make sure she returns home safely," she said. "Thank you so much for coming." Then she said something in French that he didn't catch.

The night had grown chilly, but Anthony hardly felt it. He was aware of the waves lapping the shore far below, the clink of glasses, snatches of conversation as Moncrieff and Stirling discussed stock markets and investment opportunities abroad, but paid little attention as he downed the excellent cognac that someone had placed in his hand. He was used to being alone in a strange land, comfortable with his own company, but tonight he felt unbalanced, irritable.

He glanced at the three women, the two brunettes and the blonde.

Jennifer Stirling was holding out a hand, perhaps to show off some new piece of jewelry. The other two were murmuring, their laughter breaking into the conversation. Periodically Mariette would glance at him and smile. Was there a hint of conspiracy in it? *Seventeen*, he warned himself. *Too young.*

He heard crickets, the women's laughter, jazz music from deep within the house. He closed his eyes, then opened them and checked his watch. Somehow an hour had passed. He had the disturbing feeling that he might have nodded off. Either way, it was time to go. "I think," he said, to the men, as he hauled himself out of his chair, "I should probably get back to my hotel."

Laurence Stirling rose to his feet. He was smoking an oversize cigar. "Let me call my driver." He turned to the house.

"No, no," Anthony protested. "The fresh air will do me good. Thank you very much for a . . . a very interesting evening."

"Telephone my office in the morning if you need any further information. I'll be there until lunchtime. Then I leave for Africa. Unless you'd like to come and see the mines in person? We can always do with an old Africa hand . . ."

"Some other time," Anthony said.

Stirling shook his hand, a brief, firm handshake. Moncrieff followed suit, then tipped a finger to his head in mute salute.

Anthony turned away and headed for the garden gate. The pathway was lit by small lanterns placed in the flower beds. Ahead, he could see the lights of vessels in the black nothingness of the sea. The lowered voices carried toward him on the breeze from the veranda.

"Interesting fellow," Moncrieff was saying, in the kind of voice that suggested he thought the opposite.

"Better than a self-satisfied prig," Anthony muttered, under his breath.

"Mr. O'Hare? Would you mind if I walked with you?"

He turned unsteadily. Mariette stood behind him, clutching a little handbag, a cardigan slung around her shoulders. "I know the way to the town—there's a cliff path we can take. I suspect you will get very lost on your own."

He stumbled on the gritty path. The girl wound her slim brown hand through his arm. "It's lucky there's moonlight. At least we shall see our feet," she said.

They walked a little way in silence, Anthony hearing the shuffle of his shoes on the ground, the odd gasp escaping him as he tripped on tufts of wild lavender. Despite the balmy evening and the girl on his arm, he felt homesick for something he could not articulate.

"You're very quiet, Mr. O'Hare. Are you sure you're not falling asleep again?"

A burst of laughter carried to them from the house.

"Tell me something," he said. "Do you enjoy evenings like that?"

She shrugged. "It's a nice house."

"'A nice house.' That's your principal criterion for a pleasant evening, is it, mademoiselle?"

She raised an eyebrow, apparently untroubled by the edge in his voice. "Mariette. Please. Do I take it you didn't enjoy yourself?"

"People like that," he pronounced, aware that he sounded drunk and belligerent, "make me want to stick a revolver in my mouth and pull the trigger."

She giggled, and, a little gratified by her apparent complicity, he warmed to his theme: "The men talk about nothing but who has what. The women can't see beyond their bloody jewelry. They have the money, the opportunity, to do anything, see anything, yet nobody has an opinion on anything outside their own narrow little world." He stumbled again, and Mariette's hand tightened on his arm.

"I'd rather have spent the night chatting to the paupers outside the Hôtel du Cap. Except, no doubt, people like Stirling would have them tidied up and put somewhere less offensive. . . ."

"I thought you'd like Mme Stirling," she chided. "Half the men on the Riviera are in love with her. Apparently."

"Spoiled little tai-tai. You find them in any city, mademois— Mariette. Pretty as a peach, and not an original thought in her head."

He had continued his tirade for some time before he became aware that the girl had stopped. Sensing some change in the atmosphere, he glanced behind him and, as his gaze steadied, saw Jennifer Stirling a few feet back up the path. She was clutching his linen jacket, her blond hair silver in the moonlight.

"You left this," she said, thrusting out her hand. Her jaw was rigid, her eyes glittering in the blue light.

He moved forward and took it.

Her voice cut through the still air: "I'm sorry we were such a disappointment to you, Mr. O'Hare, that how we live caused such offense. Perhaps we would have met with your approval if we had been dark-skinned and impoverished."

"Christ," he said, and swallowed. "I'm sorry. I'm—I'm very drunk."

"Evidently. Perhaps I could just ask that, whatever your personal views of me and my spoiled life, you don't attack Laurence in print." She began to walk back up the hill.

As he winced and swore silently, her parting line caught on the breeze: "In fact, perhaps the next time you face the prospect of having to endure the company of such bores, you might find it easier just to say, 'No, thank you.'"

Chapter 4

NOVEMBER 1960

"I'm going to start on the vacuuming, madam, if it won't disturb you."

She had heard the footsteps coming across the landing and sat back on her heels.

Mrs. Cordoza, vacuum cleaner in hand, stopped in the doorway. "Oh! All your things . . . I didn't know you were sorting out this room. Would you like me to help?"

Jennifer wiped her forehead, surveying the contents of her wardrobe, which were strewn across the bedroom floor around her. "No, thank you, Mrs. Cordoza. You get along. I'm just rearranging my things so that I can find them."

The housekeeper hovered. "If you're sure. I'll be going to the shops after I've finished. I've put some cold cuts in the refrigerator. You did say you didn't want anything too heavy for lunch."

"That will be quite sufficient. Thank you."

And then she was alone again, the dull roar of the vacuum cleaner receding down the corridor. Jennifer straightened her back and lifted the lid from another box of shoes. She had been doing this for days, spring cleaning in the depths of winter, the other rooms with Mrs. Cordoza's help. She had pulled out the contents of shelves and cupboards, examining, restacking, tidying with a fearsome efficiency, stamping herself on her belongings, imprinting her way of doing things on a house that still resolutely refused to feel like her own.

It had started as a distraction, a way of not thinking too much about how she felt: that she was fulfilling a role everyone else seemed to have assigned to her. Now it had become a way of anchoring herself to this home, a way of finding out who she was, who she had been. She had uncovered letters, photographs, scrapbooks from her childhood that showed her as a scowling, pigtailed child on a fat white pony. She deciphered the careful scrawl of her school days, the flippant jokes of her correspondence, and realized with relief that she could recall whole chunks of it. She had begun to calculate the gulf between what she had been, a buoyant, adored, perhaps even spoiled creature, and the woman she now inhabited.

She knew almost everything it was possible to know about herself, but that didn't ameliorate her ever-present sense of dislocation, of having been dropped into the wrong life.

"Oh, darling, everyone feels like that." Yvonne had patted her shoulder sympathetically when Jennifer had broached this, after two martinis, the previous evening. "I can't tell you how many times I've woken up, gazed at the unadulterated loveliness that is my snoring, stinking, hung-over husband, and thought, How on earth did I end up here?"

Jennifer had tried to laugh. No one wanted to hear her prattling on. She had no alternative but to get on with it. The day after the dinner party, anxious and upset, she had traveled alone to the hospital and asked to speak to Dr. Hargreaves. He had ushered her into his office immediately—a sign less of conscientiousness, she suspected, than of professional courtesy to the wife of an extremely wealthy customer. His response, while less flippant than Yvonne's, had essentially told her the same thing. "A bump on the head can affect you in all sorts of ways," he said, stubbing out his cigarette. "Some people find it difficult to concentrate, others are tearful at inappropriate moments or find they're angry for a long time. I've had gentlemen patients who became uncharacteristically violent. Depression is not an unusual reaction to what you've been through."

"It's more than that, though, Dr. Hargreaves. I really thought I'd feel more . . . myself by now."

"And you don't feel yourself?"

"Everything seems wrong. Misplaced." She gave a short, diffident laugh. "Sometimes I've thought I was going mad."

He nodded, as if he had heard this many times before. "Time really is a great healer, Jennifer. I know it's a terrible cliché, but it's true. Don't fret about conforming to some correct way of feeling. With head injuries there really are no precedents. You may well feel odd—dislocated, as you put it—for a time. In the meantime I'll give you some tablets that will help. Do try not to dwell on matters."

He was already scribbling. She waited for a moment, accepted the prescription, then stood up to leave. *Do try not to dwell on matters.*

An hour after she returned home, she had begun to sort out the house. She possessed a dressing room full of clothes. She had a walnut jewelry box that contained four good rings with gemstones and a secondary box that contained a large amount of costume jewelry. She owned twelve hats, nine pairs of gloves, and eighteen pairs of shoes, she noted, as she stacked the last box. She had written a short description at each end—pumps, claret, and evening, green silk. She had held each shoe, trying to leach from it some memory of a previous occasion. A couple of times a fleeting image had passed through her mind: her feet, clad in the green silk, descending from a taxi—to a theater?—but they were frustratingly ephemeral, gone before she could fix them.

Do try not to dwell on matters.

She was just placing the last pair of shoes back in their box when she spied the paperback. It was a cheap historical romance, tucked between the tissue paper and the side of the box. She gazed at the cover, wondering why she couldn't recall the plot when she had been able to do so with many of the books on her shelves.

Perhaps I bought it and decided against it, she thought, flicking through the first few pages. It looked rather lurid. She'd skim a little tonight and perhaps give it to Mrs. Cordoza, if it wasn't her cup of tea. She placed it on her bedside table and dusted off her skirt.

Now she had more pressing matters to attend to, such as tidying this mess away and working out what on earth she was going to wear this evening.

There were two in the second post. They were almost carbon copies of each other, Moira thought, as she read them, the same symptoms, the same complaints. They were from the same factory, where each man had started work almost two decades before. Perhaps it was something to do with the unions, as her boss had said, but it was a little unnerving that the faint trickle of such correspondence several years ago had become a regular drip, drip, drip.

Glancing up, she saw him returning from lunch and wondered what to tell him. He was shaking hands with Mr. Welford, their faces wreathed in the satisfied smiles that told of a successful meeting. After the briefest hesitation, she swept both letters from the table and into her top drawer. She would put them with the others. There was no point in worrying him. She knew, after all, what he would say.

She let her gaze rest on him for a moment, as he saw Mr. Welford out of the boardroom toward the lifts, recalling their conversation of that morning. It had been just the two of them in the office. The other secretaries rarely turned up before nine, but she regularly arrived an hour earlier to start the coffee machine, lay out his papers, check for overnight telegrams, and make sure his office was running smoothly by the time he stepped into it. That was her job. Besides, she preferred eating her breakfast at her desk: it was less lonely somehow than it was at home, now that Mother was gone.

He had motioned her into his office, standing and half raising one hand. He knew she would catch the gesture: she always had an eye half open in case he needed something. She had straightened her skirt and walked in briskly, expecting a piece of dictation, a request for figures, but instead he had crossed the room and closed the door quietly after her. She had tried to suppress a shiver of excitement. He had never closed the door behind her before, not in five years. Her hand had reached unconsciously to her hair.

His voice dropped as he took a step toward her. "Moira, the matter we discussed some weeks ago."

She had stared at him, stunned into paralysis by his proximity, the unexpected turn of events. She shook her head—a little foolishly, she suspected afterward.

"The matter we discussed"—his voice carried a hint of impatience—"after my wife's accident. I thought I should check. There was never anything . . ."

She recovered, her hand fluttering at her collar. "Oh. Oh, no, sir. I went twice, as you asked. And no. There was nothing." She waited a moment, then added, "Nothing at all. I'm quite sure."

He nodded, as if reassured. Then he smiled at her, one of his rare, gentle smiles. "Thank you, Moira. You know how much I appreciate you, don't you?"

She felt herself prickle with pleasure.

He walked toward the door and opened it again. "Your discretion has always been one of your most admirable qualities."

She had to swallow hard before she spoke. "I . . . You can always rely on me. You know that."

"What's up with you, Moira?" one of the typists had asked, later that day in the ladies' powder room. She had realized she was humming. She had reapplied her lipstick carefully and added just the lightest squirt of scent. "You look like the cat that got the cream."

"Perhaps Mario in the post room's got past her stockings after all." An unpleasant cackle followed from the cubicle.

"If you paid half as much attention to your work as you do to silly tittle-tattle, Phyllis, you might actually progress beyond junior typist," she said, as she left. But even the giggling catcall as she walked out into the office couldn't dampen her pleasure.

There were Christmas lights all around the square, large white tulip-shaped bulbs. They were draped between the Victorian lampposts and strung in jagged spirals around the trees that bordered the communal gardens.

"Earlier every year," Mrs. Cordoza remarked, turning from the big bay window in the drawing room as Jennifer walked in. She had been about to draw the curtains. "It's not even December."

"But very pretty," Jennifer said, putting on an earring. "Mrs. Cordoza, would you mind terribly fastening this button at my neck? I can't seem to reach." Her arm was improved, but still lacked the flexibility that would have allowed her to dress unaided.

The older woman drew the collar together, fastened the dark blue silk-covered button, and stood back, waiting for Jennifer to turn. "That dress always looked lovely on you," she observed.

Jennifer had become accustomed to such moments, the times when she had to catch herself so that she didn't ask, "Did it? When?" She had grown adept at hiding them, at convincing the world around her that she was sure of her place in it.

"I can't seem to remember when I last wore it," she mused, after a beat.

"It was your birthday dinner. You were going to a restaurant in Chelsea."

Jennifer hoped that this might dislodge a memory. But nothing. "So I did," she said, raising a quick smile, "and it was a lovely evening."

"Is it a special occasion tonight, madam?"

She checked her reflection in the mirror over the mantelpiece. Her hair was set in soft blond waves, her eyes outlined with artfully smudged kohl. "Oh, no, I don't believe so. The Moncrieffs have invited us out. Dinner and dancing. The usual crowd."

"I'll stay an extra hour, if you don't mind. There's some linen that needs starching."

"We do pay you for all your extra work?" She had spoken without thinking.

"Oh, yes," Mrs. Cordoza said. "You and your husband are always very generous."

Laurence—she still couldn't think of him as Larry, no matter what everyone else called him—had said he would not be able to leave work early, so she had said she would take a taxi to his office and that

they could go on from there. He had seemed a little reluctant, but she
had insisted. During the last couple of weeks she had been trying to
force herself out of the house a little more often to reclaim her independence. She had been shopping, once with Mrs. Cordoza and
once by herself, walking slowly up and down Kensington High Street,
trying not to let the sheer numbers of people, the constant noise and
jostling, overwhelm her. She had bought a wrap from a department
store two days previously, not because she particularly wanted or
needed it but so that she could return home having fulfilled a purpose.

"Can I help you on with this, madam?"

The housekeeper was holding a sapphire brocade swing coat. She
held it up by the shoulders, allowing Jennifer to slide her arms into
the sleeves one at a time. The lining was silk, the brocade pleasingly
heavy around her. She turned as she put it on, straightening the collar
around her neck. "What do you do? After you leave here?"

The housekeeper blinked, a little taken aback. "What do I do?"

"I mean, where do you go?"

"I go home," she said.

"To . . . your family?" *I spend so much time with this woman,* she thought.
And I know nothing about her.

"My family are in South Africa. My daughters are grown up. I
have two grandchildren."

"Of course. Please forgive me, but I still can't remember things as
well as I might. I don't remember you mentioning your husband."

The woman looked at her feet. "He passed away almost eight years
ago, madam." When Jennifer didn't speak, she added, "He was a manager at the mine in the Transvaal. Your husband gave me this job so
I could continue to support my family."

Jennifer felt as if she had been caught snooping. "I'm so sorry. As
I said, my memory is a little unreliable at the moment. Please don't
think it reflects . . ."

Mrs. Cordoza shook her head.

Jennifer had flushed a deep red. "I'm sure in normal circumstances
I would have—"

"Please, madam. I can see . . . ," the housekeeper said carefully, "that you are not quite yourself yet."

They stood there, facing each other, the older woman apparently mortified by her overfamiliarity.

But Jennifer didn't see it that way. "Mrs. Cordoza," she said, "do you find me much changed since my accident?" She saw the woman's eyes search her face briefly before she answered. "Mrs. Cordoza?"

"Perhaps a little."

"Can you tell me in what way?"

The housekeeper looked awkward, and Jennifer saw that she feared giving a truthful response. But she couldn't stop now. "Please. There's no right or wrong answer, I assure you. I've just . . . Things have been a little strange since . . . I'd like to get a better idea of how things were."

The woman's hands were clasped tightly in front of her. "Perhaps you're quieter. A little less . . . sociable."

"Would you say I was happier beforehand?"

"Madam, please . . ." The older woman fiddled with her necklace. "I don't—I really should go. I might leave the linen until tomorrow, if you wouldn't mind."

Before Jennifer could speak again, the housekeeper had disappeared.

The Beachcomber restaurant at the Mayfair Hotel was one of the hottest tables around. When Jennifer walked in, her husband close behind her, she could see why: only yards from the chilly London street, she found herself in a beach paradise. The circular bar was clad in bamboo, as was the ceiling. The floor was sea grass, while fishing nets and buoys hung from the rafters. Hula music wafted from speakers set into fake stone cliffs, only just audible above the noise of a crowded Friday night. A mural of blue skies and endless white sands took up most of one wall, and the oversize bust of a woman, taken from the prow of a ship, jutted into the bar area. It was there, attempting to hang his hat upon one of her carved breasts, that they spotted Bill.

"Ah, Jennifer . . . Yvonne . . . have you met Ethel Merman here?" He picked up his hat and waved it at them.

"Watch out," Yvonne muttered as she stood up to greet them. "Violet's stuck at home, and Bill's already three sheets to the wind."

Laurence released Jennifer's arm as they were shown to their seats. Yvonne sat opposite her, then waved an elegant hand, beckoning Anne and Dominic, who had just arrived. Bill, at the other end of the table, had snatched Jennifer's hand and kissed it as she passed him.

"Oh, you are a creep, Bill, really." Francis shook his head. "I'll send a car for Violet if you're not careful."

"Why is Violet at home?" Jennifer let the waiter pull out the chair for her.

"One of the children is ill, and she didn't feel able to let the nanny cope alone." Yvonne managed to convey everything she thought about that decision in one beautifully arched eyebrow.

"Because the children must always come first," Bill intoned. He winked at Jennifer. "Best to stay as you are, ladies. We men need a surprising amount of looking after."

"Shall we get a jug of something? What do they do that's good?"

"I'll have a mai tai," said Anne.

"I'll have a Royal Pineapple," said Yvonne, gazing at the menu, which bore a picture of a woman in a hula skirt and was marked "Grog List."

"What'll you have, Larry? Let me guess. A Bali Hai Scorpion. Something with a sting in its tail?" Bill had grabbed the drinks menu.

"Sounds disgusting. I'll have a whiskey."

"Then let me choose for the lovely Jennifer. Jenny darling, how about a Hidden Pearl? Or a Hula Girl's Downfall? Fancy that?"

Jennifer laughed. "If you say so, Bill."

"And I'll have a Suffering Bastard because I am one," he said cheerfully. "Right. When do we start dancing?"

Several drinks in, the food arrived: Polynesian pork, shrimp almond, and peppered steak. Jennifer, made swiftly tipsy by the strength of the cocktails, found she could barely pick at hers. Around her the room had grown noisier; a band struck up in the corner, couples moved onto the dance floor, and the tables competed in volume to be heard. The lights dimmed, a swirling red and gold glow emanating from the colored-glass table lamps. She let her gaze wander around her friends. Bill kept shooting her looks, as if he was keen for her approval. Yvonne's arm was draped over Francis's shoulder as she told some story. Anne broke off from sucking her multicolored drink through a straw to laugh uproariously. The feeling was creeping in again, as relentless as a tide: that she should be somewhere else. She felt as if she were in a glass bubble, distanced from those around her—and homesick, she realized, with a start. *I've drunk too much,* she scolded herself. *Stupid girl.* She met her husband's eye and smiled at him, hoping she didn't look as uncomfortable as she felt. He didn't smile back. I'm too transparent, she thought mournfully.

"So what is this?" Laurence said, turning to Francis. "What exactly are we celebrating?"

"Do we need a reason to enjoy ourselves?" Bill said. He was now drinking from Yvonne's pineapple through a long striped straw. She didn't appear to notice.

"We have some news, don't we, darling?" Francis said.

Yvonne leaned back in her chair, reached into her handbag, and lit a cigarette. "We certainly do."

"We wanted to gather you—our best friends—here tonight to let you know before anyone else that"—Francis glanced at his wife—"in about six months from now we're going to have a little Moncrieff."

There was a short silence. Anne's eyes widened. "You're having a baby?"

"Well, we're certainly not buying one." Yvonne's heavily lipsticked mouth twitched with amusement. Anne was already out of her seat, moving round the table to hug her friend. "Oh, that's wonderful news. You clever thing."

Francis laughed. "Trust me. It was nothing."

"Certainly felt like nothing," Yvonne said, and he nudged her.

Jennifer felt herself getting up, making her way around the table, as if propelled by some automatic impulse. She stooped to kiss Yvonne. "That's absolutely wonderful news," she said, unsure why she felt suddenly even more unbalanced. "Congratulations."

"I would have told you before"—Yvonne's hand was on hers—
"but I thought I should wait until you felt a little more . . ."

"Myself. Yes." Jennifer straightened up. "But it really is marvelous.
I'm so happy for you."

"Your turn next." Bill pointed with exaggerated deliberation at
Laurence and her. His collar was undone, his tie loosened. "You two
will be the only ones left. Come on, Larry, chop chop. Mustn't let the
side down."

Jennifer, returning to her seat, felt the color rise to her face, and
hoped that in the lighting it wouldn't show.

"All in good time, Bill," Francis cut in smoothly. "It took us years
to get round to it. Best to get all your fun out of the way first."

"What? That was meant to be fun?" queried Yvonne.

There was a burst of laughter.

"Quite. There's no hurry."

Jennifer watched her husband pull a cigar from his inside pocket
and slice off the end with careful deliberation. "No hurry at all," she
echoed.

They were in a taxi, heading for home. On the icy pavement Yvonne
was waving, Francis's arm protectively around her shoulders. Dominic
and Anne had left a few minutes before, and Bill appeared to be ser-
enading some passersby.

"Yvonne's news is rather wonderful, isn't it?" she said.

"You think so?"

"Why, yes. Don't you?"

He was gazing out of the window. The city streets were near black,
apart from the occasional streetlamp. "Yes," he said. "A baby is wonderful news."

"Bill was terribly drunk, wasn't he?" She pulled her compact from
her handbag and checked her face. It had finally ceased to surprise
her.

"Bill," her husband said, still staring out at the street, "is a fool."

Some distant alarm bell was ringing. She closed her bag and folded her hands in her lap, struggling to work out what else she might say. "Did you . . . What did you think when you heard?"

He turned to her. One side of his face was illuminated by the sodium light, the other in darkness.

"About Yvonne, I mean. You didn't say much. In the restaurant."

"I thought," he said, and she detected infinite sadness in his voice, "what a lucky bastard Francis Moncrieff was."

They said nothing else on the short journey home. When they arrived, he paid off the taxi driver while she made her way carefully up the gritted stone steps. The lights were on, casting a pale yellow glow over the snow-covered paving. It was the only house still aglow in the silent square. He was drunk, she realized, watching the heavy, uneven fall of his feet on the steps. She tried, briefly, to remember how many whiskeys he had consumed and couldn't. She had been locked in her own thoughts, wondering how she appeared to everyone else. Her brain had seemed to fizz with the effort of seeming normal.

"Would you like me to fetch you a drink?" she said, as she let them in. The hall echoed to their footfall. "I could make some tea, if you'd like."

"No," he said, dropping his overcoat onto the hall chair. "I'd like to go to bed."

"Well, I think I'll—"

"And I'd like you to come with me."

So that was how it was. She hung her coat neatly in the hall cupboard and followed him up the stairs to their bedroom. She wished, suddenly, that she had drunk more. She would have liked them to be carefree, like Dominic and Anne, collapsing onto each other with giggles in the street. But her husband, she knew now, was not the giggling kind.

The alarm clock said it was a quarter to two. He peeled off his clothes, leaving them in a heap on the floor. He looked suddenly, desperately tired, she thought, and the faint hope dawned within her that he might simply fall asleep. She kicked off her shoes and realized she wouldn't be able to undo the button at the collar of her dress.

"Laurence?"

"What?"

"Would you mind undoing . . . ?" She turned her back to him, and tried not to wince as his fingers clumsily ripped at the fabric. His breath was sharp with whiskey and the bitter tang of cigar smoke. He pulled, several times catching hairs at the back of her neck, causing her to flinch. "Bugger," he said, eventually. "I've torn it."

She peeled it from her shoulders, and he put the silk-covered button into her palm. "That's all right," she said, trying not to mind. "I'm sure Mrs. Cordoza will be able to mend it."

She was about to hang the dress up when he caught her arm. "Leave that," he said. He was gazing at her, his head nodding slightly, his lids at half-mast over shadowed eyes. He lowered his face, took hers between his hands, and began to kiss her. She closed her eyes as his hands wandered down her neck, her shoulders, both of them stumbling as he lost his balance. Then he pulled her onto the bed, his large hands covering her breasts, his weight already shifting onto her. She met his kisses politely, trying not to acknowledge her revulsion at his breath. "Jenny," he was murmuring, breathing faster now, "Jenny . . ." At least it might not take too long.

She became aware that he had stopped. She opened her eyes to find him gazing at her. "What's the matter?" he said thickly.

"Nothing."

"You look as if I'm doing something distasteful to you. Is that how you feel?"

He was drunk, but there was something else in his expression, some bitterness she could not account for.

"I'm sorry, darling. I didn't mean to give you that impression." She pushed herself up onto her elbows. "I'm just tired, I suppose." She reached out a hand to him.

"Ah. Tired."

They sat up beside each other. He ran a hand through his hair, disappointment oozing from him. She was overwhelmed with guilt, and also, to her shame, relief. When the silence became unbearable, she took his hand. "Laurence . . . do you think I'm all right?"

"All right? What's that supposed to mean?"

She felt a lump rise in the back of her throat. He was her husband: surely she should be able to confide in him. She thought briefly of Yvonne draped over Francis, the constant looks that passed between them and spoke of a hundred other conversations to which no one else was party. She thought of Dominic and Anne, laughing their way into their taxi. "Laurence . . ."

"Larry!" he exploded. "You call me Larry. I don't see why you can't remember that."

Her hands flew to her face. "Larry, I'm sorry. It's just I . . . I still feel so strange."

"Strange?"

She winced. "As if something's missing. I feel as if there's some puzzle to which I don't hold all the pieces. Does that sound terribly silly?" *Please reassure me*, she begged him silently. Put your arms around me. Tell me I am being silly, that it will all come back to me. Tell me that Hargreaves was right, and this awful feeling will go. Love me a little. Keep me close, until I can feel like it is the right thing for you to do. Just understand me.

But when she looked up, his eyes were on his shoes, which lay a few feet away from him on the carpet. His silence, she grasped gradually, was not a questioning one. It didn't speak of things that he was trying to work out. His terrible stillness spoke of something darker: barely suppressed anger.

His voice was quiet and icily deliberate when he said, "What do you think is missing from your life, Jennifer?"

"Nothing," she said hurriedly. "Nothing at all. I'm perfectly happy. I—" She got up and made for the bathroom. "It's nothing. As Dr. Hargreaves said, it will soon pass. I'll soon be completely myself again."

When she woke, he had already gone, and Mrs. Cordoza was knocking softly on her door. She opened her eyes, feeling an ominous ache as she moved her head.

"Madam? Would you like me to bring you a cup of coffee?"

"That would be very kind. Thank you," she croaked.

She pushed herself up slowly, squinting into the bright light. It was a quarter to ten. Outside, she could hear a car engine, the dull scrape of someone clearing snow from the pavement, and sparrows squabbling in the trees. The clothes that had been strewn across the bedroom the previous evening had somehow been tidied away. She lay flat against the pillows, letting the night's events pierce her consciousness.

He had turned away from her when she had returned to the bed, his broad, strong back an unbridgeable barrier. She had felt relief, but something more perplexing, too. Now a melancholic weariness stole over her. I'll have to do better, she thought. I'll stop talking about my feelings. I'll be nicer to him. I'll be generous. I hurt him last night, and that was what did it.

Do try not to dwell on matters.

Mrs. Cordoza knocked. She had brought up coffee and two thin slices of toast on a tray. "I thought you might be hungry."

"Oh, you're kind. I'm sorry. I should have been up hours ago."

"I'll put it here." She laid it carefully on the bedspread, then picked up the coffee cup and placed it on Jennifer's bedside table.

"I'll stay downstairs for now so that I don't disturb you." She glanced briefly at Jennifer's bare arm, the scar vivid in the bright light, and averted her gaze.

She left the room as Jennifer caught sight of the book, the romantic novel she had meant to read or give away. She would have her coffee first, she thought, and take it downstairs afterward. It would be good to restore things between herself and Mrs. Cordoza after their odd exchange the previous evening.

Jennifer sipped her coffee and picked up the paperback, flicking through its pages. This morning she could barely see straight enough to read. A sheet of paper dropped out of it. Jennifer laid the book on the bedside table and picked it up. She unfolded it slowly and began to read.

Dearest,
    I couldn't make you listen, when you left in such a hurry, but I was not rejecting you. You were so far from the truth I can hardly bear it.

Here is the truth: you are not the first married woman I have made love to. You know my personal circumstances, and to be frank, these relationships, such as they are, have suited me. I did not want to be close to anyone. When we first met, I chose to think you would be no different.

But when you arrived at my room on Saturday, you looked so wonderful in your dress. And then you asked me to unfasten that button at your neck. And as my fingers met your skin I realized in that moment that to make love to you would be a disaster for both of us. You, dearest girl, have no idea of how you would feel to be so duplicitous. You are an honest, delightful creature. Even if you do not feel it now, there is pleasure to be had from being a decent person. I do not want to be the man responsible for making you someone less than that.

And me? I knew in the moment you looked up at me that if we did this I would be lost. I would not be able to put you aside, as I had with the others. I would not be able to nod agreeably to Laurence as we passed each other in some restaurant. I would never be satisfied with just a part of you. I had been fooling myself to think otherwise. It was for that reason, darling girl, that I redid that wretched button at your neck. And for that reason I have lain awake for the last two nights, hating myself for the one decent thing I have ever done.

Forgive me.

B.

Jennifer sat in her bed, staring at the one word that had leapt out at her. *Laurence.*

Laurence.

Which could mean only one thing.

The letter was addressed to her.

Chapter 5

AUGUST 1960

Anthony O'Hare woke up in Brazzaville. He stared at the fan that rotated lazily above his head, dimly aware of the sunlight slicing through the shutters, and wondered, briefly, if this time he was going to die. His head was trapped in a vise, and arrows shot from temple to temple. His kidneys felt as if someone had hammered them enthusiastically for much of the previous night. The inside of his mouth was dry and foul tasting, and he was faintly nauseated. A vague sense of panic assailed him. Had he been shot? Beaten in a riot? He closed his eyes, waiting for the sounds of the street outside, the food vendors, the ever-present buzz of the wireless as people gathered, sitting on their haunches, trying to hear where the next outbreak of trouble would be. Not a bullet. It was yellow fever. This time it would surely finish him off. But even as the thought formed, he realized there were no Congolese sounds: no yelling from an open window, no bar music, no smells of *kwanga* cooking in banana leaves. No gunshots. No shouting in Lingala or Swahili. Silence. The distant sound of seagulls.

Not Congo. France. He was in France.

He felt a fleeting gratitude, until the pain became distinct. The consultant had warned him it would feel worse if he drank again, he observed with some distant, still analytical part of his mind. Dr.

Robertson would be gratified to know just how accurate his prediction had been.

When he became confident that he could do so without disgracing himself, he shifted to an upright position. He swung his legs over the side of the bed and walked tentatively to the window, conscious of the smell of stale sweat and the empty bottles on the table that told of the long night behind him. He drew back the curtain a fraction of an inch and could see the glittering bay below, bathed in a pale gold light. The red roofs on the hillsides were of terra-cotta tiles, not the painted rust of the Congolese bungalows, their inhabitants healthy, happy people milling on the seafront, chatting, walking, running. White people. Wealthy people.

He squinted. This scene was blameless, idyllic. He let the curtain fall, stumbled to the bathroom, and threw up, cradling the lavatory, spitting and miserable. When he could stand again, he climbed unsteadily into the shower and slumped against the wall, letting the warm water wash over him for twenty minutes, wishing it could clean away what ran through him.

Come on, get a grip.

He dressed, rang down for some coffee, and, feeling a little steadier, sat at the desk. It was almost a quarter to eleven. He needed to send his copy through, the profile he had worked on the previous afternoon. He gazed at his scrawled notes, recalling the end of the evening. The memory came back to him haltingly: Mariette, her face raised to him outside this hotel, demanding to be kissed. His determined refusal, even as he still muttered about what a fool he was: the girl was desirable and had been his for the taking. But he wanted to feel the tiniest bit glad about one thing he'd done that evening.

Oh, Christ. Jennifer Stirling, brittle and wounded, holding his jacket toward him. She had overheard him ranting mindlessly, ungraciously, about them all. What had he said about her? *Spoiled little tai-tai . . . not an original thought in her head.* He closed his eyes. War zones, he thought, were easier. Safer. In war zones you could always tell who the enemy was.

The coffee arrived. He took a deep breath, then poured a cupful. He lifted the telephone receiver and asked the operator wearily to put him through to London.

Mrs. Stirling,

> *I am an ungracious pig. I'd like to be able to blame exhaustion, or some uncharacteristic reaction to shellfish, but I'm afraid it was a combination of alcohol, which I shouldn't take, and the choleric temper of the socially inept. There is little you could say about me that I have not already deduced about myself in my more sober hours.*
>
> *Please allow me to apologize. If I could buy you and Mr. Stirling lunch before I return to London I'd be very glad to make it up to you.*
>
> *Yours shamefacedly,*

Anthony O'Hare

> *P.S. I enclose a copy of the report I sent to London to assure you that I have, at least, behaved honorably in that regard.*

Anthony folded the letter into an envelope, sealed it, and turned it over. It was possible he was still a little drunk: he couldn't remember ever having been so honest in a letter.

It was at that point that he remembered he had no address to which he could send it. He swore softly at his own stupidity. The previous evening Stirling's driver had collected him, and he could remember little of the journey home, aside from its various humiliations.

The hotel's reception desk offered little help. *Stirling?* The concierge shook his head.

"You know him? Rich man. Important," he said. His mouth still tasted powdery.

"Monsieur," the concierge said wearily, "everyone here is rich and important."

The afternoon was balmy, the air white, almost phosphoric under the clear sky. He began to walk, retraced the route that the car had taken the previous evening. It had been a drive of less than ten minutes: How hard could it be to find the house again? He would drop the letter at the door and leave. He refused to think about what he would do when he returned to town: since that morning his body, reminded of its long relationship with alcohol, had begun a low, perverse hum of desire. *Beer*, it urged. *Wine. Whiskey.* His kidneys ached, and he still trembled a little. The walk, he told himself, nodding in greeting at two smiling, sun-hatted women, would do him good.

The sky above Antibes was a searing blue, the beaches dotted with holidaymakers basting themselves on the white sand. He remembered turning left at this roundabout and saw that the road, dotted with clay-tiled villas, led him into the hills. This was the way he had come. The sun was beating hard on the back of his neck and straight through his hat. He removed his jacket, slinging it over his shoulder as he walked.

It was in the hills behind the town that things began to go wrong. He had turned left at a church that had looked vaguely familiar and begun to make his way up the side of a hill. The pine and palm trees thinned, then disappeared altogether, leaving him unprotected by shade, the heat bouncing off the pale rocks and tarmac. He felt his exposed skin tighten, and knew that by evening it would be burned and sore.

Occasionally a car would pass, sending sprays of flint over the growing precipice. It had seemed such a brief journey the previous evening, speeded by the scent of the wild herbs, the cool breezes of dusk. Now the milestones stretched before him, and his confidence ebbed as he was forced to contemplate the possibility that he was lost.

Don Franklin would love this, he thought, pausing to wipe his head with his handkerchief. Anthony could make his way from one end of Africa to the other, fight his way across borders, yet here he was, lost in what should have been a ten-minute journey across a millionaires' playground. He stepped back to let another car pass, then squinted into the light as, with a low squeal of brakes, it stopped. With a whine, it reversed toward him.

Yvonne Moncrieff, sunglasses tilted back on her head, leaned out of a Daimler SP250. "Are you mad?" she said cheerfully. "You'll fry up here."

He peered across and saw Jennifer Stirling at the wheel. She gazed at him from behind oversize dark sunglasses, her hair tied back, her expression unreadable.

"Good afternoon," he said, removing his hat. He was suddenly conscious of the sweat seeping through his crumpled shirt and his face shining with it.

"What on earth are you doing so far out of town, Mr. O'Hare?" Jennifer asked. "Chasing some hot story?"

He took his linen jacket from his shoulder, reached into his pocket, and thrust the letter toward her. "I—I wanted to give you this."

"What is it?"

"An apology."

"An apology?"

"For my ungraciousness last night."

She made no move to stretch across her friend and take it.

"Jennifer, shall I?" Yvonne Moncrieff glanced at her, apparently perturbed.

"No. Can you read it out loud, Mr. O'Hare?" she said.

"Jennifer!"

"If Mr. O'Hare has written it, I'm sure he's perfectly capable of saying it." Behind the glasses her face was impassive.

He stood there for a moment, looked behind him at the empty road and down at the sunbaked village below. "I'd really rather—"

"Then it's not much of an apology, is it, Mr. O'Hare?" she said sweetly. "Anyone can scribble a few words."

Yvonne Moncrieff was looking at her hands, shaking her head. Jennifer's blank sunglasses were still focused on him, his silhouette visible in their dark lenses.

He opened the envelope, pulled out the sheet of paper, and after a moment read the contents to her, his voice unnaturally loud on the mountain. He finished and tucked it back into his pocket. He felt oddly embarrassed in the silence, broken only by the quiet hum of the engine.

"My husband," Jennifer said eventually, "has gone to Africa. He left this morning."

"Then I'd be delighted if you'd let me buy you and Mrs. Moncrieff lunch." He looked at his watch.

"Obviously rather a late lunch now."

"Not me, darling. Francis wants me to look at a yacht this afternoon. I've told him a man can but dream."

"We'll give you a lift back to town, Mr. O'Hare," Jennifer said, nodding toward the tiny rear seat. "I don't want to be responsible for the *Nation's* most honorable correspondent getting sunstroke, as well as alcohol poisoning."

She waited while Yvonne climbed out and tilted the seat forward for Anthony to climb in, then rummaged in the glove compartment. "Here," she said, throwing a handkerchief at him. "And you do know you were walking in completely the wrong direction? We live over there." She pointed toward a distant, tree-lined hill. Her mouth twitched at the corners, just enough for him to think he might be forgiven, and the two women burst into laughter. Deeply relieved, Anthony O'Hare rammed his hat onto his head, and they were off, speeding down the narrow road back toward the town.

The car became stuck in traffic almost as soon as they had dropped Yvonne at Hôtel St. Georges. "Behave yourselves now," the older woman had said as she waved them good-bye. She spoke, he noted, with the cheerful insouciance of one who knows the alternative to be out of the question.

Once it was just the two of them, the mood had altered. Jennifer Stirling had grown silent, seemingly preoccupied by the road ahead in a way that she hadn't been twenty minutes earlier. He glanced surreptitiously at her lightly tanned arms, her profile, as she gazed ahead at the long line of taillights. He wondered, briefly, if she was angrier with him than she had been prepared to let on.

"So how long will your husband be in Africa?" he said, to break the silence.

"A week probably. He rarely stays longer." She peered over the side of her door briefly, apparently to gauge what was causing the holdup.

"Quite a journey for such a short stay."

"You'd know, Mr. O'Hare."

"Me?"

She raised an eyebrow. "You know everything about Africa. You said so last night."

"'Everything'?"

"You knew that most of the men who do business out there are crooks."

"I said that?"

"To M. Lafayette."

Anthony sank a little lower in his seat. "Mrs. Stirling—," he began.

"Oh, don't worry. Laurence didn't hear you. Francis did, but he only does a little business out there, so he didn't take it too personally."

The cars began to move.

"Let me buy you lunch," he said. "Please. I'd like the chance to show you, even if only for half an hour, that I'm not a complete ass."

"You think you can change my mind so swiftly?" That smile again.

"I'm game if you are. You show me where we should go."

The waiter brought her a tall glass of lemonade. She took a sip, then sat back in her chair and surveyed the seafront.

"Lovely view," he said.

"Yes," she conceded.

Her hair fell from her head like paint from a pot, in a sheet of silky blond ripples that ended just above her shoulders. Not his normal type. He liked less conventionally pretty women, those with a hint of something darker, whose charms were less obvious to the eye. "Aren't you drinking?"

He looked at his glass. "I'm not really meant to."

"Wife's orders?"

"Ex-wife," he corrected. "And no, doctor's."

"So you really did find last night unbearable."

He shrugged. "I don't spend much time in society."

"An accidental tourist."

"I admit it. I find armed conflict a less daunting prospect."

Her smile, when it came this time, was slow and mischievous. "So you're William Boot," she said. "Out of your depth in the war zone of Riviera society."

"Boot . . ." At the mention of Evelyn Waugh's hapless fictional character, he found himself smiling properly for the first time that day. "I suppose you could legitimately have said much worse."

A woman entered the restaurant, clutching a button-eyed dog to her vast bosom. She walked through the tables with a kind of weary determination, as if she could allow herself to focus on nothing but where she was headed. When she sat down at an empty table, a few seats away from them, it was with a little sigh of relief. She placed the dog on the floor, where it stood, its tail clamped between its legs, trembling.

"So, Mrs. Stirling—"

"Jennifer."

"Jennifer. Tell me about yourself," he said, leaning forward over the table.

"You're meant to be telling me. Showing me, in fact."

"What?"

"That you're not a complete ass. I do believe you gave yourself half an hour."

"Ah. How long have I got left?"

She checked her watch. "About nine minutes."

"And how am I doing so far?"

"You can't possibly expect me to give anything away quite so soon."

They were silent then, he because, uncharacteristically, he didn't know what to say, she perhaps regretting her choice of words. Anthony O'Hare thought of the last woman he had been involved with, the wife of his dentist, a redhead with skin so translucent he was reluctant to look too hard in case he saw what lay beneath it. She had been flattened by her husband's long-term indifference to her. Anthony had half suspected that her receptiveness to his advances had been as much an act of revenge as anything else.

"What do you do with your days, Jennifer?"

"I'm afraid to tell you."

He raised an eyebrow.

"I do so little of any worth that I'm afraid you'd be terribly disapproving." The way in which she said this told him she was not afraid at all.

"You run two houses."

"I don't. There's a part-time staff. And in London Mrs. Cordoza is much cleverer than I am at housekeeping."

"So what do you do?"

"I host cocktail parties, dinners. I make things beautiful. I look decorative."

"You're very good at that."

"Oh, an expert. It's a specialized skill, you know."

He could have stared at her all day. It was something about the way her top lip turned up a little as it joined the soft skin below her nose. There was a special name for that part of the face, and he was sure that if he stared at her long enough he would remember it.

"I did what I was bred to do. I bagged a rich husband, and I keep him happy."

The smile faltered. Perhaps a man without his experience might have missed it, a slight give around the eyes, a suspicion of something more complex than the surface might suggest.

"Actually, I'm going to have a drink," she said. "Would you mind awfully?"

"You should absolutely have a drink. I shall enjoy it vicariously."

"*Vicariously,*" she repeated, holding up a hand to the waiter. She ordered a Martini vermouth, lots of ice.

A recreational drink, he thought: she wasn't out to hide anything, to lose herself in alcohol. He was a little disappointed. "If it makes you feel any better," he said lightly, "I don't know how to do anything but work."

"Oh, I think you do," she responded. "Men find it easier to work than to deal with anything else."

"Anything else?"

"The messiness of everyday life. People not behaving as you'd like and feeling things you'd rather they didn't feel. At work you can achieve results, be the master of your domain. People do as you say."

"Not in my world." He laughed.

"But you can write a story and see it on the newsstands the next day just as you wrote it. Doesn't that make you feel rather proud?"

"It used to. That wears off after a while. I don't think I've done much I can feel proud of for some time. Everything I write is ephemeral. Tomorrow's fish-and-chip paper."

"No? Then why work so hard?"

He swallowed, pushing an image of his son from him. Suddenly he wanted a drink very much. He forced a smile. "All the reasons you say. So much easier than dealing with everything else."

Their eyes met, and in that unguarded moment, her smile fell away. She flushed a little, and stirred her drink slowly with a cocktail stick. "'Vicariously,'" she said slowly. "You'll have to tell me what that means, Anthony."

The way she said his name induced a kind of intimacy. It promised something, a repetition in some future time.

"It means"—Anthony's mouth had dried—"it means pleasure gained through the pleasure of someone else."

After she had dropped him at his hotel, he lay on the bed and stared at the ceiling for almost an hour. Then he went down to reception, asked for a postcard, and wrote a note to his son, wondering if Clarissa would bother to pass it on.

When he returned to his room, a note had been pushed under the door:

Dear Boot,

While I'm not yet convinced you're not an ass, I'm willing to give you another chance to convince me. My dinner plans have fallen through for this evening. I'll be dining in the Hôtel des Calypsos on rue St. Jacques and would welcome company, 8 p.m.

He read this twice, then ran downstairs and sent a telegram
to Don:

IGNORE LAST TELEGRAM STOP AM STAYING ON TO WORK ON
SERIES ABOUT RIVIERA HIGH SOCIETY STOP WILL INCLUDE
FASHION TIPS STOP

He grinned, folded it, and handed it over, picturing his editor's
face when he read it, then tried to work out how to get his suit laundered before the evening.

That night Anthony O'Hare was utterly charming. He was the person
he should have been the previous evening. He was the person he perhaps should have been when he was married. He was witty, courteous,
chivalrous. She had never been to Congo—her husband said it was
"not for your sort"—and, perhaps because he now had some built-in
need to contradict Stirling, Anthony was determined to make her want
to love it. He talked to her of the elegant, tree-lined streets of Léopoldville, of the Belgian settlers who imported all their food, tinned and
frozen, at hideous expense rather than eat in one of the world's most
glorious cornucopias of produce. He told her of the shock of the city's
Europeans when an uprising at the Léopoldville garrison ended with
their pursuit and flight to the relative safety of Stanleyville.

He wanted her to see him at his best, to look at him with admiration instead of that air of pity and irritation. And something strange
happened: as he acted the charming, upbeat stranger, he found that
he briefly became him. He thought of his mother: "Smile," she would
tell him, when he was a boy, it would make him happier. He hadn't
believed her.

Jennifer, in turn, was lighthearted. She listened more than she
talked, as socially clever women were wont to do, and when she laughed
at something he said, he found himself expanding, keen to make her
do it again. He realized, with gratification, that they drew admiring
glances from those around them—*that terribly gay couple at table 16.* She

was curiously unabashed at being seen with a man who was not her husband. Perhaps this was how Riviera society functioned, he thought, an endless social duet with other people's husbands and wives. He didn't like to think of the other possibility: that a man of his stature, his class, could not be seen as a threat.

Shortly after the main course, a tall man in an immaculately cut suit appeared at their table. He kissed Jennifer on both cheeks, then waited, after they had exchanged pleasantries, to be introduced. "Richard, darling, this is Mr. Boot," she said, straight-faced. "He's been working on a profile of Larry for the newspapers back in England. I'm filling in the details, and trying to show him that industrialists and their wives are not entirely dull."

"I don't think anyone could accuse you of being dull, Jenny." He held out his hand for Anthony to shake it. "Richard Case."

"Anthony . . . ah . . . Boot. There's nothing dull about Riviera society, as far as I can see. Mr. and Mrs. Stirling have been wonderful hosts," he said. He was determined to be diplomatic.

"Perhaps Mr. Boot will write something about you, too. Richard owns the hotel at the top of the hill. The one with the fabulous views. He's at the absolute epicenter of Riviera society."

"Perhaps we can accommodate you on your next visit, Mr. Boot," the man said.

"I should like that very much, but I'll wait and see if Mr. Stirling enjoys what I've written before I predict whether I'll be allowed back," he said. They had both been so careful to mention Laurence repeatedly, he thought afterward, to keep him, invisibly, between them.

That evening she glowed. She gave off a vibration of energy that he suspected only he could detect. Do I do this to you? he wondered, as he watched her eat. Or is it just the relief of being out from under the forbidding eye of that husband of yours? Remembering how Stirling had humiliated her the previous evening, he asked her opinion on the markets, Mr. Macmillan, the royal wedding, refusing to let her defer to his own judgment. She was not greatly aware of the world beyond hers, but was astute on human nature and interested enough in what he had to say to be flattering company. He thought briefly of

Clarissa, of her sour pronouncements on the people around her, her readiness to see slights in the most cursory gestures. He had not enjoyed an evening so much for years.

"I should be going soon," she said, after a glance at her watch. The coffee had arrived, accompanied by a small silver plate of perfectly arranged petits fours.

He laid his napkin on the table, feeling the drag of disappointment. "You can't," he said, and added hurriedly, "I'm still not sure if I've overridden your previous opinion of me."

"Really? Oh, I suppose there is that." She turned her head, saw Richard Case at the bar with friends. He looked away swiftly, as if he had been watching them.

She studied Anthony's face. If she had been testing him, he appeared to have passed. She leaned forward and lowered her voice: "Can you row?"

"Can I *row*?"

They walked down to the quay. There, she peered down at the water, as if she wasn't confident of recognizing the boat without double-checking its name, and finally pointed him toward a small dinghy. He climbed down into it, then gave her his hand so that she could take the seat opposite him. The breeze was warm, the lights of the lobster boats winking peaceably in the inky darkness.

"Where are we headed?" He removed his jacket, laid it on the seat beside him, and picked up the oars.

"Oh, just row that way. I'll show you when we're there."

He pulled slowly, listening to the slap of the waves against the sides of the little boat. She sat opposite, her wrap loose around her shoulders. She was twisted away from him, the better to watch where she was guiding him.

Anthony's thoughts had stalled. In normal circumstances he would have been thinking strategically, working out when he would make his move, excited at the prospect of the night ahead. But even though he was alone with this woman, even though she had invited him onto a boat in the middle of a black sea, he wasn't convinced he knew which way this evening would go.

"There," she said, pointing. "It's that one."

"A boat, you said." He stared at the vast, sleek white yacht.

"A biggish boat," she conceded. "I'm not really a yacht person. I only pop aboard a couple of times a year."

They secured the dinghy and climbed aboard the yacht. She told him to sit on the cushioned bench and, a few minutes later, emerged from the cabin. She had shed her shoes, he noted, trying not to stare at her impossibly small feet. "I've made you an alcohol-free cocktail," she said, holding it toward him. "I wasn't sure you could face more tonic water."

It was warm, even so far out in the harbor, and the waves were so gentle that the yacht barely moved beneath them. Behind her he could see the lights of the harbor, the occasional car making its way up the coast road. He thought of Congo and felt like someone airlifted out of hell to a heaven he might only have imagined.

She had poured herself another martini and tucked her feet neatly under her on the bench opposite.

"So," he said, "how did you and your husband meet?"

"My husband? Are we still working?"

"No. I'm intrigued."

"By what?"

"By how he—" He checked himself. "I'm interested in how people end up together."

"We met at a ball. He was donating money to wounded servicemen. He was seated at my table, asked me out to dinner, and that was it."

"That was it?"

"It was very straightforward. After a few months he asked me to marry him, and I agreed."

"You were very young."

"I was twenty-two. My parents were delighted."

"Because he's rich?"

"Because they thought he was a suitable match. He was a solid sort, and he had a good reputation."

"And those things are important to you?"

"Aren't they important to everyone?" She fiddled with the hem of her skirt, straightening and smoothing it. "Now I ask the questions. How long were you married for, Boot?"

"Three years."

"Not very long."

"I knew pretty quickly that we'd made a mistake."

"And she didn't mind you divorcing her?"

"She divorced me." She eyed him, and he could see her assessing all the ways in which he might have deserved it. "I wasn't a faithful husband," he added, not sure, as he spoke, why he should tell her this.

"You must miss your son."

"Yes," he said. "I sometimes wonder whether I'd have done what I did if I'd known how much."

"Is that why you drink?"

He raised a wry smile. "Don't try to fix me, Mrs. Stirling. I've been the hobby of far too many well-meaning women."

She looked down at her drink. "Who said I wanted to fix you?"

"You have that . . . charitable air about you. It makes me nervous."

"You can't hide sadness."

"And you would know?"

"I'm not a fool. Nobody gets everything. I know that as well as you do."

"Your husband did."

"It's nice of you to say so."

"I'm not saying it nicely."

Their eyes locked, and then she looked away, toward the shore. The mood had become almost combative, as if they were quietly furious with each other. Away from the constraints of real life on the shore, something had loosened between them. *I want her,* he thought, and was almost reassured that he could feel something so ordinary.

"How many married women have you slept with?" Her voice cut through the still air.

He almost choked on his drink. "It's probably simpler to say that I've slept with few who weren't married."

She pondered this. "Are we a safer bet?"

"Yes."

"And why do these women sleep with you?"

"I don't know. Perhaps because they're unhappy."

"And you make them happy."

"For a little while, I suppose."

"Doesn't that make you a gigolo?" That smile again, playing at the corners of her mouth.

"No, just someone who likes to make love to married women."

This time the silence seemed to enter his bones. He would have broken it if he'd had the slightest idea what to say.

"I'm not going to make love to you, Mr. O'Hare."

He played the words over twice in his head before he could be sure of what she'd said. He took another sip of his drink, recovering. "That's fine."

"Really?"

"No"—he forced a smile—"it's not. But it'll have to be."

"I'm not unhappy enough to sleep with you."

God, when she looked at him, it was if she could see everything. He wasn't sure he liked it.

"I've never even kissed another man since I got married. Not one."

"That's admirable."

"You don't believe it."

"Yes, I do. It's rare."

"Now you do think I'm terribly dull." She stood up and walked around the edge of the yacht, turning toward him when she got to the bridge. "Do your married women fall in love with you?"

"A little."

"Are they sad when you leave them?"

"How do you know they don't leave me?"

She waited.

"As to whether they fall in love," he added eventually, "I don't generally speak to them afterward."

"You ignore them?"

"No. I'm often abroad. I tend not to spend much time in one place.

And, besides, they have their husbands, their lives . . . I don't believe any of them ever intended to leave their husbands. I was just . . . a diversion."

"Did you love any of them?"

"No."

"Did you love your wife?"

"I thought so. Now I'm not sure."

"Have you ever loved anyone?"

"My son."

"How old is he?"

"Eight. You'd make a good journalist."

"You really can't bear it that I do nothing useful, can you?" She burst out laughing.

"I think you may be wasted in the life you're in."

"Is that so? And what would you have me do instead?" She came a few steps closer to him. He could see the moon reflecting light on her pale skin, the blue shadow in the hollow of her neck. She took another step, and her voice lowered, even though nobody was near. "What was it you said to me, Anthony? 'Don't try to fix me.' "

"Why should I? You've told me you're not unhappy." His breath had caught at the back of his throat. She was so close now, her eyes searching his. He felt drunk, his senses heightened, as if every part of her was ruthlessly imprinting itself on his consciousness. He breathed in her scent, something floral, Oriental.

"I think," she said slowly, "that everything you have said to me tonight is what you would say to any of your married women."

"You're wrong," he said. But he knew she was entirely correct. It was all he could do not to crush that mouth, bury it under his own. He didn't think he had ever been more aroused in his life.

"I think," she said, "that you and I could make each other terribly unhappy."

And as she spoke, something deep inside him keeled over a little, as if in defeat. "I think," he said slowly, "that I'd like that very much."

Chapter 6

DECEMBER 1960

The women were tapping again. She could just see them from her bedroom window: one dark, one with unfeasibly red hair, seated at the window of the first-floor flat on the corner. When any man walked past, they would tap at the glass, waving and smiling if he was unwise enough to look up.

They infuriated Laurence. There had been a High Court case earlier that year in which the judge had warned such women against doing this. Laurence said that their soliciting, low-key as it might be, was lowering the tone of the area. He couldn't understand why if they were breaking the law, no one did a damn thing about it.

Jennifer didn't mind them. To her, they seemed imprisoned behind the glass. Once she had even waved to them, but they had stared blankly at her, and she had hurried on.

That aside, her days had fallen into a new routine. She would rise when Laurence did, make him coffee and toast, and fetch the newspaper from the hallway while he shaved and dressed. Often she was up before him, fixing her hair and makeup so that while she moved around the kitchen in her dressing gown, she appeared pleasing and put-together for those few occasions when he looked up from his newspaper. It was somehow easier to start the day without him sighing in irritation.

He would leave the table, allow her to help him with his overcoat, and usually some time after eight, his driver would knock discreetly at the front door. She would wave until the car disappeared around the corner.

Some ten minutes later she would greet Mrs. Cordoza, and as the older woman made them a pot of tea, perhaps remarking on the cold, she would run through the list of things she had prepared that detailed what might need doing that day. On top of the usual tasks, the vacuuming, dusting, and washing, there was often a little sewing: a button might have fallen off Laurence's shirt cuff, or some shoes needed cleaning. Mrs. Cordoza might be required to sort through the linen cupboard, checking and refolding what was within, or to polish the canteen of silver, sitting at the kitchen table, which would be spread with newspaper while she completed the task, listening to the wireless.

Jennifer, meanwhile, would bathe and dress. She might pop next door for coffee with Yvonne, take her mother for a light lunch, or hail a taxi and go into the center of town to do a little Christmas shopping. She made sure she had always returned by early afternoon. It was at that point that she usually found some other task for Mrs. Cordoza: a bus trip to buy curtain material; a search for a particular type of fish that Laurence had said he might like. Once, she gave the housekeeper an afternoon off—anything to grant herself an hour or two alone in the house, buy time to search for more letters.

In the two weeks that had passed since she'd discovered the first, she had found two more. They, too, were addressed to a post-office box, but were clearly for her. The same handwriting, the same passionate, direct way of speaking. The words seemed to echo some sound deep within. They described events that, while she couldn't remember them, held a deep resonance, like the vibrations of a huge bell long after it had stopped ringing.

None was signed other than with "B." She had read them, and read them again until the words were imprinted on her soul.

> *Dearest girl,*
> *It's 4 a.m. I can't sleep, knowing he is returning to you tonight. It is the road to madness, but I lie here imagining him lying next to you, his*

license to touch you, to hold you, and I would do anything to make that freedom mine.

You were so angry with me when you found me drinking at Alberto's. You called it an indulgence, and I'm afraid my response was unforgivable. Men hurt themselves when they lash out, and as cruel and stupid as my words may have been, I think you know your words hurt me more. Felipe told me I was a fool when you left, and he was right.

I am telling you this because I need you to know that I'm going to be a better man. Hah! I can barely believe I'm writing such a cliché. But it's true. You make me want to be a better version of myself. I have sat here for hours, staring at the whiskey bottle, and then, not five minutes ago, I finally got up and poured the whole darned lot into the sink. I will be a better person for you, darling. I want to live well, wish for you to be proud of me. If all we are allowed is hours, minutes, I want to be able to etch each of them onto my memory with exquisite clarity so that I can recall them at moments like this, when my very soul feels blackened.

Take him to you, if you must, my love, but don't love him. Please don't love him.

Yours selfishly,

B.

Her eyes had welled with tears at these last lines. Don't love him. Please don't love him. Everything had become a little clearer to her now: she had not imagined the distance she felt between herself and Laurence. It was the result of her having fallen in love with someone else. These were passionate letters: this man had opened himself to her in a way that Laurence never could. When she read his notes, her skin prickled, her heart raced. She recognized these words. But for all that she knew them, there was still a great hole at their heart.

Her mind buzzed with questions. Had the affair been going on for long? Was it recent? Had she slept with this man? Is that why things felt so physically stilted with her husband?

And, most incomprehensible of all: Who *was* this lover?

She had gone over the three letters forensically, searching for clues.

She could think of no one she knew whose name began with B, save Bill, or her husband's accountant, whose name was Bernard. She knew without a shadow of doubt that she had never been in love with him. Had B seen her at the hospital, in the days when her mind had not been her own, when everyone had been indistinct around her? Was he watching at a distance now? Waiting for her to get in touch? He existed somewhere. He held the key to everything.

Day after day, she tried to imagine her way back into her former self: this woman of secrets. Where would the Jennifer of old have hidden letters? Where were the clues to her other, secret existence? Two of the letters she had uncovered in books, another folded neatly in a balled-up stocking. All were in places her husband would never have thought of looking. I was clever, she thought. And then, a little more uncomfortably: I was duplicitous.

"Mother," she said, one lunchtime, over a sandwich on the top floor of John Lewis, "who was driving when I had my accident?"

Her mother had glanced up sharply. The restaurant around them was packed with customers, laden with shopping bags and heavy coats, the dining room thick with chatter and the clatter of crockery.

She glanced around before she turned back to Jennifer, as if the question was almost subversive. "Darling, do we really need to revisit that?"

Jennifer sipped her tea. "I know so little about what happened. It might help if I could put the pieces together."

"You nearly died. I really don't want to think about it."

"But what happened? Was I driving?"

Her mother inspected her plate. "I don't recall."

"And if it wasn't me, what happened to the driver? If I was hurt, he must have been, too."

"I don't know. How would I? Laurence always looks after his staff, doesn't he? I assume he wasn't badly hurt. If he needed treatment, I dare say Laurence would have paid for it."

Jennifer thought of the driver who had picked them up when she left the hospital: a tired-looking man in his sixties with a neat mustache and a balding head. He had not looked as if he had suffered any great trauma—or as if he might have been her lover.

Her mother pushed away the remains of her sandwich. "Why don't you ask him?"

"I will." But she knew she wouldn't. "He doesn't want me to dwell on things."

"Well, I'm sure he's quite right, darling. Perhaps you should heed his advice."

"Do you know where I was going?"

The older woman was flustered now, a little exasperated by this line of questioning. "I've no idea. Shopping, probably. Look, it happened somewhere near Marylebone Road. I believe you hit a bus. Or a bus hit you. It was all so awful, Jenny darling, we could only think about you getting better." Her mouth closed in a thin line, which told Jennifer that the conversation was at an end.

In a corner of the canteen, a woman wrapped in a dark green coat was gazing into the eyes of a man who traced her profile with a finger. As Jennifer watched, she took his fingertip between her teeth. The casual intimacy of the gesture sent a little electric shock through her. No one else seemed to have noticed the pair.

Mrs. Verrinder wiped her mouth with her napkin. "What does it really matter, dear? Car accidents happen. The more cars there are, the more dangerous it seems to be. I don't think half of the people on the roads can drive. Not like your father could. Now, he was a careful driver."

Jennifer wasn't listening.

"Anyway, you're all fixed up now, aren't you? All better?"

"I'm fine." Jennifer turned a bright smile on her mother. "Just fine."

When she and Laurence went out in the evenings now, to dinner or for drinks, she found herself looking at their wider circle of friends and acquaintances with new eyes. When a man's focus lingered on her a little longer than it should have, she found herself unable to tear her gaze away. Was it him? Was there some meaning behind his pleasant greeting? Was that a knowing smile?

There were three possible men, if B was in fact a nickname. There was Jack Amory, the head of a motor-spares company, who was unmarried and kissed her hand ostentatiously whenever they met. But he did it almost with a wink to Laurence, and she couldn't work out if this was a double bluff.

There was Reggie Carpenter, Yvonne's cousin, who sometimes made up the numbers at dinner. Dark-haired, with tired, humorous eyes, he was younger than she imagined her letter-writer to be, but he was charming, and funny, and seemed always to ensure that he was sitting at her side when Laurence wasn't there.

And then there was Bill, of course. Bill, who told jokes as if they were only for her approval, who laughingly declared he adored her, even in front of Violet. He definitely had feelings for her. But could she have had feelings for him?

She began to pay more attention to her appearance. She made regular visits to the hairdresser, bought some new dresses, became chattier, "more your old self," as Yvonne said approvingly. In the weeks after the accident she had hidden behind her girlfriends, but now she asked questions, quizzed them politely, but with some determination, seeking the chink in the armor that might lead to some answers. Occasionally she dropped clues into conversations, inquiring whether anyone might like a whiskey, then scanning the men's faces for a spark of recognition. But Laurence was never far away, and she suspected that even if they had picked up on her clues, they could have conveyed little to her in response.

If her husband noticed a particular intensity in her conversations with their friends, he didn't remark on it. He didn't remark on much. He hadn't approached her once, physically, since the night they had argued. He was polite but distant. She knew she should feel worse about it than she did, but increasingly she wanted the freedom to retreat into her private parallel world, where she could retrace her mythical, passionate romance, see herself through the eyes of the man who adored her.

Somewhere, she told herself, B was still out there. Waiting.

"These are to sign, and on the filing cabinet there are several gifts that arrived this morning. There's a case of champagne from Citroën, a hamper from the cement people in Peterborough, and a box of chocolates from your accountants. I know you don't like soft centers, so I was wondering if you'd like me to hand them round the office. I know Elsie Machzynski is particularly partial to fondants."

He barely looked up. "That will be fine." Moira observed that Mr. Stirling's thoughts were far from Christmas gifts.

"And I hope you don't mind, but I've gone ahead and organized the bits and pieces for the Christmas party. You decided it would be better held here than in a restaurant, now that the company is so much larger, so I've asked caterers to lay on a small buffet."

"Good. When is it?"

"The twenty-third. After we finish for the day. That's the Friday before we break up."

"Yes."

Why should he seem so preoccupied? So miserable? Business had never been better. Their products were in demand. Even with the credit squeeze predicted by the newspapers, Acme Mineral and Mining had one of the healthiest balance sheets in the country. There had been no more of the troublemaking letters, and those she had received the previous month still lingered, unseen by her boss, in her top drawer.

"I also thought you might like to—"

He glanced up suddenly at a sound outside, and Moira turned, startled, to see what he was looking at. There she was, walking through the office, her hair set in immaculate waves, a little red pillbox hat perched on her head, the exact shade of her shoes. What was she doing here? Mrs. Stirling gazed around her, as if she was looking for someone, and then Mr. Stevens, from Accounts, walked up to her, holding out his hand. She took it, and they chatted briefly before they looked across the office toward where she and Mr. Stirling were standing. Mrs. Stirling raised a hand in greeting.

Moira's hand was reaching for her hair. Some women managed always to look as if they had stepped out of the pages of a fashion magazine, and Jennifer Stirling was one of them. Moira didn't mind: she had always preferred to focus her energies on work, on more substantial achievements. But it was hard when the woman walked into the office, her skin glowing from the cold outside, two fiery diamond studs glinting in her ears, not to feel the tiniest bit dull in comparison. She was like a perfectly wrapped Christmas parcel, a glittering bauble.

"Mrs. Stirling," Moira said politely.

"Hello," she said.

"This is an unexpected pleasure." Mr. Stirling stood to greet her, looking rather awkward but perhaps secretly pleased. Like an unloved student who had been approached by the school sweetheart.

"Would you like me to leave?" Moira felt ill at ease, standing between them. "I've got some filing I could be—"

"Oh, no, not on my account. I'll only be a minute." She turned back to her husband. "I was passing and I thought I'd check whether you were likely to be late this evening. If you are, I might pop over to the Harrisons'. They're doing mulled wine."

"I . . . Yes, you do that. I can meet you there if I finish early."

"That would be nice," she said.

She gave off a faint scent of Nina Ricci. Moira had tried it the previous week in D. H. Evans, but had thought it a little pricey. Now she regretted not having bought it.

"I'll try not to be too late."

Mrs. Stirling didn't seem in any hurry to leave. She stood in front of her husband, but she seemed more interested in looking at the office, the men at their desks. She surveyed it all with some concentration. It was as if she had never seen the place before.

"It's been a while since you were here," he said.

"Yes," she said. "I suppose it has."

There was a short silence.

"Oh," she said abruptly. "What are your drivers' names?"

He frowned. "My drivers?"

She gave a little shrug. "I thought you might like me to organize a Christmas gift for each of them."

He seemed nonplussed. "A Christmas gift? Well, Eric's been with me the longest. I usually buy him a bottle of brandy. Have done for the last twenty years, I think. Simon fills in on the odd occasion. He's a teetotaler, so I put a little extra in his last pay packet. I don't think it's anything you need to worry about."

Mrs. Stirling seemed oddly disappointed. "Well, I'd like to help. I'll buy the brandy," she said finally, clutching her bag in front of her.

"That's very . . . thoughtful of you," he said.

She let her gaze wander across the office, then returned it to them. "Anyway, I imagine you must be terribly busy. As I said, I just thought I'd call in. Nice to see you . . . er . . ." Her smile wavered.

Moira was stung by the woman's casual dismissal. How many times had they met over the last five years? And she couldn't even be bothered to remember her name.

"Moira," Mr. Stirling prompted, when the silence became uncomfortable.

"Yes. Moira. Of course. Nice to see you again."

"I'll be right back." Moira watched as Mr. Stirling steered his wife to the door. They exchanged a few more remarks, and then, with a little wave of her gloved hand, Mrs. Stirling was gone.

The secretary took a deep breath, trying not to mind. Mr. Stirling stood immobile as his wife left the building.

Almost before she knew what she was doing, Moira walked out of the office and swiftly to her desk. She pulled a key from her pocket and opened the locked drawer, hunting through the various pieces of correspondence until she found it. She was back in Mr. Stirling's office before he was.

He closed the door behind him, glancing through the glass wall, as if he was half expecting his wife to come back. He seemed softened, a little more at ease. "So," he said, sitting down, "you were mentioning the office party. You'd been planning something." A small smile played about his lips.

Her breath was tight in her chest. She had to swallow before she could speak normally. "Actually, Mr. Stirling, there's something else."

He had pulled out a letter, ready to sign. "Right-oh. What is it?"

"This arrived two days ago." She handed him the handwritten envelope. "At the PO box you mentioned." When he said nothing, she added, "I've been keeping an eye on it, as you asked."

He stared at the envelope, then looked up at her, the color draining from his face so rapidly that she thought he might pass out. "Are you sure? This can't be right."

"But it—"

"You must have got the wrong number."

"I can assure you I got the right PO box. Number thirteen. I used Mrs. Stirling's name, as you . . . suggested."

He ripped it open, then stooped forward over the desk as he read the few lines. She stood on the other side, not wanting to appear curious, aware that the atmosphere in the room had become charged. She was already afraid of what she had done.

When he looked up, he seemed to have aged several years. He cleared his throat, then crumpled up the sheet of paper with one hand and threw it with some force into the bin beneath his desk. His expression was fierce. "It must have been lost in the postal system. Nobody must know about this. Do you understand?"

She took a step backward. "Yes, Mr. Stirling. Of course."

"Close the PO box down."

"Now? I still have the audit report to—"

"This afternoon. Do whatever you need to do. Just close it down. Do you understand?"

"Yes, Mr. Stirling." She tucked her file under her arm and let herself out of his office. She gathered up her handbag and coat and prepared to go to the post office.

Jennifer had planned to go home. She was tired, the trip to the office had been fruitless, and it had begun to rain, sending pedestrians hurrying along the pavement, collars up and heads down. But standing on the steps of her husband's workplace, she had known she couldn't go back to that silent house.

She stepped off the curb and hailed a cab, waving until she saw the yellow light swerve toward her. She climbed in, brushing raindrops from her red coat. "Do you know a place called Alberto's?" she said, as the driver leaned back toward the dividing window.

"Which part of London is it in?" he said.

"I'm sorry, I have no idea. I thought you might know."

He frowned. "There's an Alberto's club in Mayfair. I can take you there, but I'm not sure it'll be open."

"Fine," she said, and settled back in the seat.

It took only fifteen minutes to get there. The taxi drew up, and the driver pointed across the road. "That's the only Alberto's I know," he said. "Not sure if it's your kind of place, ma'am."

She wiped the window with her sleeve and peered out. Metal railings surrounded a basement entrance, the steps disappearing out of view. A weary sign bore the name, and two bedraggled yew trees stood in large pots at each side of the door. "That's it?"

"You think it's the right place?"

She managed a smile. "Well, I'll soon find out."

She paid him, and was left standing, in the thin rain, on the pavement. The door was half open, propped by a dustbin. As she entered, she was bombarded by the smell of alcohol, stale cigarette smoke, sweat, and perfume. She let her eyes adjust to the dim light. To her left a cloakroom was empty and unattended, a beer bottle and a set of keys on its counter. She walked along the narrow hall and pushed open double doors to find herself in a huge empty room, chairs stacked up on round tables in front of a small stage. Weaving in and out of them, an old woman dragged a vacuum cleaner, muttering to herself occasionally in apparent disapproval. A bar ran along one wall. Behind it a woman was smoking and talking to a man stacking the illuminated shelves with bottles. "Hold up," the woman said, catching sight of her. "Can I help you, love?"

Jennifer felt the woman's assessing gaze on her. It was not entirely friendly. "Are you open?"

"Do we look open?"

She held her bag to her stomach, suddenly self-conscious. "I'm sorry. I'll come back another time."

"Who d'you want, lady?" said the man, straightening up. He had dark, slicked-back hair and the kind of pale, puffy skin that told of too much alcohol and too little fresh air.

She stared at him, trying to work out if what she felt was a glimmer of recognition. "Have you . . . have you seen me in here before?" she asked.

He looked mildly amused. "Not if you say I haven't."

The woman cocked her head. "We have a very bad memory for faces in this place."

Jennifer walked a few steps toward the bar. "Do you know someone called Felipe?"

"Who are you?" the woman demanded.

"I—it doesn't matter."

"Why do you want Felipe?"

Their faces had hardened. "We have a mutual friend," she explained.

"Then your friend should have told you that Felipe would be a bit difficult to get hold of."

She bit her lip, wondering how much she could reasonably explain. "It's not someone I'm in touch with very—"

"He's dead, lady."

"What?"

"Felipe. Is dead. The place is under new management. We've had all sorts down here saying he owed them this and that, and I might as well tell you that you'll get nothing from me."

"I didn't come here for—"

"Unless you can show me Felipe's signature on an IOU, you're getting nothing." Now the woman was looking closely at her clothes, her jewelry, smirking, as if she had decided why Jennifer might be there. "His family gets his estate. What's left of it. That would include his wife," she said nastily.

"I had nothing to do with Mr. Felipe personally. I'm sorry for your loss," Jennifer said primly. As quickly as she could, she walked out of the club and back up the stairs into the gray daylight.

Moira rummaged through the boxes of decorations until she had found what she wanted, then sorted and laid out what was within. She pinned two pieces of tinsel around each door. She sat at her desk for almost half an hour and restuck the paper chains that had come apart during the year, then taped them in garlands above the desks. To the wall she pinned several pieces of string, and hung on them the greetings cards that had been sent by commercial partners. Above the light fittings she draped shimmering strands of foil, making sure that they were not so close to the bulbs as to be a fire risk.

Outside, the skies had darkened, the sodium lights coming on down the length of the street. Gradually, in much the same order that they always did, the staff of Acme Mineral and Mining's London office left the building. First Phyllis and Elsie, the typists, who always left at five on the dot, even though they seemed to carry no such sense of rigorous punctuality when it came to clocking in. Then David Moreton, in Accounts, and shortly after him, Stevens, who would retreat to the pub on the corner for several bracing shots of whiskey before he made his way home. The rest left in small groups, wrapping themselves in scarves and coats, the men picking up theirs from the stands in the corner, a few waving good-bye to her as they passed Mr. Stirling's office. Felicity Harewood, in charge of the payroll, lived only one stop away from Moira in Streatham, but never once suggested they catch the same bus. When Felicity had first been hired, in May, Moira had thought it might be rather nice to have someone to chat to on the way home, a woman with whom she could exchange recipes or pass a few comments on the day's events in the fuggy confines of the 159. But Felicity left each evening without even a backward look. On the one occasion Moira and she had been on the same bus, she had kept her head stuck in a paperback novel for most of the journey, even though Moira was almost certain she knew that she was only two seats behind.

Mr. Stirling left at a quarter to seven. He had been distracted and impatient for most of the afternoon, telephoning the factory manager to berate him about sickness rates, and canceling a meeting he had arranged for four. When she had returned from the post office, he had glanced at her, as if to confirm that she had done what he had asked, then returned to his work.

Moira pulled the two spare desks to the edge of the room beside Accounts. She spread them with festive tablecloths and pinned some strands of tinsel to the edges. In ten days' time this would be the base for the buffet; in the meantime it would be useful to have somewhere to put the gifts that arrived from suppliers, and the Christmas postbox through which the staff were supposed to send each other seasonal greetings.

By almost eight o'clock it was done. Moira surveyed the empty office, made glittering and festive through her efforts, smoothed her skirt, and allowed herself to picture the expressions of pleasure on people's faces when they walked back through the door in the morning.

She wouldn't get paid for it, but it was the little gestures, the extras, that made all the difference. The other secretaries had little idea that a personal assistant's job was not just a matter of typing personal correspondence and making sure the filing was in order. It was a far greater role than that. It was about making sure that an office didn't just run smoothly but that the people within it felt part of . . . well, a family. A Christmas postbox and some cheerful decorations were what ultimately tied an office together, and made it a place one might look forward to coming to.

The little Christmas tree she had set up in the corner looked nicer there. There was little point in having it at home, now that there was no one but her to see it. Here it could be enjoyed by lots of people. And if someone happened to remark on the very pretty angel at the top, or the lovely baubles with the frosted crystals, she might tell them casually, as if it had just occurred to her, that those had been Mother's favorites.

Moira put on her coat. She gathered up her belongings, tied her scarf, and placed her pen and pencil neatly on the desk ready for the morning. She went to Mr. Stirling's office, keys in hand, to lock the door, and then, with a glance at the door, she moved swiftly into the room and reached under his desk for the wastepaper bin.

It took her only a moment to locate the handwritten letter. She barely hesitated before she picked it up and, after checking again through the glass to make sure that she was still alone, she smoothed out the creases on the desk and began to read.

She stood very, very still.

Then she read it again.

The bell outside chimed eight. Startled by the sound, Moira left Mr. Stirling's office, placed his bin outside for the cleaners to empty, and locked the door. She put the letter at the bottom of her desk drawer, locked it, and dropped the key into her pocket.

For once, the bus ride to Streatham seemed to take no time at all. Moira Parker had an awful lot to think about.

Chapter 7

AUGUST 1960

They met every day, sitting outside sun-drenched cafés, or heading into the scorched hills in her little Daimler to eat at places they picked without care or forethought. She told him about her upbringing in Hampshire and Eaton Place, the ponies, boarding school, the narrow, comfortable world that had made up her life until her marriage. She told him how, even at twelve, she had felt stifled, had known she would need a bigger canvas, and how she had never suspected that the wide stretches of the Riviera could contain a social circle just as restricted and monitored as the one she had left behind.

She told him of a boy from the village with whom she had fallen in love at fifteen, and how, when he discovered the relationship, her father had taken her into an outbuilding and thrashed her with his braces.

"For falling in love?" She had told the story lightly, and he tried to hide how disturbed he was by it.

"For falling in love with the wrong sort of boy. Oh, I suppose I was a bit of a handful. They told me I'd brought the whole family into disrepute. They said I had no moral compass, that if I didn't watch myself no decent man would want to marry me." She laughed, without humor. "Of course, the fact that my father had a mistress for years was quite a different matter."

"And then Laurence came along."

She smiled at him slyly. "Yes. *Wasn't* I lucky?"

He talked to her in the way that people tell lifelong secrets to fellow passengers in railway carriages: an unburdened intimacy, resting on the unspoken understanding that they were unlikely to meet again. He told her about his three-year tenure as the *Nation*'s Central Africa correspondent, how at first he had welcomed the chance to escape his failing marriage, but hadn't adopted the personal armory necessary to cope with the atrocities he witnessed: Congo's steps to independence had meant the death of thousands. He had found himself spending night after night in Léopoldville's Foreign Correspondents' Club, anesthetizing himself with whiskey or, worse, palm wine, until the combined horrors of what he had seen and a bout of yellow fever almost ended him. "I had something of a breakdown," he said, attempting to emulate her light tone, "although no one is impolite enough to say so, of course. They blame the yellow fever and urge me not to go back."

"Poor Boot."

"Yes. Poor me. Especially as it gave my ex-wife yet another good reason not to let me see my son."

"And there I was, thinking it was that little matter of serial infidelity." She laid her hand on his. "I'm sorry. I'm teasing. I don't mean to be trite."

"Am I boring you?"

"On the contrary. It's not often that I spend time with a man who actually wants to talk to me."

He didn't drink in her company, and no longer missed it. The challenge she posed was an adequate substitute for alcohol, and besides, he liked being in control of who he was when he was with her. Having spoken little since his last months in Africa, afraid of what he might reveal, the weaknesses he might expose, he now found he wanted to talk. He liked the way she watched him when he did, as if nothing he might say would change her fundamental opinion of him, as if nothing he confided would later be used in evidence against him.

"What happens to former war correspondents when they become weary of trouble?" she asked.

"They're pensioned off to dark corners of the newsroom and bore everyone with tales of their glory days," he said. "Or they stay out in the field until they get killed."

"And which kind are you?"

"I don't know." He lifted his eyes to hers. "I haven't yet become weary of trouble."

He sank easily into the gentle rhythms of the Riviera: the long lunches, the time spent outdoors, the endless chatting with people of whom one had only limited acquaintance. He had taken to long walks in the early morning, when once he had been dead to the world, enjoying the sea air, the friendly greetings exchanged by people not bad-tempered with hangovers and lack of sleep. He felt at ease, in a way he had not for many years. He fended off telegrams from Don, threatening dire consequences if he didn't file something useful soon.

"You didn't like the profile?" he had asked.

"It was fine, but it ran in the business section last Tuesday, and Accounts wants to know why you're still filing expenses four days after you wrote it."

She took him to Monte Carlo, spinning the car around the vertiginous bends of the mountain roads while he watched her slim strong hands on the wheel and imagined placing each finger reverently in his mouth. She took him to a casino, and made him feel like a god when he translated his few pounds into a sizable win at roulette. She ate mussels at a seafront café, plucking them delicately but ruthlessly from their shells, and he lost the power of speech. She had seeped into his consciousness so thoroughly, absorbing all lucid thought, that not only could he think of nothing else but no longer cared to. In his hours alone, his mind wandered to a million possible outcomes, and he marveled at how long it had been since he had felt so preoccupied by a woman.

It was because she was that rare thing, genuinely unobtainable. He should have given up days ago. But his pulse quickened when another note was pushed under his door, wondering if he'd like to join her for drinks at the Piazza, or perhaps a quick drive to Menton?

What harm could it do? He was thirty, and couldn't remember the last time he had laughed so much. Why shouldn't he enjoy briefly the kind of gaiety that other people took for granted? It was all so far removed from his habitual life that it seemed unreal.

It was on the Saturday evening that he received the telegram telling him what he had half expected for days: his train home had been booked for tomorrow, and he was expected at the *Nation*'s offices on Monday morning. When he read it, he experienced a kind of relief: this thing with Jennifer Stirling had become strangely disorienting. He would never normally have spent so much time and energy on a woman whose passion was not a foregone conclusion. The thought of not seeing her again was upsetting, but some part of him wanted to return to his old routines, to rediscover the person he was.

He pulled his suitcase from the rack and placed it on his bed. He would pack, and then he would send her a note, thanking her for her time and suggesting that if she ever wanted to meet for lunch in London, she should telephone him. If she chose to contact him there, away from the magic of this place, perhaps she would become like all of the others: a pleasant physical diversion.

It was as he put his shoes into the case that the call came from the concierge: a woman was waiting in reception for him.

"Blond hair?"

"Yes, sir."

"Would you mind asking her to come to the telephone?"

He heard a brief burst of French, then her voice, a little breathless, uncertain. "It's Jennifer. I just wondered . . . if we might have a quick drink."

"Delighted, but I'm not quite ready. Do you want to come up and wait?"

He tidied his room rapidly, kicking stray items under the bed. He rearranged the sheet of paper in his typewriter, as if he had been working on the piece he had wired across an hour earlier. He pulled on a clean shirt, although he didn't have time to do it up. When he heard a soft knock, he opened the door. "What a lovely surprise," he said. "I was just finishing something, but do come in."

She stood awkwardly in the corridor. When she caught sight of his bare chest, she looked away. "Would you rather I waited downstairs?"

"No. Please. I'll only be a few minutes."

She stepped in and walked to the center of the room. She was wearing a pale gold sleeveless dress with a mandarin collar. Her shoulders were slightly pink where the sun had touched them as she drove. Her hair was loose around her shoulders, a little windblown, as if she had driven there in a hurry.

Her gaze took in the bed, littered with notepads, the near-packed suitcase. They were briefly silenced by proximity. She recovered first. "Aren't you going to offer me a drink?"

"Sorry. Inconsiderate of me." He telephoned down for a gin and tonic, which arrived in minutes. "Where are we going?"

"Going?"

"Have I time to shave?" He went into the bathroom.

"Of course. Go ahead."

He had done this on purpose, he thought afterward, made her party to the enforced intimacy. He looked better: the sick man's yellow pallor had left his skin, the lines of strain had been ironed from his eyes. He ran the hot water, and watched her in the bathroom mirror as he lathered his chin.

She was distracted, preoccupied. As his razor scraped against his skin, he watched her pace, like a restless animal. "Are you all right?" he called, rinsing his blade in the water.

"I'm fine." She had drunk half the gin and tonic already, and poured another.

He finished shaving, toweled dry his face, splashed on some of the aftershave he had bought from the *pharmacie*. It was sharp, with notes of citrus and rosemary. He did up his shirt and straightened his collar in the mirror. He loved this moment, the convergence of appetite and possibility. He felt oddly triumphant. He stepped out of the bathroom and found her standing by the balcony. The sky was dimming, the lights of the seafront glowing as dusk fell. She held her drink in one hand, the other arm laid slightly defensively across her waist. He took a step closer to her.

"I forgot to say how lovely you look," he said. "I like that color on you. It's—"

"Larry's back tomorrow."

She drew away from the balcony and faced him. "I had a wire this afternoon. We'll be flying to London on Tuesday."

"I see," he said. There were tiny blond hairs on her arm. The sea breeze lifted and laid them down.

When he looked up, her eyes locked with his. "I'm not unhappy," she said.

"I know that."

She was studying him, her lovely mouth serious. She bit her lip, then turned her back to him. She stood very still. "The top button," she said.

"I'm sorry?"

"I can't undo it myself."

Something ignited inside him. He experienced it almost as relief, that this would happen, that the woman he had dreamed about, conjured at night in this bed, was to be his after all. Her distance, her resistance, had almost overwhelmed him. He wanted the release that comes with release, wanted to feel spent, the ache of perpetual unrelieved desire soothed.

He took her drink from her, and her hand went to her hair, lifting it from the nape of her neck. He obeyed the silent instruction, lifting his hands to her skin. Usually so certain, his fingers fumbled, were thick and clumsy. He watched them as if from afar, wrestling with the silk-covered button, and as he released it, he saw that his hands were trembling. He stilled, and gazed at her neck: exposed now, it was bent forward slightly, as if in supplication. He wanted to place his mouth on it, could already taste that pale, lightly freckled skin. His thumb rested there, tender, luxuriating in the prospect of what lay ahead. She let out a small breath at the pressure, so subtle that he felt rather than heard it. And something in him stalled.

He stared at the down where her golden hair met her skin, at the slender fingers still holding it up. And he understood, with horrible certainty, what was going to happen.

Anthony O'Hare closed his eyes very tightly, and then, with exquisite deliberation, he refastened her dress. He took a small step backward.

She hesitated, as if she were trying to work out what he had done, perhaps registering the absence of his skin on hers.

Then she turned, her hand on the back of her neck, establishing what had taken place. She gazed at him, and her face, at first questioning, colored.

"I'm sorry," he began, "but I—I can't."

"Oh . . ." She flinched. Her hand went to her mouth, and a deep blush stained her neck. "Oh, God."

"No. You don't understand, Jennifer. It's not anything that—"

She pushed past him, grabbing her handbag. And then, before he could say anything else, she was wrestling with the door handle and running down the corridor.

"Jennifer!" he yelled. "Jennifer! Let me explain!" But by the time he had reached the door, she was gone.

The French train plodded through the parched countryside to Lyon, as if it was determined to grant him too long to think of all the things he had got wrong and all the things he couldn't have changed even if he'd wanted to. Several times an hour he thought about ordering himself a large whiskey from the dining car; he watched the stewards move deftly up and down the carriage, carrying glasses on silver trays, a choreographed ballet of stooping and pacing, and knew it would take only the lifting of a finger to have that consolation for himself. Afterward he was barely sure what had prevented him doing so.

At night, he settled into the *couchette*, pulled out with disdainful efficiency by the steward. As the train rumbled on through the darkness, he clicked on his bedside light and picked up a paperback book he had found at the hotel, left by some former traveler. He read the same page several times, took nothing in, and eventually threw it down in disgust. He had a French newspaper, but the space was too cramped to unfold the pages properly, and the print too small in the dim light. He dozed, and awoke, and as England drew closer, the future settled on him like a big black cloud.

Finally, as dawn broke, he found pen and paper. He had never written a letter to a woman, other than brief thank-you notes to his mother, for whatever small gift she had sent, to Clarissa about financial matters, and his brief apology to Jennifer after that first night. Now, consumed by an aching melancholy, haunted by the mortified look in Jennifer's eyes, freed by the prospect that he might never see her again, he wrote unguardedly, wanting only to explain himself.

Dearest,

I couldn't make you listen, when you left in such a hurry, but I was not rejecting you. You were so far from the truth I can hardly bear it.

Here is the truth: you would not be the first married woman I have made love to. You know my personal circumstances, and to be frank, these relationships, such as they are, have suited me. I did not want to be close to anyone. When we first met, I chose to think you would be no different.

But when you arrived at my room on Saturday, you looked so wonderful in your dress. And then you asked me to unfasten that button at your neck. And as my fingers met your skin I realized in that moment that to make love to you would be a disaster for both of us. You, dearest girl, have no idea of how you would feel to be so duplicitous. You are an honest, delightful creature. Even if you do not feel it now, there is pleasure to be had from being a decent person. I do not want to be the man responsible for making you someone less than that.

And me? I knew in the moment you looked up at me that if we did this I would be lost. I would not be able to put you aside, as I had with the others. I would not be able to nod agreeably to Laurence as we passed each other in some restaurant. I would never be satisfied with just a part of you. I had been fooling myself to think otherwise.

It was for that reason, darling girl, that I redid that wretched button at your neck. And for that reason I have lain awake for the last two nights, hating myself for the one decent thing I have ever done.

Forgive me.

B.

He folded it carefully into his breast pocket, and then, at last, he slept.

Don stubbed out his cigarette and studied the typewritten sheet while the young man standing awkwardly to the side of his desk shifted from one foot to the other. "You can't spell *bigamy*. It's an *a*, not an *o*." He swiped his pencil belligerently across three lines. "And this intro's terrible. You've got a man who married three women called Hilda, all within two miles of each other. That's a gift of a story. The way you've written it I'd rather be reading *Hansard* on municipal drainage."

"Sorry, Mr. Franklin."

"Bugger sorry. Get it right. This was for an early page, and it's already twenty to four. What the hell is the matter with you? 'Bigomy'! You want to take a lesson from O'Hare here. He spends so much time in Africa that we can't tell whether the bloody spellings are right or wrong anyway." He threw the sheet of paper at the young man, who scrabbled for it and left the office quickly.

"So," Don tutted, "where's my bloody feature, then? 'Riviera Secrets of the Rich and Famous?' "

"It's coming," Anthony lied.

"You'd better make it quick. I've got half a page put by for it on Saturday. Did you have a good time?"

"It was fine."

Don tilted his head. "Yeah. Looks like it. So. Anyway. I've got good news."

The windows of Don's office were so covered with nicotine that anyone who brushed innocently against them would find their shirtsleeves stained yellow. Anthony stared out through the golden fug at the newsroom. For two days now he had walked around with the letter in his pocket, trying to work out how he could get it to her. He kept seeing her face, the flush of horror as she realized what she thought had been her mistake.

"Tony?"

"Yes."

"I've got good news for you."

"Right. Yes."

"I've been talking to the foreign desk, and they want someone to go to Baghdad. Take a look at this man from the Polish embassy who's claiming to be some sort of super-spy. Hard news, son. Right up your street. It'll get you out of the office for a week or two."

"I can't go now."

"You need a day or two?"

"I've got some personal business to sort out."

"Shall I tell the Algerians to hold off on the ceasefire too? Just in case it gets in the way of your domestic arrangements? Are you kidding me, O'Hare?"

"Then send someone else. I'm sorry, Don."

Don's metronomic clicking of his ballpoint pen became increasingly uneven. "I don't understand. You spend all your time hanging around the office bitching that you need to be off doing 'real' news, so I give you a story that Peterson would gnaw his right arm off for, and all of a sudden you want to be deskbound."

"Like I said, I'm sorry."

Don's mouth fell open. He closed it, stood up heavily, made his way across the office, and closed the door. Then he came back to his seat. "Tony, this is a good story. You should be all over it like a bad suit. More than that, you need this story. You need to show them they can rely on you." He peered at him. "You lost your appetite? You telling me you want to stick with the soft stuff?"

"No. I'm just . . . Just give me a day or two."

Don sat back, lit a cigarette, and inhaled noisily. "Good God," he said. "It's a woman."

Anthony said nothing.

"It is. You met a woman. What's the matter? You can't go anywhere until you've cracked her?"

"She's married."

"Since when did that stop you?"

"She's . . . It's the wife. Stirling's wife."

"And?"

"And she's too good."

"For him? Don't tell me."

"For me. I don't know what to do."

Don raised his eyes to the ceiling.

"An attack of conscience, eh? I wondered why you looked so bloody awful." He shook his head, spoke as if someone else was in the little room. "I don't believe it. O'Hare, of all people." He placed his pen on his desk with a chubby hand. "Okay. Here's what you're going to do. Go and see her, do what you have to do, get it out of your system. Then be on the flight that leaves tomorrow lunchtime. I'll tell the desk you left this evening. How does that sound? And write me some bloody decent stories."

" 'Get it out of your system'? You old romantic."

"You got a prettier phrase?"

Anthony felt the letter in his pocket. "I owe you one," he said.

"You owe me eighty-three," Don grumbled.

It had not been hard to find Stirling's address. He had scanned the office copy of *Who's Who*, and there it was, at the bottom of his entry, underneath "m: Jennifer Louisa Verrinder, b. 1934." That evening, after work, he had driven to Fitzrovia and parked in the square a few doors up from the white-stuccoed house.

A Nash-style Regency villa, with pillars that flanked the front porch, it had the air of an expensive consultant's office in Harley Street. He sat in the car and wondered what she was doing behind those net curtains. He pictured her sitting with a magazine, perhaps gazing blankly across the room and thinking of a lost moment in a hotel room in France. At around half past six a middle-aged woman left the house, drawing her coat around her and glancing up, as if checking the sky for rain. She tied a waterproof bonnet over her hair and hurried down the street. The curtains were drawn by an unseen hand and the humid evening gave way to night, but he sat in his Hillman, staring at Number 32.

He had begun to drift off when at last the front door opened. As he pushed himself upright, she stepped out. It was almost nine o'clock. She was wearing a sleeveless white dress, a little wrap over her shoulders, and walked down the steps carefully, as if she didn't quite trust her feet. Then Stirling was behind her, saying something that Anthony couldn't hear, and she nodded. Then they were climbing into a big black car. As it pulled out into the road, Anthony charged the ignition. He drove into the road, one car behind them, and followed.

They didn't travel far. The driver paused at the door of a Mayfair casino to let them out. She straightened her dress, then walked inside, taking off her wrap as she went.

Anthony waited until he was sure Stirling had gone in, then pulled his Hillman into the spot behind the black car. "Park that for me, will you?" he called to the incredulous doorman, threw him the keys, and pressed a ten-shilling note into his hand.

"Sir? Can I see your membership card?" He was hastening through the lobby when a man in a casino uniform stopped him. "Sir? Your membership card?"

The Stirlings were about to step into the elevator. He could just see her through the crowd. "I need to speak to someone. I'll be two minutes."

"Sir, I'm afraid I can't let you in without—"

Anthony reached into his pocket and pulled out everything in it—wallet, house keys, passport—and dumped it into the man's open hands. "Take it—take it all. I promise I'll only be two minutes." And as the man stared, openmouthed, he pushed his way through the crowd and edged into the lift as the doors closed.

Stirling was to the right, so Anthony pulled the brim of his hat low over his face, moved past him, and, confident that the man hadn't seen him, edged backward until his own back was pressed to the wall.

Everyone faced the doors. Stirling, in front of him, was talking to someone he seemed to know. Anthony heard him murmur something about markets, a crisis in credit, the other man's muttered agreement. His own pulse was thumping in his ears, and sweat trickled down his back. She held her bag in front of her with two gloved hands, her face composed, only a stray blond strand of hair creeping down from her chignon to confirm that she was human, not some heavenly apparition.

"Second floor."

The doors opened, allowing two people out and one man in. The remaining passengers shuffled obligingly, making space for the new arrival. Stirling was still talking, his voice low and sonorous. It was a warm evening, and in the close confines of the lift, Anthony was acutely aware of the bodies around him, the smells of perfume, setting lotion, and Brylcreem that hung in the sticky air, the faint breeze as the doors closed.

He lifted his head a little and stared at Jennifer. She was less than a foot away, so close that he could detect the spice of her scent and each tiny freckle on her shoulders. He kept staring, until she turned her head a little—and saw him. Her eyes widened, her cheeks colored. Her husband was still deep in conversation.

She looked at the floor, then her eyes slid back to Anthony's, the rise and fall of her chest revealing how much he'd shocked her. Their eyes met, and in those few silent moments, he told her everything. He told her that she was the most astonishing thing he had ever encountered. He told her that she haunted his waking hours, and that every feeling, every experience he had had in his life up to that point was flat and unimportant compared to the enormity of this.

He told her he loved her.

"Third floor."

She blinked, and they moved apart as a man at the back excused himself, walked between them, and stepped out of the lift. As the gap closed behind him, Anthony reached into his pocket and retrieved the letter. He took a step to his right, and held it out to her behind the evening jacket of a man who coughed, making them jump a little. Her husband was shaking his head at something his companion had said. Both men laughed humorlessly. For a moment, Anthony thought she wouldn't take it from him, but then her gloved hand shot out surreptitiously, and as he stood there, the envelope disappeared into her bag.

"Fourth floor," said the bellboy. "Restaurant."

Everyone except Anthony moved forward. Stirling glanced to his right, apparently remembering his wife's presence, and reached out a hand—not in affection, Anthony observed, but to propel her forward. The doors closed behind her, and he was alone as, with the bellboy's cry of "Ground floor," the lift began to descend.

Anthony had barely expected a response. He hadn't even bothered to check his post until he left his house, late, and found two letters on the mat. He half walked, half ran along the baked, busy pavement, ducking in and out of the nurses and patients leaving the vast St. Bartholomew's Hospital, his suitcase bashing against his legs. He was meant to be at Heathrow by half past two, was barely sure even now how he would make it in time. The sight of her handwriting had induced a kind of shock in him, followed by panic when he realized it was already ten to twelve, and he was at the wrong end of London.

Postman's Park. Midday.

There had, of course, been no taxis. He had jumped on the Tube part of the way and run the rest. His shirt, neatly pressed, now stuck to his skin; his hair flopped over his sweaty forehead. "Excuse me," he muttered, as a woman in high-heeled sandals tutted, forced to step out of his way. "Excuse me." A bus stopped, belching purple fumes, and he heard the conductor ring the bell for it to move off again. He hesitated as the passengers poured across the pavement, trying to catch his wind, and checked his watch. It was a quarter past twelve. It was entirely possible she would already have given up on him.

What the hell was he doing? If he missed this flight, Don would personally see to it that he was on Golden Weddings and Other Anniversaries for the next ten years. They would view it as another example of his inability to cope, a reason to give the next good story to Murfett or Phipps.

He ducked down King Edward Street, gasping, and then he was in a tiny oasis of peace in the middle of the City. Postman's Park was a small garden, created by a Victorian philanthropist to mark the lives of ordinary heroes. He walked, breathing hard, into the center.

It was blue, a gently moving swarm of blue. As his vision steadied, he saw postmen in their blue uniforms, some walking, some lying on the grass, a few lined up along the bench in front of the glazed Royal Doulton tablets that commemorated each act of bravery. The postmen of London, freed from their rounds and postbags, were enjoying the midday sun, in their shirtsleeves with their sandwich boxes, chatting, exchanging food, relaxing on the grass under the dappled shade of the trees.

His breathing had steadied. He dropped his suitcase and fished for a handkerchief, mopped his forehead, then turned in a slow circle, trying to see behind the large ferns, the wall of the church, and into the shadowed enclaves of the office buildings. He scanned the park for a jeweled emerald dress, the flash of pale gold hair that would mark her out.

She was not there.

He looked at his watch. Twenty past. She had come and gone. Perhaps she had changed her mind. Perhaps Stirling had found the ruddy letter. It was then that he remembered the second envelope, the one from Clarissa, which he had stuffed into his pocket as he left home. He pulled it out now and read it swiftly. He could never see her handwriting without hearing her tight, disappointed voice or seeing her neat blouses, always buttoned to the neck when she saw him, as if he might gain some advantage from a glimpse of her skin.

Dear Anthony,
   This is to let you know as a matter of courtesy that I am to be married.

He felt a vague sense of proprietary shock at the idea that Clarissa might find happiness with someone else. He had thought her incapable of it with anybody.

   I have met a decent man who owns a chain of drapery shops, and he is willing to take on me and Phillip. He is kind, and says he will treat him as his own. The wedding will be in September. This is difficult for me to broach, but you might want to think about how much contact you wish to maintain with the boy. I would like him to be able to live as a normal family, and it may well be that continued, erratic contact with you will make it harder for him to settle.
   Please consider this, and let me know what you think.
   We will not require further financial assistance from you, as Edgar can provide for us. I enclose our new address below.
   Yours sincerely,

   Clarissa

He read it twice, but it was not until the third time that he grasped what she was proposing: Phillip, his boy, should be brought up by some upright curtain merchant, free from his father's "continued, erratic contact." The day closed in on him. He felt a sudden urgent desire for alcohol, and saw an inn across the road through the park gates.

"Oh, Christ," he said aloud, his hands dropping to his knees, his head sinking. He stayed there, bent double, for a minute, trying to collect his thoughts, to allow his pulse rate to return to normal. Then, with a sigh, he pushed himself upright.

She was in front of him. She wore a white dress, patterned with huge red roses, and a pair of oversize sunglasses. She pushed them to the top of her head. A great sigh forced itself from his chest at the sheer sight of her.

"I can't stay," he began, when he found his voice. "I've got to fly to Baghdad. My plane leaves in—I have no idea how—"

She was so beautiful, outshining the blooms in their neat borders, dazzling the postmen, who had stopped talking to look at her.

"I don't . . ." He shook his head. "I can say it all in letters. Then when I see you I—"

"Anthony," she said, as if she was affirming him to herself.

"I'll be back in a week or so," he said. "If you'll meet me then, I'll be able to explain. There's so much—"

But she had stepped forward and, taking his face in her two gloved hands, pulled him to her. There was the briefest hesitation, and then her lips met his, her mouth warm, yielding, yet surprisingly demanding. Anthony forgot the flight. He forgot the park and his lost child and his ex-wife. He forgot the story that his boss believed should have consumed him. He forgot that emotions, in his experience, were more dangerous than munitions. He allowed himself to do as Jennifer demanded: to give himself to her, to do it freely.

"Anthony," she had said, and with that one word, had given him not only herself but a new, better edited version of his future.

Chapter 8

DECEMBER 1960

Once again he wasn't talking to her. For such an undemonstrative man, Laurence Stirling's moods could be perversely mercurial. Jennifer eyed her husband silently over breakfast as he read his newspaper. Although she was downstairs before him, had laid out breakfast as he liked it, he had uttered, in the thirty-three minutes since he had first laid eyes on her that morning, not one word.

She glanced down at her dressing gown, checked her hair. Nothing out of place. Her scar, which she knew disgusted him, was covered with her sleeve. What had she done? Should she have waited up for him? He had returned home so late the previous evening that she had been only briefly roused by the sound of the front door. Had she said something in her sleep?

The clock ticked its melancholy way toward eight o'clock, interrupted only by the intermittent rustle of Laurence's newspaper as it was opened and refolded. Outside, she heard footsteps on the front steps, the brief rattle as the postman pushed the mail through the letterbox, then a child's voice, lifted querulously, as it passed the window.

She attempted to make some remark about the snow, a headline about the increasing cost of fuel, but Laurence merely sighed, as if in irritation, and she said no more.

My lover wouldn't treat me like this, she told him silently, butter-

ing a piece of toast. He would smile, touch my waist as he passed me
in the kitchen. In fact, they probably wouldn't even have breakfast in
the kitchen: he would bring a tray of delicious things up to bed,
handing her coffee as she awoke, when they would exchange joyous,
crumby kisses. In one of the letters, he had written

> *When you eat, just for that moment you give yourself over entirely to*
> *the experience of it. I watched you that first time at dinner, and I wished*
> *you would give the same concentration to me.*

Laurence's voice broke into her reverie. "It's drinks at the Moncrieffs'
tonight, before the company Christmas party. You do remember?"

"Yes." She didn't look up.

"I'll be back at around half past six. Francis is expecting us then."
She felt his eyes linger on her, as if he was waiting for some further
response, but she felt too mulish to try. And then he was gone, leaving
Jennifer to a silent house, and dreams of an imaginary breakfast far
preferable to her own.

> *Do you remember that first dinner? I was such a fool, and you knew*
> *it. And you were so utterly, utterly charming, darling J, even faced with*
> *my ungracious behavior.*
> *I was so angry that night. Now I suspect I was in love with you even*
> *then, but we men are so thumpingly incapable of seeing what is before us.*
> *It was easier to pass off my discomfort as something else entirely.*

She had now unearthed seven letters from their hiding places
around her house; seven letters that laid out before her the kind of
love she had known, the kind of person she had become as a result of
it. In those handwritten words, she saw herself reflected in myriad
ways: impulsive, passionate, quick to temper and to forgive.

He seemed her polar opposite. He challenged, proclaimed, promised. He was an acute observer; of her, of the things around him. He
kept nothing hidden. She seemed to be the first woman he had ever

truly loved. She wondered, when she read his words again, whether he was the first man she had truly loved in return.

> *When you looked at me with those limitless, deliquescent eyes of yours, I used to wonder what it was you could possibly see in me. Now I know that is a foolish view of love. You and I could no more not love each other than the earth could stop circling the sun.*

Although the letters were not always dated, it was possible to place them in some kind of chronology: this one had come soon after they had first met, another after some kind of argument, a third after a passionate reunion. He had wanted her to leave Laurence. Several of them asked her to. She had apparently resisted. Why? She thought now of the cold man in the kitchen, the oppressive silence of her home. *Why did I not go?*

She read the seven letters obsessively, trawling for clues, trying to work out the man's identity. The last was dated September, a matter of weeks before her accident. Why had he not made contact? They had plainly never telephoned each other, nor had any specific meeting place. When she observed that some of the letters shared a PO box, she had gone to the post office to find out if there were any more. But the box had been reallocated, and there were no letters for her.

She became convinced that he would make himself known to her. How could the man who had written these letters, the man whose emotions were suffused with urgency, just sit and wait? She no longer believed it might be Bill; it was not that she couldn't believe she'd had feelings for him, but the idea of deceiving Violet seemed beyond her, if not him. Which left Jack Amory and Reggie Carpenter. And Jack Amory had just announced his engagement to a Miss Victoria Nelson of Camberley, Surrey.

Mrs. Cordoza entered the room as Jennifer was finishing her hair. "Could you make sure my midnight blue silk is pressed for this evening?" she said. She held a string of diamonds against her pale neck. He loved her neck:

I have never yet been able to look at it without wanting to kiss the back of it.

"I've laid it out on the bed there. And would you mind fetching me a drink?"

Mrs. Cordoza walked past her to pick it up. "I'll do it now, Mrs. Stirling," she said.

Reggie Carpenter was flirting. There was no other word for it. Yvonne's cousin was leaning up against Jenny's chair, his eyes fixed on her mouth, which was twitching mischievously as if they had shared a private joke.

Yvonne watched them as she handed Francis a drink where he sat, a few feet away. She stooped to murmur into her husband's ear, "Can't you get Reggie over with the men? He's been virtually sitting in Jennifer's lap since she got here."

"I tried, darling, but short of physically hauling him away, there wasn't a lot I could do."

"Then grab Maureen. She looks as if she's going to cry."

From the moment she had opened the door to the Stirlings—Jennifer in a mink coat and apparently already loaded, he grim-faced—her skin had prickled, as if in anticipation of something awful. There was tension between them, and then Jennifer and Reggie had latched on to each other in a way that was frankly exasperating.

"I do wish people would confine their quarrels to home," she muttered.

"I'll give Larry a large whiskey. He'll warm up eventually. Probably a bad day at the office." Francis stood up, touched her elbow, and was gone.

The cocktail sausages had hardly been tried. With a sigh, Yvonne picked up a plate of small eats and prepared to hand it around.

"Have one, Maureen."

Reggie's twenty-one-year-old girlfriend barely registered that she had spoken. Immaculate in her rust-colored wool dress, she was seated stiffly on a dining chair, casting dark looks at the two people to her right, both of whom seemed oblivious to her. Jennifer was leaning back in the armchair, while Reggie perched neatly on the arm. He whispered something, and they burst into peals of laughter.

"Reggie?" Maureen said. "Didn't you say we were going into town to meet the others?"

"Oh, they can wait," he said dismissively.

"They were going to meet us in the Green Rooms, Bear. Half past seven, you said."

"Bear?" Jenny, her laughter silenced, was staring at Reggie.

"His nickname," said Yvonne, offering her the plate. "He was the most ridiculously hairy baby. My aunt said at first she thought she had given birth to one."

"Bear," Jenny repeated.

"Yup. I'm irresistible. Soft. And never happier than when I'm tucked into bed . . ." He raised an eyebrow and leaned closer to her.

"Reggie, can I have a word?"

"Not when you wear that face, dear cousin. Yvonne thinks I'm flirting with you, Jenny."

"Not just thinking it," said Maureen, coldly.

"Oh, come on, Mo. Don't be a bore." His voice, while still joking, held a note of irritation. "I haven't had a chance to talk to Jenny for far too long. We're just catching up."

"Has it really been that long?" Jennifer said innocently.

"Oh, an age," he said fervently.

Yvonne saw the girl's face fall. "Maureen, darling, would you care to come and help me make some more drinks? Goodness only knows where my useless husband has gone."

"He's just there. He—"

"Come on, Maureen. Through here."

The girl followed her into the dining room and took the bottle of crème de menthe Yvonne handed her. She radiated impotent fury. "What does that woman think she's doing? She's married, isn't she?"

"Jennifer's just . . . Oh, she doesn't mean anything by it."

"She's all over him! Look at her! How would she like it if I mooned at her husband like that?"

Yvonne glanced into the living room where Larry, his face a mask of contained disapproval, was now sitting, only half listening to what Francis was saying. She probably wouldn't notice, she thought.

"I know she's your friend, Yvonne, but as far as I'm concerned she's an absolute bitch."

"Maureen, I know Reggie's behaving badly, but you can't speak like that about my friend. You have no idea what she's gone through recently. Now, pass me that bottle, would you?"

"And what about what she's putting me through? It's humiliating. Everyone knows I'm with Reggie, and she's got him wrapped around her little finger."

"Jennifer had the most awful car crash. She's not very long out of hospital. Like I said, she's just letting her hair down a little."

"And her knickers with it."

"Mo . . ."

"She's drunk. And she's ancient. How old must she be? Twenty-seven? Twenty-eight? My Reggie's at least three years younger than she is."

Yvonne took a deep breath. She lit a cigarette, handed another to the girl, and pulled the double doors closed behind her. "Mo—"

"She's a thief. She's trying to steal him from me. I can see it, even if you can't."

Yvonne lowered her voice. "You have to understand, Mo, darling, that there's flirting and then there's flirting. Reggie and Jenny are having a high old time together out there, but neither of them would ever think of cheating. They're flirting, yes, but they're doing it in a roomful of people, not attempting to hide it. If there was the slightest seriousness in it, do you really think she'd be like that in front of Larry?" It sounded convincing, even to herself. "Darling girl, you will find, as you get older, that a bit of conversational parrying is part of life." She popped a cashew into her mouth. "It's one of the great consolations for having to be married to one man for years and years."

The girl scowled, but deflated a little. "I suppose you're right," she said. "But I still don't think it's a nice way for a lady to behave." She opened the doors and went back into the living room. Yvonne took a deep breath and followed her.

The cocktails slid down as the conversation grew louder and livelier. Francis returned to the dining room and made more Snowballs, while Yvonne deftly threaded cherries onto cocktail sticks to decorate them. She found now that she felt frankly dreadful if she had more than two proper drinks, so she had one made with blue curaçao, then limited herself to Jaffa Juice. The champagne was going down like no one's business. Francis turned off the music in the hope that people might take the hint and leave, but Bill and Reggie turned it on again and tried to get everyone to dance. At one point both men had hold of Jennifer's hands, while they danced around her. As Francis was busy with the drinks, Yvonne moved to where Laurence was sitting and planted herself next to him. She had sworn to herself that she would get a smile out of him.

He said nothing, but took a long swig of his drink, glanced at his wife, and looked away again. Dissatisfaction radiated from him. "She's making a fool of herself," he muttered, when the silence between them became too great.

She's making a fool of you, Yvonne thought. "She's just merry. It's been a strange time for her, Larry. She's . . . trying to enjoy herself."

When she looked at him, he was gazing at her intently. Yvonne felt a little uncomfortable. "Didn't you tell me the doctor said she might not be herself?" she added. He had told her this when Jennifer had been in the hospital—back when he still talked to people.

He took another swig of his drink, his eyes not leaving hers. "You knew, didn't you?"

"Knew what?"

His eyes strafed hers for clues.

"Knew what, Larry?"

Francis had put on a rhumba. Behind them Bill was entreating Jennifer to dance with him, and she was pleading with him to stop.

Laurence drained his glass. "Nothing."

She leaned forward and put a hand on his. "It's been tough on both of you. I'm sure you need a little time to—" She was interrupted by another peal of laughter from Jennifer. Reggie had put one of the cut flowers between his teeth and was engaging her in an impromptu tango.

Laurence shrugged her off delicately, just as Bill, breathless, flopped down beside them. "That Reggie character's a bit much, isn't he? Yvonne, shouldn't you have a word?"

She dared not look at Laurence, but his voice, when it came, was steady. "Don't worry, Yvonne," he said, his eyes fixed somewhere in the far distance. "I'll sort it out."

She found Jennifer in the bathroom shortly before eight thirty. She was leaning across the marble washbasin, retouching her makeup. Her eyes slid to Yvonne as she entered, then returned to her reflection. She was flushed, Yvonne noted. Giddy, almost. "Would you like some coffee?" she said.

"Coffee?"

"Before you go on to Larry's work do."

"I think," Jennifer said, outlining her lips with an unusually careful hand, "for that shindig I'm more likely to need another stiff drink."

"What are you doing?"

"I'm putting on my lipstick. What does it look like I'm—"

"With my cousin. You're coming on awfully strong." It had come out more sharply than she had intended. But Jennifer seemed not to have noticed.

"When did we last go out with Reggie?"

"What?"

"When did we last go out with him?"

"I have no idea. Perhaps when he came to France with us in the summer."

"What does he drink when he's not drinking cocktails?"

Yvonne took a deep, steadying breath. "Jenny, darling, don't you think you should tone it down a little?"

"What?"

"This thing with Reggie. You're upsetting Larry."

"Oh, he doesn't care a fig what I do," she said dismissively. "What does Reggie drink? You must tell me. It's terribly important."

"I don't know. Whiskey. Jenny, is everything all right at home? With you and Larry?"

"I don't know what you mean."

"I'm probably talking out of turn, but Larry really does seem dreadfully unhappy."

"Larry does?"

"Yes. I wouldn't be too cavalier with his feelings, darling."

Jenny turned to her. "His feelings? Do you think anyone gives a damn what I've been through?"

"Jenny, I—"

"No one could care less. I'm just supposed to get on with it, keep my mouth shut, and play the adoring wife. As long as *Larry* hasn't got a long face."

"But if you want my opinion—"

"No, I don't. Just mind your own business, Yvonne. Really."

Both women stood very still. The air vibrated around them, as if a physical blow had been struck.

Yvonne felt something tighten in her chest. "You know, Jennifer, just because you can have any man in this house, it doesn't mean you have to." Her voice was steely.

"What?"

Yvonne rearranged the towels on the rail. "Oh, that helpless-little-princess shtick wears a bit thin sometimes. We know you're beautiful, Jennifer, yes? We know all our husbands adore you. Just have a care for other people's feelings for a change."

They stared at each other. "Is that what you think of me? That I behave like a princess?"

"No. I think you're behaving like a bitch."

Jennifer's eyes widened. She opened her mouth, as if to speak, then closed it, replaced the top on her lipstick, straightened her shoulders, and glared at Yvonne. Then she walked out.

Yvonne sat down heavily on the lid of the lavatory and wiped her nose. She stared at the bathroom door, hoping it might open again, and when it didn't, her head sank into her hands.

It was some moments later that she heard Francis's voice. "You all right in here, old girl? I was wondering where you were. Darling?"

When she looked up, he saw the expression in her eyes and knelt swiftly, taking her hands. "Are you all right? Is it the baby? Do you need me to do something?"

She gave a great shudder and allowed him to enfold her hands in his. They stayed where they were for some minutes, listening to the music and chatting downstairs, then Jennifer's high-pitched laughter. Francis reached into his pocket and lit his wife a cigarette.

"Thank you." She took it and inhaled deeply. Finally she looked up at him, her dark eyes serious. "Promise me we'll be happy even after the baby comes, Franny darling."

"What's—"

"Just promise me."

"Now, you know I can't do that," he said, cupping her cheek. "I've always prided myself on keeping you downtrodden and miserable."

She couldn't help but smile. "Beast."

"I do my best." He stood up and straightened the creases in his trousers. "Look. I should imagine you're exhausted. I'll get this show out of here, and you and I can slope off to bed. How does that sound?"

"Sometimes," she said fondly, as he offered a hand and she got to her feet, "you're not such a waste of a good wedding ring, after all."

The air was cold and the pavement around the square almost empty. Alcohol had warmed her; she felt giddy, intoxicated.

"I don't suppose we'll get a taxi around here," Reggie said cheerfully, pulling up his collar. "What are you chaps going to do?" His breath clouded in the night air.

"Larry has a driver," she said. Her husband was standing on the curb nearby, peering down the street.

"Except it looks as if he's disappeared." She found this suddenly very funny, and fought to stop herself giggling.

"I gave him the night off," Laurence muttered. "I'll drive. You stay here, and I'll fetch the car keys." He walked up the steps to their house.

Jennifer wrapped her coat tightly around her. She couldn't stop staring at Reggie. It was him. *Bear.* It had to be. He had barely left her side all evening. She was sure there were hidden messages in many of the remarks he'd made. *I haven't had a chance to talk to Jenny for ages.* There had been something in the way he'd said it. She was sure she hadn't imagined it. He drank whiskey. *Bear.* Her head was spinning. She'd drunk too much, but she didn't care. She had to know for sure.

"We're going to be awfully late," Reggie's girlfriend said mournfully, and Reggie cast a conspiratorial glance at Jennifer.

He glanced at his watch. "Oh, we've probably missed them. They'll have gone on for a meal now."

"So what will we do?"

"Who knows?" He shrugged.

"Ever been to Alberto's club?" Jennifer said suddenly.

Reggie's smile was slow, and ever so slightly sly. "You know I have, Mrs. Stirling."

"I do?" Her heart was thumping. She was amazed nobody else could hear it.

"I believe I saw you at Alberto's the very last time I was there." His expression was playful, mischievous almost.

"Well, some night out this has been," Maureen said petulantly, her hands thrust deep into the pockets of her coat. She glared at Jennifer, as if she was to blame.

Oh, if only you weren't here, Jennifer thought, her pulse racing. "Come with us," she said suddenly.

"What?"

"To Laurence's party. It'll probably be deathly dull, but I'm sure you can liven it up a bit. Both of you. There'll be lots to drink," she added.

Reggie looked delighted. "Count us in," he said.

"Do I get a say in this?" Maureen's displeasure was written across her face.

"Come on, Mo. It'll be fun. Otherwise it'll just be you and me in some dreary restaurant."

Jennifer felt a twinge of guilt at Maureen's now obvious despair, but hardened herself against it. She had to know. "Laurence?" she called. "Laurence, darling? Reggie and Maureen are going to come with us. Won't that be fun?"

Laurence hesitated on the top step, his keys in his hand, his gaze flicking between them. "Marvelous," he said, walked steadily down the steps, and opened the rear door of the big black car.

Jennifer appeared to have undersold the potential for riotous behavior at the Christmas celebrations of Acme Mineral and Mining. Perhaps it had been the decorations, or the copious amounts of food and drink, or even the prolonged absence of the boss, but when they arrived, the office party was in full swing. Someone had brought a portable gramophone, the lights were dimmed, and the desks had been moved to the side to create a dance floor upon which a throng of people squealed and shimmied to Connie Francis.

"Larry! You never told us your staff were such hep cats!" Reggie exclaimed.

Jennifer left him standing in the doorway, gazing at the scene before him, as she joined the cluster of dancers. His place of work, his domain, his haven, was unrecognizable to him, his staff no longer under his control, and he hated it. She saw his secretary rise from her chair, where she might have sat all evening, and say something to him. He nodded, attempting to smile.

"Drinks!" Jennifer called, wanting to get as far from him as possible. "Fight your way through, Reggie! Let's get sloshed."

She was dimly aware of a few looks of surprise as she passed her husband's staff, many of whom had loosened their ties, their faces flushed with drink and dancing. Their eyes went from her to Laurence.

"Hello, Mrs. Stirling."

She recognized the accountant who had spoken to her in the office a couple of weeks previously and smiled at him. His face was shiny with sweat, and he had an arm around a giggling girl in a party hat. "Why, hello! You couldn't show us where the drinks are, could you?"

"Over there. By the typing pool."

A huge vat of punch had been made. Paper cups were being filled and handed over people's heads. Reggie handed her one and she drank the contents in one, laughing when its unexpected potency made her cough and splutter. Then she was dancing, lost in a sea of bodies, dimly aware of Reggie's smile, his hand occasionally touching her waist. She saw Laurence watching her impassively from the wall, then, apparently reluctantly, engaged in conversation with one of the older, more sober men. She didn't want to be anywhere near him. She wished he would go home and leave her there to dance. She didn't see Maureen again. It was possible the girl had left. Things blurred, time stretched, became elastic. She was having fun. She felt hot, raised her arms above her head, let herself ride the music, ignoring the other women's curiosity. Reggie spun her around and she laughed uproariously. God, but she was alive! This was where she belonged. It was the first time she hadn't felt alien in a world that everyone insisted was hers.

Reggie's hand touched hers, shocking and electric. His glances at her had become meaningful, his smile knowing. Bear. He was mouthing something at her.

"What?" She pushed a sweaty lock of hair off her face.

"It's hot. I need another drink."

His hand felt radioactive on her waist. She followed close behind him, camouflaged by the bodies around them. When she glanced behind her for Laurence, he had vanished. Probably to his office, she thought. In it, the light was on. Laurence would hate this. He hated fun of any kind, her husband. Sometimes, these last weeks, she had wondered if he even hated her.

Reggie was thrusting another paper cup into her hand. "Air," he shouted. "I need some air."

And then they were out in the main hallway, just the two of them, where it was cool and silent. The sounds of the party faded as the door closed behind them.

"Here," he said, steering her past the lift to a fire escape. "Let's go out on the stairs." He wrestled with the door, and then they were in the chill night air, Jennifer gulping it as if to quench a great thirst. Below them she could see the street, the odd car's brake lights.

"I'm soaked!" He pulled at his shirt. "And I have absolutely no idea where I left my jacket."

She found herself staring at his body, now clearly outlined by the damp fabric, and made herself look away. "Fun, though," she murmured.

"I'll say. Didn't see old Larry dancing."

"He doesn't dance," she said, wondering how she could say this with such certainty. "Ever."

They were quiet for a moment, staring out into the darkness of the city. In the distance they could hear traffic, and behind them the muffled sounds of the party. She felt charged, breathless with anticipation.

"Here." Reggie took a packet of cigarettes from his pocket and lit one for her.

"I don't—" She stopped herself. What did she know? She might have smoked hundreds. "Thank you," she said. She took it gingerly, between two fingers, inhaled and coughed.

Reggie laughed.

"I'm sorry," she said, smiling at him. "I appear to be hopeless at it."

"Go on anyway. It'll make you lightheaded."

"I'm already lightheaded." She felt herself color a little.

"Proximity to me, I'll wager," he said, grinning, and taking a step closer to her. "I wondered when I'd get you alone." He touched the inside of her wrist. "It's pretty hard speaking in code, with everyone else around."

She wondered if she'd heard him correctly. "Yes," she said, when she could speak, and her voice was filled with relief. "Oh, God, I wanted to say something earlier. It's been so difficult. I'll explain later, but there was a time . . . Oh, hold me. Hold me, Bear. Hold me."

"Glad to."

He took another step forward and put his arms around her, pulling her close to him. She said nothing, just trying to absorb how it felt to be in his arms. He brought his face to hers, and she closed her eyes, ready, breathing in the male scent of his sweat, feeling the unexpected narrowness of his chest, wanting to be transported. *Oh, but I've waited so long for you,* she told him silently, lifting her face to his.

His lips met hers, and just for a moment she thrilled to their touch. But the kiss became clumsy, overbearing. His teeth mashed against hers, his tongue forcing its way into her mouth so that she had to pull back.

He seemed untroubled. His hands slid over her buttocks, pulling her so close that she could feel him pressed against her. He was gazing at her, eyes dulled with desire. "You want to find a hotel room? Or . . . here?"

She stared at him. It must be him, she told herself. Everything said so. But how could B feel so—so altered from what he had written?

"What's the matter?" he said, seeing some of this pass across her face. "Too cold for you? Or you don't want a hotel—too risky?"

"I—"

This was wrong. She backed out of his embrace. "I'm sorry. I don't think . . ." She lifted a hand to her head.

"You don't want to do it here?"

She frowned. Then she looked up at him. "Reggie, do you know what *deliquescent* means?"

"De-li—what?"

She closed her eyes, then opened them again. "I need to go," she mumbled. Suddenly she felt horribly sober.

"But you like playing away. You like a bit of action."

"I like a bit of what?"

"Well, I'm hardly the first, am I?"

She blinked. "I don't understand."

"Oh, don't play the innocent, Jennifer. I saw you, remember? With your other fancy man. At Alberto's. All over him. I knew what you were saying to me earlier, making that reference to it in front of everyone."

"My fancy man?"

He inhaled on his cigarette, then stubbed it out sharply under his heel.

"So that's how you want to play it, huh? What is it? Do I not measure up because I didn't understand some stupid word?"

"What man?" She had hold of his shirtsleeve now, unable to help herself. "Who are you talking about?"

He shook her off angrily. "Are you playing games with me?"

"No," she protested. "I just need to know who you saw me with."

"Jesus! I knew I should have gone with Mo when I had the chance. At least she appreciates a man. She's not a—a prick-tease," he spat.

Suddenly his features, flushed and angry, were flooded with light. Jennifer spun round to see Laurence holding open the fire escape door. He took in the illuminated spectacle of his wife and the man who was stepping away from her. Reggie, head down, swept past Laurence and into the building without a word, wiping his mouth.

She stood, frozen. "Laurence, it's not what you—"

"Get inside," he said.

"I just—"

"Get inside. Now." His voice was low, apparently calm. After the briefest hesitation, she stepped forward and into the stairwell. She made for the door, preparing to rejoin the party, still trembling with confusion and shock, but as they passed the lift he grabbed her wrist and spun her around.

She looked down at his hand, gripping her, then up at his face.

"Don't think you can humiliate me, Jennifer," he said quietly.

"Let go of me!"

"I mean it. I'm not some fool you can—"

"Let go of me! You're hurting me!" She pulled backward.

"Listen to me." A muscle pulsed in his jaw. "I won't have it. Do you understand me? I won't have it." He was gritting his teeth. There was so much anger in his voice.

"Laurence!"

"Larry! You call me Larry!" he shouted, his free fist lifting. The door opened, and that man from Accounts stepped out. He was laughing, his arm around the girl from earlier. He registered the scene, and his smile faded. "Ah . . . We were just stepping out for some air, sir," he said awkwardly.

It was at that moment that Laurence let go of her wrist, and Jennifer, seizing her chance, pushed past the couple and ran down the stairs.

Chapter 9

Anthony sat on a bar stool, one hand around an empty coffee cup, watching the staircase that led to street level for any sign of a pair of slim legs descending. Occasionally a couple would walk down the stairs into Alberto's, exclaiming about the unseasonal heat, their outrageous thirst, passing Sherrie, the bored cloakroom girl, slumped on her stool with a paperback. He would scan their faces and turn back to the bar.

It was a quarter past seven. Six thirty, she had said in the letter. He pulled it from his pocket again, thumbing its creases, examining the large, looping handwriting that confirmed she would be there. *Love, J.*

For five weeks they had traded letters, his forwarded to the sorting office on Langley Street, where she had taken out PO Box 13—the one, the postmistress had confided, that nobody ever wanted. They had seen each other only five or six times, and their meetings tended to be brief—too brief—confined to the few occasions that either his or Laurence's work schedule allowed.

But what he could not always convey to her in person, he had said in print. He wrote almost every day, and he told her everything, without shame or embarrassment. It was as if a dam had been breached. He told her how much he missed her, of his life abroad, how until now he had felt perpetually restless, as if in constant earshot of a conversation that was going on somewhere else.

He laid his faults before her—selfish, stubborn, often uncaring—and told her how she had caused him to start ironing them out. He told her he loved her, again and again, relishing the appearance of the words on paper.

In contrast, her letters were short and to the point. *Meet me here,* they said. Or *Not at that time, make it half an hour later.* Or, simply, *Yes. Me too.* At first he had been afraid that such brevity meant she felt little for him, and found it hard to square the person she was when they were together, intimate, affectionate, teasing, concerned for his welfare, with the words she wrote.

One night when she had arrived very late—Laurence, he discovered, had come home early, and she had been forced to invent a sick friend to get out of the house at all—she had found him drunk and churlish at the bar.

"Nice of you to stop by," he had said sarcastically, raising a glass to her. He had drunk four double whiskeys in the two hours he had waited.

She had pulled off her headscarf, ordered a martini, and, a second later, canceled it.

"Not staying?"

"I don't want to watch you like this."

He had berated her for the lack of all the things he felt from her—the lack of time, the lack of anything on paper that he could hold to him—ignoring the restraining hand that Felipe, the barman, had laid on his arm. What he felt terrified him, and he wanted to hurt her for it. "What's the matter? Scared of putting down anything that might be used in evidence against you?"

He had hated himself as he said the words, knew he had become ugly, the object of pity he had tried so desperately to conceal from her.

Jennifer had turned on her heel and walked swiftly up the stairs, ignoring his yelled apology, his demand for her to return.

He had left a one-word message—"Sorry"—in the PO box the following morning, and two long, guilt-ridden days later he had received a letter.

Boot. I do not give my feelings easily to paper. I do not give them easily at all. You deal in the business of words, and I cherish each one you write to me. But do not judge my feelings by the fact that I don't respond in kind.

I am afraid that if I tried to write as you do you would feel badly let down. Like I once said, my opinion is rarely sought on anything—let alone something as important as this—and I don't find it easy to volunteer it. Trust that I am here. Trust me by my actions, my affections. Those are my currency.

Yours,

J.

He had cried with shame and relief when he got it. He suspected afterward that part of it, the part she did not talk about, was that she still bore the humiliation of that hotel room, no matter how hard he tried to convince her of his reason for not making love to her. For all that he said, he suspected she was still not convinced that she was more than just another of his married women.

"Your girlfriend not coming?" Felipe slid into the seat beside him. The club had filled up now. Tables buzzed with chatter, a pianist played in the corner, and there was another half hour before Felipe would take up his trumpet. Overhead, the fan whirred lazily, hardly stirring the thick air. "Now, you ain't going to end up slaughtered again, are you?"

"It's coffee."

"You want to be careful, Tony."

"I told you, it's coffee."

"Not the drink. One of these days, you're going to fool around with the wrong woman. One day a husband's going to do for you."

Anthony held up his hand for more coffee. "I'm flattered, Felipe, that you take my welfare so seriously but, first, I've always been careful in my choice of partner." He flashed a sideways grin. "Believe me, you have to have a certain confidence in your powers of discretion to let a dentist loose with a drill in your mouth less than an hour after you've . . . um . . . entertained his wife."

Felipe couldn't help but laugh. "You're shameless, man."

"Not at all. Because, second, there will be no more married women."

"Just single ones, eh?"

"No. No more women. This is The One."

"The one hundred and one, you mean." Felipe barked a laugh. "You're gonna tell me you've taken up Bible studies next."

And there was the irony: the more he wrote and the harder he tried to convince her of what he felt, the more it seemed she suspected that the words were meaningless, that they tripped from his pen too easily. She had teased him about it several times—but he could taste the gunmetal bite of truth underneath.

She and Felipe saw the same thing: someone incapable of real love. Someone who would desire the unobtainable for just as long as it took to get it.

"One day, Felipe, my friend, I might just surprise you."

"Tony, you sit in this place long enough, there are no more surprises. And, look, talk of the devil. Here comes your birthday present. And so nicely wrapped, too."

Anthony glanced up and saw a pair of emerald green silk shoes negotiating the stairs. She walked slowly, one hand on the rail, as she had the first time he watched her coming down her front steps, revealing herself inch by inch until her face, flushed and slightly damp, was directly before him. At the sight of her, his breath was briefly knocked from his chest.

"I'm so sorry," she said, as she kissed his cheek. He got a warm waft of perfume, could feel the moisture on her cheeks transferring to his own. Her fingers squeezed his lightly. "It was . . . difficult getting here. Is there somewhere we can sit?"

Felipe showed them to a booth, and she attempted to smooth her hair.

"I thought you weren't coming," he said, after Felipe had brought her a martini.

"Laurence's mother made one of her unannounced visits. She will go on and on. I sat there pouring tea and thought I was going to scream."

"Where is he?" He reached out a hand under the table and enclosed hers in it. God, he loved the feel of it.

"Trip to Paris. He's meeting someone from Citroën about brake linings or something."

"If you were mine," Anthony said, "I wouldn't leave you alone for a minute."

"I bet you say that to all the girls."

"Don't," he said. "I hate that."

"Oh, you can't pretend you haven't used all your best lines on other women first. I know you, Boot. You told me, remember?"

He sighed. "So this is where honesty gets you. No wonder I never felt like trying it before." He felt her shuffle along the seat so that they were close to each other, her legs curling around his, and something in him relaxed. She drank her martini, then a second, and there, in the snug booth, with her beside him, he enjoyed a fleeting sense of possession. The band struck up, Felipe began to play his trumpet, and as she watched, her face illuminated by candlelight and pleasure, he watched her secretly, knowing with unfathomable certainty that she would be the only woman who could ever make him feel like this.

"Dance?"

There were other couples already on the floor, swaying to the music in the near darkness. He held her, breathing in the scent of her hair, feeling the pressure of her body against his, allowing himself to believe it was just the two of them, the music and the softness of her skin.

"Jenny?"

"Yes?"

"Kiss me."

Every kiss since that first in Postman's Park had been a hidden thing: in his car, in a quiet suburban street, at the back of a restaurant. He could see the protest forming on her lips: *Here? In front of all these people?* He waited for her to tell him it was too much of a risk. But perhaps something in his expression chimed in her, and, her face softening as it always did when it was just millimeters from his own, she lifted a hand to his cheek and kissed him, a tender, passionate kiss.

"You do make me happy, you know," she said quietly, confirming to him that she hadn't been before. Her fingers entwined in his; possessive, certain. "I can't pretend this does, but you do."

"So leave him." The words were out of his mouth before he knew what he was saying.

"What?"

"Leave him. Come and live with me. I've been offered a posting. We could just disappear."

"Don't."

"Don't what?"

"Talk like that. You know it's impossible."

"Why?" he said. He could hear the demanding note in his voice. "Why is it impossible?"

"We—we don't really know each other at all."

"Yes, we do. You know we do."

He lowered his head and kissed her again. He felt her resist a little this time, and pulled her to him, his hand on the small of her back, feeling her meld against him. The music receded, he lifted her hair from the nape of her neck with one hand, feeling the dampness underneath, and paused. Her eyes were closed, her head tilted slightly to one side, her lips very slightly parted.

Her blue eyes opened, bored into his, and then she smiled, a heady half smile that spoke of her own desire. How often did a man see a smile like that? Not an expression of tolerance, of affection, of obligation. *Yes, all right, dear, if you really want to.* Jennifer Stirling wanted him. She wanted him like he wanted her. "I'm awfully hot," she said, her eyes not leaving his.

"Then we should get some air." He took her hand, and led her through the dancing couples. He could feel her laughing, reaching for the shirt at his back. They reached the comparative privacy of the corridor, where he stifled her laughter with kisses, his hands entwined in her hair, her warm mouth under his lips. She kissed him back with increasing fervor, not hesitating even when they heard footsteps pass. He felt her hands reach under his shirt, and the touch of her fingers was so intensely pleasurable that he briefly lost the power of thought.

What to do? What to do? Their kisses grew deeper, more urgent. He knew that if he didn't take her, he would explode. He broke off, his hands on her face, saw her eyes, heavy with longing. Her flushed skin was his answer.

He looked to his right. Sherrie was still deep in her book, the cloakroom redundant in the sticky September heat. She was blind to them after years of amorous fumblings around her. "Sherrie," he said, pulling a ten-shilling note from his pocket, "how'd you fancy a tea break?"

She raised an eyebrow, then took the money and slid off her stool. "Ten minutes," she said baldly. And then Jennifer, giggling, was following him into the cloakroom, breathless as he pulled the dark curtain as far across the little alcove as it would go.

Here the dark was soft and total, the scent of a thousand discarded coats lingering in the air. Wrapped around each other, they stumbled to the end of the coat rail, the wire hangers clashing around their heads like whispering cymbals. He couldn't see her, but then she was facing him, her back against the wall, her lips on his, with a greater urgency now, murmuring his name.

Some part of him knew, even then, that she would be his undoing. "Tell me to stop," he whispered, his hand on her breast, his breath thick in his throat, knowing this would be the only possible brake. "Tell me to stop." The shake of her head was a mute refusal. "Oh, God," he murmured. And then they were frantic, her breath coming in short gasps, her leg lifted around his. He slid his hands underneath her dress, palms sliding against the silk and lace of her underwear. He felt her fingers threaded in his hair, one hand reaching for his trousers, and he found he was mildly shocked, as if he had imagined her natural sense of decorum would preclude such an appetite.

Time slowed, the air became a vacuum around them, their breath mingling. Fabrics were pushed aside. Legs became damp, his braced to support her weight. And then—oh, God—he was finally inside her, and just for a moment everything stilled: her breath, movement, his heart. The world, possibly. He felt her open mouth against his, heard her intake of breath. And then they were moving, and he was one thing, could feel only one thing, deaf to the clashing hangers, the muffled music on the other side of the wall, the muted exclamation of someone greeting a friend in the corridor. It was he and Jennifer, moving slowly, then faster, her hold on him tighter, the laughter gone now, his lips on her skin, her breath in his ear. He felt the increasing violence of her movements, felt her disappear into some distant part of herself. He knew, with what remained of his sensibility, that she mustn't make a sound. And as he heard the cry build at the back of her throat, as her head tipped back, he stopped it with his mouth, absorbing the sound, her pleasure, so surely that it became his own.

Vicariously.

And then they were stumbling, his legs cramping as he lowered her, and they were pressed together, holding each other, he feeling the tears on her cheeks as she shivered, limp in his arms. Afterward he couldn't recall what he told her at that point. *I love you. I love you. Never let me go. You are so beautiful.* He remembered wiping the tears from her eyes tenderly, her whispered reassurances, half smiles, her kisses, her kisses, her kisses.

And then, as if at the end of a distant tunnel, they heard Sherrie's conspicuous cough. Jennifer straightened her clothes, allowed him to smooth her skirt, and he felt the pressure of her hand as she led him the few feet back into the light, the real world, his legs still weak, his breathing not yet regular, already regretting leaving that dark heaven behind.

"Fifteen minutes," Sherrie said into her paperback, as Jennifer stepped out into the corridor. Her dress was neat, but the flattening of the back of her hair hinted at what had transpired.

"If you say so." He slipped the girl another note.

Jennifer turned to him, her face still flushed. "My shoe!" she exclaimed, holding up one stockinged foot. She burst out laughing, covered her mouth. He wanted to rejoice at her mischievous expression—he had feared she might be suddenly pensive or regretful.

"I'll get it," he said, ducking back in.

"Who says chivalry's dead?" Sherrie muttered.

He fumbled in the dark for the emerald silk shoe, his free hand lifting to his hair, lest it should be as evidential as hers. He fancied he could smell the musty scent of sex now mingling with the traces of perfume. Oh, but he had never felt anything like that. He closed his eyes for a moment, conjuring up the feel of her, the feel of . . .

"Well, hello, Mrs. Stirling!"

He located the shoe under an upturned chair, and heard Jennifer's voice, a brief murmur of conversation.

As he emerged, a young man had stopped by the cloakroom. A cigarette was wedged in the corner of his mouth, and he had his arm around a dark-haired girl who was clapping enthusiastically in the direction of the music.

"How are you, Reggie?" Jennifer was holding out a hand, which he took briefly.

Anthony saw the young man's eyes slide toward him. "I'm fine. Mr. Stirling with you?"

She barely missed a beat. "Laurence is away on business. This is Anthony, a friend of ours. He's very kindly taking me out this evening."

A hand snaked across. "How do you do?"

Anthony's smile felt like a grimace.

Reggie stood there, his eyes lifting to Jennifer's hair, the faint flush on her cheeks, something unpleasantly knowing in his gaze. He nodded toward her feet. "You seem to be . . . missing a shoe."

"My dancing shoes. I checked them in and got a mixed pair back. Silly of me." Her voice was cool, seamless.

Anthony held it out. "Found it," he said. "I've put your outdoor shoes back under the coat." Sherrie sat motionless beside him, her face buried in her book.

Reggie smirked, clearly enjoying the hiatus he had caused. Anthony wondered briefly whether he was waiting to be offered a drink or asked to join them, but he was damned if he'd do either.

Thankfully, Reggie's female companion tugged at his arm. "Come on, Reggie. Look, Mel's over there."

"Duty calls." Reggie waved, and was gone, weaving through the tables. "Enjoy your . . . dancing."

"Damn," she said, under her breath. "Damn. Damn. Damn."

He steered her back into the main room. "Let's get a drink."

They slid into their booth, the rapture of fifteen minutes ago already a distant memory. Anthony had disliked the young man on sight—but for that loss he could have thumped him.

She downed a martini in a single gulp. In other circumstances he would have found it amusing. Now, however, it signified her anxiety.

"Stop fretting," he said. "There's nothing you can do."

"But what if he tells—"

"So leave Laurence. Simple."

"Anthony . . ."

"You can't go back to him, Jenny. Not after that. You know it."

She pulled out a compact and rubbed at the mascara under her eyes. Apparently dissatisfied, she snapped it shut.

"Jenny?"

"Think about what you're asking me. I'd lose everything. My family . . . everything my life is. I'd be disgraced."

"But you'd have me. I'd make you happy. You said so."

"It's different for women. I'd be—"

"We'll get married."

"You really think Laurence would ever divorce me? You think he'd let me go?" Her face had clouded.

"I know he's not right for you. I am." When she didn't reply, he said, "Are you happy with him? Is this the life you want for yourself? To be a prisoner in a gilded cage?"

"I'm not a prisoner. Don't be ridiculous."

"You just can't see it."

"No. That's how you want to see it. Larry isn't a bad man."

"You can't see it yet, Jenny, but you're going to become more and more unhappy with him."

"Now you're a fortune-teller as well as a hack?"

He still felt raw, and it made him reckless. "He'll squash you, extinguish the things that make you you. Jennifer, the man's a fool, a dangerous fool, and you're too blind to see it."

Her face whipped around. "How dare you? How *dare* you?"

He saw the tears in her eyes, and the heat within him dissipated. He reached into his pocket for a handkerchief, made to wipe her eyes with it, but she blocked his hand. "Don't," she murmured. "Reggie might be watching."

"I'm sorry. I didn't want to make you cry. Please don't cry."

They sat in an unhappy silence, staring at the dance floor.

"It's just so hard," she murmured. "I thought I was happy. I thought my life was fine. And then you came along, and nothing . . . nothing makes sense anymore. All the things I'd had planned—houses, children, holidays—I don't want them now. I don't sleep. I don't eat. I think about you all the time. I know I won't be able to stop thinking about that." She gestured toward the cloakroom. "But the thought of actually leaving"—she sniffed—"it's like looking into an abyss."

"An abyss?"

She blew her nose. "Loving you would come at such a cost. My parents would disown me. I'd have nothing to bring with me. And I can't do anything, Anthony. I'm no good for anything but living as I do. What if I couldn't even run your house for you?"

"You think I care about that?"

"You would. Eventually. A spoiled little tai-tai. That was what you first thought of me, and you were right. I can make men love me, but I can't do anything else."

Her bottom lip was trembling. He wished, furious with himself, that he had never used that word against her. They sat in silence, watching Felipe play, both locked in thought.

"I've been offered a job," he said eventually. "In New York, reporting on the United Nations."

She turned to him. "You're leaving?"

"Listen to me. For years I've been a mess. When I was in Africa, I fell apart. When I was at home, I couldn't wait to get back there. I could never settle, could never escape the feeling that I should be somewhere else, doing something else." He took her hand. "And then I met you. Suddenly I can see a future. I can see the point of staying still, of building a life in one place. Working at the UN would be fine. I just want to be with you."

"*I can't.* You don't understand."

"What?"

"I'm afraid."

"Of what he'd do?" Rage built within him. "You think I'm frightened of him? You think I couldn't protect you?"

"No. Not of him. Please lower your voice."

"Of those ridiculous people you hang around with? You really care about their opinions? They're empty, stupid people with—"

"Stop it! It's not them!"

"What, then? What are you afraid of?"

"I'm afraid of you."

He battled to understand. "But I wouldn't—"

"I'm afraid of what I feel for you. I'm afraid to love somebody this much." Her voice broke. She folded her cocktail napkin, twisting it between her slim fingers. "I love him, but not like this. I've been fond of him and I've despised him, and much of the time we exist reasonably well together and I've made my accommodations and I know I can live like this. Do you understand? I know I can live like this for the rest of my life, and it won't be so bad. Plenty of women have worse."

"And with me?"

She didn't answer for so long that he almost repeated the question. "If I let myself love you, it would consume me. There would be nothing but you. I would be constantly afraid that you might change your mind. And then, if you did, I would die."

He took her hands, raised them to his lips, ignoring her whispered protests. He kissed her fingertips. He wanted to take her whole self into him. He wanted to wrap himself around her and never let her go. "I love you, Jennifer," he said. "I will never stop loving you. I have never loved anyone before you, and there will never be anyone after you."

"You say that now," she said.

"Because it's true." He shook his head. "I don't know what else you want me to say."

"Nothing. You've said everything. I have them all on paper, your beautiful words." She pulled her hand from his and reached for her martini. When she spoke again it was as if she was talking to herself. "But that doesn't make it any easier."

She had withdrawn her leg from his. He felt its absence like a pain. "What are you saying?" He fought to keep his voice under control. "You love me, but there's no hope for us?"

Her face crumpled a little. "Anthony, I think we both know . . ." She didn't finish.

She didn't need to.

Chapter 10

DECEMBER 1960

She had watched Mrs. Stirling disappear from the office party and Mr. Stirling grow increasingly agitated until he had slammed down his tumbler and strode out into the hallway after her. Almost vibrating with excitement, she had wanted to follow, to see what was happening, but Moira Parker had enough self-control to stay where she was. No one else seemed to notice he had gone.

Finally he walked back into the party. She watched him over the rise and fall of people's heads, utterly marooned. His face betrayed little emotion, yet she saw strain in his features that even she had never witnessed before.

What happened out there? What had Jennifer Stirling been doing with that young man?

An almost indecent spark of gratification burst into life within her, feeding her imagination until it was glowing. Perhaps he had been forced to see his wife for the selfish creature she was. Moira knew that when the office reopened, just a few words would cause the woman's behavior to become the talk of it. But, she thought with sudden melancholy, that would mean Mr. Stirling would be too, and the prospect of that brave, dignified, stoic man as the butt of flippant secretarial gossip made her heart constrict. How could she humiliate him in the one place he should be considered above everyone?

Moira stood, helpless, on the other side of the room, afraid to attempt to comfort her boss but so far removed from the revelry of her coworkers that she might have been in a different room. She watched as he went toward the makeshift bar and, with a grimace, accepted a cup of what looked like whiskey. He downed it in one gulp and demanded another. After a third, he nodded to those around him and went to his office.

Moira made her way through the throng. It was a quarter to eleven. The music had stopped, and people had begun to go home. Those who were not leaving were evidently taking themselves somewhere else, away from their colleagues' eyes. Behind the coat stand, Stevens was kissing that redhead from the typing pool as if nobody could see them. The girl's skirt had ridden halfway up her thighs, and his pudgy fingers plucked at the flesh-colored garters now exposed to view. She realized that the post boy had not returned after taking Elsie Machzynski to fetch a taxi, and she wondered what she might say to Elsie later to let her know that she was aware of this, even if nobody else had noticed. Was everyone except her obsessed with matters of the flesh? Were the formal greetings, the polite conversation of every day, simply a cover for a bacchanalian nature that she lacked?

"We're going on to the Cat's Eye Club. Fancy joining us, Moira? Let your hair down a little?"

"Oh, she won't come," Felicity Harewood said, so dismissively that, for just a moment, Moira thought she might surprise them all and say, "Why, yes, actually, I'd love to join you." But the light was on in Mr. Stirling's office. Moira did what any other responsible personal assistant to a chief executive would do. She stayed behind to clear up.

It was almost one in the morning by the time she finished. She didn't do it *all* herself: the new girl in Accounts held a bag for her when she collected the empty bottles, and the head of sales, a tall South African man, helped collect the paper cups, singing loudly from his spot in the ladies' cloakroom. Eventually it was just Moira, scrubbing at the stains on the linoleum that might yet be removed, and using a dust-pan and brush to pick up the crisps and peanuts that had somehow become trodden into the tiles. The men could move the desks back when they returned to the office. Apart from a few fluttering foil streamers, the place looked almost workmanlike again.

She looked at the battered Christmas tree, its decorations broken or missing, and the little postbox, which had become rather squashed since someone had sat on it, the crepe paper peeling away forlornly from the sides. She was glad that her mother wasn't alive to see her precious baubles tossed aside so carelessly.

She was packing away the last of it when she caught sight of Mr. Stirling. He was sitting in his leather chair, his head in his hands. The table near the door supported the remnants of the drink, and almost on impulse, she poured two fingers of whiskey. She walked across the office and knocked. He was still wearing his tie. Formal, even at this hour.

"I've just been clearing up," she said, when he stared at her. She felt suddenly embarrassed.

He glanced out of the window, and she realized he had not been aware that she was still there.

"Very kind of you, Moira," he said quietly. "Thank you." He took the whiskey from her and drank it, slowly this time.

Moira took in her boss's collapsed face, the tremor of his hands. She stood close to the corner of his desk, certain for once that she was justified in simply being there. On his desk, in neat piles, sat the letters she had left out for signing earlier that day. It felt like an age ago.

"Would you like another?" she said, when he had finished it. "There's a little more in the bottle."

"I suspect I've had quite enough." There was a lengthy silence. "What am I supposed to do, Moira?" He shook his head, as if engaged in some ongoing internal argument that she couldn't hear. "I give her everything. *Everything.* She has never wanted for a thing."

His voice was halting, broken.

"They say everything's changing. Women want something new . . . God knows what. Why does everything have to change?"

"Not all women," she said quietly. "An awful lot of women think a husband who would provide for them, and who they could look after, make a home for, would be a wonderful thing to have."

"You think so?" His eyes were red-rimmed with exhaustion.

"Oh, I know it. A man to make a drink for when he came home, to cook for and fuss over a little. I—it would be perfectly lovely." She colored.

"Then why . . ." He sighed.

"Mr. Stirling," she said suddenly, "you're a wonderful boss. A wonderful man. Really." She plowed on. "She's awfully lucky to have you. She must know that. And you don't deserve . . . you didn't deserve . . ." She trailed off, knowing even as she spoke that she was breaching some unspoken protocol. "I'm so sorry," she said, when the silence stretched uncomfortably beyond her words. "Mr. Stirling, I didn't mean to presume . . ."

"Is it wrong," he said, so quietly that at first she wasn't sure what he was saying, "for a man to want to be held? Does that make him less of a man?"

She felt tears prick her eyes . . . and something underneath them, something shrewder and sharper. She moved over a little and placed an arm lightly around his shoulders. Oh, the feel of him! Tall and broad, his jacket sitting so beautifully on his frame. She knew she would revisit this moment again and again for the rest of her life. The feel of him, the liberty to touch . . . She was almost faint with pleasure.

When he did nothing to stop her, she perched on the arm of his chair, leaned over a little, and, holding her breath, placed her head on his shoulder. A gesture of comfort, of solidarity. This is how it would feel, she thought blissfully. She wished, just briefly, that someone would take a picture of them pressed together so intimately. Then he lifted his head, and she felt a sudden pang of alarm—and shame.

"I'm so sorry—I'll get . . ." She straightened, choking on the words. But his hand was on hers. Warm. Close. "Moira," he said, and his eyes were half closed, his voice a croak of despair and desire. His hands were on her face, tilting it, pulling it down to meet his, and his mouth, searching, desperate, determined. A sound escaped her, a gasp of shock and delight, and then she was returning his kiss. He was only the second man she had kissed, and this instance was beyond the realm of what had preceded it, colored as it was by years of unrequited longing. Little explosions took place inside her as her blood raced around at super speed and her heart fought to escape her chest.

She felt him easing her back across the desk, his murmuring voice hoarse and urgent, his hands at her collar, her breasts, his breath warm on her collarbone. Inexperienced, she knew little of where to put her hands, her limbs, but found herself clutching him, wanting to please, lost in new sensations. *I adore you*, she told him silently. *Take what you want from me.*

But even as she gave herself up to pleasure, Moira knew she must keep some part of her aware enough to remember. Even as he enveloped her, entered her, her skirt hitched above her hips, his ink bottle digging uncomfortably into her shoulder, she knew she was no threat to Jennifer Stirling. The Jennifers of this world would always be the ultimate prize in a way that a woman like her never could. But Moira Parker had one advantage: she was appreciative in a way that Jennifer Stirling, that those who had always had things handed to them, never were. And she knew that even one brief night could be the most precious of all precious things, and that if this was to be the defining event of her romantic life, some part of her should be conscious enough to file it safely somewhere. Then, when it was over, she could relive it on those endless evenings when she was alone again.

She was sitting in the large drawing room at the front of the house when he returned home. She was wearing a raspberry tweed swing coat and hat, her black patent handbag and matching gloves resting neatly on her lap. She heard his car pull up, saw the lights outside dim, and stood. She pulled back the curtain a few inches and watched him sitting in the driving seat, letting his thoughts tick over with the dying engine.

She glanced behind her at her suitcases, then moved away from the window.

He came in and dropped his overcoat on the hall chair. She heard his keys fall into the bowl they kept for that purpose on the table, and the clatter of something falling over. The wedding photograph? He hesitated for a moment outside the drawing-room door, then opened it and found her.

"I think I should leave." She saw his eyes go to the packed suitcase at her feet, the one she had used when she'd left the hospital all those weeks earlier.

"You think you should leave."

She took a deep breath. Spoke the words she had rehearsed for the last two hours. "This isn't making either of us very happy. We both know that."

He walked past her to the drinks cabinet and poured himself three fingers of whiskey. The way he held the decanter made her wonder how much he had drunk since she had returned home. He took the cut-glass tumbler to a chair and sat down heavily. He lifted his eyes to hers, held them for a few minutes. She fought the urge to fidget.

"So . . ." he said. "Do you have something else in mind? Something that might make you happier?" His tone was sarcastic, unpleasant; drink had unleashed something in him. But she was not afraid. She had the freedom of knowing he was not her future.

They stared at each other, combatants locked in an uneasy battle.

"You know, don't you?" she said.

He drank some of his whiskey, his eyes not leaving her face. "What do I know, Jennifer?"

She took a breath. "That I love someone else. And that it's not Reggie Carpenter. It never was." She fiddled with her handbag as she spoke. "I worked it out this evening. Reggie was a mistake, a diversion from the truth. But you're so angry with me all the time. You have been ever since I got out of hospital. Because you know, just as I do, that someone else loves me, and isn't afraid to tell me so. That's why you didn't want me to ask too many questions. That's why my mother—and everyone else—has been so keen for me to simply get on with things. You didn't want me to remember. You never have."

She had half expected him to explode with anger. But instead he nodded. Then, as she held her breath, he raised his glass to her. "So . . . this lover of yours, what time will he be here?" He peered at his watch, then at her cases. "I assume he's picking you up."

"He . . ." She swallowed. "I . . . It's not like that."

"So you're going to meet him somewhere."

He was so calm. As if he was almost enjoying this. "Eventually. Yes."

"Eventually," he repeated. "What's the delay?"

"I . . . I don't know where he is."

"You don't know where he is." Laurence downed the whiskey. He stood laboriously and poured himself another.

"I can't remember, you know I can't. Things are coming back to me, and I don't have it clear in my head yet, but I know now that this"—she gestured around the room—"feels wrong for a reason. It feels wrong because I'm in love with someone else. So I'm very sorry, but I have to go. It's the right thing to do. For both of us."

He nodded. "May I ask what this gentleman—your lover—has that I don't?"

The streetlight outside the window sputtered.

"I don't know," she admitted. "I just know that I love him. And that he loves me."

"Oh, you do, do you? And what else do you know? Where he lives? What he does for a living? How he's going to keep you, with your extravagant tastes? Will he buy you new frocks? Allow you a house-keeper? Jewelry?"

"I don't care about any of that."

"You certainly used to care about it."

"I'm different now. I just know he loves me, and that's what really matters. You can mock me all you want, Laurence, but you don't know—"

He sprang up from his seat, and she shrank back. "Oh, I know all about your lover, Jenny," he bellowed. He pulled a crumpled envelope from his inside pocket, brandishing it at her. "You really want to know what happened to you? You really want to know where your lover is?" Flecks of spittle flew, and his eyes were murderous.

She froze, her breath stalled in her chest.

"This isn't the first time you've left me. Oh, no. I know, just like I know about him, because I found his letter in your bag after the accident."

She saw the familiar handwriting on the envelope and was unable to tear her eyes from it.

"This is from him. In it, he asks you to meet him. He wants to run away with you. Just the two of you. Away from me. To start a new life together." He grimaced, half in anger, half in grief. "Is it coming back to you now, darling?" He thrust it at her, and she took it with trembling fingers. She opened it and read,

> *My dearest and only love. I meant what I said. I have come to the conclusion that the only way forward is for one of us to make a bold decision.*
>
> *I am not as strong as you. When I first met you, I thought you were a fragile little thing. Someone I had to protect. Now I realize I had us all wrong. You are the strong one, the one who can endure living with the possibility of a love like this, and the fact that we will never be allowed it.*
>
> *I ask you not to judge me for my weakness. The only way I can endure is to be in a place where I will never see you, never be haunted by the possibility of seeing you with him. I need to be somewhere where sheer necessity forces you from my thoughts minute by minute, hour by hour. I cannot do that here.*
>
> *I am going to take the job. I'll be at Platform 4 Paddington at 7:15 on Monday evening, and there is nothing in the world that would make me happier than if you found the courage to come with me.*
>
> *If you don't come, I'll know that whatever we might feel for each other, it isn't quite enough. I won't blame you, my darling. I know the past weeks have put an intolerable strain on you, and I feel the weight of that keenly. I hate the thought that I could cause you any unhappiness.*

I'll be waiting on the platform from a quarter to seven. Know that you hold my heart, my hopes, in your hands.

Your

B.

"Ring a bell, does it, Jenny?"

"Yes," she whispered. Images flashed in her mind's eye. Dark hair. A crumpled linen jacket. A little park, dotted with men in blue.

Boot.

"Yes, you know him? Yes, it's all coming back to you?"

"Yes, it's coming back to me . . ." She could almost see him. He was so close now.

"Obviously not all of it."

"What do you—"

"He's dead, Jennifer. He died in the car. You survived the crash, and your gentleman friend died. Dead at the scene, according to the police. So nobody's out there waiting for you. There's no one at Paddington Station. There's nobody left for you to bloody remember."

The room had started to move around her. She heard him speak, but the words refused to make sense, to take root in anything meaningful. "No," she said, trembling now.

"Oh, I'm afraid so. I could probably dig out the newspaper reports, if you really wanted proof. We—your parents and I—kept your name out of the public eye, for obvious reasons. But they reported his death."

"No." She pushed at him, her arms swinging rhythmically at his torso. *No no no.* She wouldn't hear what he was saying.

"He died at the scene."

"Stop it! Stop saying that!" She launched herself at him now, wild, uncontrolled, shrieking. She heard her voice as if at a distance, was dimly aware of her fists coming into contact with his face, his chest, and then his stronger hands grabbing her wrists until she couldn't move.

He was immovable. What he had said was immovable.

Dead.

She sank onto the chair, and eventually he released her. She felt as if she had shrunk, as if the room had expanded and swallowed her. *My dearest and only love.* Her head lowered, so that she could see only the floor, and tears slid down her nose and onto the expensive rug.

A long time later she looked up at him. His eyes were closed, as if the scene was too unpleasant for him to contemplate. "If you knew," she began, "if you could see I was beginning to remember, why . . . why didn't you tell me the truth?"

He was no longer angry. He sat down in the chair opposite, suddenly defeated. "Because I hoped . . . when I realized you remembered nothing, that we could put it behind us. I hoped we might just carry on as if none of it had happened."

My dearest and only love.

She had nowhere to go. Boot was dead. He had been dead the whole time. She felt foolish, bereft, as if she had imagined the whole thing in a fit of girlish indulgence.

"And," Laurence's voice broke the silence, "I didn't want you to have to bear the guilt of knowing that, without you, this man might still be alive."

And there it was. A pain so sharp she felt as if she had been impaled.

"Whatever you think of me, Jennifer, I believed you might be happier this way."

Time passed. She couldn't say afterward whether it had been hours or minutes. After a while Laurence stood up. He poured and drank another glass of whiskey, as easily as if it had been water. Then he placed his tumbler neatly on the silver tray.

"So, what happens now?" she said dully.

"I go to bed. I'm really very tired." He turned and walked toward the door. "I suggest you do the same."

After he had gone, she sat there for some time. She could hear him moving heavily on the floorboards upstairs, the wearied, drunken path of his footsteps, the creak of the bedstead as he climbed in. He was in the master bedroom. Her bedroom.

She read the letter again. Read of a future that wouldn't be hers. A love she had not been able to live without. She read the words of the man who had loved her more than even he could convey, a man for whose death she had been unwittingly responsible. She finally saw his face: animated, hopeful, full of love.

Jennifer Stirling fell to the floor, curled up with the letter clutched to her chest, and silently began to cry.

Chapter 11

SEPTEMBER 1960

He saw them through the window of the coffee shop, half obscured by steam, even on this late-summer evening. His son was seated at the table nearest the window, his legs swinging as he read the menu. He paused on the pavement, taking in the longer limbs, the loss of the soft edges that had marked him out as a child. He could just make out the man he might become. Anthony felt his heart constrict. He tucked his parcel under his arm and walked in.

The café had been Clarissa's choice, a large, bustling place where the waitresses wore old-fashioned uniforms and white pinafores. She had called it a tearoom, as if she was embarrassed by the word *café*.

"Phillip?"

"Daddy?"

He stopped beside the table, noting with pleasure the boy's smile as he caught sight of him.

"Clarissa," he added.

She was less angry, he thought immediately. There had been a tautness about her face for the past few years that had made him feel guilty whenever they met. Now she looked back at him with a kind of curiosity, as one might examine something that might turn around and snap: forensically, and from a distance.

"You look very well," he said.

"Thank you," she said.

"And you've grown," he said, to his son. "Goodness, I think you've shot up six inches in two months."

"Three months. And they do, at that age." Clarissa's mouth settled into the moue of mild disapproval he knew so well. It made him think briefly of Jennifer's lips. He didn't think he'd ever seen her do that thing with her mouth; perhaps the way she was designed forbade it.

"And you're . . . well?" she said, pouring him a cup of tea and pushing it toward him.

"Very, thank you. I've been working hard."

"As always."

"Yes. How about you, Phillip? School all right?"

His son's face was buried in the menu.

"Answer your father."

"Fine."

"Good. Keeping your marks up?"

"I have his report here. I thought you might want to see it." She fished in her bag, and handed it to him.

Anthony noted, with unexpected pride, the repeated references to Phillip's "decent character," his "genuine efforts."

"He's captain of the football team." She couldn't quite keep the pleasure from her voice.

"You've done well." He patted his son's shoulder.

"He does his homework every night. I make sure of that."

Phillip wouldn't look at him now. Had Edgar already filled the father-shaped hole that he feared existed in Phillip's life? Did he play cricket with him? Read stories to him? Anthony felt something in him cloud over and took a gulp of tea, trying to gather himself. He called over a waitress and ordered a plate of cakes. "The biggest you have. An early celebration," he said.

"He'll spoil his supper," Clarissa said.

"It's just one day."

She turned away, as if she was struggling to bite her tongue.

Around them the clamor of the café seemed to increase. The cakes arrived on a tiered silver platter. He saw his son's eyes slide toward them and gestured that he should help himself.

"I've been offered a new job," he said, when the silence grew too weighty.

"With the *Nation?*"

"Yes, but in New York. Their man at the UN is retiring, and they've asked me if I'd like to take his place for a year. It comes with an apartment, right in the heart of the city." He had barely believed Don when he'd told him. It showed their faith in him, Don had said. If he got this right, who knew? This time next year he might be on the road again.

"Very nice."

"It's come as a bit of a surprise, but it's a good opportunity."

"Yes. Well. You always did like traveling."

"It's not traveling. I'll be working in the city."

It had been almost a relief when Don had mentioned it. This would decide things. It gave him a better job and meant that Jennifer could come too, start a new life with him . . . and, although he tried not to think of this, he knew that if she said no, it would give him an escape route. London had already become inextricably tied up with her: landmarks everywhere were imprinted with their time together.

"Anyway, I'll be over a few times a year, and I know what you said, but I would like to send letters."

"I don't know . . ."

"I'd like to tell Phillip a little of my life over there. Perhaps he could even come and visit when he's a bit older."

"Edgar thinks it will be better for all of us if things are kept simple. He doesn't like . . . disruption."

"Edgar is not Phillip's father."

"He's as much of a father as you've ever been."

They glared at each other.

Phillip's cake was sitting in the middle of his plate; his hands were wedged under his thighs.

"Let's not discuss this now, anyway. It's Phillip's birthday." He brightened his voice. "I expect you'd like to see your present, wouldn't you?"

His son said nothing. Christ, thought Anthony. What are we doing to him? He reached under the table and pulled out a large, rectangular parcel. "You can keep it for the big day, if you like, but your mother told me you were—you were all going out tomorrow, so I thought you might prefer it now."

He handed it over. Phillip took it and glanced warily at his mother.

"I suppose you can open it, as you won't have much time tomorrow," she said, trying to smile. "If you'll excuse me, I'm going to powder my nose." She rose, and he watched her walk through the tables, wondering if she was as disheartened by these exchanges as he was. Perhaps she was off to find a public telephone from which she could ring Edgar and complain about how unreasonable her ex-husband was.

"Go on, then," he said, to the boy. "Open it."

Freed from the eye of his mother, Phillip became a little more animated. He ripped at the brown paper and stopped, in awe, when he saw what it had concealed.

"It's a Hornby," Anthony said. "The best you can get. And that's the Flying Scotsman. You've heard of it?"

Phillip nodded.

"There's a fair bit of track with it, and I got the man to throw in a little station and some men. They're in this bag here. Think you can set it up?"

"I'll ask Edgar to help me."

It was like a sharp kick to the ribs. Anthony forced himself to ride the pain. It wasn't the boy's fault, after all.

"Yes," he said, through gritted teeth. "I'm sure he would."

They were quiet for a few moments. Then Phillip's hand snaked out, snatched up his cake, and stuffed it into his mouth, an unthinking act conducted with greedy pleasure. Then he selected another, a chocolate fancy, and gave his father a conspiratorial wink before it followed the first.

"Still happy to see your old dad, then?"

Phillip reached over and laid his head against Anthony's chest. Anthony looped his arms around him, holding him tightly, breathing in the smell of his hair, feeling the visceral pull that he tried so hard not to acknowledge.

"Are you better now?" the boy said, when he pulled back. He had lost a front tooth.

"I'm sorry?"

Phillip began to prize the engine from its box. "Mother said you weren't yourself, that that was why you didn't write."

"I am better. Yes."

"What happened?"

"There—were unpleasant things going on when I was in Africa. Things that upset me. I got ill, and then I was rather silly and drank too much."

"That was rather silly."

"Yes. Yes, it was. I shan't do it again."

Clarissa came back to the table. He saw, with a jolt, that her nose was pink, her eyes red-rimmed. He attempted a smile, and received a wan one in return.

"He likes his present," Anthony said.

"Goodness. Well, that's quite a present." She gazed at the gleaming engine, at her child's patent delight, and added, "I hope you said thank you, Phillip."

Anthony put a cake on a plate and handed it to her, then took one for himself, and they sat there in some strained facsimile of family life.

"Let me write," Anthony said, after a beat.

"I'm trying to start a new life, Anthony," she whispered. "Trying to start afresh." She was almost pleading.

"It's just *letters.*"

They stared at each other across the Formica. Beside them, their son spun the wheels of his new train, humming with pleasure.

"A letter. How disruptive could it be?"

Jennifer unfolded the newspaper that Laurence had left, smoothed it open on the kitchen table, and turned a page. He was visible through the open door, checking his reflection in the hall mirror, straightening his tie.

"Don't forget the dinner at Henley tonight. Wives are invited, so you might want to start thinking about what you're going to wear."

When she didn't respond, he said testily, "Jennifer? It's tonight. And it will be in a marquee."

"I'm sure a whole day is quite enough time for me to sort out a dress," she replied.

Now he was standing in the doorway. He frowned when he saw what she was doing. "What are you bothering with that for?"

"I'm reading the newspaper."

"Hardly your thing, is it? Have your magazines not arrived?"

"I just . . . thought I might try to read up a little. See what's going on in the world."

"I can't see that there's anything in it that might concern you."

She glanced at Mrs. Cordoza, who was pretending not to listen as she washed dishes at the sink.

"I was reading," she said, with slow deliberation, "about the Lady Chatterley trial. It's actually rather fascinating."

She felt, rather than saw, his discomfort—her eyes were still on the newspaper. "I really don't see what everyone's making such a fuss about. It's just a book. From what I understand it's just a love story, between two people."

"Well, you don't understand very much, do you? It's filth. Moncrieff has read it and said it's subversive."

Mrs. Cordoza was scrubbing a pan with intense vigor. She had begun to hum under her breath. Outside the wind picked up, sending a few ginger leaves skittering past the kitchen window.

"We should be allowed to judge these things for ourselves. We're all adults. Those who think it would offend them needn't read it."

"Yes. Well. Don't go offering your half-baked opinions on such matters at this dinner, will you? They're not the type of crowd who want to hear a woman pontificating on things she knows nothing about."

Jennifer took a breath before she responded. "Well, perhaps I'll ask Francis if he can lend me his copy. Then I might know what I'm talking about. How would that suit you?" Her jaw set, a small muscle working in her cheek.

Laurence's tone was dismissive. He reached for his briefcase. "You've been in an awful mood these last few mornings. I hope you can make yourself a little more agreeable this evening. If this is what reading the newspaper does for you, I might have it delivered to the office."

She didn't rise from her chair to kiss his cheek, as she might once have done. She bit her lip and continued to stare at the newspaper until the sound of the front door closing told her that her husband had left for the office.

For three days she had barely slept or eaten. Most nights now she lay awake through the small hours, waiting for something biblical to fall out of the dark above her head. All the time she was quietly furious with Laurence; she would see him suddenly through Anthony's eyes, and find herself concurring with his damning assessment. Then she would hate Anthony for making her feel that way about her husband, and be even more furious that she couldn't tell him so. At night she remembered Anthony's hands on her, his mouth, pictured herself doing things to him that, in the light of morning, made her blush. On one occasion, desperate to quell her confusion, to weld herself back to her husband's side, she woke him, slid one pale leg across him, kissed him into wakefulness. But he had been appalled, had asked her what on earth had got into her, and all but pushed her off. He had turned his back on her, leaving her to cry silent tears of humiliation into her pillow.

During those sleepless hours, along with the toxic conflagration of desire and guilt, she tossed around endless possibilities: she could leave, somehow survive the guilt, the loss of money, and her family's anguish. She could have an affair, find some level on which she and Anthony could exist, parallel to their ordinary lives. It wasn't just

Lady Chatterley who did it, surely. Their social circle was rife with tales of who was having whom. She could break it off and be a good wife. If her marriage was not working, then it was her fault for not trying hard enough. And you could turn such things around: all the women's magazines said so. She could be a little kinder, a little more loving, present herself more beautifully. She could stop, as her mother would say, looking at the greener grass beyond.

She had reached the front of the queue. "Will this make the afternoon post? And could you check my PO box? It's Stirling, box thirteen."

She hadn't come here since the night in Alberto's, convincing herself that it was for the best. The thing—she dared not think of it as an affair—had become overheated. They needed to let it cool a little so that they could think with clearer heads. But after her unpleasant exchange with her husband that morning, her resolve had collapsed. She had written the letter in haste, perched at her little bureau in the drawing room while Mrs. Cordoza was vacuuming. She had implored him to understand. She didn't know what to do: she didn't want to hurt him . . . but she couldn't bear to be without him:

> *I am married. For a man to walk away from his marriage is one thing, but for a woman? At the moment I can do nothing wrong in your eyes. You see the best in everything I do. I know there would come a day when that would change. I don't want you to see in me all that you despised in everyone else.*

It was confused, jumbled, her writing scrawled and uneven.

The postmistress took the letter from her and returned with another.

Her heart still fluttered at the sight of his handwriting. His words were so beautifully strung together that she could recite whole swathes of them to herself in the dark, like poetry. She opened it impatiently, still standing at the counter, moving along to allow the next person in the queue to be served. This time, however, the words were a little different.

If anyone else noticed the acute stillness of the blond woman in the blue coat, the way she reached out a hand to steady herself on the counter as she finished reading her letter, they were probably too busy with their own parcels and forms to pay much attention. But the change in her demeanor was striking. She stood there for a moment longer, her hand trembling as she thrust the letter into her bag and walked slowly, a little unsteadily, out into the sunshine.

She wandered the streets of central London all afternoon, patrolling the shop windows with a vague intensity. Unable to return home, she waited on the crowded pavements for her thoughts to clear. Hours later, when she walked through the front door, Mrs. Cordoza was in the hallway, two dresses over her arm.

"You didn't tell me which you wanted for the dinner this evening, Mrs. Stirling. I've pressed these, in case you thought one might be suitable." The sun flooded the hallway with the peachy light of late summer as Jennifer stood in the doorway. The gray gloom returned as she closed the door behind her.

"Thank you." She walked past the housekeeper and into the kitchen. The clock told her it was almost five. Was he packing now?

Jennifer's hand closed over the letter in her pocket. She had read it three times. She checked the date: he did, indeed, mean this evening. How could he decide something like that so quickly? How could he do it at all? She cursed herself for not picking up the letter sooner, not giving herself time to plead with him to reconsider.

> *My dearest and only love. I meant what I said. I have come to the conclusion that the only way forward is for one of us to make a bold decision.*
>
> *I am not as strong as you. When I first met you, I thought you were a fragile little thing. Someone I had to protect. Now I realize I had us all wrong. You are the strong one, the one who can endure living with the possibility of a love like this, and the fact that we will never be allowed it.*
>
> *I ask you not to judge me for my weakness. The only way I can endure is to be in a place where I will never see you, never be haunted by*

*the possibility of seeing you with him. I need to be somewhere where sheer
necessity forces you from my thoughts minute by minute, hour by hour.
That cannot happen here.*

At one moment she was furious with him for attempting to force
her hand. At the next she was gripped by the terrible fear of his going
away. How would it feel to know she would never see him again? How
could she remain in this life, having glimpsed the alternative he had
shown her?

> *I am going to take the job. I'll be at Platform 4 Paddington at 7:15
> on Monday evening, and there is nothing in the world that would make
> me happier than if you found the courage to come with me.*
> *If you don't come, I'll know that whatever we might feel for each other,
> it isn't quite enough. I won't blame you, my darling. I know the past
> weeks have put an intolerable strain on you, and I feel the weight of that
> keenly. I hate the thought that I could cause you any unhappiness.*

She had been too honest with him. She shouldn't have confessed
the confusion, the haunted nights. If he'd thought she was less upset,
he wouldn't have felt the need to act like this.

> *I'll be waiting on the platform from a quarter to seven. Know that
> you hold my heart, my hopes, in your hands.*

And then this: this great tenderness. Anthony, who couldn't bear
the thought of making her less than she was, who wanted to protect
her from the worst of her feelings, had given her the two easiest ways
out: come with him, or remain where she was blamelessly, knowing
she was loved. What more could he have done?

How could she make a decision so momentous in so little time? She
had thought of traveling to his house, but she couldn't be sure he would
be there. She had thought of going to the newspaper, but she was
afraid some gossip columnist would see, that she would become the
object of curiosity or, worse, embarrass him. Besides, what could she

say to change his mind? Everything he had said was right. There was no other possible end to this. There was no way to make it right.

"Oh. Mr. Stirling rang to say he'll pick you up at around a quarter to seven. He's running a little late at the office. He sent his driver for his dinner suit."

"Yes," she said, absently. She felt suddenly feverish, reached out a hand to the balustrade.

"Mrs. Stirling, are you all right?"

"I'm fine."

"You look as if you need some rest." Mrs. Cordoza laid the dresses carefully over the hall chair and took Jennifer's coat from her. "Shall I run you a bath? I could make you a cup of tea while it's filling, if you like."

She turned to the housekeeper. "Yes. I suppose so. Quarter to seven, you say?" She began to walk up the stairs.

"Mrs. Stirling? The dresses? Which one?"

"Oh. I don't know. You choose."

She lay in the bath, almost oblivious to the hot water, numbed by what was about to happen. I'm a good wife, she told herself. I'll go to the dinner tonight, and I'll be entertaining and gay and not pontificate on things I know nothing about.

What was it Anthony had once written? That there was pleasure to be had in being a decent person. *Even if you do not feel it now.*

She got out of the bath. She couldn't relax. She needed something to distract her from her thoughts. She wished, suddenly, that she could drug herself and sleep through the next two hours. Even the next two months, she thought mournfully, reaching for the towel.

She opened the bathroom door, and there, on the bed, Mrs. Cordoza had laid out the two dresses: on the left was the midnight blue she had worn on the night of Laurence's birthday. It had been a merry night at the casino. Bill had won a large amount of money at roulette and insisted on buying champagne for everyone. She had drunk too much, had been giddy, unable to eat. Now, in the silent room, she recalled other parts of the evening that she had obediently excised in her retelling of it. She remembered Laurence criticizing her for spending too much money on gambling chips. She remembered him muttering that she was embarrassing him—until Yvonne had told him, charmingly, not to be so grumpy. *He'll squash you, extinguish the things that make you you.* She remembered him standing in the kitchen doorway this morning. *What are you bothering with that for? I hope you can make yourself a little more agreeable this evening.*

She looked at the other dress on the bed: pale gold brocade, with a mandarin collar and no sleeves. The dress she had worn on the evening that Anthony O'Hare had declined to make love to her.

It was as if a heavy mist had lifted. She dropped the towel and threw on some clothes. Then she began to hurl things onto the bed. Underwear. Shoes. Stockings. What on earth did one pack when one was leaving forever?

Her hands were shaking. Almost without knowing what she was doing, she pulled her case down from the top of the wardrobe and opened it. She tossed things into it with a kind of abandon, fearing that if she stopped to think about what she was doing, she wouldn't do it at all.

"Are you going somewhere, madam? Would you like help packing?" Mrs. Cordoza had appeared in the doorway behind her, holding a cup of tea.

Jennifer's hand flew to her throat. She turned, half hiding the case behind her. "No—no. I'm just taking some clothes to Mrs. Moncrieff. For her niece. Things I've grown tired of."

"There are some things in the laundry room that you said didn't fit you anymore. Do you want me to bring them up?"

"No. I can do it myself."

Mrs. Cordoza peered past her. "But that's your gold dress. You love it."

"Mrs. Cordoza, please will you let me sort out my own wardrobe?" she snapped.

The housekeeper flinched. "I'm very sorry, Mrs. Stirling," she said, and withdrew in hurt silence.

Jennifer began to cry, sobs forcing their way out in ugly bursts. She crawled on top of the bedspread, her hands over her head, and howled, not knowing what she should do, only that, with every second of indecision, the direction of her life hung in the balance. She heard her mother's voice, saw her appalled face at the news of her family's disgrace, the whispers of delighted shock in church. She saw the life she had planned, the children that would surely soften Laurence's coldness, force him to unbend a little. She saw a poky series of rented rooms, Anthony out all day working, herself afraid in a strange country without him. She saw him wearying of her in her drab clothes, his gaze already on some other married woman.

I will never stop loving you. I have never loved anyone before you, and there will never be anyone after you.

When she pushed herself up, Mrs. Cordoza was at the foot of the bed.

She wiped her eyes and her nose and was prepared to apologize for snapping when she saw that the older woman was packing her bag.

"I've put in your flat shoes and your brown slacks. They don't need so much laundering."

Jennifer stared at her, still hiccuping.

"There are undergarments and a nightdress."

"I—I don't—"

Mrs. Cordoza continued to pack. She removed things from the suitcase, refolding them with tissue paper and putting them back with the same reverent care one might lavish on a newborn. Jennifer was hypnotized by the sight of those hands smoothing, replacing.

"Mrs. Stirling," Mrs. Cordoza said, without looking up, "I never told you this. Where I lived in South Africa, it was customary to cover your windows with ash when a man died. When my husband died, I kept my windows clear. In fact, I cleaned them so that they shone."

Sure she had Jennifer's attention, she continued folding. Shoes now, placed sole to sole in a thin cotton bag, tucked neatly in the base, a pair of white tennis shoes, a hairbrush.

"I did love my husband when we were young, but he was not a kind man. As we grew older, he cared less and less how he behaved toward me. When he died suddenly, God forgive me, I felt as if someone had set me free." She hesitated, gazing into the half-packed suitcase. "If someone had given me the chance, many years ago, I would have gone. I think I would have had the chance of a different life."

She placed the last folded clothes on top and closed the lid, securing the buckles on each side of the handle.

"It's half past six. Mr. Stirling said he would be home by a quarter to seven, in case you'd forgotten." Without another word, she straightened and left the room.

Jennifer checked her watch, then shrugged on the rest of her clothes. She ran across the room, sliding her feet into the nearest pair of shoes. She went to her dressing table, fumbled in the back of a drawer for the emergency supply of shopping money she always kept balled up in a pair of stockings, and thrust the notes into her pocket, with a handful of rings and necklaces from her jewelry box. Then she grabbed her suitcase and wrenched it down the stairs.

Mrs. Cordoza was holding out her mackintosh. "Your best chance of a taxi will be New Cavendish Street. I would suggest Portland Place, but I believe Mr. Stirling's driver uses it."

"New Cavendish Street."

Neither woman moved, stunned, perhaps, by what they had done. Then Jennifer stepped forward and gave Mrs. Cordoza an impulsive hug. "Thank you. I—"

"I'll inform Mr. Stirling that, to my knowledge, you're on a shopping trip."

"Yes. Yes, thank you."

She was outside in the night air that suddenly felt loaded with possibility. She tripped carefully down the steps, scanning the square for the familiar yellow light of a taxi. When she reached the pavement, she set off at a run into the city dusk.

She felt an overwhelming sense of relief—she no longer had to be Mrs. Stirling, to dress, behave, love, in a certain way. She realized, giddily, that she had no idea who or where she might be in a year's time and almost laughed at the thought.

The streets were packed with marching pedestrians, the streetlamps coming to life in the encroaching dusk. Jennifer ran, her suitcase banging against her legs, her heart pounding. It was almost a quarter to seven. She pictured Laurence arriving home and calling irritably for her, Mrs. Cordoza tying her scarf over her head and observing that madam seemed to be a long time shopping. It would be another half an hour before he became properly concerned, and by that time she would be on the platform.

I'm coming, Anthony, she told him silently, and the bubble that rose in her chest might have been excitement or fear or a heady combination of both.

The endless movement of people along the platform made watching impossible. They swam in front of him, weaving in and out of each other so that he no longer knew what he was watching for. Anthony stood by a cast-iron bench, his cases at his feet, and checked his watch for the thousandth time. It was almost seven. If she was going to come, surely she would have been here by now?

He glanced up at the announcements board and then at the train that would carry him to Heathrow. *Get a grip, man,* he told himself. *She'll come.*

"You for the seven-fifteen, sir?"

The guard was at his shoulder. "Train's leaving in a few moments, sir. If this is yours, I'd advise you to get on."

"I'm waiting for someone."

He peered along the platform to the ticket barrier. An old woman stood there, scrabbling for a long-lost ticket. She shook her head in a way that suggested this was not the first time her handbag had seemingly swallowed some important document. Two porters stood chatting. No one else came through.

"Train won't wait, sir. Next one's at nine forty-five, if that's any help."

He began to pace between the two cast-iron benches, trying not to look at his watch again. He thought of her face that night at Alberto's when she had said she loved him. There had been no guile in it, just honesty. It was beyond her to lie. He dared not think of how it might feel to wake up next to her every morning, the sheer elation of being loved by her, having the freedom to love her in return.

It had been something of a gamble, the letter he had sent her, the ultimatum it contained, but that night he had recognized that she was right: they couldn't go on as they were. The sheer force of their feelings would convert to something toxic. They would come to resent each other for their inability to do what they wanted so badly. If the worst happened, he told himself, again and again, at least he would have behaved honorably. But somehow he didn't believe the worst would happen. She would come. Everything about her told him she would.

He glanced at his watch again, and ran his fingers through his hair, his eyes darting over the few commuters emerging through the ticket barrier.

"This will be a good move for you," Don had told him. "Keep you out of trouble." He had wondered whether his editor was secretly relieved to have him in some other part of the world.

It might be, he answered him, moving out of the way as a crowd of bustling businessmen pushed past and climbed aboard the train. *I have fifteen minutes to find out if that's true.*

It was barely believable. It had begun to rain shortly after she reached New Cavendish Street, the sky turning first a muddy orange, then black. As if at some silent instruction, every taxi was occupied. Every black outline she saw had its yellow light dimmed; some shadowy passenger already en route to wherever they needed to be. She took to waving her arm anyway. *Don't you realize how urgent this is?* she wanted to shout at them. *My life depends on this journey.*

The rain was torrential now, coming down in sheets, like a tropical storm. Umbrellas shot up around her, their spikes jabbing into her as she shifted her weight from foot to foot on the curb. She grew damp, then properly wet.

As the minute hand of her watch crept closer to seven o'clock, the vague thrill of excitement had hardened into a lump of something like fear. She wasn't going to get there in time. Any minute now Laurence would be searching for her. She couldn't make it on foot, even if she ditched her suitcase.

Anxiety rose like a tide within her, and the traffic sloshed past, sending great sprays across the legs of the unwary.

It was when she saw the man in the red shirt that she thought of it. She began to run, pushing past the people who blocked her way, for once uncaring of the impression she made. She ran along the familiar streets until she found the one she was looking for. She parked her suitcase at the top of the stairs and ran down, hair flying, into the darkened club.

Felipe was standing at the bar, polishing glasses. Nobody else was there other than Sherrie, the cloakroom girl. The bar felt petrified in an overwhelming air of stillness, despite the low music in the background.

"He's not here, lady." Felipe didn't even look up.

"I know." She was so breathless she could barely speak. "But this is terribly important. Do you have a car?"

The look he gave her was not friendly. "I might."

"Could you possibly give me a lift to the station?"

"You want me to give you a lift?" He took in her wet clothes, the hair plastered to her head.

"Yes. Yes! I only have fifteen minutes. Please."

He studied her. She noticed a large, half-empty glass of Scotch in front of him.

"Please! I wouldn't ask if it wasn't terribly important." She leaned forward. "It's to meet Tony. Look, I have money—" She rummaged in her pocket for the notes. They came out damp.

He reached behind him through a door and pulled out a set of keys. "I don't want your money."

"Thank you, oh, thank you," she said breathlessly. "Hurry. We have less than fifteen minutes."

His car was a short walk away, and by the time they reached it he, too, was soaked. He didn't open the door for her, and she wrenched at it, hurling her dripping case with a grunt onto the backseat. "Please! Go!" she said, wiping wet fronds of hair from her face, but he was motionless in the driver's seat, apparently thinking. *Oh, God, please don't be drunk,* she told him silently. *Please don't tell me now that you can't drive, that your car's out of petrol, that you've changed your mind.* "Please. There's so little time." She tried to keep the anguish from her voice.

"Mrs. Stirling? Before I drive you?"

"Yes?"

"I need to know . . . Tony, he is a good man, but . . ."

"I know he was married. I know about his son. I know about it all," she said impatiently.

"He is more fragile than he lets on."

"What?"

"Don't break his heart. I have never seen him like this with a woman. If you are not sure, if you think there is even a chance you might go back to your husband, please don't do this."

The rain beat down on the roof of the little car. She reached out a hand, placed it on his arm. "I'm not . . . I'm not who you think I am. Really."

He looked sideways at her.

"I—just want to be with him. I'm giving it all up for him. It's just him. It's Anthony," she said, and the words made her want to laugh with fear and anxiety. "Now go! Please!"

"Okay," he said, wrenching the car around so that the tires squealed. "Where to?" He pointed the car toward Euston Road, bashing the button in an attempt to make the windscreen wipers work. She thought distantly of Mrs. Cordoza's windows, washed until they shone, then pulled the letter from the envelope.

> *My dearest and only love. I meant what I said. I have come to the conclusion that the only way forward is for one of us to make a bold decision. . . .*
>
> *I am going to take the job. I'll be at Platform 4 Paddington at 7:15 on Monday evening . . .*

"Platform four," she yelled. "We have eleven minutes. Do you think we'll—"

Part 2

Chapter 12

SUMMER 1964

The nurse moved slowly down the ward, pushing a trolley on which sat neat rows of paper cups containing brightly colored pills. The woman in Bed 16c muttered, "Oh, God, not more . . ."

"Not going to make a fuss, are we?" The nurse placed a beaker of water on the bedside table.

"If I have any more of those things, I'll start to rattle."

"Yes, but we've got to get that blood pressure down now, haven't we?"

"Do we? I hadn't realized it was catching . . ."

Jennifer, perched on the chair beside the bed, lifted the beaker and handed it to Yvonne Moncrieff, whose swollen middle rose, domelike, beneath the blankets, curiously divorced from the rest of her body.

Yvonne sighed. She tipped the pills into her mouth, swallowed obediently, then smiled sarcastically at the young nurse, who pushed her way along the maternity ward to the next patient. "Jenny, darling, stage a breakout. I don't think I can bear another night in here. The moaning and groaning—you wouldn't believe it."

"I thought Francis was going to put you in a private ward."

"Not now that they think I'm going to be here for weeks. You know how careful he is with money. 'What's the point of it, darling, given that we can get perfectly good care for free? Besides, you'll have the other ladies to chat to.'" She sniffed, tilting her head toward the large, freckled woman in the next bed. "Yes, because I have so much in common with Lilo Lil there. Thirteen children! Thirteen! I'd thought we were awful with three in four years, but goodness, I'm an amateur."

"I brought you some more magazines." Jennifer took them out of her bag.

"Oh, *Vogue*. You are a sweetie, but I'm going to ask you to take that one away. It'll be months before I can get into anything in their pages, and it'll only make me want to cry. I'm booking a fitting for a new girdle the day after this little one finally gets here. . . . Tell me something exciting."

"Exciting?"

"What are you up to for the rest of this week? You don't know what it's like being stuck here for days on end, the size of a whale, being force-fed milk pudding and wondering what on earth's actually happening in the world."

"Oh . . . it's rather dull. Drinks at some embassy tonight. I'd really rather stay at home, but Larry's insistent I go with him. There's been some conference in New York about people getting ill from asbestos, and he wants to go and tell them he thinks this man Selikoff, who's something to do with it all, is a troublemaker."

"But cocktails, pretty dresses . . ."

"Actually, I was rather looking forward to curling up with *The Avengers*. It's too hot to get dressed up."

"Ugh. You're telling me. I feel like I'm trapped with my own little stove here." She patted her stomach. "Oh! I knew there was something I wanted to tell you. Mary Odin popped in yesterday. She told me that Katherine and Tommy Broughton have agreed to divorce. And you'll never guess what they're doing?"

Jennifer shook her head.

"A hotel divorce. Apparently he's agreed to be 'caught' in a hotel with some woman so they can be released without the usual delays. But that's not the half of it."

"No?"

"Mary says the woman who's agreed to be pictured with him is actually his mistress. The one who sent those letters. Poor old Katherine thinks he's paying someone to do it. She's already using one of the love letters as evidence. Apparently he told Katherine he got a friend to write it and make it authentic. Isn't that the most awful thing you ever heard?"

"Awful."

"I'm praying Katherine doesn't come to see me. I know I'll end up giving the game away. Poor woman. And everyone but her knowing."

Jennifer picked up a magazine and leafed through it, observing companionably on that recipe or this dress pattern. She became aware that her friend wasn't listening. "Are you all right?" She put a hand on the bedcover. "Anything I can get you?"

"Keep an eye open for me, won't you?" Yvonne's voice was calm, but her swollen fingers beat a restless tattoo on the sheet.

"What do you mean?"

"Francis. Keep an eye open for any unexpected visitors. Female visitors." Her face was turned resolutely toward the window.

"Oh, I'm sure Francis—"

"Jenny? Just do it for me, will you?"

A brief pause. Jennifer examined a stray thread on the lap of her skirt. "Of course."

"Anyway," Yvonne changed the subject, "let me know what you wear tonight. As I said, I simply can't wait to be back in civilian clothes. Did you know my feet have gone up two sizes? I'll be walking out of here in Wellington boots if they get any worse."

Jennifer stood up and reached for her bag, which she had left on the back of the chair. "I almost forgot. Violet said she'd be here after tea."

"Oh, Lord. More updates on little Frederick's terrible poop problem."

"I'll come tomorrow if I can."

"Have fun, darling. I'd give my eyeteeth to be at a cocktail party rather than stuck here listening to Violet drone on." Yvonne sighed. "And pass me that copy of *Queen* before you go, would you? What do you think of Jean Shrimpton's hair? It's a little like how you wore yours to that disastrous supper at Maisie Barton-Hulme's."

Jennifer stepped into her bathroom and locked the door behind her, letting the dressing gown fall at her feet. She had laid out the clothes she would wear this evening: a raw silk shift dress with a scoop collar, the color of good claret, with a silk wrap. She would pin up her hair, and put on the ruby earrings Laurence had bought her for her thirtieth birthday. He complained that she rarely wore them. In his opinion, if he spent money on her, she should at least demonstrate the evidence of it.

That being settled, she would soak in her bath until she had to polish her fingernails. Then she would get dressed, and by the time Laurence returned home, she would be putting the finishing touches to her makeup. She turned off the taps and looked at her reflection in the mirror of the medicine cabinet, wiping the glass when it became obscured by steam. She stared at herself until it had clouded again. Then she opened the cabinet and sorted through the brown bottles on the top shelf until she found what she wanted. She swallowed two Valium, washing them down with water from the tooth mug. She eyed the pentobarbital, but decided that would be too much if she wanted to drink. And she definitely did.

She climbed into the bath as she heard the slam of the front door, which announced that Mrs. Cordoza was back from the park, and slid down into the comforting water.

Laurence had rung to say he would be late again. She sat in the back of the car while Eric, the driver, negotiated the hot, dry streets, finally coming to a halt outside her husband's offices. "Will you be waiting in the car, Mrs. Stirling?"

"Yes, thank you."

She watched as the young man walked briskly up the steps and disappeared into the foyer. She no longer cared to go into her husband's offices. She made the odd appearance at functions, and to wish the staff a happy Christmas, when he insisted, but the place made her uncomfortable. His secretary regarded her with a kind of curious disdain, as if Jennifer had wronged her. Perhaps she had. It was often hard to tell what she had done wrong, these days.

The door opened and Laurence walked out, followed by the driver, in his dark gray tweed. No matter that the temperature was in the low seventies, Laurence Stirling would wear what he considered appropriate. He found the new trends in men's clothing incomprehensible.

"Ah. You're here." He slid into the backseat beside her, bringing with him a burst of warm air.

"Yes."

"Everything all right at home?"

"Everything is fine."

"Did the boy call to wash the steps?"

"Just after you left."

"I wanted to be away by six—bloody transatlantic calls. They always come in later than they say they will."

She nodded. She knew she wasn't required to answer.

They pulled out into the evening traffic. Across Marylebone Road, she could picture the green mirage of Regent's Park, and watched girls walking toward it in lazy, laughing groups on the shimmering pavements, pausing to exclaim to each other. Just lately she had started to feel old, matronly, faced with these girdle-free dolly birds in their short, blunt skirts and bold makeup. They seemed not to care what anyone thought of them. There were probably only ten years between them and herself, Jennifer thought, but she might as well be from her own mother's generation.

"Oh. You wore that dress." His voice was loaded with disapproval.

"I hadn't realized you disliked it."

"I don't have any feelings about it one way or another. I just thought you might want to wear something that made you look less . . . bony."

It never ended. Even though she'd thought she'd covered her heart with a permanent porcelain shell, he still found a way to chip at it.

She swallowed. "Bony. Thank you. I don't suppose there's a lot I can do about it now."

"Don't make a fuss. But you could think a little more carefully about how you present yourself." He turned to her briefly. "And you might want to use some more of whatever you put on your face here." He pointed under his eyes. "You look rather tired." He leaned back in his seat and lit a cigar. "Right, Eric. Crack on—I want to be there by seven."

With an obedient purr, the car surged forward. Jennifer stared out at the busy streets, and said nothing.

Gracious. Even-tempered. Calm. These were the words her friends, Laurence's friends, and his business associates used to describe her. Mrs. Stirling, a paragon of female virtue, always perfectly put together, never prone to the excitement and shrill hysterics of other, lesser wives. Occasionally, if this was said in his earshot, Laurence would say, "Perfect wife? If only they knew, eh, darling?" The men in his presence would laugh obligingly, and she would smile, too. It was often those evenings that ended badly. Occasionally, when she caught the fleeting glances that traveled between Yvonne and Francis at one of Laurence's sharper comments, or Bill's blush, she suspected that their relationship might indeed have been the subject of private speculation. But no one pressed her. A man's domestic life was private, after all. They were good friends, far too good to intrude.

"And here is the lovely Mrs. Stirling. Don't you look gorgeous?" The South African attaché took her hands in his and kissed her cheeks.

"Not too bony?" she asked innocently.

"What?"

"Nothing." She smiled. "You look terribly well, Sebastian. Getting married has evidently been good for you."

Laurence clapped the younger man on the back. "Despite all my warnings, eh?"

The two men laughed, and Sebastian Thorne, who still carried the glow of the genuinely well matched, beamed proudly. "Pauline's over there, if you'd like to say hello, Jennifer. I know she's looking forward to seeing you."

"I'll do that," she said, filled with gratitude for such an early exit. "Do excuse me."

Four years had gone by since the accident. Four years in which Jennifer had struggled with grief, guilt, the loss of a love affair she could only half recall, and had made flailing attempts to salvage the one she belonged in.

On the few occasions when she had let her thoughts drift that way, she decided that a kind of madness must have overcome her after she had first found those letters. She remembered her manic efforts to uncover Boot's identity, her misidentification and reckless pursuit of Reggie, and felt almost as if those events had happened to someone else. She couldn't imagine feeling passion like that now. She couldn't imagine that intensity of wanting. For a long time, she had been penitent. She had betrayed Laurence, and her only hope was to make it up to him. It was the least he might expect from her. She had bent herself to the task, tried to banish thoughts of anyone else. The letters, those that remained, had finally been consigned to a shoebox.

She wished she had known then that Laurence's anger would be such a corrosive and enduring thing. She had asked for understanding, for another chance, and he had taken an almost perverse pleasure in reminding her of all the ways in which she had offended him. He never liked to mention her betrayal explicitly—that, after all, implied a loss of control on his part, and she understood now that Laurence liked to be seen to be in control of all parts of his life—but he let her know, daily and in myriad ways, of her failures. The way she dressed. The way she ran their home. Her inability to make him happy. She suspected, some days, that she would pay for the rest of her life.

For the past year or so, he had been less volatile. She suspected he had taken a mistress. This knowledge didn't trouble her; in fact, she was relieved. His demands on her had lessened, were less punishing. His verbal digs seemed almost cursory, like a habit he couldn't be bothered to break.

The pills helped, as Dr. Hargreaves had said they would. If they left her feeling oddly flat, she thought it was probably a price worth paying. Yes, as Laurence often pointed out, she could be dull. Yes, she might no longer sparkle at the dinner table, but the pills meant that she no longer cried at inappropriate moments or struggled to get out of bed. She no longer feared his moods, and cared less when he came to her at night. Most importantly, she was no longer eviscerated by pain over all that she had lost or for which she had been responsible.

No. Jennifer Stirling moved in a stately fashion through her days, her hair and makeup perfect, a lovely smile across her face. Gracious, even-tempered Jennifer, who gave the finest dinner parties, kept a beautiful home, knew all the best people. The perfect wife for a man of his standing.

And there were compensations. She had been allowed that.

"I do absolutely love having our own place. Didn't you feel like that when you and Mr. Stirling first married?"

"I can't remember so far back." She glanced at Laurence, talking to Sebastian, one hand raised to his mouth as he puffed on the ever-present cigar. Fans whirred lazily overhead, and the women stood in jeweled clusters beneath them, occasionally patting their necks with fine lawn handkerchiefs.

Pauline Thorne pulled out a small wallet that contained photographs of their new house. "We've gone for modern furniture. Sebastian said I could do whatever I wanted."

Jennifer thought of her own house, its heavy mahogany, the portentous decor. She admired the clean white chairs in the snapshots, so smooth they might have been eggshells, the brightly colored rugs, the modern art on the walls. Laurence believed his house should be a reflection of himself. He saw it as grand, filled with a sense of history. Looking at these photographs, Jennifer realized she saw it as pompous, unmoving. Stifling. She reminded herself not to be unkind. Many people would love to live in a house like hers.

"It's going to feature in *Your House* next month. Seb's mother absolutely hates it. She says every time she sets foot in our living room, she thinks she's going to be abducted by aliens." The girl laughed, and

Jennifer smiled. "When I said I might convert one of the bedrooms to a nursery, she said that judging by the rest of the decor, I'd probably drop a baby out of a plastic egg."

"Are you hoping for children?"

"Not yet. Not for ages . . ." She laid a hand on Jennifer's arm. "I hope you don't mind me telling you, but we're only just off our honeymoon. My mother gave me The Talk before I left. You know— how I must submit to Seb, how it might be 'a bit unpleasant.' "

Jennifer blinked.

"She really thought I'd be traumatized. But it isn't like that at all, is it?"

Jennifer took a sip of her drink.

"Oh, am I being terribly indiscreet?"

"Not at all," she said politely. She suspected her face might have taken on a terrifying blankness.

"Would you like another drink, Pauline?" she said, when she could speak again. "I do believe my glass is empty."

She sat in the ladies' and opened her handbag. She unscrewed the little brown bottle and took another Valium. Just one, and perhaps one drink more. She sat on the lavatory seat, waiting for her heartbeat to return to normal, and opened her compact to powder a nose that needed no powder.

Pauline had seemed almost hurt when she'd walked off, as if her confidences had been rebuffed. The younger woman was girlish, excited, delighted to have been allowed into this new adult world.

Had she ever felt like that about Laurence? she wondered dully. Sometimes she passed their wedding picture in the hallway, and it was like looking at strangers. Most of the time she tried to ignore it. If she was in the wrong frame of mind, as Laurence said she often was, she wanted to shout at that trusting, wide-eyed girl, tell her not to marry at all. Plenty of women didn't now. They had careers and money of their own, and didn't feel obliged to watch everything they said or did in case it offended the one man whose opinion apparently mattered.

She tried not to imagine Pauline Thorne in ten years' time when Sebastian's words of adoration would have been long forgotten, when the demands of work, children, worries about money, or the sheer tedium of day-to-day routine would have caused her glow to fade. She mustn't be sour. Let the girl have her day. Her story might turn out differently.

She took a deep breath and reapplied her lipstick.

When she returned to the party, Laurence had moved to a new group. She stood in the doorway, watching him stoop to greet a young woman she didn't recognize. He was listening attentively to what she said, nodding. She spoke again, and all the men laughed. Laurence put his mouth to her ear and murmured something, and the woman nodded, smiling. She would think him utterly charming, Jennifer thought.

It was a quarter to ten. She would have liked to leave, but knew better than to press her husband. They would go when he was ready.

The waiter was on his way over to her. He proffered a silver tray, loaded with glasses of champagne. "Madam?" Home seemed suddenly an impossible distance away. "Thank you," she said, and took one.

It was then that she saw him, half hidden by some potted palms. She watched almost absently at first, some distant part of her mind observing that she had once known someone whose hair met his collar just like that man's did. There had been a time—perhaps a year ago or more—when she had seen him everywhere, a phantom, his torso, his hair, his laugh transplanted onto other men.

His companion guffawed, shaking his head as if pleading with him not to continue. They lifted their glasses to each other. And then he turned.

Jennifer's heart stopped. The room stilled, then tilted. She didn't feel the glass drop from her fingers, was only dimly aware of the crash that echoed through the vast atrium, a brief lull in the conversation, the brisk footsteps of a waiter hurrying toward her to clear it up. She heard Laurence, a short distance away, say something dismissively. She was rooted to the spot, until the waiter placed a hand on her arm, telling her, "Step back, madam, please step back."

The room refilled with conversation. The music continued. And as she stared, the man with the dark hair looked back at her.

Chapter 13

SEPTEMBER 1964

"I don't know. I thought you were done with that part of the world. Why would you want to head back there?"

"It's a big story, and I'm the best person for the job."

"You're doing good stuff at the UN. Upstairs is happy."

"But the real story is back in Congo, Don, you know that."

Despite the seismic changes that had taken place, despite his promotion from news to executive editor, Don Franklin's office and the man himself had changed little since Anthony O'Hare had left England. Every year Anthony had returned to visit his son and show his face in the newsroom, and every year the windows were a little more nicotine stained, the mammoth piles of press cuttings teetering a little more chaotically. "I like it like that," Don would say, if asked. "Why the hell would I want a clear view of that sorry shower anyway?"

But Don's scruffy, paper-strewn office was an anomaly. The *Nation* was changing. Its pages were bolder and brighter, speaking to a younger audience. There were features sections, filled with makeup tips and discussions on the latest musical trends, letters about contraception, and gossip columns detailing people's extramarital affairs. In the newspaper offices, among the men with rolled-up shirtsleeves, girls in short skirts staffed the photocopier and stood in huddles along corridors. They would break off their conversations to eye him speculatively as he passed. London girls had become bolder. He was rarely alone on visits to the city.

"You know as well as I do. No one here has the Africa experience I do. And it's not just the U.S. consulate staff that are being taken hostage now, it's whites everywhere. There are terrible tales coming out of the country—the Simba leaders don't care what the rebels are doing. Come on, Don. Are you telling me Phipps is the better man for the job? MacDonald?"

"I don't know, Tony."

"Believe me, the Americans don't like their missionary, Carlson, being paraded around like a bargaining chip." He leaned forward. "There's talk of a rescue operation. . . . The name being bandied about is Dragon Rouge."

"Tony, I don't know that the editor wants anyone out there right now. These rebels are lunatics."

"Who has better contacts than I do? Who knows more about Congo, more about the UN? I've done four years in that rabbit warren, Don, four bloody years. You need me out there. I need to be out there." He could see Don's resolve wavering. The authority of Anthony's years outside the newsroom, his polished appearance, added weight to his claims. For four years he had faithfully reported the political to-and-fros of the labyrinthine United Nations.

During the first year he had given little thought to anything except getting up in the morning and making sure he could do his job. But since then he had struggled with the familiar nagging conviction that the real story, his life, even, was taking place somewhere far from where he was. Now Congo, teetering on the brink since Lumumba's assassination, was threatening to implode, and its siren call, once a distant hum, was insistent.

"It's a different game out there now," Don said. "I don't like it. I'm not sure we should have anyone in the country until it settles down a bit."

But Don knew as well as Anthony did that this was the curse of reporting conflict: it gave you clear-cut rights and wrongs; the adrenaline surged, and you were filled with humor, desperation, and camaraderie. It might well burn you out, but anyone who had been there found it hard to relish the mundane slog of "normal" life at home.

Every morning Anthony made calls, searched the newspapers for the few lines that had made it out, interpreting what was happening. It was going to go big: he could feel it in his bones. He needed to be there, tasting it, bringing it back on paper. For four years he had been half dead. He needed it around him to feel alive again.

Anthony leaned over the desk. "Look, Philmore told me the editor asked specifically for me. You want to disappoint him?"

Don lit another cigarette. "Of course not. But he wasn't here when you were . . ." He tapped the cigarette on the edge of the overflowing ashtray.

"That's it? You're afraid I'm going to crack up again?"

Don's embarrassed chuckle told him everything he needed to know. "I haven't had a drink in years. I've kept my nose clean. I'll get inoculated against yellow fever, if that's what you're worried about."

"I'm just thinking about you, Tony. It's risky. Look. What about your son?"

"He's not a factor." One visit, two letters a year, if he was lucky. Clarissa was only thinking of Phillip, of course: it was better for him not to have the disruption of too much face-to-face contact. "Let me go for three months. It'll be over by the end of the year. They're all saying as much."

"I don't know . . ."

"Have I ever missed a deadline? Haven't I pulled in some good stories? For Christ's sake, Don, you need me out there. The paper needs me out there. It's got to be someone who knows their way around. Someone with contacts. Picture it." He ran his hand along an imaginary headline. "'Our man in Congo as the white hostages are rescued.' Look, do this for me, Don, and then we'll talk."

"You've still got itchy feet, eh?"

"I know where I should be."

Don blew out his cheeks, like a human hamster, then exhaled noisily. "Okay. I'll talk to Him Upstairs. I can't promise anything—but I'll talk to him."

"Thank you." Anthony got up to leave.

"Tony."

"What?"

"You look good."

"Thanks."

"I mean it. Fancy a drink tonight? You, me, and some of the old crowd? Miller's in town. We could grab a few beers—iced water, Coca-Cola, whatever."

"I said I'd go to some do with Douglas Gardiner."

"Oh?"

"At the South African embassy. Got to keep up the contacts."

Don shook his head resignedly. "Gardiner, eh? Tell him I said he couldn't write his way out of a paper bag."

Cheryl, the news-desk secretary, was standing by the stationery cupboard and winked at him as he passed her on the way out. She actually winked at him. Anthony O'Hare sighed, shook his head, and reached for his jacket.

"Winked at you? Tony, old son, you were lucky she didn't pull you into the damned cupboard."

"I've only been gone a few years, Dougie. It's still the same country."

"No." Douglas's eyes darted round the room. "No, it's not, old chap. London's now at the center of the universe. It's all happening here, old chum. Equality between men and women is only the half of it."

There was, he had to acknowledge, truth in what Douglas had said. Even the appearance of the city had changed: gone were many of the sober streets, the elegant, shabby facades and echoes of postwar penury. They had been replaced by illuminated signage, women's boutiques with names like Party Girl and Jet Set, foreign restaurants, and high-rise towers. Every time he returned to London, he felt increasingly a stranger: familiar landmarks disappeared, and those that remained were overshadowed by the Post Office Tower or other examples of its architect's futuristic craft. His old apartment building had been torn down and replaced by something brutally modernistic. Alberto's jazz club was now some rock-and-roll setup. Even clothes were brighter. The older generation, stuck in brown and navy, looked somehow more dated and faded than they actually were.

"So . . . you miss being out in the field?"

"Nah. We'll all have to lay down our tin helmets one day, won't we? Better-looking women in this job, that's for sure. How's New York? What do you think of Johnson?"

"He's no Kennedy, that's for sure. . . . So, what do you do now? Weave your way through high society?"

"It's not like when you left, Tony. They don't want ambassadors' wives and tittle-tattle about indiscretions. Now it's pop stars—the Beatles and Cilla Black. No one with any breeding. It's all egalitarian, the society column."

The sound of smashing glass echoed in the vast ballroom. The two men broke off their conversation.

"Whoops. Someone's had one too many," Douglas observed. "Some things don't change. The ladies still can't hold their drink."

"Well, I have a feeling that some of the girls in the newspaper office could have drunk me under the table." Anthony shuddered.

"Still off the sauce?"

"More than three years now."

"You wouldn't last long in this job. Don't you miss it?"

"Every damned day."

Douglas had stopped laughing and was looking past him. Anthony glanced over his shoulder. "You need to speak to someone?" He shifted to one side obligingly.

"No." Douglas squinted. "I thought someone was staring at me. But I think it's you. She familiar?"

Anthony turned—and his mind went blank. Then it hit him with the brutal inevitability of a demolition ball. Of course she'd be here. The one person he had tried not to think about. The one person he had hoped never to see again. He had come to England for a little less than a week, and there she was. On his first evening out.

He took in the dark red dress, the almost perfect posture that marked her out from any other woman in the room. As their eyes met, she seemed to sway.

"Nope. Can't have been you," Douglas remarked. "Look, she's headed for the balcony. I know who that is. She's . . ." He clicked his fingers. "Stirling. Thingy Stirling's wife. The asbestos magnate." He cocked his head. "Mind if we go over? It might make a paragraph. She was quite the society hostess a few years back. They'll probably drop in some piece about Elvis Presley instead, but you never know . . ."

Anthony swallowed. "Sure." He straightened his collar, took a deep breath, and followed his friend through the crowd toward the balcony.

"Mrs. Stirling."

She was looking down at the busy London street, her back to him. Her hair was in a sculptural arrangement of glossy bubble curls, and rubies hung at her throat. She turned slowly, and her hand lifted to her mouth.

It had to happen, he told himself. Perhaps seeing her like this, having to meet her, would mean he could finally lay it to rest. Even as he thought this, he had no idea what to say to her. Would they engage in some polite social exchange? Perhaps she would make an excuse and walk straight past him. Was she embarrassed about what had happened? Guilty? Had she fallen in love with someone else? His thoughts careened wildly.

Douglas extended his hand to her, and she took it, but her eyes settled on Anthony. All color had drained from her face.

"Mrs. Stirling? Douglas Gardiner, the *Express*. We met at Ascot, I believe, back in the summer?"

"Oh, yes," she said. Her voice shook. "I'm sorry," she whispered. "I—I—"

"I say, are you all right? You look awfully pale."

"I . . . Actually I'm feeling a little faint."

"Would you like me to fetch your husband?" Douglas took her elbow.

"No!" she said. "No." She took a breath. "Just a glass of water. If you'd be so kind."

Douglas shot him a fleeting look. What have we here? "Tony . . . you'll stay with Mrs. Stirling for a minute, won't you? I'll be right back." Douglas stepped into the party, and as the door closed behind him, muffling the music, it was just the two of them. Her eyes were wide and terrible. She didn't seem able to speak.

"Is it that bad? To see me, I mean?" There was a slight edge to his voice—he couldn't help it.

She blinked, looked away, looked back at him, as if to check he was actually there.

"Jennifer? Would you like me to leave? I'm sorry. I wouldn't have bothered you. It's just that Dougie—"

"They said—they said you. Were. Dead." Her voice emerged as a series of coughs.

"Dead?"

"In the crash." She was perspiring, her skin pale and waxy. He wondered, briefly, if she was indeed going to pass out. He took a step forward and steered her to the ledge of the balcony, removing his jacket so that she could sit on it. Her head dropped into her hands, and she gave a low moan. "You can't be here." It was as if she was talking to herself.

"What? I don't understand." He wondered, briefly, if she had gone mad.

She looked up. "We were in a car. There was a crash . . . It can't be you! It can't be." Her eyes traveled down to his hands, as if she was half expecting them to evaporate.

"A crash?" He knelt beside her. "Jennifer, the last time I saw you was at a club, not in a car."

She was shaking her head, apparently uncomprehending.

"I wrote you a letter—"

"Yes."

"—asking you to come away with me."

She nodded.

"And I was waiting at the station. You didn't turn up. I thought you'd decided against it. Then I received your letter, forwarded on to me, in which you made the point, repeatedly, that you were married."

He could say it so calmly, as if it had held no more importance than if he had been waiting for an old friend. As if her absence had not skewed his life, his happiness, for four years.

"But I was coming to you."

They stared at each other.

Her face fell back into her hands, and her shoulders shook. He stood up, glancing behind her at the lit ballroom, and laid a hand on her shoulder. She flinched as though she'd been burned. He was conscious of the outline of her back through her dress, and his breath stalled in his throat. He couldn't think clearly. He could barely think at all.

"All this time"—she looked at him, tears in her eyes—"all this time . . . and you were alive."

"I assumed . . . you just didn't want to come with me."

"Look!" She pulled up her sleeve, showing the jagged, raised silver line that scored her arm. "I had no memory. For months. I still remember little of that time. He told me you'd died. He told me—"

"But didn't you see my name in the newspaper? I have pieces in it almost daily."

"I don't read newspapers. Not anymore. Why would I?"

The full ramifications of what she had said were beginning to sink in, and Anthony was feeling a little unsteady on his feet. She turned to the French windows, now half obscured by steam, then wiped her eyes with her fingers. He offered her his handkerchief, and she took it tentatively, as if she was still afraid to make contact with his skin.

"I can't stay out here," she said, when she had recovered her composure. Mascara had left a black smear under her eye, and he resisted the urge to wipe it away. "He'll be wondering where I am." There were new lines of strain around her eyes; the dewiness of her skin had been supplanted by something tighter. The girlishness had gone, replaced by subtle new knowledge. He couldn't stop staring at her. "How can I reach you?" he asked.

"You can't." She shook her head a little, as if she was trying to clear it.

"I'm staying at the Regent," he said. "Ring me tomorrow." He reached into his pocket, scribbled on a business card.

She took it and gazed at it, as if imprinting the details on her memory.

"Here we are." Douglas had appeared between them. He held out a glass of water. "Your husband is talking to some people just inside the door. I can fetch him, if you like."

"No—no, I'll be fine." She took a sip from the glass. "Thank you so much. I have to go, Anthony."

The way she had said his name. Anthony. He realized he was smiling. She was there, inches from him. She had loved him, grieved for him. She had tried to come to him that night. It was as if the misery of four years had been wiped away.

"Do you two know each other, then?"

Anthony heard, as if from a distance, Douglas talking, saw him motioning toward the doors. Jennifer sipped the water, her eyes not leaving his face. He knew that in the coming hours he would curse whichever gods had thought it amusing to send their lives careering away from each other, and grieve for the time they had lost. But for now he could only feel a welling joy that the thing he had thought lost forever had been returned to him.

It was time for her to go. She stood up, smoothed her hair. "Do I look . . . all right?"

"You look—"

"You look wonderful, Mrs. Stirling. As always." Douglas opened the door.

Such a small smile, heartbreaking in what it told Anthony. As she passed him, she reached out a slim hand and touched his arm just above the elbow. And then she walked into the crowded ballroom.

Douglas raised an eyebrow as the door closed behind her. "Don't tell me," he said. "Not another of your conquests? You old dog. You always did get what you wanted."

Anthony's eyes were still on the door. "No," he said quietly. "I didn't."

Jennifer was silent during the short drive back to the house. Laurence had offered a lift to a business colleague she didn't know, which meant she could sit quietly while the men talked.

"Of course, Pip Marchant was up to his old tricks, all his capital tied up in one project."

"He's a hostage to fortune. His father was the same."

"I expect if you go far enough back in that family tree you'll find the South Sea Bubble."

"I think you'll find several! All filled with hot air."

The interior of the big black car was thick with cigar smoke. Laurence was garrulous, opinionated, in the way he often was when surrounded by businessmen or marinated in whiskey. She barely heard him, swamped by this new knowledge. She stared out at the still streets as the car glided along, seeing not the beauty of her surroundings, the occasional person dawdling on their way home, but Anthony's face. His brown eyes, when they had fixed on hers, his face a little more lined, but perhaps more handsome, more at ease. She could still feel the warmth of his hand on her back.

How can I reach you?

Alive, these past four years. Living, breathing, sipping cups of coffee and typing. Alive. She could have written to him, spoken to him. Gone to him.

She swallowed, trying to contain the tumultuous emotion that threatened to rise within her. There would be a time to deal with everything that must have led to this, to her being here, now, in this car with a man who no longer thought it necessary even to acknowledge her presence. Now was not it. Her blood fizzed within her. *Alive*, it sang.

The car pulled up on Upper Wimpole Street. Eric climbed out of the driver's seat and opened the passenger door. The businessman climbed out, puffing at his cigar. "Much obliged, Larry. You at the club this week? I'll buy you dinner."

"I'll look forward to it." The man made his way heavily toward his front door, which opened, as if someone had been waiting for his arrival. Laurence watched his colleague disappear, then turned back to the front. "Home, please, Eric." He shifted in his seat.

She felt his eyes on her. "You're very quiet." He always made it sound disapproving.

"Am I? I didn't think I had anything to add to your conversation."

"Yes. Well. Not a bad evening, all in all." He settled back, nodding to himself.

"No," she said quietly. "Not a bad evening at all."

Chapter 14

Your hotel, midday. J.

Anthony stared at the letter, with its single line of text.

"Delivered by hand this morning." Cheryl stood in front of him, a pencil between her index and middle fingers. Her short, astonishingly blond hair was so thick that he wondered briefly if she was wearing a wig. "I wasn't sure whether to phone you, but Don said you'd be coming in."

"Yes. Thank you." He folded the note carefully and put it into his pocket.

"Cute."

"Who—me?"

"Your new girlfriend."

"Very funny."

"I mean it. I thought she looked far too classy for you, though." She sat on the edge of his desk, gazing up at him through impossibly blackened eyelashes.

"She is far too classy for me. And she's not my girlfriend."

"Oh, yes, I forgot. You have one of those in New York. This one's married, right?"

"She's an old friend."

"Hah! I have old friends like that. Are you whisking her off to Africa with you?"

"I don't know that I'm going to Africa." He leaned back in his chair, linked his fingers behind his head. "And you're extremely nosy."

"This is a newspaper, in case you hadn't noticed. Nosiness is our business."

He had barely slept, his senses hypersensitive to everything around him. He had given up trying at three and instead sat in the hotel bar, nursing cups of coffee, going over their conversation, trying to make sense of what had been said. He had fought the urge, in the small hours, to take a taxi to the square and sit outside her house for the pleasure of knowing that she was inside, a matter of feet away.

I was coming to you.

Cheryl was still watching him. He tapped his fingers on the desk. "Yes," he said. "Well. In my opinion, everyone's far too interested in everyone else's affairs."

"So it is an affair. You know the subs desk's opened a book on it."

"Cheryl . . ."

"Well, there's not much copy going through at this time of the morning. And what's in the letter? Where are you meeting her? Anywhere nice? Does she pay for everything, given that she's plainly loaded?"

"Good God!"

"Well, she can't be very practiced at affairs, then. Tell her that the next time she leaves a love note, she should take her wedding ring off first."

Anthony sighed. "You, young lady, are wasted as a secretary."

She lowered her voice to a whisper: "If you tell me her name, I'll split the sweepstake with you. There's a tidy sum."

"Send me to Africa, for God's sake. The Congolese Army Interrogation Unit is nothing compared to you."

She laughed throatily and went back to her typewriter.

He unfolded the note. The mere sight of that looped script transported him back to France, to notes pushed under his door in an idyllic week a million years ago. Some part of him had known she would contact him. He jumped when he realized Don had come in.

"Tony. The editor wants a word. Upstairs."

"Now?"

"No. Three weeks on Tuesday. Yes, now. He wants to talk to you about your future. And, no, you're not for the chop, sadly. I think he's trying to suss out whether or not to send you back to Africa." Don poked his shoulder. "Hello? Cloth Ears? You need to look like you know what you're doing."

Anthony barely heard him. It was a quarter past eleven already. The editor was not a man who liked to do anything in a hurry, and it was entirely possible he would be with him for a good hour. He turned to Cheryl as he stood. "Blondie, do me a favor. Ring my hotel. Tell them a Jennifer Stirling is due to meet me at twelve, and ask someone to tell her I'll be late but not to leave. I'll be there. She mustn't leave."

Cheryl's smile was laced with satisfaction. "Mrs. Jennifer Stirling?"

"As I said, she's an old friend."

Don was wearing yesterday's shirt, Anthony noted. He was always wearing yesterday's shirt. He was also shaking his head. "Jesus. That Stirling woman again? How much of an appetite for trouble have you got?"

"She's just a friend."

"And I'm Twiggy. Come on. Come and explain to the Great White Chief why you should be allowed to sacrifice yourself to the Simba rebels."

She was still there, he was relieved to see. It was more than half an hour after their supposed meeting time. She was seated at a small table in the extravagantly frothy salon, where the plaster moldings resembled the icing on an overadorned Christmas cake and most of the other tables were occupied by elderly widows exclaiming in shocked, hushed tones at the wickedness of the modern world.

"I ordered tea," she said, as he sat down opposite her, apologizing for the fifth time. "I hope you don't mind."

Her hair was down. She wore a black sweater and tailored fawn trousers. She was thinner than she had been. He supposed it was the fashion.

He attempted to regulate his breathing. He had pictured this moment so many times, sweeping her into his arms, their passionate reunion. Now he felt vaguely wrong-footed by her self-possession, the formality of the surroundings.

A waitress arrived, pushing a trolley from which she took a teapot, milk jug, some precision-cut sandwiches on white bread, cups, saucers, and plates. He realized he could probably fit four of the sandwiches into his mouth at once.

"Thank you."

"You don't . . . take sugar." She frowned, as if she was trying to remember.

"No."

They sipped their tea. Several times he opened his mouth to speak, but nothing came out. He kept stealing glances at her, noting tiny details. The familiar shape of her nails. Her wrists. The way she periodically lifted herself from her waist, as if some distant voice was telling her to sit up straight.

"Yesterday was such a shock," she said finally, placing her cup on the saucer. "I . . . must apologize for how I behaved. You must have thought I was very odd."

"Perfectly understandable. Not every day you see someone risen from the dead."

A small smile. "Quite."

Their eyes met and slid away. She leaned forward and poured more tea. "Where do you live now?"

"I've been in New York."

"All this time?"

"There wasn't really a reason to come back."

Another heavy silence, which she broke: "You look well. Very well."

She was right. It was impossible to live in the heart of Manhattan and stay scruffy. He had returned to England this year with a wardrobe of good suits and a host of new habits: hot shaves, shoe polishing, teetotalism. "You look lovely, Jennifer."

"Thank you. Are you in England for long?"

"Probably not. I may be going overseas again." He watched her face to see what effect this news might have on her. But she merely reached for the milk. "No," he said, lifting a hand. "Thank you."

Her hand stilled, as if she was disappointed in herself for having forgotten.

"What does the newspaper have in mind for you?" She put a sandwich on a plate and placed it in front of him.

"They'd like me to stay here, but I want to return to Africa. Things have become very complicated in Congo."

"Isn't it very dangerous there?"

"That's not the point."

"You want to be in the thick of it."

"Yes. It's an important story. Plus I have a horror of being desk-bound. These last few years have been"—he tried to think of an expression he could use safely: *These years in New York kept me sane? Allowed me to exist away from you? Stopped me throwing myself on a grenade in a foreign field?*—"useful," he said finally, "in that the editor probably needed to see me in a different light. But I'm keen to move on now. Back to what I do best."

"And there are no safer places you could satisfy that need?"

"Do I look like someone who wants to shuffle paper clips or do the filing?"

She smiled a little. "And what about your son?"

"I've barely seen him. His mother would prefer me to stay away." He took a sip of his tea. "A posting to Congo wouldn't make a huge amount of difference when we largely communicate by letter."

"That must be very hard."

"Yes. Yes, it is."

A string quartet had started up in the corner. She looked behind her briefly, which gave him a moment to gaze at her unhindered, that profile, the small tilt to her upper lip. Something in him constricted, and he knew with a painful pang that he would never again love anyone as he loved Jennifer Stirling. Four years had not freed him, and another ten were unlikely to do so. When she turned back to him, he was aware that he couldn't speak or he would reveal everything, spill out his guts like someone mortally wounded.

"Did you like New York?" she asked.

"It was probably better for me than staying here."

"Where did you live?"

"Manhattan. Do you know New York?"

"Not enough to have any real idea of where you're talking about," she admitted. "And did you . . . are you remarried?"

"No."

"Do you have a girlfriend?"

"I've been dating someone."

"An American?"

"Yes."

"Is she married?"

"No. Funnily enough."

Her expression didn't flicker. "Is it serious?"

"I haven't decided yet."

She allowed herself to smile. "You haven't changed."

"Neither have you."

"I have," she said quietly.

He wanted to touch her. He wanted to knock all the crockery off the damned table, reach across, and take hold of her. He felt furious suddenly, hampered by this ridiculous place, its formality. She had been odd the previous evening, but at least the tumultuous emotions had been genuine. "And you? Has life been good?" he said, when he saw she wasn't going to speak.

She sipped her tea. She seemed almost lethargic. "Has life been good?" She pondered the question. "Good and bad. I'm sure I'm no different from anyone else."

"And you still spend time on the Riviera?"

"Not if I can help it."

He wanted to ask: *Because of me?* She didn't seem to want to volunteer anything. Where was the wit? The passion? That simmering sense she had held within her of something threatening to erupt out of her, whether unexpected laughter or a flurry of kisses? She seemed flattened, buried under glacial good manners.

In the corner, the string quartet paused between movements. Frustration rose in Anthony. "Jennifer, why did you invite me here?"

She looked tired, he realized, but also feverish, her cheekbones lit by points of high color.

"I'm sorry," he continued, "but I don't want a sandwich. I don't want to sit in this place listening to ruddy string music. If I've earned anything through being apparently dead for the last four years, it must be the right not to have to sit through tea and polite conversation."

"I . . . just wanted to see you."

"You know, when I saw you across the room yesterday, I was still so angry with you. All this time I'd assumed you chose him—a lifestyle—over me. I've rehearsed arguments with you in my head, berated you for not replying to my last letters—"

"Please don't." She held up a hand, cutting him off.

"And then I see you, and you tell me you were trying to come with me. And I'm having to rethink everything I believed about the last four years—everything I thought was true."

"Let's not talk about it, Anthony, what might have been . . ." She placed her hands on the table in front of her, like someone laying down cards. "I . . . just can't."

They sat opposite each other, the immaculately dressed woman and the tense man. The thought, brief and darkly humorous, occurred to him that to onlookers they appeared miserable enough to be married.

"Tell me something," he said. "Why are you so loyal to him? Why have you stayed with someone who so clearly cannot make you happy?"

She lifted her eyes to his. "Because I was so disloyal, I suppose."

"Do you think he'd be loyal to you?"

She held his gaze for a moment, then glanced at her watch. "I need to leave."

He winced. "I'm sorry. I won't say another thing. I just need to know—"

"It's not you. Really. I do need to be somewhere."

He caught himself. "Of course. I'm sorry. I'm the one who was late.

I'm sorry to have wasted your time." He couldn't help the anger in his voice. He cursed his editor for losing him that precious half hour, cursed himself for what he already knew were wasted opportunities—and for allowing himself to come close to something that still had the power to burn him.

She stood up to leave, and a waiter appeared to help her with her coat. There would always be someone to help her, he thought absently. She was that kind of woman. He was immobilized, stuck at the table.

Had he misread her? Had he misremembered the intensity of their brief time together? He was saddened by the idea that this was it. Was it worse to have the memory of something perfect sullied, replaced by something inexplicable and disappointing?

The waiter held her coat by the shoulders. She put her arms into the sleeves, one at a time, her head dipped.

"That's it?"

"I'm sorry, Anthony. I really do have to go."

He stood up. "We're not going to talk about anything? After all this? Did you even *think* of me?"

Before he could say more, she had turned on her heel and walked out.

Jennifer splashed her reddened, blotchy eyes with cold water for the fifteenth time. In the bathroom mirror her reflection showed a woman defeated by life. A woman so far removed from the "tai-tai" of five years ago that they might have been different species, let alone different people. She let her fingers trace the shadows under her eyes, the new lines of strain on her brow, and wondered what he had seen when he looked at her.

He'll squash you, extinguish the things that make you you.

She opened the medicine cabinet and gazed at the neat row of brown bottles. She couldn't tell him that she had been so afraid before she met him that she had taken twice the recommended dose of Valium. She couldn't tell him that she had heard him as if through a fog, had been so dissociated from what she was doing that she could barely hold the teapot. She couldn't tell him that to have him so close that she could see every line on his hands and breathe the scent of his cologne had paralyzed her.

Jennifer turned on the hot tap and the water rushed down the plughole, splashing off the porcelain and leaving dark spots on her pale trousers. She took the Valium from the top shelf and unscrewed the lid.

> *You are the strong one, the one who can endure living with the possibility of a love like this, and the fact that we will never be allowed it.*

Not as astute as you thought, Boot.

She heard Mrs. Cordoza's voice downstairs and locked the bathroom door. She placed both hands on the side of the washbasin. *Can I do this?*

She lifted the bottle and tipped its contents down the plughole, watching the water carry away the little white pills. She unscrewed the next, barely pausing to check its contents. Her "little helpers." Everyone took them, Yvonne had said blithely, the first time Jennifer had sat in her kitchen and found she couldn't stop crying. Doctors were only too happy to supply them. They would even her out a little. *I'm so evened out that nothing's left*, she thought, and reached for the next bottle.

Then they were all gone, the shelf empty. She stared at herself in the mirror as, with a gurgle, the last of the pills was washed out of sight.

There was trouble in Stanleyville. A note had arrived from the foreign desk at the *Nation* informing Anthony that the Congolese rebels, the self-styled Simba Army, had begun to herd more white hostages into the Victoria Hotel in retaliation against the Congolese government forces and their white mercenaries. "Have bags ready. Moving story," it said. "Editor has given special approval you go. With request that do not get yourself killed/captured."

For the first time, Anthony did not rush to the office to check the late newswires. He did not telephone his contacts at the UN or the army. He lay on his hotel bed, thinking of a woman who had loved him enough to leave her husband and then, in the space of four years, had disappeared.

He was startled by a knock on his door. The maid seemed to want to clean every half hour. She had an annoying way of whistling as she worked so he could never quite ignore her presence. "Come back later," he called, and shifted onto his side.

Had it simply been the shock of finding him alive that had caused her literally to vibrate in front of him? Had she realized today that the feelings she had once held for him had evaporated? Had she just gone through the motions, entertaining him as anyone would an old friend? Her manners had always been immaculate.

Another knock, tentative. It was almost more irritating than if the girl had just opened the door and walked in. At least then he could have yelled at her. He got up and went to the door. "I'd really rather—"

Jennifer stood in front of him, her belt tied tightly around her waist, her eyes bright. "Every day," she said.

"What?"

"Every month. Every day. Every hour." She paused, then added, "For four years. I tried not to, but . . . you were always there."

The corridor was silent around them.

"I thought you were dead, Anthony. I grieved for you. I grieved for the life I hoped I might have with you. I read and reread your letters until they fell apart. When I believed I might have been responsible for your death, I loathed myself so much I could barely get through each day. If it hadn't been . . ."

She corrected herself: "And then, at a drinks party I hadn't even wanted to go to, I saw you. *You.* And you ask me why I wanted to see you?" She took a deep breath, as if to steady herself.

There were footsteps at the other end of the corridor. He held out a hand. "Come inside," he said.

"I couldn't sit at home. I had to say something before you were gone again. I had to tell you."

He stepped back, and she walked past him into the large double bedroom, its generous dimensions and decent position testament to his improved standing at the newspaper. He was glad that for once he had left it tidy, a laundered shirt hanging on the back of the chair, his good shoes against the wall. The window was open, allowing in the noise of the street outside, and he went over to close it. She put her bag on the chair, laid her coat over it.

"It's a step up," he said awkwardly. "The first time I came back I got a hostel in Bayswater Road. Do you want a drink?" He felt oddly self-conscious as she sat down on the side of the bed. "Shall I ring for something? Coffee, maybe?" he continued.

God, he wanted to touch her.

"I haven't slept," she said, rubbing her face ruefully. "I couldn't think straight when I saw you. I've been trying to work it all out. Nothing makes any sense."

"That afternoon, four years ago, were you in the car with Felipe?"

"Felipe?" She looked puzzled.

"My friend from Alberto's. He died around the time I left, in a car crash. I looked up the cuttings this morning. There's a reference to an unnamed woman passenger. It's the only way I can explain it."

"I don't know. As I said yesterday, there are still bits I can't remember. If I hadn't found your letters, I might never have remembered you. I might never have known—"

"But who told you I was dead?"

"Laurence. Don't look like that. He's not cruel. I think he really believed you were." She waited a moment. "He knew there was . . . someone, you see. He read your last letter. After the accident he must have put two and two—"

"My last letter?"

"The one asking me to meet you at the station. I was carrying it when the car crashed."

"I don't understand—that wasn't my last letter—"

"Oh, let's not," she interrupted. "Please . . . It's too—"

"Then what?" She was watching him intently. "Jennifer, I—"

She stood up and stepped so close to him that even in the dim light he could see every tiny freckle on her face, each eyelash tapering into a black point sharp enough to pierce a man's heart. She was with him and yet removed, as if she was coming to some decision.

"Boot," she said softly, "are you angry with me? Still?"

Boot.

He swallowed. "How could I be?"

She lifted her hands and traced the shape of his face, her fingertips so light they barely touched him. "Did we do this?"

He stared at her.

"Before?" She blinked. "I don't remember. I only know your words."

"Yes." His voice broke. "Yes, we did this." He felt her cool fingers on his skin and remembered her scent.

"Anthony," she murmured, and there was sweetness in the way she said his name, an unbearable tenderness that spoke of all the love and loss he, too, had felt.

Her body rested against his, and he heard the sigh that traveled through her, then felt her breath on his lips. The air stilled around them. Her lips were on his, and something broke open in his chest. He heard himself gasp, and realized, with horror, that his eyes had filled with tears. "I'm sorry," he whispered, mortified. "I'm sorry. I don't know . . . why . . ."

"I know," she said. "I know." She put her arms around his neck, kissing the tears that ran down his cheeks, murmuring to him. They clung together, elated, despairing, neither quite able to believe the turn of events. Time became a blur, the kisses more urgent, the tears drying. He pulled her sweater over her head, stood, almost helpless, as she undid the buttons of his shirt. And in a joyful wrench it was off him, his skin against hers, and they were on the bed, wrapped around each other, their bodies fierce, almost clumsy with urgency.

He kissed her, and knew he was trying to tell her the depth of how he felt. Even as he lost himself in her, felt her hair sweep across his face, his chest, her lips meet his skin, her fingers, he understood that there were people for whom one other was their missing part.

She was alive beneath him; she set him alight. He kissed the scar that ran up to her shoulder, ignored her flinching reluctance until she accepted what he was telling her: this silvered ridge was beautiful to him; it told him she had loved him. It told him she had wanted to come to him. He kissed it because there was no part of her that he didn't want to make better, no part of her that he didn't adore.

He watched desire grow in her as if it were a gift shared between them, the infinite variety of expressions that crossed her face, saw her unguarded, locked in some private struggle, and when she opened her eyes, he felt blessed.

When he came he wept again, because some part of him had always known, even though he had chosen not to believe it, that there must be something that could make you feel like this. And that to have it returned to him was more than he could have hoped for.

"I know you," she murmured, her skin sticky against his, her tears wet on his neck. "I do know you."

For a moment he couldn't speak but stared up at the ceiling, feeling the air cool around them, her limbs pressed damply against his own. "Oh, Jenny," he said. "Thank God."

When her breathing had returned to normal, she raised herself on one elbow and looked down at him. Something in her had altered: her features had lifted, the strain had vanished from around her eyes. He enclosed her in his arms, pulling her to him so tightly that their bodies felt welded together. He felt himself hardening again, and she smiled.

"I want to say something," he said, "but nothing seems . . . momentous enough."

Her smile was glorious: satiated, loving, full of wry surprise. "I've never felt like that in my whole life," she said.

They looked at each other.

"Have I?" she said.

He nodded. She gazed into the distance. "Then . . . thank you."

He laughed, and she collapsed, giggling, onto his shoulder.

Four years had dissolved, become nothing. He saw, with a new clarity, the path of his life to come. He would stay in London. He would break things off with Eva, the girlfriend in New York. She was a sweet girl, breezy and cheerful, but he knew now that every woman he had dated over the past four years had been a pale imitation of the woman beside him. Jennifer would leave her husband. He would take care of her. They would not miss their chance a second time. He had a sudden vision of her with his son, the three of them on some family outing, and the future glowed with unforeseen promise.

His train of thought was broken by her kissing his chest, his shoulder, his neck, with intense concentration. "You do realize," he said, rolling her over so that her legs were entwined with his, her mouth inches away, "that we're going to have to do that again. Just to make sure you remember."

She said nothing, just closed her eyes.

This time when he made love to her, he did so slowly. He spoke to her body with his own. He felt her inhibitions fall away, her heart beat against his own, the mirroring of that faint tattoo. He said her name a million times, for the sheer luxury of being able to do so. In whispers, he told her everything he had ever felt for her.

When she told him she loved him, it was with an intensity that stopped his breath. The rest of the world slowed and closed in, until it was just the two of them, a tangle of sheets and limbs, hair and soft cries.

"You are the most exquisite . . ." He watched her eyes open with shy recognition of where she had been. "I would do that with you a hundred times just for the sheer pleasure of watching your face." She said nothing, and he felt greedy now. "*Vicariously*," he said suddenly. "Remember?"

Afterward, he was not sure how long they had lain there together, as if each wished to absorb the other through their skin. He heard the sounds of the street, the occasional pad of feet up and down the corridor outside the room, a distant voice. He felt the rhythm of her breathing against his chest. He kissed the top of her head, let his fingers rest in her tangled hair. A perfect peace had descended on him, spreading to his very bones. I'm home, he thought. This is it.

She shifted in his arms. "Let's order up something to drink," he said, kissing her collarbone, her chin, the space where her jaw met her ear. "A celebration. Tea for me, champagne for you. What do you say?"

He saw it then, an unwelcome shadow, her thoughts transferring to somewhere outside the room.

"Oh," she said, sitting upright. "What's the time?"

He checked his watch. "Twenty past four. Why?"

"Oh, no! I've got to be downstairs at half past." She was off the bed, stooping to pick up her clothes.

"Whoa! Why do you have to be downstairs?"

"Mrs. Cordoza."

"Who?"

"My housekeeper's meeting me. I'm meant to be shopping."

"Be late for her. Is shopping really that important? Jennifer, we have to talk—work out what we're going to do next. I've got to tell my editor I'm not going to Congo."

She was pulling on her clothes inelegantly, as if nothing mattered but speed, brassiere, trousers, pullover. The body he had taken, made his own, disappeared from view.

"Jennifer?" He slid out of the bed, reached for his trousers, belted them around his waist. "You can't just go."

She had her back to him.

"We've got things to talk about, surely, how we're going to sort it all out."

"There's nothing to sort out." She opened her handbag, pulled out a brush, and attacked her hair with short, fierce strokes.

"I don't understand."

When she turned to him, her face had closed, as though a screen had been pulled across it.

"Anthony, I'm sorry, but we—we can't meet again."

"What?"

She pulled out a compact, began to wipe the smudged mascara from under her eyes.

"You can't say that after what we've just done. You can't just turn it all off. What the hell is going on?"

She was rigid. "You'll be fine. You always are. Look, I—I have to go. I'm so sorry."

She swept up her bag and coat. The door closed behind her with a decisive click.

Anthony was after her, wrenching it open. "Don't do this, Jennifer! Don't leave me again!" His voice echoed down the already empty corridor, bouncing off the blank doors of the other bedrooms. "This isn't some kind of game! I'm not going to wait another four years for you!"

He was frozen with shock until, cursing, he collected himself and sprinted back into the room, wrestled into his shirt and shoes.

He grabbed his jacket and ran out into the corridor, his heart thudding. He tore down the stairs, two at a time, to the foyer. He saw the lift doors open, and there she was, her heels clicking briskly across the marble floor, composed, recovered, a million miles from where she'd been only minutes earlier. He was about to shout to her when he heard the cry: "Mummy!"

Jennifer went down, her arms already outstretched. A middle-aged woman was walking toward her, the child breaking free from her grasp. The little girl threw herself into Jennifer's arms and was lifted up, her voice bubbling across the echoing concourse. "Are we going to Hamleys? Mrs. Cordoza said we were."

"Yes, darling. We'll go right now. I just have to sort something out with reception."

She put the child down and took her hand. Perhaps it was the intensity of his gaze, but something made her look back as she walked to the desk. She saw him. Her eyes locked on his, and in them he caught a hint of apology—and guilt.

She looked away, scribbled something, then turned back to the receptionist, her handbag on the desk. A few words were exchanged, and she was away, walking out through the glass doors into the afternoon sunshine, the little girl chattering beside her.

The implication of what he had seen sank into Anthony, like feet into quicksand. He waited until she had disappeared, and then, like a man waking from a dream, shouldered on his jacket.

He was about to walk out when the concierge hurried up to him. "Mr. Boot? The lady asked me to give you this." A note was thrust into his hand.

He unfolded the little piece of hotel writing paper.

Forgive me. I just had to know.

Chapter 15

Moira Parker walked up to the typing pool and switched off the transistor radio that had been balanced on a pile of telephone directories.

"Hey!" Annie Jessop protested. "I was listening to that."

"It is not appropriate to have popular music blaring out in an office," Moira said firmly. "Mr. Stirling doesn't want to be distracted by such a racket. This is a place of work." It was the fourth time that week.

"More like a funeral parlor. Oh, come on, Moira. Let's have it on low. It helps the day go by."

"Working hard helps the day go by."

She heard the scornful laughter and tilted her chin a little higher. "You'd do well to learn that you'll only progress at Acme Mineral and Mining with a professional attitude."

"And loose knicker elastic," muttered someone behind her.

"I beg your pardon?"

"Nothing, Miss Parker. Shall we switch it on to Wartime Favorites? Will that make you happy? *'We're going to hang out the washing on the Siegfried Line . . .'*" There was another burst of laughter.

"I'll put it in Mr. Stirling's office. Perhaps you can ask him what *he* prefers."

She heard the mutters of dislike as she crossed the office, and made herself deaf to them. As the company had grown, the standards of the staff had sunk commensurately. Nowadays nobody respected their superiors, the work ethic, or what Mr. Stirling had achieved. Quite frequently she found herself in such a poor humor on her way home that she was at Elephant and Castle before even her crocheting could distract her. Sometimes it felt as if only she and Mr. Stirling—and perhaps Mrs. Kingston from Accounts—understood how to behave.

And the clothes! Dolly birds they called themselves, and it was horribly apt. Primping and preening, vacuous and childish, the girls in the typing pool spent far more time thinking about how they looked, all short skirts and ridiculous eye makeup, than about the letters they were supposed to type. She had had to send back three yesterday afternoon. Misspellings, forgotten date lines, even a "Yours sincerely" where she had clearly stated "Yours faithfully." When she pointed it out, Sandra had raised her eyes to the ceiling, not caring that Moira saw her.

Moira sighed, tucked the transistor under her arm, and, noting briefly that Mr. Stirling's office door was rarely shut at lunchtime, pushed on the handle and walked in.

Marie Driscoll was sitting opposite him—and not on the chair that Moira used when she was taking dictation, but *on his desk*. It was such an astonishing sight that it took her a moment to register that he had stepped back suddenly as she entered.

"Ah, Moira."

"I'm sorry, Mr. Stirling. I didn't know anybody else was in here." She shot the girl a pointed look. What on earth did she think she was doing? Had everyone gone mad? "I—I've brought in this wireless. The girls had it on ridiculously loudly. I thought if they had to explain themselves to you, it might give them pause for thought."

"I see." He sat down in his chair.

"I was concerned they might be disturbing you."

There was a long silence. Marie made no effort to move, just picked at something on her skirt—which ended halfway up her thigh. Moira waited for her to leave.

But Mr. Stirling spoke. "I'm glad you came in. I wanted a private word. Miss Driscoll, could you give us a minute?"

With evident reluctance, the girl lowered her feet to the floor and stalked past Moira, eyeing her as she passed. She wore too much perfume, Moira thought. The door closed behind her, and then it was just the two of them. As she liked it.

Mr. Stirling had made love to her twice more in the months after that first time. Perhaps "made love" was a slight exaggeration: on both occasions he had been very drunk, it was briefer and more functional than it had been the first time, and the following day he had made no reference to it.

Despite her attempts to let him know he would not be rebuffed—the homemade sandwiches she had left on his desk, the especially nice way she had kept her hair—it had not happened again. Still, she had known she was special to him, had relished her private knowledge when her coworkers discussed the boss in the canteen. She understood the strain such duplicity would cause him, and even while she wished things were different, she respected his admirable restraint. On the rare occasions when Jennifer Stirling dropped in, she no longer felt cowed by the woman's glamour. *If you had been wife enough, he would never have needed to turn to me.* Mrs. Stirling had never been able to see what she had in front of her.

"Sit down, Moira."

She perched in a far more decorous manner than the Driscoll girl, arranging her legs carefully, suddenly regretting that she had not worn her red dress. He liked her in it, had said so several times. From outside the office she heard laughter and wondered absently if they'd got hold of another transistor somehow. "I'll tell those girls to pull themselves together," she murmured. "I'm sure they must make an awful racket for you."

He didn't seem to hear her. He was shuffling papers on his desk. When he looked up, he didn't quite meet her eye. "I'm moving Marie, with immediate effect—"

"Oh, I think that's a very good—"

"—to be my personal assistant."

There was a brief silence. Moira tried not to show how much she minded. The workload had gotten heavier, she told herself. It was understandable that he would think a second pair of hands was needed. "But where will she sit?" she asked. "There's only room for one desk in the outer office."

"I'm aware of that."

"I suppose you could move Maisie—"

"That won't be necessary. I've decided to lighten your workload a little. You'll be . . . moving to the typing pool."

She couldn't have heard him correctly. "The typing pool?"

"I've told Payroll you'll remain on the same salary, so it should be rather a good move for you, Moira. Perhaps give you a bit more of a life outside the office. A little more time to yourself."

"But I don't want time to myself."

"Let's not make a fuss, now. As I said, you'll be on the same salary, and you'll be the most senior of the girls in the pool. I'll make that quite clear to the others. As you said, they need someone capable to take charge of them."

"But I don't understand. . . ." She stood up, her knuckles white on the transistor. Panic rose in her chest. "What have I done wrong? Why would you take my job away from me?"

He looked irritated. "You've done nothing wrong. Every organization moves people around once in a while. Times are changing, and I want to freshen things up a bit."

"Freshen things up?"

"Marie is perfectly capable."

"Marie Driscoll's going to be doing my job? But she knows nothing of how the office runs. She doesn't know the Rhodesian wage system, the telephone numbers, or how to book your air tickets. She doesn't know the filing system. She spends half her time in the ladies' room doing her makeup. And she's late! All the time! Why, twice this week I've had to reprimand her. Have you seen the figures on the clocking-in cards?" The words tumbled out of her.

"I'm sure she can learn. It's just a secretarial job, Moira."

"But—"

"I really don't have any more time to discuss this. Please move your things out of the drawers this afternoon, and we'll start afresh with the new setup tomorrow."

He reached into his cigar box, signaling that the conversation was over. Moira stood up, putting out a hand to steady herself on the edge of his desk. Bile rose in her throat, blood thumped in her ears. The office felt as if it was collapsing on her, brick by brick.

He put the cigar into his mouth, and she heard the sharp snip of the clippers as they sheared off the end.

She walked slowly toward the door and opened it, hearing the sudden hush in the outer office that told her others had known this was taking place before she had been told.

She saw Marie Driscoll's legs, stretched against her desk. Long, spindly legs in ridiculous colored tights. Who on earth would wear royal blue tights to an office and expect to be taken seriously?

She snatched her handbag from her desk and made her way unsteadily through the office to the ladies', feeling the stares of the curious and the smirks of the less than sympathetic burning into the back of her blue cardigan.

"Moira! They're playing your song! 'Can't Get Used to Losing You' . . ."

"Oh, don't be mean, Sandra." There was another noisy burst of laughter, and then the cloakroom door was closing behind her.

Jennifer stood in the middle of the bleak little play park, watching the frozen nannies chatting over their Silver Cross prams, hearing the cries of small children who collided and tumbled, like skittles, to the ground.

Mrs. Cordoza had offered to bring Esmé, but Jennifer had told her she needed the air. For forty-eight hours she had not known what to do with herself, her body still sensitized by his touch, her mind reeling with what she had done. She was almost felled by the enormity of what she had lost. She couldn't anesthetize her way through this with Valium: it had to be endured. Her daughter would be a reminder that she had done the right thing. There had been so much she had wanted to say to him. Even as she told herself she had not set out to seduce him, she knew she was lying. She had wanted one small piece of him, one beautiful, precious memory to carry with her. How could she have known she would be opening Pandora's box? Worse, how could she have imagined he would be so destroyed by it?

That night at the embassy he had looked so pulled together. He couldn't have suffered as she had; he couldn't have felt what she had. He was stronger, she had believed. But now she couldn't stop thinking about him, his vulnerability, his joyful plans for them. And the way he had looked at her when she had walked across the hotel lobby toward her child.

She heard his voice, anguished and confused, echoing down the corridor behind her: *Don't do this, Jennifer! I'm not going to wait another four years for you!*

Forgive me, she told him silently, a thousand times a day. *But Laurence would never have let me take her. And you, of all people, couldn't ask me to leave her. You, more than anyone, should understand.*

Periodically she wiped the corners of her eyes, blaming the high wind or yet another piece of grit that had mysteriously found its way into one. She felt emotionally raw, acutely aware of the least change in temperature, buffeted by her shifting emotions.

Laurence is not a bad man, she told herself, repeatedly. He's a good father, in his way. If he found it hard to be nice to Jennifer, who could blame him? How many men could forgive a wife for falling in love with someone else? Sometimes she had wondered whether, if she hadn't got pregnant so quickly, he would have tired of her, chosen to cut her loose. But she didn't believe it: Laurence might not love her anymore, but he wouldn't contemplate the prospect of her existing somewhere else without him.

And she is my consolation. She pushed her daughter on the swing, watching her legs fly up, the bouncing curls flying in the breeze. This is so much more than many women have. As Anthony had once told her, there was comfort to be had in knowing you had done the right thing.

"Mama!"

Dorothy Moncrieff had lost her hat, and Jennifer was briefly distracted by the search, the two little girls walking with her around the swings, the spinning roundabout, peering under the benches until it was located on the head of some other child.

"It's wrong to steal," said Dorothy, solemnly, as they walked back across the play park.

"Yes," said Jennifer, "but I don't think the little boy was stealing. He probably didn't know the hat was yours."

"If you don't know what's right and wrong, you're probably stupid," Dorothy announced.

"Stupid," echoed Esmé, delightedly.

"Well, that's possible," Jennifer said. She retied her daughter's scarf and sent them off again, this time to the sandpit, with instructions that they were absolutely not to throw sand at each other.

Dearest Boot, she wrote, in another of the thousand imaginary letters she had composed over the past two days, *Please don't be angry with me. You must know that if there was any way on earth I could go with you, I would do so . . .*

She would send no letter. What was there to say, other than what she had already said? He'll forgive me in time, she told herself. He'll have a good life.

She tried to shut her mind to the obvious question: How would she live? How could she carry on, knowing what she now knew? Her eyes had reddened again. She pulled her handkerchief out of her pocket and dabbed them again, turning away so that she wouldn't attract attention. Perhaps she would pay a quick visit to her doctor, after all. Just a little help to get her through the next couple of days.

Her attention was drawn to the tweed-coated figure walking across the grass toward the play park. The woman's feet tramped determinedly forward with a kind of mechanical regularity, despite the muddiness of the grass. She realized, with surprise, that it was her husband's secretary.

Moira Parker walked right up to her and stood so close that Jennifer had to take a step backward. "Miss Parker?"

Her lips were tightly compressed, her eyes bright with purpose. "Your housekeeper told me where you were. May I have a quick word?"

"Um . . . yes. Of course." She turned briefly. "Darlings? Dottie? Esmé? I'll just be over here."

The children looked up, then resumed digging.

They walked a few paces, Jennifer positioning herself so that she could see the little girls. She had promised the Moncrieffs' nanny she would have Dorothy home by four, and it was nearly a quarter to. She pasted on a smile. "What is it, Miss Parker?"

Moira reached into a battered handbag and wrenched out a fat folder.

"This is for you," she said brusquely.

Jennifer took it from her. She opened it, and immediately placed her hand on top of the papers as the wind threatened to whip them away.

"Don't lose any of them." It was an instruction.

"I'm sorry . . . I don't understand. What are these?"

"They are the people he has paid off."

When Jennifer looked blank, Moira continued, "Mesothelioma. Lung disease. They are workers he paid off because he wanted to hide the fact that working for him has given them terminal illnesses."

Jennifer lifted a hand to her head. "What?"

"Your husband. The ones who have already died are at the bottom. Their families had to sign legal waivers that stopped them saying anything in order to get the money."

Jennifer struggled to keep up with what the woman was saying. "Died? Waivers?"

"He got them to say he wasn't responsible. He paid them all off. The South Africans got hardly anything. The factory workers here were more expensive."

"But asbestos doesn't hurt anyone. It's just troublemakers in New York who are trying to blame him. Laurence told me."

Moira didn't seem to be listening. She ran her hand down a list on the top sheet. "They're all in alphabetical order. You can speak to the families, if you want. Most of their addresses are at the top. He's terrified that the newspapers will get hold of it all."

"It's just the unions . . . He told me . . ."

"Other companies are having the same problem. I listened in on a couple of telephone conversations he had with Goodasbest in America. They're funding research that makes asbestos look harmless."

The woman was speaking so fast that Jennifer's head reeled. She glanced at the two children, now throwing handfuls of sand at each other.

Moira Parker said pointedly: "You do realize it would ruin him if anyone found out what he'd done. It'll come out eventually, you know. It'll have to. Everything does."

Jennifer held the folder gingerly, as if it, too, might be contaminated. "Why are you giving this to me? Why on earth do you think I'd want to do anything that might harm my husband?"

Moira Parker's expression changed and became almost guilty. Her lips had pursed into a thin red line. "Because of this." She pulled out a creased piece of paper and thrust it into Jennifer's hand. "It came a few weeks after your accident. All those years ago. He doesn't know I kept it."

Jennifer unfolded it, the wind whipping it against her fingers. She knew the handwriting.

> *I swore I wouldn't contact you again. But six weeks on, and I feel no better. Being without you—thousands of miles from you—offers no relief at all. The fact that I am no longer tormented by your presence, or presented with daily evidence of my inability to have the one thing I truly desire, has not healed me. It has made things worse. My future feels like a bleak, empty road.*
>
> *I don't know what I'm trying to say, darling Jenny. Just that if you have any sense at all that you made the wrong decision, this door is still wide open.*
>
> *And if you feel that your decision was the right one, know this at least: that somewhere in this world is a man who loves you, who under-*

stands how precious and clever and kind you are. A man who has always
loved you and, to his detriment, suspects he always will.
  Your

  B.

Jennifer stared at the letter as the blood drained from her face. She
glanced at the date. Almost four years ago. Just after the accident.
"Did you say Laurence had this?"

Moira Parker looked at the ground. "He made me shut down the
post-office box."

"He knew Anthony was still alive?" She was shaking.

"I don't know about any of that." Moira Parker hoisted up her
collar. She managed to look disapproving.

A cold stone had settled inside Jennifer. She felt the rest of herself
harden around it.

Moira Parker clipped her handbag shut. "Anyway, do what you
want with it all. He can go hang for all I care."

She was still muttering to herself as she began to walk back across
the park. Jennifer sank onto a bench, ignoring the two children, who
were now joyfully rubbing sand into each other's hair. She read the
letter again.

She took Dorothy Moncrieff home to her nanny, and asked Mrs.
Cordoza if she would walk Esmé to the sweet shop. "Buy her a lollipop, and perhaps a quarter of a pound of boiled sweets." She stood
at the window to watch them go down the road, her daughter's every
step a little bounce of anticipation. As they turned the corner, she
opened the door to Laurence's study, a room she rarely entered, and
from which Esmé was banned, lest her inquisitive little fingers presume to displace one of its many valuable items.

Afterward she was not sure why she had even gone in there. She
had always hated it: the gloomy mahogany shelves, full of books he

had never read, the lingering smell of cigar smoke, the trophies and certificates for achievements she could not recognize as such—"Round Table Businessman of the Year," "Best Shot, Cowbridge Deer Stalk 1959," "Golfing Trophy 1962." He rarely used it: it was an affectation, a place he promised his male guests where they might "escape" the women, a refuge in which he professed to find peace.

Two comfortable armchairs stood on each side of the fireplace, their seats barely dented. In eight years a fire had never been lit in the grate. On the sideboard the cut-glass tumblers had never been filled with fine whiskey from the decanter that stood beside them. The walls were lined with photographs of Laurence shaking hands with fellow businessmen, visiting dignitaries, the South African trade minister, the duke of Edinburgh. It was a place for other people to see, yet another reason for the men to admire him. *Laurence Stirling, lucky bugger.*

Jennifer stood in the doorway beside the caddy of expensive golf clubs, the shooting stick in the corner. A knot, tight and hard, had formed in her chest, just at the point of her windpipe where air was meant to expand her lungs. She realized she could not breathe. She picked up a golf club and walked into the center of the room. A small sound escaped her, like the gasp of someone ending a long race. She lifted the club above her head, as if to imitate a perfect swing, and let it go so that the full force met the decanter. Glass splintered across the room, and then she swung again, at the walls, the photographs shattering in their frames, the dented trophies knocked from their stands. She swung at the leather-bound books, the heavy glass ashtrays. She hit fiercely, methodically, her slim frame fueled by an anger that even now continued to build in her.

She beat the books from their cases, sent the frames flying from the mantelpiece. She brought the club down like an ax, splintering the heavy Georgian desk, then sent it whistling sideways. She swung until her arms ached and her whole body was beaded with sweat, her breath coming in short, sharp bursts. Finally, when there was nothing left to break, she stood in the center of the room, her shoes crunching on broken glass, wiping a sweaty frond of hair off her forehead as she surveyed what she had done. *Lovely Mrs. Stirling, sweet-tempered Mrs. Stirling. Even, calm, tamped down. Her fire extinguished.*

Jennifer Stirling dropped the bent club at her feet. Then she wiped her hands on her skirt, picked out a small shard of glass, which she dropped neatly on the floor, and left the room, closing the door behind her.

Mrs. Cordoza was sitting in the kitchen with Esmé when Jennifer announced that they were going out again. "Does the child not want her tea? She'll be hungry."

"I don't want to go out," Esmé chimed in.

"We won't be long, darling," she said coolly. "Mrs. Cordoza, you can take the rest of the day off."

"But I—"

"Really. It's for the best."

She scooped up her daughter, the suitcase she had just packed, the sweets in the brown-paper bag, ignoring the housekeeper's perplexity. Then she was outside, down the steps and hailing a taxi.

She saw him even as she opened the double doors, standing outside his office, talking to a young woman at his desk. She heard a greeting, heard her own measured response, and was dimly surprised that she could be responsible for such a normal exchange.

"Hasn't she grown!"

Jennifer looked down at her daughter, who was stroking her string of pearls, then at the woman who had spoken. "Sandra, isn't it?" she said.

"Yes, Mrs. Stirling."

"Would you mind terribly letting Esmé have a little play on your typewriter while I nip in to see my husband?"

Esmé was delighted to be let loose on the keyboard, cooed and fussed over by the women who immediately surrounded her, delighted by a legitimate diversion from work. Then Jennifer pushed her hair off her face and went to his office. She walked into the secretary's area, where he was standing.

"Jennifer." He raised an eyebrow. "I wasn't expecting you."

"A word?" she said.

"I have to go out at five."

"It won't take long."

He shepherded her into his own office, closing the door behind him, and motioned her toward the chair. He seemed mildly irritated when she declined to sit and sank heavily into his own leather chair.

"Well?"

"What did I do to make you hate me so much?"

"What?"

"I know about the letter."

"What letter?"

"The one you intercepted at the post office four years ago."

"Oh, that," he said dismissively. He wore the expression of someone who had been reminded that he had forgotten to pick up some item from the grocer.

"You knew, and you let me think he was dead. You let me think I was *responsible*."

"I thought he probably was. And this is all history. I can't see the point of dragging it up again." He leaned forward and pulled a cigar from the silver box on his desk.

She thought briefly of the dented one in his study, shimmering with broken glass. "The point is, Laurence, that you've punished me day after day, let me punish myself. What did I ever do to you to deserve that?"

He threw a match into the ashtray. "You know very well what you did."

"You let me think I'd killed him."

"What you thought has nothing to do with me. Anyway, as I said, it's history. I really don't see why—"

"It's not history. Because he's back."

That got his attention. She had a faint inkling that the secretary might be listening outside the door, so she kept her voice low. "That's right. And I'm leaving to be with him—Esmé, too, of course."

"Don't be ridiculous."

"I mean it."

"Jennifer, no court in the land would let a child stay with an adulterous mother—a mother who can't get through the day without a pharmacy of pills. Dr. Hargreaves would testify to the sheer number you get through."

"They're gone. I've thrown them away."

"Really?" He consulted his watch again. "Congratulations. So, you've made it a whole . . . twenty-four hours without pharmaceutical help? I'm sure the courts would find that admirable." He laughed, pleased with his response.

"Do you think they would find the lung-disease file admirable, too?"

She caught the sudden rigidity of his jaw, the flash of uncertainty. "What?"

"Your secretary gave it to me. I have the name of every one of your employees who has become ill and died over the past ten years. What was it?" She pronounced the word carefully, emphasizing its unfamiliarity. "Me-so-the-lio-ma."

The color drained so quickly from his face that she thought he might pass out. He got up and walked past her to the door. He opened it, peered out, then closed it again firmly. "What are you talking about?"

"I have all the information, Laurence. I even have the bank slips for the money you paid them."

He wrenched open a drawer and rifled through it. When he straightened up, he looked shaken. He took a step toward her so that she was forced to meet his gaze. "If you ruin me, Jennifer, you ruin yourself."

"Do you really think I care?"

"I'll never divorce you."

"Fine," she said, her resolve strengthened by his disquiet. "This is how it will be. Esmé and I will take a place nearby, and you can visit her. You and I will be husband and wife in name only. You will give me a reasonable stipend, to support her, and in return I'll make sure those papers are never made public."

"Are you trying to blackmail me?"

"Oh, I'm far too dim to do something like that, Laurence, as you've reminded me countless times over the years. No, I'm just telling you how my life is going to be. You can keep your mistress, the house, your fortune, and . . . your reputation. None of your business colleagues needs to know. But I will never set foot in the same house as you again."

He genuinely hadn't realized she knew about the mistress. She saw impotent fury spread over his face, mixed with wild anxiety. Then they were smothered by a conciliatory attempt at a smile. "Jennifer, you're upset. This fellow reappearing must have come as a shock. Why don't you go home and we'll talk about it?"

"I've lodged the papers with a third party. If anything were to happen to me, he has his instructions."

He had never looked at her with such venom. Her grip tightened on her handbag.

"You are a whore," he said.

"With you I was," she said quietly. "I must have been, because I certainly didn't do it for love."

There was a knock at the door, and his new secretary walked in. The manner in which the girl's gaze flicked between them was a banner of extra information. It boosted Jennifer's courage. "Anyway, I think that's all I needed to tell you. I'll be off now, darling," she said. She walked up to him and kissed his cheek. "I'll be in touch. Goodbye, Miss . . ." She waited.

"Driscoll," the girl said.

"Driscoll." She fixed her with a smile. "Of course."

She walked past the girl, collected her daughter, and, heart hammering, opened the double doors, half expecting to hear his voice, his footsteps, behind her. She skipped down the two flights of stairs to where the taxi was still waiting.

"Where are we going?" said Esmé, as Jennifer hoisted her onto the seat beside her. She was picking her way through a handful of sweets, her haul from the troupe of secretaries.

Jennifer leaned forward and opened the little window, shouting to the driver above the noise of the rush-hour traffic. She felt suddenly weightless, triumphant. "To the Regent Hotel, please. As fast as you can."

Later she would look back on that twenty-minute journey and realize she had viewed the crowded streets, the gaudy shopfronts, as if through the eyes of a tourist, a foreign correspondent, someone who had never seen them before. She noted only a few details, an overriding impression, knowing it was possible she might not see them again. Her life as she had known it was over, and she wanted to sing.

This was how Jennifer Stirling said good-bye to her old life, the days when she had walked those streets laden with shopping bags filled with things that meant nothing to her as soon as she returned home. It was at this point, near Marylebone Road, that she had felt daily the stiffening of some internal brace as she approached the house that felt no longer like a home but some kind of penance.

There was the square, flashing by, with her silent house, a world in which she had lived internally, knowing there was no thought she could express, no action she could complete, that would not invoke criticism from a man she had made so unhappy that his only course was to keep punishing her, with silence, relentless slights, and an atmosphere that left her permanently cold, even in high summer.

A child could protect you from that, but only so far. And while what she was doing meant she might be disgraced in the eyes of those around her, she could show her daughter that there was another way to live. A way that did not involve anesthetizing yourself. A way that did not mean you lived your whole life as an apology for who you were.

She saw the window where the prostitutes had displayed themselves; the tapping girls had disappeared to some other location. *I hope you're living a better life*, she told them silently. *I hope you're freed from whatever held you there. Everyone deserves that chance.*

Esmé was still eating her sweets, observing the busy streets through the other window. Jennifer put her arm around the little girl and pulled her close. She unwrapped another and put it into her mouth. "Mummy, where are we going?"

"To meet a friend, and then we're going on an adventure, darling," she replied, suddenly brimming with excitement.

"An adventure?"

"Yes. An adventure that should have taken place a long, long time ago."

The page-four story on the disarmament negotiations wouldn't make a lead, Don Franklin thought, while his deputy drew up alternatives. He was wishing his wife hadn't put raw onions in his liver sausage sandwiches. They always gave him gut ache. "If we move the tooth-paste ad to this side, we could fill this space with the dancing priest?" the deputy suggested.

"I hate that story."

"What about the theater review?"

"Already on page eighteen."

"Eyes west-southwest, boss."

Rubbing his belly, Don glanced up to see a woman hurrying through the newspaper office. She was dressed in a short black trench coat and had a blond child with her. To see a little girl in a newspaper office made Don feel uncomfortable, like seeing a soldier in a petti-coat. It was all wrong. The woman paused to ask Cheryl something, and Cheryl gestured to him.

His pencil was wedged in the corner of his mouth as she ap-proached. "I'm sorry to bother you, but I need to speak to Anthony O'Hare," she said.

"And you are?"

"Jennifer Stirling. I'm a friend of his. I've just come from his hotel, but they said he'd checked out." Her eyes were anxious.

"You brought the note a couple of days ago," Cheryl recalled.

"Yes," the woman said, "I did."

He observed the way Cheryl was looking her up and down. The

child was holding a half-eaten lollipop, which had left a sticky trail on the mother's sleeve. "He's gone to Africa," he said.

"What?"

"Gone to Africa."

She went completely still, the child, too. "No." Her voice cracked. "That's not possible. He hadn't even decided whether to go."

Don took the pencil out of his mouth and shrugged. "News moves fast. He left yesterday, got the first flight out. He'll be traveling for the next few days."

"But I need to speak to him."

"He can't be contacted." He could see Cheryl watching him. Two of the other secretaries were whispering to each other.

The woman had paled. "Surely there must be some way of reaching him. He can't have been gone long."

"He could be anywhere. It's Congo. They don't have telephones. He'll telegraph when he gets a chance."

"Congo? But why on earth did he go so soon?" Her voice had faded to a whisper.

"Who knows?" He looked at her pointedly. "Perhaps he wanted to get away." He was aware of Cheryl loitering, pretending to sort a pile of papers nearby.

The woman seemed to have lost the power of thought. Her hand lifted to her face. He thought, for one awful moment, that she might be about to cry. If there was one thing worse than a child in a newsroom, it was a crying woman with a child in a newsroom.

She took a deep breath, steadying herself. "If you speak to him, would you ask him to telephone me?" She reached into her bag, from which she pulled out a paper folder stuffed with documents, then several battered envelopes; she hesitated, and thrust the letters deep inside the folder. "And give him this. He'll know what it means." She scribbled a note, ripped it from her diary, and pushed it under the flap. She placed the folder on the desk in front of him.

"Sure."

She took hold of his arm. He noticed she was wearing a ring with a diamond the size of the ruddy Koh-i-Noor. "You will make sure he gets it? It's really important. Desperately important."

"I understand. Now, if you'll excuse me, I need to get on. This is our busiest time of day. We're all on deadlines here."

Her face crumpled. "I'm sorry. Please just make sure he gets it. Please."

Don nodded.

She waited, her eyes not leaving his face, perhaps trying to reassure herself that he had meant what he said. Then, with a final glance around the office, as if to check that O'Hare really wasn't there, she took her daughter's hand. "I'm—I'm sorry to have bothered you."

Looking somehow smaller than she had when she'd walked in, she made her way slowly toward the doors, as if she had no idea where she was going. The few people gathered around the sub's desk watched her leave.

"Congo," said Cheryl, after a beat.

"We need to get page four off stone." Don stared fixedly at the desk. "Let's go with the dancing priest."

It was almost three weeks later that someone thought to clear the subeditor's desk. Among the old galley proofs and dark blue carbon sheets, there was a shabby folder.

"Who's B?" Dora, the temporary secretary, opened it. "Is this something for Bentinck? Didn't he leave two months ago?"

Cheryl, who was arguing about travel expenses on the phone, shrugged without turning but cupped her hand over the mouthpiece. "If you can't see who it belongs to, send it to the library. That's where I put everything that doesn't seem to belong to anyone. Then Don can't yell at you." She thought for a moment. "Well, he can. But not for misfiling."

The folder landed on the trolley destined for the archive, with the old editions of the newspaper, *Who's Who*, and *Hansard*, in the bowels of the building.

It would not reappear for almost forty years.

Part 3

Chapter 16

Ellie Haworth emerges from the underground station and half walks, half runs along the street, dodging pedestrians, blind to the gaudy shop windows offering unmissable autumn bargains, deaf to the cacophonous queue of traffic, her gaze still on the little screen of her mobile phone. She clashes elbows with a suited man who tuts loudly, sidestepping around her, and she mutters an apology without looking up.

She comes to a brief halt outside the pub, stands still for a moment, and then punches a number into the phone.

"I'm just about to go into a meeting," Nicky says.

"Very quickly. 'Later.' With an *x*. What on earth does that mean?" She has to shout to be heard over the engine of an idling bus.

"What?"

"I mean at the end of a text message. 'Later x.' Does it mean someone is going to call later today? This week? Never?"

Bob, who runs the little coffee wagon opposite her office building, is packing up, ready to move on to his next pitch at the shopping mall. She has overslept, having lain awake until the small hours, and now realizes with a sick lurch that this means she is even later than she had feared. But the thought of going into conference without a coffee is too much. She taps him on the shoulder, her phone still pressed to her ear, and arranges her face into an expression she might call "hopeful."

Bob spins around, and registers that it is Ellie. When he realizes what she wants, he taps his watch.

"What did he say?" says Nicky.

" 'Later.' With an *x*."

She mouths a *please* to Bob. She wedges her phone in the crook of her neck and lifts both hands in a gesture of prayer.

" 'Later *x*' ?" echoes Nicky.

Shaking his head resignedly, Bob pulls the cover off his coffee machine and with an ostentatious air of martyrdom begins to make her an Americano, just as she likes it.

"Nicky?"

"Oh, Lord. I don't know what it means. It could mean anything. 'Later' when he remembers who you are. 'Later' when his wife lets him out of the cellar."

"Funny."

"Well, it's meaningless. It's one of those things men say so that they're not committed to anything."

"But he's—"

"I don't know, Ellie. You know him better than I do. Look, I'm really sorry, but I've got to go. They're waiting for me. I'll call you tonight, okay?"

"Do you think a big X means more than a little *x*?" Ellie begins, but the phone has gone dead.

She stares at it for a moment, then shoves the phone into her pocket, grabs the coffee, hands a fistful of change to Bob, and with a hurried "Thank you thank you Bob you're a lifesaver," turns and runs across the road toward her office.

It has never even occurred to her to tell Nicky the rest of the message. Sorry couldn't make it last night. Things tricky at home. Later x.

The *Nation* is being packed up, box by box, for transfer to its new glass-fronted home on a gleaming, reclaimed quay to the east of the

City. The office, week by week, has been thinning: where once there were towers of press releases, files, and archived cuttings, now empty desks, unexpected shiny lengths of laminated surface, are exposed to the harsh glare of the strip lighting. Souvenirs of past stories have been unearthed, like prizes from an archaeologist's dig, flags from royal jubilees, dented metal helmets from distant wars, and framed certificates for long-forgotten awards. Banks of cables lie exposed; carpet tiles have been dislodged and great holes opened in the ceilings, prompting histrionic visits from health and safety experts and endless visitors with clipboards. Advertising, Classified, and Sport have already moved to Compass Quay. The Saturday magazine, Business, and Personal Finance are preparing to transfer in the next weeks. Features, Ellie Haworth's department, will follow along with News, moving in a carefully choreographed sleight of hand so that while Saturday's newspaper will emanate from the old Turner Street offices, Monday's will spring, as if by magic, from the new address.

The building, home to the newspaper for almost a hundred years, is no longer fit-for-purpose, in that unlovely phrase. According to the management, it does not reflect the dynamic, streamlined nature of modern newsgathering. It has too many places to hide, the hacks observe bad-temperedly as they are prised from their positions, like limpets clinging stubbornly to a holed hull.

"We should celebrate it," says Melissa, head of Features, from the editor's almost-cleared office. She's wearing a wine-colored silk dress. On Ellie, this would have looked like her grandmother's nightie; on Melissa it looks like what it is—defiantly high fashion.

"The move?" Ellie is glancing at her mobile phone, set to silent, beside her. Around her, the other feature writers are silent, notepads on knees.

"Yes. I was talking to one of the librarians the other evening. He says there are lots of old files that haven't been looked at in years. I want something on the women's pages from fifty years ago. How attitudes have changed, fashions, women's preoccupations. Case studies, side by side, then and now." Melissa opens a file and pulls out several photocopied A3 sheets. She speaks with the easy confidence of someone accustomed to being listened to. "For instance, from our problem pages: 'What on earth can I do to get my wife to dress more smartly and to make herself more attractive? My income is £1,500 a year, and I am beginning to make my way in a sales organization. I am very often getting invitations from customers, but in recent weeks I have had to dodge them because my wife, frankly, looks a mess.' "

There is a low chuckle around the room.

" 'I have tried to put it to her in a gentle way, and she says that she doesn't care about fashions or jewelry or makeup. Frankly she doesn't look like the wife of a successful man, which is what I want her to be.' "

John had once told Ellie that, after the children, his wife had lost interest in her appearance. He had changed the subject almost as soon as he had introduced it, and never referred to it again, as if he felt what he had said was even more of a betrayal than sleeping with another woman. Ellie had resented that hint of gentlemanly loyalty even while a bit of her admired him for it.

But it had stuck in her imagination. She had pictured his wife: slatternly in a stained nightdress, clutching a baby and haranguing him for some supposed deficit.

She wanted to tell him she would never be like that with him.

"One could put the questions to a modern advice columnist." Rupert, the Saturday editor, leans forward to peer at the other photocopied pages.

"I'm not sure you'd need to. Listen to the response: 'It may never have occurred to your wife that she is meant to be part of your shop window. She may, insofar as she thinks about these things at all, tell herself that she's married, secure, happy, so why should she bother?' "

"Ah," says Rupert. " 'The deep, deep peace of the double bed.' "

" 'I have seen this happen remarkably quickly to girls who fall in love just as much as to women who potter about in the cozy wrap of an old marriage. One moment they're smart as new paint, battling heroically with their waistlines, seams straight, anxiously dabbed with perfume. Some man says, "I love you," and the next moment that shining girl is, as near as makes no difference, a slattern. A happy slattern.' "

The room fills briefly with polite, appreciative laughter.

"What's your choice, girls? Battle heroically with your waistline, or become a happy slattern?"

"I think I saw a film of that name not long ago," says Rupert. His smile fades when he realizes the laughter has died.

"There's a lot we can do with this stuff." Melissa gestures toward the folder. "Ellie, can you dig around a bit this afternoon? See what else you might find. We're looking at forty, fifty years ago. A hundred will be too alienating. The editor's keen for us to highlight the move in a way that will bring readers along with us."

"You want me to go through the archive?"

"Is that a problem?"

Not if you like sitting in dark cellars full of mildewing paper policed by dysfunctional men with Stalinist mindsets, who apparently haven't seen daylight for thirty years. "Not at all," she says brightly. "I'm sure I'll find something."

"Get a couple of interns to help you, if you like. I've heard there's a couple lurking in the fashion cupboard."

Ellie doesn't register the malevolent satisfaction crossing her editor's features at the thought of sending the latest batch of Anna Wintour wannabes deep into the bowels of the newspaper. She's busy thinking, *Bugger. No mobile reception underground.*

"By the way, Ellie, where were you this morning?"

"What?"

"This morning. I wanted you to rewrite that piece about children and bereavement. Yes? Nobody seemed to know where you were."

"I was out doing an interview."

"Who with?"

A body-language expert, Ellie thinks, would have identified correctly that Melissa's blank smile was more of a snarl.

"Lawyer. Whistleblower. I was hoping to work something up on sexism in chambers." It's out almost before she knows what she's saying.

"Sexism in the City. Hardly sounds groundbreaking. Make sure you're at your desk at the right time tomorrow. Speculative interviews on your own time. Yes?"

"Right."

"Good. I want a double-page spread for the first Compass Quay edition. Something along the lines of *plus ça change*." She is scribbling in her leather-backed notebook. "Preoccupations, ads, problems . . . Bring me a few pages later this afternoon, and we'll see what you've got."

"Will do." Ellie's smile is the brightest and most workmanlike in the whole room as she follows the others out of the office.

Spent today in modern-day equivalent of purgatory, she types, pausing to take a sip of her wine. Newspaper archive office. You want to be grateful you only make stuff up.

He has messaged her from his hotmail account. He calls himself Penpusher; a joke between the two of them. She curls her feet under her on the chair and waits, willing the machine to signal his response.

You're a cultural heathen. I love archives, the screen responds. Remind me to take you to the British Newspaper Library for our next hot date.

The only human librarian has given me a great wedge of loose papers. Not the most exciting bedtime reading.

Afraid this sounds sarcastic, she follows it with a smiley face, then curses as she remembers he once wrote an essay for the *Literary Review* on how the smiley face represented all that was wrong with modern communication.

That was an ironic smiley face, she adds, and stuffs her fist into her mouth.

Hold on. Phone. The screen stills.

Phone. His wife? He was in a hotel room in Dublin. It overlooked the water, he had told her. You would love it. What was she meant to say to that? Then bring me next time? Too demanding. I'm sure I would? Sounded almost sarcastic. Yes, she had replied, finally, and let out a long, unheard sigh.

It's all her own fault, her friends tell her. Unusually for her, Ellie Haworth can't disagree.

She had met him at a book festival in Suffolk, sent to interview this thriller writer who had made a fortune after he had given up on more-literary offerings. His name is John Armor, his hero, Dan Hobson, an almost cartoonish amalgam of old-fashioned masculine traits. She had interviewed him over lunch, expecting a rather chippy defense of the genre, perhaps a few moans about the publishing industry—she always found writers rather wearying to interview. She had expected someone paunchy, middle-aged, puddingy after years of being desk-bound. But the tall, tanned man who rose to shake her hand had been lean and freckly, resembling a weathered South African farmer. He was funny, charming, self-deprecating, and attentive. He had turned the interview on her, asking her questions about herself, then told her his theories on the origin of language and how he believed communication was morphing into something dangerously flaccid and ugly.

When the coffee arrived, she realized she hadn't put pen to note-pad for almost forty minutes.

"Don't you love the sound of them, though?" she'd said, as they left the restaurant and headed back toward the literary festival. It was late in the year and the winter sun had dipped below the low buildings of the quieting high street. She had drunk too much, had reached the point at which her mouth would race off defiantly before she had worked out what she should say. She hadn't wanted to leave the restaurant.

"Which ones?"

"Spanish. Mostly Italian. I'm sure it's why I love Italian opera, and I can't stand the German ones. All those hard, guttural noises." He had considered this, and his silence unnerved her. She began to stutter: "I know it's terribly unfashionable, but I love Puccini. I love that high emotion. I love the curling r, the staccato of the words . . ." She tailed away as she heard how ridiculously pretentious she sounded.

He paused in a doorway, gazed briefly up the road behind them, then turned back to her. "I don't like opera." He had stared at her directly as he said it. As if it was a challenge. She felt something give, deep in the pit of her stomach. Oh, God, she thought.

"Ellie," he said, after they had stood there for almost a minute. It was the first time he had called her by name. "Ellie, I have to pick up something from my hotel before I go back to the festival. Would you like to come with me?"

Even before he shut the bedroom door behind them, they were on each other, bodies pressed together, mouths devouring, locked together as their hands performed the urgent, frantic choreography of undressing.

Afterward she would look back on her behavior and marvel as if at some kind of aberration seen from afar. In the hundreds of times she had replayed it, she had rubbed away the significance, the overwhelming emotion, and was left only with details. Her underwear, everyday, inappropriate, flung across a trouser press; the way they had giggled insanely on the floor afterward underneath the multipatterned synthetic hotel quilt; how he had cheerfully, and with inappropriate charm, handed back his key to the receptionist later that afternoon.

He had called two days later, as the euphoric shock of that day was segueing into something more disappointing.

"You know I'm married," he said. "You read my cuttings."

I've Googled every last reference to you, she told him silently.

"I've never been . . . unfaithful before. I still can't quite articulate what happened."

"I blame the quiche," she quipped, wincing.

"You do something to me, Ellie Haworth. I haven't written a word in forty-eight hours." He paused. "You make me forget what I want to say."

Then I'm doomed, she thought, because as soon as she had felt his weight against her, his mouth on hers, she had known—despite everything she had ever said to her friends about married men, everything she had ever believed—that she required only the faintest acknowledgment from him of what had happened for her to be lost.

A year on, she still hadn't begun to look for a way out.

He comes back online almost forty-five minutes later. In this time she has left her computer, fixed herself another drink, wandered the flat aimlessly, peering at her skin in a bathroom mirror, then gathering up stray socks and hurling them into the laundry basket. She hears the ping of a message and hurls herself into her chair.

Sorry. Didn't mean to be so long. Hope to speak tomorrow.

No mobile-phone calls, he had said. Mobile bills were itemized.

Are you in hotel now? she types rapidly. I could call you in your room. The spoken word was a luxury, a rare opportunity. God, but she just needed to hear his voice.

Got to go to a dinner, gorgeous. Sorry—behind already. Later x.

And he is gone.

She stares at the empty screen. He will be striding off through the hotel foyer now, charming the reception staff, climbing into whatever car the festival has organized for him. Tonight he will give a clever off-the-cuff speech over dinner and then be his usual bemused, slightly wistful self to those lucky enough to sit at his table. He will be out there, living his life to the full, when she seems to have put hers perennially on hold.

What the hell is she doing?

"What the hell am I doing?" she says aloud, hitting the off button. She shouts her frustration at the bedroom ceiling, flops down on her vast, empty bed. She can't call her friends: they've endured these conversations too many times, and she can guess what their response will be—what it can only be. The irony is, if it had been any of them, she would have said exactly the same thing.

She sits on the sofa, flicks on the television. Finally, glancing at the pile of papers at her side, she hauls them on to her lap, cursing Melissa. A miscellaneous pile, the librarian had said, cuttings that bore no date and had no obvious category—"I haven't got time to go through them all. We're turning up so many piles like this." He was the only librarian under fifty down there. She wondered, fleetingly, why she'd never noticed him before.

"See if there's anything that's of use to you." He had leaned forward conspiratorially. "Throw away whatever you don't want, but don't say anything to the boss. We're at the stage now when we can't afford to go through every last bit of paper."

It soon becomes apparent why: a few theater reviews, a passenger list for a cruise ship, some menus from celebratory newspaper dinners. She flicks through them, glancing up occasionally at the television. There's not much here that'll excite Melissa.

Now she's leafing through a battered file of what looks like medical records. All lung disease, she notes absently. Something to do with mining. She's about to tip the whole lot into the bin when a pale blue corner catches her eye. She tugs at it with her index finger and thumb and pulls out a hand-addressed envelope. It's been opened, and the letter inside is dated October 4, 1960.

My dearest and only love. I meant what I said. I have come to the conclusion that the only way forward is for one of us to make a bold decision.

I am not as strong as you. When I first met you, I thought you were a fragile little thing. Someone I had to protect. Now I realize I had us all wrong. You are the strong one, the one who can endure living with the possibility of a love like this, and the fact that we will never be allowed it.

I ask you not to judge me for my weakness. The only way I can endure is to be in a place where I will never see you, never be haunted by the possibility of seeing you with him. I need to be somewhere where sheer necessity forces you from my thoughts minute by minute, hour by hour. I cannot do that here.

I am going to take the job. I'll be at Platform 4 Paddington at 7:15 on Monday evening, and there is nothing in the world that would make me happier than if you found the courage to come with me.

If you don't come, I'll know that whatever we might feel for each other, it isn't quite enough. I won't blame you, my darling. I know the past weeks have put an intolerable strain on you, and I feel the weight of that keenly. I hate the thought that I could cause you any unhappiness.

I'll be waiting on the platform from a quarter to seven. Know that you hold my heart, my hopes, in your hands.

Your

B.

Ellie reads it a second time, and finds her eyes welling inexplicably with tears. She can't take her eyes off the large, looped handwriting; the immediacy of the words springs out to her more than forty years after they were written. She turns it over, checks the envelope for clues. It's addressed to PO Box 13, London. It could be a man or a woman. *What did you do, PO Box 13?* she asks silently.

Then she gets up, replaces the letter carefully in the envelope, and walks over to her computer. She opens the mail file and presses refresh. Nothing since the message she had received at seven forty-five.

Got to go to a dinner, gorgeous. Sorry—behind already. Later x

Chapter 17

Tuesday lunch. Red Lion? Any good? John x

She waits for twenty minutes before he arrives, all cold air and apologies. A radio interview had gone on longer than he'd expected. He'd bumped into a sound engineer he'd known at university who wanted to catch up. It would have been rude to rush away.

But not rude to leave me sitting in a pub, she replies silently, but she doesn't want to upset the mood, so she smiles.

"You look lovely," he says, touching the side of her face. "Had your hair done?"

"No."

"Ah. Just habitually lovely, then." And, with one sentence, his lateness is forgotten.

He's wearing a dark blue shirt and a khaki jacket; she had once teased him that it was a writer's uniform. Understated, muted, expensive. It's the outfit she imagines him in when she's not with him. "How was Dublin?"

"Hurried. Harried." He unwinds his scarf from his neck. "I have this new publicist, Ros, and she seems to think it her duty to pack something into every last fifteen-minute slot. She'd actually allocated me loo breaks."

She laughs.

"Are you drinking?" He motions to a waiter, having spotted her empty glass.

"White wine." She hadn't been planning to have more: she's trying to cut down, but now he's here and her stomach has those knots that only alcohol can loosen.

He chats on about his trip, the books sold, the changes in the Dublin waterfront. She watches him as he talks. She'd read somewhere that you only truly saw what someone looked like in the first few minutes of meeting them, that after then it was only an impression, colored by what you thought of them. It gave her comfort on the mornings when she woke up puffy-faced after drinking too much, or with eyes pixellated from lack of sleep.

"Not working today, then?"

She hauls herself back into the conversation. "It's my day off. I worked last Sunday, remember? But I'm going to pop into the office anyway."

"What are you working on?"

"Oh, nothing very exciting. I found an interesting letter and wanted to have a root around in the archive in case there were more like it."

"A letter?"

"Yes."

He raises an eyebrow.

"Nothing to tell, really." She shrugs. "It's old. From 1960." She doesn't know why she's being reticent, but she would feel strange showing him the raw emotion on the page. She's afraid he might think she had some hidden reason for showing it to him.

"Ah. Strictures were so much firmer then. I love writing about that period. It's so much more effective for creating tension."

"Tension?"

"Between what we want and what we're allowed."

She looks at her hands. "Yup. I know all about that."

"The pushing against boundaries . . . all those rigid codes of conduct."

"Say that again." Her eyes meet his.

"Don't," he murmurs, grinning. "Not in a restaurant. Bad girl."

The power of words. She gets him every time.

She feels the pressure of his leg against hers. After this they will return to her flat, and she will have him to herself for at least an hour. It isn't enough, it never is, but the thought of it, his body against hers, is already making her giddy.

"Do you . . . still want to eat?" she asks slowly.

"That depends . . ."

Their eyes linger on each other. For her there is nothing in the bar but him.

He shifts in his chair. "Oh, before I forget, I'm going to be away from the seventeenth."

"Another tour?" His legs are enclosing hers under the table. She struggles to focus on what she's saying. "Those publishers are keeping you busy."

"No," he says, his voice neutral. "Holiday."

The briefest pause. And there it is. An actual pain, something like a punch, just under her ribs. Always the softest part of her.

"Nice for you." She pulls her legs back. "Where are you going?"

"Barbados."

"Barbados." She can't help the surprise in her voice. Barbados. Not camping in Brittany. Not some distant cousin's cottage in rain-soaked Devon. Barbados doesn't suggest the drudgery of a family holiday. It suggests luxury, white sand, a wife in a bikini. Barbados suggests a treat, a destination that implies their marriage is still of value. It suggests they might have sex.

"I don't suppose there will be Internet access, and the phone will be difficult. Just so you know."

"Radio silence."

"Something like that."

She doesn't know what to say. She feels quietly furious with him, while conscious that she has no right to be. What has he ever promised her, after all?

"Still. There's no such thing as a holiday with small children," he says, taking a swig of his drink. "Just a change of venue."

"Really?"

"You wouldn't believe the amount of stuff you have to cart around. Bloody prams, high chairs, nappies . . ."

"I wouldn't know."

They sit in silence until the wine arrives. He pours her a glass, hands it to her. The silence expands, becomes overwhelming, catastrophic.

"I can't help the fact that I'm married, Ellie," he says eventually. "I'm sorry if it hurts you, but I can't not go on holiday because—"

"—it makes me jealous," she finishes. She hates the way it makes her sound. Hates herself for sitting there like some sulking teenager. But she's still absorbing the significance of Barbados, the knowledge that for two weeks she will be trying not to imagine him making love to his wife.

This is where I should walk away, she tells herself, picking up her glass. This is where any sensible person pulls together the remnants of their self-respect, announces that they deserve more, and walks off to find someone who can give them a whole self, not snatched lunchtimes and haunted, empty evenings.

"Do you still want me to come back to yours?"

He is watching her carefully, his whole face an apology, etched with the understanding of what he's doing to her. This man. This minefield. "Yes," she says.

There is a hierarchy in newspaper offices, and librarians are somewhere near the bottom. Not quite as low as canteen staff or security guards, but nowhere near the columnists, editors, and reporters who compose the action section, the face of the publication. They are support staff, invisible, undervalued, there to do the bidding of those who are more important. But no one seems to have explained this to the

man in the long-sleeved T-shirt. "We're not taking requests today."
He points up at a handwritten notice taped to what had been the
counter.

Sorry—no access to archive until Monday.
Most requests can be answered online—pls try their first,
and x3223 in an emergency.

When she looks up again, he's gone.

She might have been offended, but she's still thinking about John,
the way he shook his head as he pulled his shirt back over his head an
hour previously. "Wow," he had said, tucking the tail into his waist-
band. "I've never had angry sex before."

"Don't knock it," she had replied, made flippant by temporary
release. She was lying on top of the duvet, staring out through the
skylight at the gray October clouds. "It's better than angry no-sex."

"I liked it." He had leaned over and kissed her. "I quite like the
idea of you using me. A mere vehicle for your pleasure."

She had thrown a pillow at him. He had been wearing that look,
his face somehow softened, the look he'd worn when he was still
locked into her. The look he'd worn when he was hers.

"Do you think it would be easier if the sex wasn't so good?" she
asked, pushing her hair out of her eyes.

"Yes. And no."

Because you wouldn't be here if it wasn't for the sex?

She had pushed herself upright, suddenly awkward. "Right," she
had said briskly. She had kissed his cheek, and then, for good measure, his ear. "I need to get to the office. Lock the door on your way
out." She padded into the bathroom.

Conscious of his surprise, she had closed the door behind her and
turned on the cold tap so that it gushed noisily down the plughole.
She perched on the rim of the bath and listened to him walking
through to the living room, perhaps to get his shoes, then the footfall
outside the door.

"Ellie? Ellie?"

She didn't respond.

"Ellie, I'm going now."

She waited.

"I'll speak to you soon, gorgeous." He rapped twice on the door, and then he was gone.

She had sat there for almost ten minutes after she'd heard the front door slam.

The man reappears as she's about to leave. He's carrying two teetering boxes of files and is about to push open a door with his rear and disappear again. "Still here?"

"You've spelt 'there' wrong." She points at the notice.

He glances at it. "Just can't get the staff these days, can you?" He turns toward the door.

"Don't go! Please!" She leans over the counter, brandishes the folder he'd given her. "I need to look at some of your 1960s newspapers. And I wanted to ask you something. Can you remember where you found that stuff you gave me?"

"Roughly. Why?"

"I . . . There was something in it. A letter. I thought it might make a good feature if I could flesh it out a little."

He shakes his head. "Can't do it now. Sorry—we're flat out with the move."

"Please, please, please! I need to get something together by the end of the weekend. I know you're really busy, but I only need you to show me. I'll do the rest."

He has untidy hair, and his long-sleeved T-shirt is tracked with dust. An unlikely librarian—he looks as if he should be surfing on books, rather than stacking them.

He blows out his cheeks, dumps the box on the end of the counter. "Okay. What kind of letter?"

"It's this." She pulls the envelope out of her pocket.

"Not a lot to go on," he says, glancing at it. "A PO box and an initial."

He's curt. She wishes she hadn't made that crack about the spelling. "I know. I just thought if you had any more in there, I might be able to—"

"I haven't got time to—"

"Read it," she urges. "Go on. Just read it . . ." She tails off as she remembers she doesn't know his name. She's worked there for two years and she doesn't know any of the librarians' names.

"Rory."

"I'm Ellie."

"I know who you are."

She raises her eyebrows.

"Down here we like to be able to put a face to a byline. Believe it or not, we talk to each other, too." He looks at the letter. "I'm pretty busy—and personal correspondence isn't the kind of thing we hold on to. I don't even know how it ended up in there." He pushes it back to her, looks her in the eye. "That's t-h-e-r-e."

"Two minutes." She shoves it at him. "Please, Rory."

He takes the envelope from her, pulls out the letter, and reads, lingering. He finishes, and looks up at her.

"Tell me you aren't interested."

He shrugs.

"You are." She grins. "You are."

He flips open the counter and motions her through with an expression of resignation. "I'll have the newspapers you want on the counter in ten minutes. I've been putting all the loose stuff in garbage bags for throwing away, but yes, come on through. You can plow through them, and see if you can put anything else together. But don't tell my boss. And don't expect me to help."

She's there for three hours. She forgets the 1960 newspaper file, and instead sits in the corner of the dusty basement, barely noticing as men pass her carrying boxes marked "Election 67," "Train Disasters," or "June–July 1982." She works through the garbage bags, peeling apart reams of dusty paper, sidetracked by advertisements for cold cures, tonics, and long-forgotten cigarette brands, her hands black-ened with dust and old printing ink. She sits on an upturned crate, stacking the papers around her in chaotic piles, searching for some-thing smaller than A3, something handwritten. She's so lost in it that she forgets to check her mobile phone for messages. She even forgets, briefly, the hour she had spent at home with John that normally would have stamped itself on her imagination for several days after-ward.

Above, what remains of the newsroom is rumbling on, digesting and spewing out the day's news, its newslists changing again and again within the hour, whole stories written and discarded, according to the latest digital alterations of the newswires. In the dark corridors of the basement, it might as well have been happening on a different continent.

At almost five thirty Rory appears with two polystyrene cups of tea. He hands one to her, blowing on his own as he leans against an empty filing cabinet. "How'd you get on?"

"Nothing. Plenty of innovative health tonics, or cricket-match re-sults from obscure Oxford colleges, but no devastating love letters."

"It was always going to be a long shot."

"I know. It was just one of those . . ." She lifts her tea to her lips. "I don't know. I read it and it stayed with me. I wanted to know what happened. How's the packing going?"

He sits on a crate a few feet from her. His hands are ingrained with dust, and there's a smudge on his forehead.

"Nearly there. I can't believe my boss wouldn't let the professionals handle this."

The chief librarian had been at the newspaper for as long as any-one could remember, and was legendary for being able to pinpoint the date and copy of any newspaper from the most vague description.

"Why not?"

Rory sighed. "He was worried they'd put something in the wrong place or lose a box. I keep telling him it's all going to end up digitally recorded anyway, but you know how he is about hard copies . . ."

"How many years' worth of newspapers?"

"I think it's eighty of filed newspapers, and something like sixty of clippings and associated documents. And the scary thing is, he knows where every last one belongs."

She begins to move some of the papers back into a garbage bag. "Perhaps I should tell him about this letter. He could probably tell me who wrote it."

Rory whistles. "Only if you don't mind giving it back. He can't bear to let go of a single thing. The others have been sneaking the real junk out after he's gone home, or we'd have to fill several more rooms with it. If he knew I'd given you that file of old papers, he'd probably sack me."

She grimaces. "Then I'll never know," she says theatrically.

"Know what?"

"What happened to my star-crossed lovers."

Rory considers this. "She said no."

"Oh, you old romantic."

"She had too much to lose."

She cocks her head at him. "How do you know it was addressed to a she?"

"Women didn't have jobs then, did they?"

"It's dated 1960. It's hardly the bloody suffragettes."

"Here. Give it to me." He holds out his hand for the letter. "Okay, so maybe she had a job. But I'm sure it said something about going on a train. I should think a woman would be much less likely to say she was headed off to a new job." He reads it again, pointing at the lines. "He's asking her to follow him. A woman wouldn't have asked a man to follow her. Not then."

"You have a very stereotypical view of men and women."

"No. I just spend a lot of time here immersed in the past." He gestures around him. "And it's a different country."

"Perhaps it wasn't addressed to a woman at all," she teases. "Perhaps it's to another man."

"Unlikely. Homosexuality was still illegal then, wasn't it? There would have been references to secrecy or something."

"But there are references to secrecy."

"It's just an affair," he says. "Obviously."

"What's this? The voice of experience?"

"Hah! Not me." He hands the letter back to her, and drinks some of his tea.

He has long, squared-off fingers. Working hands, not a librarian's, she thinks absently. But what would a librarian's hands look like anyway? "So, you've never been involved with anyone married?" She glances at his finger. "Or you are married and have never had an affair?"

"Nope. And nope. Never had any kind of affair. With someone involved, that is. I like my life simple." He nods at the letter, which she's tucking back into her bag. "Those things never end well."

"What? All love that isn't simple and straightforward has to end tragically?" She hears defensiveness in her voice.

"That's not what I said."

"Yes, it is. You said earlier that you thought she said no."

He finishes his tea, crumples his cup, and throws it into the garbage bag. "We'll be done in ten minutes. You'd better grab what you want. Show me what you haven't had a chance to go through, and I'll try to keep it to one side."

As she gathers up her belongings, he says, "For what it's worth, I do think she probably said no." His expression is unfathomable. "But why does that have to be the worst outcome?"

Chapter 18

Ellie Haworth is living the dream. She often tells herself so when she wakes up, hungover from too much white wine, feeling the ache of melancholy, in her perfect little flat that nobody ever messes up in her absence. (She secretly wants a cat, but is afraid of becoming a cliché.) She holds down a job as a feature writer on a national newspaper, has obedient hair, a body that is basically plump and slender in the right places, and is pretty enough to attract attention that she still pretends offends her. She has a sharp tongue—too sharp, according to her mother—a ready wit, several credit cards, and a small car she can manage without male help. When she meets people she knew at school, she can detect envy when she describes her life: she has not yet reached an age where the lack of a husband or children could be regarded as failure. When she meets men, she can see them ticking off her attributes—great job, nice rack, sense of fun—as if she's a prize to be won.

If, recently, she has become aware that the dream is a little fuzzy, that the edge she was once famed for at the office has deserted her since John came, that the relationship she had once found invigorating has begun to consume her in ways that are not exactly enviable, she chooses not to look too hard. After all, it's easy when you're surrounded by people like you, journalists and writers who drink hard, party hard, have sloppy, disastrous affairs and unhappy partners at home who, tired of their neglect, will eventually have affairs. She is one of them, one of their cohorts, living the life of the glossy magazine pages, a life she has pursued since she first knew she wanted to write. She is successful, single, selfish. Ellie Haworth is as happy as she can be. As anyone can be, considering.

And nobody gets everything, so Ellie tells herself, when occasionally she wakes up trying to remember whose dream she's meant to be living.

"Happy birthday, you old tart!" Corinne and Nicky are waiting in the coffee shop, waving and patting a seat as she rushes in, bag flying. "Come on, come on! You're sooo late. We're meant to be at work by now."

"Sorry. I got a bit held up coming out."

They glance at each other, and she can tell they suspect she's been with John. She decides not to tell them that she was actually waiting for the post. She'd wanted to see if he had sent her something. Now she feels foolish for making herself twenty minutes late for her friends.

"How does it feel to be ancient?" Nicky has cut her hair. It's still blond, but now short and choppy. She looks cherubic. "I got you a skinny latte. I'm assuming you're going to need to watch your weight from now on."

"Thirty-two is hardly ancient. At least, that's what I'm telling myself."

"I'm dreading it," says Corinne. "Somehow thirty-one sounds like you might only just be past thirty, still almost technically in your twenties. Thirty-two sounds ominously close to thirty-five."

"And thirty-five is obviously just a short step to forty." Nicky checks her hair in the mirror behind the banquette.

"And a happy birthday to you, too," Ellie says.

"Aw! We'll still love you when you're wrinkly and alone and in flesh-colored big knickers." They place two bags on the table. "Here are your presents. And, no, you can't exchange either of them."

They have chosen perfectly, as only friends of many years' standing can. Corinne has bought her cashmere socks in dove gray, so soft that it's all Ellie can do not to put them on there and then. Nicky has given her a voucher for a prohibitively expensive beauty salon. "It's for an antiaging facial," she says wickedly. "It was that or Botox."

"And we know how you feel about injections."

She's filled with love, with gratitude for her friends. There have been many evenings in which they've said they're one another's new family, airing their fear that the others will find mates first and leave them single and alone. Nicky has a new man who, unusually, seems promising. He's solvent, kind, and has her on her toes just enough to keep her interested. Nicky has spent ten years running away from men who behave well toward her. Corinne has just ended a relationship of a year. He was nice, she says, but they had become like brother and sister, "and I'd expected marriage and a couple of kids before that happened."

They don't talk seriously of the dread that they may have missed the boat their aunts and mothers are so fond of mentioning. They don't discuss the fact that most of their male friends are now in relationships with women a good five to ten years younger than themselves. They make jokes about growing old disgracefully. They line up gay friends who promise to have children with them "in ten years' time" if they're both single, while neither party believes that could possibly end up happening.

"What did he get you?"

"Who?" Ellie says innocently.

"Mr. Paperback Writer. Or was what he *gave* you the reason you were late?"

"She already got her injection." Corinne cackles.

"You're both disgusting." She sips her coffee, which is lukewarm. "I—I haven't seen him yet."

"But he *is* taking you out?" Nicky says.

"I think so," she replies. She's suddenly furious with them for looking at her like that, for seeing through it already. She's furious with herself for not having thought up an excuse for him. She's furious with him for needing one.

"Have you heard from him at all, El?"

"No. But it is only eight thirty—Oh, Christ, I'm meant to be at a Features meeting at ten, and I haven't got a single good idea."

"Well, sod him." Nicky leans over and hugs her. "We'll buy you a little birthday cake, won't we, Corinne? Stay there and I'll get one of those muffins with icing. We'll have an early birthday tea."

It's then that she hears the muffled tone of her mobile phone. She flips it open.

Happy Birthday gorgeous. Present to come later. X

"Him?" says Corinne.

"Yes." She grins. "My present's coming later."

"Like him." Nicky snorts, back at the table with the iced muffin. "Where's he taking you?"

"Um . . . it doesn't say."

"Show me." Nicky snatches it. "What the hell is that supposed to mean?"

"Nicky . . ." Corinne's voice holds a warning note.

"Well, 'Present to come later. Kiss.' It's a bit bloody vague, isn't it?"

"It's her birthday."

"Exactly. And that's why she shouldn't have to decipher crappy halfway-house messages from some half-baked boyfriend. Ellie—darling—what are you *doing*?"

Ellie is frozen. Nicky has broken the unspoken rule that they will say nothing no matter how foolish a relationship. They will be supportive; they will express concern through what is not said; they will not say things like "What are you *doing*?"

"It's fine," she says. "Really."

Nicky looks at her. "You're thirty-two years old. You've been in a relationship—in love—with this man for almost a year, and what you really deserve for your birthday is some measly text message that may or may not mean you get a seeing-to at some unspecified date in the future? Aren't mistresses at least meant to get expensive lingerie? The odd weekend in Paris?"

Corinne is wincing.

"I'm sorry, Corinne, I'm just telling it like it is for a change. Ellie, darling, I love you to death. But, really, what are you getting out of this?"

Ellie looks down at her coffee. The pleasure of her birthday is ebbing away. "I love him," she says simply.

"And does he love you?"

She feels sudden hatred for Nicky.

"Does he know you love him? Can you actually tell him so?"

Ellie looks over at Corinne, hoping for support. But Corinne is stirring her coffee, her eyes fixed on her spoon.

"Do you ever think about her?"

"Who?"

"John's wife. Do you think she knows?"

The mention of her dissipates the last of Ellie's good mood. She shrugs. "I don't know." And then, to fill the silence, she adds: "I'm sure I would, if I were her. I think she's more interested in the children than him. Sometimes I tell myself there might even be some little part of her that is glad she's not having to worry about him. You know, about keeping him happy."

"Now *that* is wishful thinking."

"Maybe. But if I'm honest, the answer is no. I don't think about her. I don't feel guilty. Because I don't think it would have happened if they had been happy, or . . . you know . . . connected."

"You have such a misguided view of men."

"You think he's happy with her." She studies Nicky's face.

"I have no idea if he's happy or not, Ellie. I just don't think he needs to be unhappy with his wife to be sleeping with you."

The café falls silent around them. Or perhaps that's just how it feels. Ellie shifts in her chair.

Corinne finally stops stirring her coffee. She makes a despairing face at Nicky, who shrugs and lifts the muffin aloft. "Still. Happy birthday, eh? Anyone want another coffee?"

She slides into her desk in front of her computer. There is nothing on her desk. No note alerting her to flowers in Reception. No chocolates or champagne. There are eighteen e-mails in her in-box, not including the junk. Her mother—who bought a computer the previous year and still punctuates every e-mailed sentence with an exclamation mark—has sent her a message to wish her happy birthday and to tell her, "the dog is doing well after having had his hip replaced!" And that "the operation cost more than Grandma Haworth's!!!" The features editor's secretary has sent a reminder about this morning's meeting. And Rory, the librarian, has sent her a message telling her to pop down later, but not after 2:00 p.m., as they'll be at the new building then. There's nothing from John. Not even a thinly disguised greeting. She deflates a little, and winces when she sees Melissa striding toward her office, followed closely by Rupert.

She is in trouble, she realizes, rifling through her desk. She has allowed herself to become so caught up in the letter that she has almost nothing to present from the 1960 edition, none of the contrasting examples that Melissa had asked for. She curses herself for having spent so long in the coffee shop, smoothes her hair, grabs the nearest folder of papers—so that at least she looks as if she's on top of things—and runs into the meeting.

"So, the health pages are pretty much done and dusted, are they? And do we have the arthritis feature? I wanted that sidebar with the alternative remedies. Any celebrity arthritics? It would liven up the pictures. These are a bit dull."

Ellie is fiddling with her papers. It's almost eleven. What would it have cost him to send some flowers? He could have paid cash at the florist's, if he was really afraid of something showing up on his credit card; he'd done it before.

Perhaps he's cooling. Perhaps the Barbados trip is his way of trying to reconnect with his wife. Perhaps telling her about it was his cowardly way of communicating that she's of less importance than she had been. She flicks through the saved text messages on her phone, trying to see if there has been a noticeable cooling-off in his communications.

Nice piece on the war veterans. X

Free for lunch? I'm your way around 12:30. J

You are something else. Can't talk tonight. Will message you
first thing.

It's almost impossible to tell if there's any change in tone: there's
so little to go on. Ellie sighs, flattened by the direction of her thoughts,
by her friend's too-blunt comments. What the hell is she doing? She
asks for so little. Why? Because she's afraid that if she asks for more,
he'll feel backed into a corner and the whole thing will crash down
around them. She's always known what the deal was. She can't claim
to have been misled. But just how little could she reasonably be expected to take? It's one thing when you know you're loved passion-
ately, and only circumstances are keeping you apart. But when there's
no sign of that to keep the whole thing afloat . . .

"Ellie?"

"Hm?" She glances up to find ten pairs of eyes on her.

"You were going to talk us through the ideas for next Monday's
edition." Melissa's gaze is both blank and all-seeing. "The then-and-
now pages?"

"Yes," she says, and flips through the folder on her lap to hide her
flush. "Yes . . . Well, I thought it might be fun to lift the old pages
directly. There was an advice columnist, so I thought we could com-
pare and contrast then with now."

"Yes," says Melissa. "That's what I asked you to do last week. You
were going to show me what you'd found."

"Oh. Sorry. The pages are still in the archive. The librarians are a
bit paranoid about making sure they know where everything is, what
with the move," she stutters.

"Why didn't you take photocopies?"

"I—"

"Ellie, you're cutting this a bit fine. I thought you'd have a handle
on it days ago." Melissa's voice is icy. The others in the room look

down, not wanting to witness the inevitable decapitation. "Would you like me to give the task to someone else? One of the work-experience girls, perhaps?"

She can see, Ellie thinks, that for months this job has just been a shadow on the radar of my day. She knows my mind's elsewhere—in a rumpled hotel bed, or an unseen family house, conducting a constant parallel conversation with a man who isn't there. Melissa's eyes are on the ceiling.

Ellie realizes, with sudden clarity, the precariousness of her position.

"I, uh, have something better," she says suddenly. "I thought you'd like this more." The envelope is nestling among the papers, and she thrusts it at her boss. "I was trying to get a few leads on it."

Melissa reads the short letter, and frowns. "Do we know who this is?"

"Not yet, but I'm working on it. I thought it would be a great feature if I could find out what happened to them. Whether they ended up together."

Melissa was nodding. "Yes. It sounds extramarital. Scandal in the sixties, eh? We could use it as a peg for how morality has changed. How close are you to finding them?"

"I've got feelers out."

"Find out what happened, whether they were ostracized."

"If they stayed married, it's possible they won't want the publicity," Rupert observes. "Such things were a much bigger deal back then."

"Offer them anonymity if you have to," Melissa says, "but ideally we'd like pictures—from the period of the letter, at least. That should make it harder for them to be identified."

"I haven't found them yet." The tightening of her skin tells Ellie this is a bad idea.

"But you will. Get one of the news journos to help if you need to. They're good at investigative stuff. And, yes, I'd like that for next week. But first get those problem pages sorted out. I want examples I can lay out on a double-page spread by the end of the day. Okay? We'll meet again tomorrow, same time." She is already striding toward the door, her perfectly groomed hair bouncing like a shampoo advert.

"It's Mrs. Spelling Bee."

She finds him sitting in the canteen. He unplugs his earphones as she sits opposite. He's reading a guidebook to South America. An empty plate tells of lunch already eaten.

"Rory, I'm in such trouble."

"Spelled *antidisestablishmentarianism* with four *t*'s?"

"I let my mouth run away with me in front of Melissa Buckingham, and now I have to flesh out the Love Story to End All Love Stories for the features pages."

"You told her about the letter?"

"I got caught out. I needed to give her something. The way she was looking at me, I thought I was about to be transferred to Obits."

"Well, that's going to be interesting."

"I know. And before that, I've got to go through every problem page in the 1960 editions and find their moral equivalent in the modern day."

"That's straightforward, isn't it?"

"But it's time-consuming, and I've got loads of other things I'm meant to be doing. Even without finding out what happened to our mystery lovers." She smiled hopefully. "I don't suppose there's anything you could do to help me?"

"Sorry. Stacked up myself. I'll dig out the 1960 newspaper files for you when I go back downstairs."

"That's your job," she protests.

He grins. "Yup. And writing and researching is yours."

"It's my birthday."

"Then happy birthday."

"Oh, you're all heart."

"And you're too used to getting your own way." He smiles at her, and she watches him gather up his book and MP3 player. He salutes as he heads toward the door.

You have no idea, she thinks, as it swings shut behind him, just how wrong you are.

> *I am 25 and I have quite a good job but not a good enough job to do all the things I would like to do——to have a house and a car and a wife.*

"Because obviously you acquire one of those along with the house and the car," Ellie mutters at the faded newsprint. Or perhaps after a washing machine. Maybe that should take priority.

> *I have noticed that many of my friends have got married and their standard of living has dropped considerably. I have been going fairly regularly with a girl for three years and I would very much like to marry her. I have asked her to wait three years until we can get married and live in rather better circumstances, but she says she is not going to wait for me.*

Three years, Ellie muses. I don't blame her. You're hardly giving her the impression that yours is a great passion, are you?

> *Either we get married this year or she won't marry me at all. I think this is an unreasonable attitude since I have pointed out to her that she will have a rather lower standard of living. Do you think that there is any other argument that I can add to the ones I have made already?*

"No, pal," she says aloud, as she slides another old sheet of newspaper under the lid of the photocopier. "I think you've made yourself quite clear."

She returns to her desk, sits down, and pulls the crumpled, hand-written letter from her folder.

> *My dearest and only love . . . If you don't come, I'll know that whatever we might feel for each other, it isn't quite enough. I won't blame you, my darling. I know the past weeks have put an intolerable strain on you, and I feel the weight of that keenly. I hate the thought that I could cause you any unhappiness.*

She rereads the words again and again. They hold passion, force, even after so many years. Why would you suffer the priggish "I have pointed out to her that she will have a rather lower standard of living" when you could have "Know that you hold my heart, my hopes, in your hands"? She wishes the unknown girlfriend of the first correspondent a lucky escape.

Ellie makes a desultory check for new e-mail, then mobile-phone messages. She chews the end of a pencil. She picks up the photocopied problem page and puts it down again.

Then she clicks open a new message on her computer screen and, before she can think too hard about it, she types:

> The one present I really want for my birthday is to know what I mean to you. I need for us to have an honest conversation, and for me to be able to say what I feel. I need to know whether we have any kind of future together.

She adds:

> I love you, John. I love you more than I have ever loved anyone in my whole life, and this is starting to drive me crazy.

Her eyes have filled with tears. Her hand moves to send. The department shrinks around her. She is dimly aware of Caroline, the health editor, chatting on the phone at the next desk, of the window cleaner on his teetering cradle outside the window, of the news editor having an argument with one of his reporters somewhere on the other side of the office, the missing carpet tile at her feet. She sees nothing but the winking cursor, her words, her future, laid bare on the screen in front of her.

> I love you more than I have ever loved anyone in my whole life.

If I do this now, she thinks, it will be decided for me. It will be my way of taking control. And if it isn't the answer I want, at least it's an answer.

Her forefinger rests gently on send.

And I will never touch that face, kiss those lips, feel those hands on me again. I will never hear the way he says "Ellie Haworth," as if the words themselves are precious.

The phone on her desk rings.

She jumps, glances at it, as if she'd forgotten where she is, then wipes her eyes with her hand. She straightens, then picks it up. "Hello."

"Hey, birthday girl," says Rory, "get yourself down to the cells at chucking-out time. I might just have something for you. And bring me a coffee while you're at it. That's the charge for my labors."

She puts down the receiver, turns back to her computer, and presses delete.

"So, what did you find?" She hands a cup of coffee over the counter, and he takes it. There's a fine sprinkling of dust in his hair, and she fights the urge to ruffle it off, as one would with a child. He has already felt patronized by her once; she doesn't want to risk offending him a second time.

"Any sugar?"

"No," she says. "I didn't think you took it."

"I don't." He leans forward over the countertop. "Look—boss is lurking. I need to be discreet. What time are you finishing?"

"Whenever," she says. "I'm pretty much through."

He rubs his hair. The dust forms an apologetic cloud around him. "I feel like that character in *Peanuts*. Which was it?"

She shook her head.

"Pig Pen. The one with the dirt floating around him . . . We're shifting boxes that haven't been touched in decades. I can't really believe we're ever going to need parliamentary minutes from 1932, whatever he says. Still. The Black Horse? Half an hour?"

"The pub?"

"Yes."

"I sort of might have plans . . ." She wants to ask, *Can't you just give me what you've found?* But even she can see how ungrateful that will sound.

"It'll only take ten minutes. I've got to meet some friends afterward, anyway. But it's cool. It can wait till tomorrow if you'd prefer."

She thinks about her mobile phone, mute and recriminating in her back pocket. What's her alternative? Rushing home and waiting for John to call there? Another evening spent sitting in front of the television, knowing that the world is revolving somewhere without her? "Oh—what the hell. A quick drink would be great."

"Half a shandy. Live dangerously."

"Shandy! Huh! I'll see you in there."

He grins. "I'll be the one clutching a file marked 'Top Secret.' "

"Oh, yes? I'll be the one shouting, 'Buy me a proper drink, cheapo. It's my birthday.' "

"No red carnation in your buttonhole? Just so I can identify you?"

"No means of identification. That way it's easier for me to escape if I don't like the look of you."

He nods approvingly. "Sensible."

"And you're not even going to give me a clue as to what you've found?"

"Some birthday surprise that would be!" With that he's gone, back through the double doors and into the bowels of the newspaper.

The ladies' is empty. She washes her hands, noting that now the building's days are numbered, the company is no longer bothering to refresh the soap dispenser or the tampon machine. Next week, she suspects, they'll have to start bringing in emergency loo roll.

She checks her face, applies some mascara, and paints out the bags under her eyes. She puts on lipstick, then rubs it off. She looks tired, and tells herself the lighting in there is harsh, that this is not an inevitable consequence of being a year older. Then she sits beside a washbasin, pulls her phone from her bag, and types a message.

> Just checking—does "later" mean this evening? Am trying to work out my plans.

E

It doesn't come across as clingy, possessive, or even desperate. It suggests that she's a woman with many offers, things to do, but implies that she'll put him first, if necessary. She fiddles with it for a further five minutes, making sure she has the tone completely right, then sends it.

The reply comes back almost immediately. Her heart jumps, as it always does when she knows it's him.

> Difficult to say at the moment. Will call later if I think I can make it. J

A sudden rage ignites within her. That's it? she wants to yell at him. My birthday, and the best you can do is "Will call later if I think I can make it"?

Don't bother, she types back, her fingers jabbing at the little keys. I'll make my own plans.

And, for the first time in months, Ellie Haworth turns off her phone before she sticks it back into her bag.

She spends longer than she intended working on the problem-pages feature, writes up an interview with a woman whose child suffers from a form of juvenile arthritis, and when she arrives at the Black Horse Rory is there. She can see him across the room, his hair now free of dust. She makes her way through the crowd toward him, apologizing for the bumped elbows, the badly negotiated spaces, already preparing to say "Sorry I'm late" when she realizes he's not alone. The group of people with him are not familiar; they're not from the newspaper. He's at their center, laughing. Seeing him like this, out of context, throws her. She turns away to gather her thoughts.

"Hey! Ellie!"

She paints on a smile and turns back.

He lifts a hand. "Thought you weren't coming."

"Got held up. Sorry." She joins the group and says hello.

"Let me buy you a drink. It's Ellie's birthday. What would you like?" She accepts the flurry of greetings from the people she doesn't know, letting them falter to a few embarrassed smiles and wishing she wasn't there. Making small talk wasn't part of the deal. She wonders, briefly, if she can leave, but Rory is already at the bar buying her a drink.

"White wine," he says, turning to hand her a glass. "I would have got champagne, but—"

"I get my own way far too much already."

He laughs. "Yeah. Touché."

"Thanks anyway."

He introduces her to his friends, reels off names she's forgotten even before he's finished.

"So . . . ," she says.

"Down to business. Excuse us, for a minute," he says, and they make their way to a corner where it's emptier and quieter. There is only one seat, and he motions her to it, squatting on his haunches beside her. He unzips his backpack, and pulls out a folder marked "Asbestos/ Case studies: symptoms."

"And this is relevant because . . . ?"

"Patience," he says, handing it over. "I was thinking about the letter we found last time. It was with a load of papers on asbestos, right? Well, there's heaps of stuff on asbestos downstairs, from the group legal actions of the last few years mainly. But I decided to dig around a bit further back and found some much older stuff. It's dated from much the same period as the bits I gave you last time. I think it must have become separated from that first file." He flicks through the papers with expert fingers. "And," he says, pulling at a clear plastic folder, "I found these."

Her heart stills. Two envelopes. The same handwriting. The same address, a PO box at the Langley Street post office.

"Have you read them?"

He grins. "How much restraint do I look like I have? Of course I read them."

"Can I?"

"Go ahead."
The first is simply headed "Wednesday."

> *I understand your fear that you will be misunderstood, but I tell you it is unfounded. Yes, I was a fool that night in Alberto's, and I will never be able to think of my outburst without shame, but it was not your words that prompted it. It was the absence of them. Can't you see, Jenny, that I am predisposed to see the best in what you say, what you do? But just as nature abhors a vacuum—so does the human heart. Foolish, insecure man that I am, as we both seem so unsure what this actually comprises, and we cannot talk about where it may go, all that is left to me is reassurance about what it may mean. I simply need to hear that this is for you what it is for me: in short, everything.*
>
> *If those words still fill you with trepidation, I give you an easier option. Answer me simply, in one word: yes.*

On the second there is a date, but again, no greeting. The handwriting, while recognizable, is scrawled, as if it has been dashed off before its author could give it careful thought.

> *I swore I wouldn't contact you again. But six weeks on, and I feel no better. Being without you—thousands of miles from you—offers no relief at all. The fact that I am no longer tormented by your presence, or presented with daily evidence of my inability to have the one thing I truly desire, has not healed me. It has made things worse. My future feels like a bleak, empty road.*
>
> *I don't know what I'm trying to say, darling Jenny. Just that if you have any sense at all that you made the wrong decision, this door is still wide open.*
>
> *And if you feel that your decision was the right one, know this at least: that somewhere in this world is a man who loves you, who understands how precious and clever and kind you are. A man who has always loved you and, to his detriment, suspects he always will.*
>
> *Your*
>
> *B.*

"Jenny," he says.

She doesn't reply.

"She didn't go," he says.

"Yup. You were right."

He opens his mouth as if to speak, but perhaps something in her expression changes his mind.

She lets out a breath. "I don't know why," she says, "but that's made me feel a bit sad."

"But you have your answer. And you have a clue to the name, if you really want to write this feature."

"Jenny," she muses. "It's not a lot to go on."

"But it's the second letter that was found in files about asbestos, so perhaps she had some link to it. It might be worth going through the two files. Just to see if there's anything else."

"You're right." She takes the file from him, carefully replaces the letter in the plastic folder, and puts it all in her bag. "Thanks," she says. "Really. I know you're busy at the moment, and I appreciate it."

He studies her in the way someone might scan a file, searching for information. When John looks at her, she thinks, it's always with a kind of tender apology, for who they are, for what they have become. "You really do look sad."

"Aw . . . just a sucker for a happy ending." She forces a smile. "I guess I just thought when you said you'd found something that it might show it all ended well."

"Don't take it personally," he says, touching her arm.

"Oh, I couldn't care less, really," she says brusquely, "but it'd fit the feature much better if we could end on a high note. Melissa might not even want me to write the thing if it doesn't end well." She brushes a lock of hair from her face. "You know what she's like—'Let's keep it upbeat . . . readers get enough misery from the news pages.' "

"I feel like I rained on your birthday," he says, as they make their way back across the pub. He has to stoop and shout it into her ear.

"Don't worry about it," she shouts back. "It's a pretty apt finish to the day I've had."

"Come out with us," Rory says, stopping her with a hand on her elbow. "We're going ice-skating. Someone's pulled out, so we have a spare ticket."

"Ice-skating?"

"It's a laugh."

"I'm thirty-two years old! I can't go ice-skating!"

It's his turn to look incredulous. "Oh . . . Well, then." He nods understandingly. "We can't have you toppling off your walker."

"I thought ice-skating was for children. Teenagers."

"Then you're a very unimaginative person, Miss Haworth. Finish your drink and come with us. Have a bit of fun. Unless you really can't get out of what you'd planned."

She feels for her phone, tucked into her bag, tempted to turn it on again. But she doesn't want to read John's inevitable apology. Doesn't want the rest of this evening colored by his absence, his words, the ache for him.

"If I break my leg," she says, "you're contractually obliged to drive me in and out of work for six weeks."

"Might be interesting, as I don't own a car. Will you settle for a piggyback?"

He's not her type. He's sarcastic, a bit chippy, probably several years younger than she is. She suspects he earns significantly less than she does, and probably still shares a flat. It's possible he doesn't even drive. But he's the best offer she's likely to get at a quarter to seven on her thirty-second birthday, and Ellie has decided that pragmatism is an underrated virtue. "And if my fingers get sliced off by someone's random skate, you have to sit at my desk and type for me."

"You only need one finger for that. Or a nose. God, you hacks are a bunch of prima donnas," he says. "Right, everyone. Drink up. The tickets say we've got to be there for half past."

As Ellie walks back from the Tube some time later, she realizes the pain in her sides is not from the skating—although she hasn't fallen over so often since she was learning to walk—but because she has laughed pretty solidly for almost two hours. Skating was comic, and exhilarating, and she realized as she took her first successful baby steps onto the ice that she rarely experienced the pleasure of losing herself in simple physical activity.

Rory had been good at it; most of his friends were. "We come here every winter," he said, gesturing at the temporary rink, floodlit and surrounded by office buildings. "They put it up in November, and we probably come every fortnight. It's easier if you've had a few drinks first. You relax more. C'mon . . . let your limbs go. Just lean forward a bit." He had skated backward in front of her, his arms outstretched so that she clutched them. When she fell over, he laughed mercilessly. It was liberating to do this with someone whose opinion she cared so little for: if it had been John, she would have fretted that the chill of the ice was making her nose redden.

She would have been thinking the whole time about when he would have to leave.

They have arrived at her door. "Thanks," she says to Rory. "Tonight was going pretty badly, and I ended up having a great time."

"Least I could do, after raining all over your birthday with that letter."

"I'll get over it."

"Who'd have thought? Ellie Haworth has a heart."

"It's just an ugly rumor."

"You're not bad, you know," he says, a smile playing around his eyes. "For an old bird."

She wants to ask him if he's talking about the skating, but she's suddenly unnerved by what he might say. "And you're all charm."

"You're . . ." He blinks, glances back down the road toward the Tube station.

She wonders, briefly, if she should invite him in. But even as she considers it, she knows it won't work. Her head, her flat, her life, are full of John. There's no room for this man. Perhaps what she actually feels for him is sisterly, and only mildly confused by the fact that he is not exactly ugly.

He's studying her face again, and she has the unnerving suspicion that her deliberation was written on her face.

"I'd better go," he says.

"Yes," she says. "Thanks again, though."

"No problem. I'll see you at work." He kisses her cheek, then turns and half jogs toward the station. She watches him go, feeling oddly bereft.

Ellie makes her way up the stone steps and reaches for her key. She will reread the new letter and go through the papers, checking for clues. She'll be productive. She'll channel her energies. She feels a hand on her shoulder and jumps, stifling a scream.

John is on the step behind her, a bottle of champagne and a ridiculously large bunch of flowers under one arm. "I'm not here," he says. "I'm in Somerset, giving a lecture to a writers' group, who are talentless and include at least one interminable bore." He stands there as she catches her breath. "You can say something—as long as it's not 'Go away.' "

She's mute.

He puts the flowers and champagne on the step and pulls her into his arms. His kiss has the warmth of his car. "I've been sitting over there for almost half an hour. I started to panic that you weren't coming home at all."

Everything inside her melts. She drops her bag, feels his skin, his weight, his size, and allows herself to fall against him. He takes her cold face in his warm hands. "Happy birthday," he says, when they finally pull apart.

"Somerset?" she says, a little giddy. "Does that mean . . . ?"

"All night."

It's her thirty-second birthday, and the man she loves is there with champagne and flowers and is going to spend all night in her bed.

"So, can I come in?" he says.

She frowns at him in a way that says, *Do you really need to ask?* Then she picks up the flowers, the champagne, and heads upstairs.

Chapter 19

"Ellie? May I have a word?"

She's sliding her bag under her desk, her skin still moist from the shower she had not half an hour previously, her thoughts still elsewhere. Melissa's voice, from the glass office, is hard, a brutal reentry into real life.

"Of course." She nods and smiles obligingly. Someone has left a coffee for her; it's lukewarm, has obviously been there some time. There is a note underneath it, addressed to "Jayne Torvill," that reads: "Lunch?"

She has no time to digest this. She has whipped off her coat, is walking into Melissa's office, noting with dismay that the features editor is still standing. She perches on a chair and waits as Melissa walks slowly round her desk and sits down. She's wearing a pair of velvety black jeans and a black polo-neck, and has the toned arms and stomach of someone who does several hours of Pilates every day. She sports what the fashion pages would call "statement jewelry," which Ellie assumes is just a trendy way of saying "big."

Melissa lets out a little sigh and stares at her. Her eyes are a startling violet, and Ellie wonders briefly whether she's wearing colored contact lenses. They're the exact shade of her necklace. "This isn't a conversation I'm entirely comfortable having, Ellie, but it's become unavoidable."

"Oh?"

"It's nearly a quarter to eleven."

"Ah. Yes, I—"

"I appreciate that Features is considered the more relaxed end of the *Nation*, but I think we're generally agreed that a quarter to ten is pretty much the absolute latest I want my staff at their desks."

"Yes, I—"

"I like to give my writers a chance to prepare themselves for conference. That gives them time to read the day's newspapers, check the Web sites, talk, inspire, and be inspired." She swivels a little in her seat, checks an e-mail. "It's a privilege to be in conference, Ellie. A chance a lot of other writers would be very glad to have. I'm finding it hard to see how you can possibly be prepared to a professional degree if you're skidding in here minutes beforehand."

Ellie's skin prickles.

"With wet hair."

"I'm very sorry, Melissa. I had to wait in for a plumber, and—"

"Let's not, Ellie," she says quietly. "I'd rather you didn't insult my intelligence. And unless you're going to be able to convince me that you have a plumber in attendance almost every other day of the week, I'm afraid I have to conclude that you're not taking this job very seriously."

Ellie swallows.

"Our Web presence means there's no place to hide on this newspaper anymore. Every writer's performance can be judged not just by the quality of their work on our print pages, but by the number of hits their stories get online. Your performance, Ellie," she consults a piece of paper in front of her, "has dropped by almost forty percent in a year."

Ellie can say nothing. Her throat dries. The other editors and writers are congregating outside Melissa's office, clutching oversize notepads and polystyrene cups. She watches them glance through the glass at her, some curious, some vaguely embarrassed, as if they know what is happening to her. She wonders, briefly, if her work has been a wider topic of conversation and feels humiliated.

Melissa is leaning across her desk. "When I took you on, you were hungry. You were ahead of the game. It was why I picked you above any number of other regional reporters who, frankly, would have sold their grandmothers to be in your position."

"Melissa, I've—"

"I don't want to know what's going on in your life, Ellie. I don't want to know if you have personal problems, if someone close to you has died, if you're in mountains of debt. I don't even particularly want to know if you're seriously ill. I just want you to do the job you're paid to do. You must know by now that newspapers are unforgiving. If you don't pull in the stories, we don't get the advertising or, indeed, the circulation figures. If we don't get those things, we're all out of a job, some of us sooner than others. Am I making myself clear?"

"Very clear, Melissa."

"Good. I don't think there's any point in you coming to conference today. Get yourself sorted out, and I'll see you in the meeting tomorrow. How's that love-letters feature coming along?"

"Good. Yes." She's standing, trying to look as if she knows what she's doing.

"Right. You can show me tomorrow. Please tell the others to come in on your way out."

At a little after twelve thirty she runs the four flights of stairs down to the library, her mood still dark, the joys of the previous evening forgotten. The library is like an empty warehouse. The shelves are now bare around the counter, the misspelled paper notice ripped off, only two sides of Scotch tape remaining. Behind the second set of swing doors she can hear furniture being dragged. The chief librarian is running a finger down a list of figures, his glasses tilted at the end of his nose.

"Is Rory around?"

"He's busy."

"Can you tell him I can't meet him for lunch?"

"I'm not sure where he is."

She feels anxious about Melissa noticing she's not at her desk.

"Well, are you likely to see him? I need to tell him that I've got to go out on this feature. Can you tell him I'll pop down at the end of the day?"

"Perhaps you should leave him a note."

"But you said you didn't know where he was."

He looks up, his brow lowered. "Sorry, but we're in the final stages of our move. I don't have time to be passing on messages." He sounds impatient.

"Fine. I'll just head up to Personnel and waste their time asking for his mobile number, shall I? Just so I can make sure I don't stand him up and waste his time."

He holds up a hand. "I'll tell him if I see him."

"Oh, don't trouble yourself. So sorry to have bothered you."

He turns slowly toward her and fixes her with what her mother might have termed an old-fashioned look. "We in the library may be considered something not far short of an irrelevance by you and your ilk, Miss Haworth, but at my age I stop a little short of office dogsbody. Forgive me if that inconveniences your social life."

She remembers, with a start, Rory's claim that the librarians can all put a face to a byline. She doesn't know this man's name.

She blushes as he disappears through the swing doors. She's cross with herself for behaving like a stroppy teenager, cross with the old man for being so uncooperative. Cross that Melissa's icy assessment means she can't have a cheerful lunch outside on a day that had started so well. John had stayed till almost nine o'clock. The train from Somerset didn't get in until a quarter to eleven, he said, so there was no point in racing off. She had cooked him scrambled eggs on toast—almost the only thing she can cook well—and sat there in bed blissfully stealing bits from his plate as he ate it.

They had spent a whole night together only once before, back in the early days of their relationship when he had claimed to be obsessed with her. Last night, it had been like those early days: he had been tender, affectionate, as if his impending holiday had made him extra sensitive to her feelings.

She didn't talk about it: if this past year has taught her one thing, it is to live in the present. She immersed herself in every moment, refusing to cloud it by considering the cost. The fall would come—it always did—but she usually collected enough memories to cushion it a little.

She stands on the stairs, thinking of his bare, freckled arms wrapped around her, his sleeping face on her pillow. It had been perfect. Perfect. A small voice wonders whether one day, if only he'd think about it hard enough, he'll realize that their whole life could be like that.

It's a short taxi ride to the post office in Langley Street. Before she leaves the office, she takes care to tell Melissa's secretary. "Here is my mobile number, if she wants me," she says, her voice dripping with professional courtesy. "I'll be about an hour."

Although it's lunchtime, the post office isn't busy. She walks to the front of the nonexistent queue and waits obediently for the electronic voice to call, "Till number four, please."

"Can I talk to someone about PO boxes, please?"

"Hang on." The woman disappears, then reemerges, pointing for her to move to the end, where there is a door. "Margie will meet you down there."

A young woman sticks her head around the door. She's wearing a name tag, a large gold chain with a crucifix, and a pair of heels so high that Ellie wonders how she can bear to stand in them, let alone spend a whole day working in them. She smiles, and Ellie thinks briefly how rare it is that anyone smiles at you in the city anymore.

"This is going to sound a little strange," Ellie begins, "but is there a way of finding out who rented a PO box years ago?"

"They can change pretty frequently. When are you talking about?" Ellie wonders how much to tell her, but Margie has a nice face, so she adopts her confidential tone. She reaches into her bag and pulls out the letters, carefully enclosed in a clear plastic folder. "It's a bit of a strange one. It's some love letters I found. They're addressed to a PO box here, and I want to return them."

She has Margie's interest. It's probably a nice change from benefit payments and catalog returns.

"PO box thirteen." Ellie points at the envelope.

Margie's face reveals recognition. "Thirteen?"

"You know the one?"

"Oh, yes." Margie's lips are compressed, as if she's considering how much she's allowed to say. "Apart from a short break, that PO box has been held by the same person for, ooh, almost forty years. Not that that's particularly unusual in itself."

"So what is?"

"The fact that it's never had a letter. Not one. We've contacted the holder lots of times to give her the chance to shut it down. She says she wants to keep it open. We say it's up to her if she wants to waste her money." She peers at the letter. "Love letter, is it? Oh, how sad."

"Can you give me her name?" Ellie's stomach tenses. This could be a better story even than she'd envisaged.

The woman shakes her head. "Sorry, I can't. Data protection and all that."

"Oh, please!" She thinks of Melissa's face if she can come back with a Forbidden Love That Lasted Forty Years. "Please. You have no idea how important this is to me."

"Sorry, I really am, but it could cost me more than my job."

Ellie swears under her breath and glances behind her at the queue that has suddenly appeared. Margie is turning back to her door.

"Thank you anyway," Ellie says, remembering her manners.

"No problem." Behind them a small child is crying, trying to escape from the restraints of its pram.

"Hang on." Ellie's rustling in her bag.

"Yes?"

She grins. "Could I—you know—leave a letter in it?"

Dear Jennifer,

Please excuse the intrusion, but I have come across some personal correspondence that I believe may be yours, and I'd welcome the opportunity to return it to you.

I can be contacted on the numbers below.
Yours sincerely,

Ellie Haworth

Rory looks at it. They're sitting at the pub across from the *Nation*. It's dark, even so early in the evening, and under the sodium lights green removal lorries are still visible outside the front gate, men in overalls traveling backward and forward up the wide steps to the *Nation's* entrance. They have been an almost permanent fixture for weeks now.

"What? You think I've got the tone wrong?"

"No." He's sitting beside her on the banquette, one foot angled against the table leg in front of them.

"What, then? You're doing that thing with your face."

He grins. "I don't know, don't ask me. I'm not a journalist."

"Come on. What does the face mean?"

"Well, doesn't it make you feel a bit . . ."

"What?"

"I don't know . . . It's so personal. And you're going to be asking her to air her dirty linen in public."

"She might be glad of the chance. She might find him again." There's a note of defiant optimism in her voice.

"Or she might be married, and they've spent forty years trying to get over her affair."

"I doubt it. Anyway, how do you know it's dirty linen? They might be together now. It might have had a happy ending."

"And she kept the PO box open for forty years? It didn't have a happy ending." He hands back the letter. "She might even be mentally ill."

"Oh, so holding a torch for someone means you're mad. Obviously."

"Keeping a PO box open for forty years, without getting a single letter in it, is on the far side of normal behavior."

He has a point, she concedes. But the idea of Jenny and her

empty PO box has taken hold of her imagination. More important, it's the closest thing she has to a decent feature. "I'll think about it," she says. She doesn't tell him she posted the good copy that afternoon.

"So," he says, "did you have a good time last night? Not too sore today?"

"What?"

"The ice-skating."

"Oh. A little." She straightens her legs, feeling the tightness in her thighs, and reddens a little when she brushes his knee with her own. In-jokes have sprung up between them. She is Jayne Torvill; he is the humble librarian, there to do her bidding. He texts her with deliberate misspellings: Pls will the smart ladee com and hav a drink with the humble librarrian later?

"I heard you came down to find me."

She glances at him, and he's grinning again. She grimaces. "Your boss is so grumpy. Honestly. It was as if I'd asked him to sacrifice his firstborn when all I was doing was trying to get a message to you."

"He's all right," Rory says, wrinkling his nose. "He's just stressed. Really stressed. This is his last project before he retires, and he's got forty thousand documents to move in the right order, plus the ones that are being scanned for digital storage."

"We're all busy, Rory."

"He just wants to leave it shipshape. He's old school—you know, everything's for the good of the paper. I like him. He's of a dying breed."

She thinks of Melissa, she of the cold eyes and high heels, and cannot help but agree with him.

"He knows everything there is to know about this place. You should talk to him sometime."

"Yes. Because he's obviously taken such a shine to me."

"I'm sure he would, if you asked him nicely."

"Like I speak to you?"

"No. I said nicely."

"Are you going to go for his job?"

"Me?" Rory lifts his glass to his lips. "Nah. I want to go traveling—South America. This was only meant to be a holiday job for me. Somehow I ended up staying eighteen months."

"You've been here eighteen months?"

"You mean you hadn't noticed me?" He makes a mock-hurt face, and she blushes again.

"I just . . . I thought I would have seen you before now."

"Ah, you hacks only see what you want to see. We're the invisible drones, there merely to fulfill your bidding."

He's smiling, and spoke without malice, but she knows there's an unpleasant kernel of truth in what he said. "So I'm a selfish, uncaring hack, blind to the needs of the true workers and nasty to decent old men with a work ethic," she muses.

"That's about the size of it." Then he looks at her properly, and his expression changes. "What are you going to do to redeem yourself?"

It's astonishingly hard to meet his eye. She's trying to work out how to answer when she hears her mobile phone. "Sorry," she mutters, scrabbling in her bag. She clicks open the little envelope symbol.

> Just wanted to say hi. Away hols tomorrow, will be in touch
> when I get back, take care Jx

She's disappointed. "Say hi," after the whispered intimacies of the previous evening? The uninhibited coming together? He wants to "say hi"?

She rereads the message. He never says much via the mobile phone, she knows that. He told her at the start it was too risky, in case his wife happened to pick it up before he could delete some incriminating message. And there's something sweet in "take care," isn't there? He's telling her he wants her to be okay. She wonders, even as she calms herself, at how far she stretches these messages, finding a whole hinterland in the sparse words he sends to her. She believes they're so connected to each other that it's fine, she understands what he really wants to say. But occasionally, like today, she doubts that there really is anything beyond the shorthand.

How to reply? She can hardly say "Have a good holiday" when she wants him to have a terrible time, his wife to get food poisoning, his children to whine incessantly, and the weather to fail spectacularly, confining them all to a grumpy indoors. She wants him to sit there missing her, missing her, missing her . . .

> Take care yourself x

When she looks up, Rory's eyes are fixed on the removals lorry outside, as if he's pretending not to be interested in what's going on beside him.

"Sorry," she says, tucking her phone back into her bag. "Work thing." Aware, even as she says it, why she's not telling him the truth. He could be a friend, is already a friend: why would she not tell him about John?

"Why do you think nobody writes love letters like these anymore?" she says instead, pulling one from her bag. "I mean, yes, there are texts and e-mails and things, but nobody sends them in language like this, do they? Nobody spells it out anymore like our unknown lover did."

The removal lorry has pulled away. The front of the newspaper building is blank and empty, its entrance a dark maw under the sodium lights, its remaining staff deep inside, making last-minute changes to the front page.

"Perhaps they do," he says, and his face has lost that brief softness. "Or perhaps, if you're a man, it's impossible to know what you're meant to say."

The gym at Swiss Cottage is no longer near either of their homes, has equipment that is regularly out of order and a receptionist so bolshy that they wonder whether she's been planted there by some opposition, but neither she nor Nicky can be bothered to go through the interminable process of ending their membership and finding somewhere new. It has become their weekly meeting place. After a few desultory laps up and down the small pool, they sit in the hot tub or

the sauna for forty minutes to talk, having convinced themselves that
these things are "good for the skin."

Nicky arrives late: she's preparing for a conference in South Africa
and has been held up. Neither friend will pass comment on the other's
lateness: it's accepted that this happens, that any inconvenience caused
by one's career is beyond reproach. Besides, Ellie has never quite understood what Nicky does.

"Will it be hot out there?" She adjusts her towel on the hot bench
of the sauna as Nicky wipes her eyes.

"I think so. Not sure how much time I'll get to enjoy it, though.
New boss is a workaholic. I was hoping to take a week's holiday afterward, but she says she can't spare me."

"What's she like?"

"Oh, she's all right, not knitting herself a pair of testicles or anything. But she really does put in the hours, and can't see why the rest
of us shouldn't do the same."

"I don't know anyone who gets a proper lunch break now."

"Apart from you hacks. I thought it was all boozy lunches with
contacts."

"Hah. Not with my boss on my tail." She tells the story of her
morning meeting, and Nicky's eyes screw up in sympathy.

"You want to be careful," she says. "She sounds like she's got you
in her sights. Is this feature coming okay? Will that get her off your
back?"

"I don't know if it'll come to anything. And I feel weird about
using some of this stuff." She rubs her foot. "The letters are lovely.
And really intense. If someone had written me a letter like that, I
wouldn't want it put into the public domain."

She hears Rory's voice as she says this, and discovers she's no longer
sure what she thinks. She'd been unprepared for how much he disliked the idea of the letters being published. She's used to the idea
that everyone on the *Nation* shares a mind-set. *The paper first. Old school.*

"I'd want to blow it up and put it on a billboard. I don't know
anyone who gets love letters anymore," Nicky says. "My sister did,
when her fiancé moved to Hong Kong back in the nineties, at least

two a week." She snorts. "Mind you, most of them were about how much he missed her bum."

They break off from laughing as another woman enters the sauna. They exchange polite smiles, and the woman takes a place on the highest shelf, carefully spreading her towel beneath her.

Ellie smooths her hair off her face. "I've been thinking about what you said. On my birthday." She lowers her voice. "About John's wife."

"Ah."

"I know you're right, Nicky, but it's not like I know her. She's not like a real person. So why should I care what happens to her?"

"Interesting logic."

"Okay. She has the one thing I really, really want, the one thing that would make me happy. And she can't be that much in love with him, can she, and pay so little attention to what he needs and wants? I mean, if they were that happy, he wouldn't be with me, would he?"

Nicky shakes her head. "Dunno. When my sister had her kid, she couldn't see straight for six months."

"His youngest is almost two." She feels, rather than hears, Nicky's shrug of derision.

"You know, Ellie," Nicky says, lying back on the bench and putting her hands behind her head. "Morally, I wouldn't care either way, but you don't seem happy."

That defensive clench. "I am happy."

Nicky raises an eyebrow.

"Okay. I'm happier and unhappier than I've ever been with anyone else, if that makes sense."

Unlike her two best friends, Ellie has never lived with a man. Until she was thirty she had assigned marriageandchildren—it was always one word—to the folder of things she would do later in life, long after she had established her career, along with drinking sensibly and taking out a pension. She didn't want to end up like some girls from her school, exhausted and pushing prams in their mid-twenties, financially dependent on husbands they seemed to despise.

Her last boyfriend had complained that he had spent most of their relationship following her while she ran from place to place "barking into a mobile phone." He had been even more pissed off that she'd found this funny. But since she'd turned thirty, it had become a little less amusing. When she visited her parents in Derbyshire, they made conspicuous efforts not to mention boyfriends, so much so that it had become just another form of pressure. She's good at being on her own, she tells them and other people. And it was the truth, until she met John.

"Is he married, love?" the woman asks, through the steam.

Ellie and Nicky exchange a subtle glance.

"Yes," Ellie says.

"If it makes you feel any better, I fell in love with a married man, and we've been married four years next Tuesday."

"Congratulations," they say in tandem, Ellie conscious that it seems an odd word to use in the circumstances.

"Happy as anything, we are. Of course his daughter won't talk to him anymore, but it's fine. We're happy."

"How long did it take him to leave his wife?" Ellie asks, sitting up.

The woman is pushing her hair into a ponytail. She has no boobs, Ellie thinks, and he still left his wife for her.

"Twelve years," she says. "It meant we couldn't have children, but like I said, it was worth it. We're very happy."

"I'm glad for you," says Ellie, as the woman climbs down. The glass door opens, letting in a burp of cold air as she leaves, and then it's the two of them, sitting in the hot, darkened cabin.

There's a short silence.

"Twelve years," says Nicky, rubbing her face with her towel. "Twelve years, an alienated daughter, and no kids. Well, I bet that makes you feel loads better."

Two days later the phone rings. It's a quarter past nine, and she's at her desk, standing up to answer it so that her boss can see she's there and working. What time does Melissa come to work? She seems to be first in and last out in Features, yet her hair and makeup are always immaculate, her outfits carefully coordinated. Ellie suspects there's probably a personal trainer at six a.m., a blow-dry at some exclusive salon an hour afterward. Does Melissa have a home life? Someone once mentioned a young daughter, but Ellie finds that hard to believe.

"Features," she says, staring absently into the glass office. Melissa is on the phone, walking up and down, one hand stroking her hair.

"Do I have the right number for Ellie Haworth?" A cut-glass voice, a relic from a previous age.

"Yup. This is she."

"Ah. I believe you sent me a letter. My name is Jennifer Stirling."

Chapter 20

She walks briskly, head down against the driving rain, cursing herself for not thinking far enough ahead to bring an umbrella. Taxis follow in the slipstream of steamy-windowed buses, sending sprays of water in graceful arcs over the curb. She is in St. John's Wood on a wet Saturday afternoon, trying not to think of white sands in Barbados, of a broad freckled hand rubbing sun cream into a woman's back. It is an image that pops into her head with punishing frequency, and has done for the six days John has been gone. The foul weather feels like some cosmic joke at her expense.

The mansion block rises in a gray slab from a wide, tree-lined pavement. She trips up the stone steps, presses the buzzer for Number 8, and waits, hopping impatiently from one soaked foot to the other.

"Hello?" The voice is clear. She thanks God that Jennifer Stirling suggested today: the thought of negotiating a whole Saturday without work, without her friends, who all seem to be busy, was terrifying.

That freckled hand again.

"It's Ellie Haworth. About your letters."

"Ah. Come in. I'm on the fourth floor. You may have to wait a while for the lift. It's terribly slow."

It's the kind of building she rarely goes into, in an area she hardly knows; her friends live in new-built flats with tiny rooms and underground parking, or maisonettes squashed like layer cakes into Victorian terraced houses. This block speaks of old money, imperviousness to fashion. It makes her think of the word *dowager*—John might use it—and smile.

The hallway is lined with dark turquoise carpet, a color from another age. The brass rail that leads up the four marble steps bears the deep patina of frequent polishing. She thinks, briefly, of the communal area in her own block, with its piles of neglected mail and carelessly left bicycles.

The lift makes its stately way up the four floors, creaking and trundling, and she steps out onto a tiled corridor.

"Hello?" Ellie sees the open door.

Afterward she's not sure what she had pictured: some stooped old lady with twinkling eyes and perhaps a nice shawl amid a house full of small china animals. Jennifer Stirling is not that woman. In her late sixties she might be, but her figure is lean and still upright; only her silver hair, cut into a side-swept bob, hints at her true age. She's wearing a dark blue cashmere sweater and a belted wool jacket over a pair of well-cut trousers that are more Dries van Noten than Marks & Spencer. An emerald green scarf is tied round her neck.

"Miss Haworth?"

She senses that the woman has watched her, perhaps assessing her, before using her name.

"Yes." Ellie sticks out her hand. "Ellie, please."

The woman's face relaxes a little. Whatever test there was, she seems to have passed it—for now, at least. "Do come in. Have you come far?"

Ellie follows her into the apartment. Again, she finds her expectations defied. No animal knickknacks here. The room is huge, light, and sparsely furnished. The pale wood floors sport a couple of large Persian rugs, and two damask-clad chesterfields face each other across a glass coffee table. The only other pieces of furniture are eclectic and exquisite: a chair that she suspects is expensive, modern, and Danish, and a small antique table, inlaid with walnut. Photographs of family, small children.

"What a beautiful flat," says Ellie, who has never particularly

cared about interior decorating but suddenly knows how she wants
to live.

"It is nice, isn't it? I bought it in . . . 'sixty-eight, I think. It was
rather a shabby old block then, but I thought it would be a nice place
for my daughter to grow up, since she had to live in a city. You can
see Regent's Park from that window. Can I take your coat? Would
you like some coffee? You look terribly wet."

Ellie sits while Jennifer Stirling disappears into the kitchen. On
the walls, which are the palest shade of cream, there are several large
pieces of modern art. Ellie eyes Jennifer Stirling as she reenters the
room, and realizes that she's not surprised that she could have inspired such passion in the unknown letter writer.

The photographs on the table include one of a ridiculously beautiful young woman, posed as if for a Cecil Beaton portrait; then, perhaps a few years later, she's peering down at a newborn child, her
expression wearing the exhaustion, awe, and elation seemingly common to all new mothers—her hair, even though she has just given
birth, is perfectly set.

"It's very kind of you to go to all this trouble. I have to say, your
letter was intriguing." A cup of coffee is placed in front of her, and
Jennifer Stirling sits opposite, stirring hers with a tiny silver spoon, a
red-enamel coffee bean at the end. Jesus, thinks Ellie. Her waist is
smaller than mine.

"I'm curious to know what this correspondence is. I don't think
I've thrown anything out accidentally for years. I tend to shred everything. And that PO box was . . . well, I thought it was private."

"Well, it wasn't actually me who found it. A friend of mine has
been sorting out the archive at the *Nation* newspaper and came across
a file."

Jennifer Stirling's demeanor changes.

"And in it were these."

Ellie reaches into her bag and carefully pulls out the plastic folder
with the three love letters. She watches Mrs. Stirling's face as she
takes them. "I would have sent them to you," she continues, "but . . ."

Jennifer Stirling is holding the letters reverently in both hands.

"I wasn't sure . . . what—well, whether you would even want to see them."

Jennifer says nothing. Suddenly ill at ease, Ellie takes a sip from her cup. She doesn't know how long she sits there, drinking her coffee, but she keeps her eyes averted, she isn't sure why.

"Oh, I do want them."

When she looks up, something has happened to Jennifer's expression. She isn't tearful, exactly, but her eyes have the pinched look of someone beset by intense emotion. "You've read them, I take it."

Ellie finds she's blushing. "Sorry. They were in a file of something completely unrelated. I didn't know I'd end up finding their owner. I thought they were beautiful," she adds awkwardly.

"Yes, they are, aren't they? Well, Ellie Haworth, not many things surprise me at my age, but you have succeeded today."

"Aren't you going to read them?"

"I don't have to. I know what they say."

Ellie learned a long time ago that the most important skill in journalism is knowing when to say nothing. But now she's becoming increasingly uncomfortable as she watches an old woman who has in some way disappeared from the room. "I'm sorry," she says carefully, when the silence becomes oppressive, "if I've upset you. I wasn't sure what to do, given that I didn't know what your—"

"—situation was," Jennifer says. She smiles, and Ellie thinks again what a lovely face she has. "That was very diplomatic of you. But these can cause no embarrassment. My husband died many years ago. It's one of the things they never tell you about being old." She gives a wry smile. "That the men die off so much sooner."

For a while they listen to the rain, the hissing brakes of the buses outside.

"Well," Mrs. Stirling says, "tell me something, Ellie. What made you go to such effort to return these letters to me?"

Ellie ponders whether or not to mention the feature. Her instincts tell her not to.

"Because I've never read anything like them?"

Jennifer Stirling is watching her closely.

"And . . . I also have a lover," she says, not sure why she says this.

"A 'lover'?"

"He's . . . married."

"Ah. So these letters spoke to you."

"Yes. The whole story did. It's the thing about wanting something you can't have. And that thing of never being able to say what you really feel." She's looking down now, speaking to her lap. "The man I'm involved with, John . . . I don't really know what he thinks. We don't talk about what's happening between us."

"I don't suppose he's unusual in that," Mrs. Stirling remarks.

"But your lover did. 'B.' did."

"Yes." Again, she's lost in another time. "He told me everything. It's an astonishing thing to receive a letter like that. To know you're loved so completely. He was always terribly good with words."

The rain becomes briefly torrential and thunders against the windows, people shouting below in the street.

"I've been mildly obsessed by your love affair, if that doesn't sound too strange. I desperately wanted the two of you to reunite. I have to ask, did you . . . did you ever get back together?"

The modern parlance seems wrong, inappropriate, and Ellie feels suddenly self-conscious. There's something graceless in what she was asking, she thinks. She has pushed it too far.

Just as Ellie is about to apologize, and make to leave, Jennifer speaks: "Would you like another cup of coffee, Ellie?" she says. "I don't suppose there's much point in your leaving while the rain is like this."

Jennifer Stirling sits on the silk-covered sofa, her coffee cooling on her lap, and tells the story of a young wife in the south of France, of a husband who, in her words, was probably no worse than any others of the age. A man very much of his time, in whom expressiveness had become a sign of weakness, unbecoming. And she tells a story of his opposite, an opinionated, passionate, damaged man, who unsettled her from the first night she met him at a moonlit dinner party.

Ellie sits, rapt, pictures building in her head, trying not to think

about the tape recorder she has surreptitiously turned on in her handbag. But she no longer feels graceless. Mrs. Stirling talks animatedly,
as if this is a story she has wanted to tell for decades. She says it's a
story she has pieced together over the years, and Ellie, although she
doesn't completely understand what is being said, doesn't want to
interrupt and ask her to clarify.

Jennifer Stirling tells of the sudden palling of her gilded life, the
sleepless nights, her guilt, the terrifying, irrevocable pull of someone
forbidden, the awful realization that the life you're leading might
be the wrong one. As she speaks, Ellie bites her nails, wondering if
this is what John is thinking, right now, on some distant sun-drenched
beach. How can he love his wife and do what he does with her? How
can he not feel that pull?

The story becomes darker, the voice quieter. She tells of a car crash
on a wet road, a blameless man dead, and the four years she sleep-
walked through her marriage, held in place only by pills and the birth
of her daughter.

She breaks off, reaches behind her, and hands Ellie a photo frame.
A tall blond woman stands in a pair of shorts, a man with his arm
around her. Two children and a dog are at her bare feet. She looks like
a Calvin Klein advertisement. "Esmé's probably not that much older
than you," she says. "She lives in San Francisco with her husband, a
doctor. They're very happy." She adds, with a wry smile, "To my
knowledge."

"Does she know about the letters?" Ellie places the frame carefully
on the coffee table, trying not to begrudge the unknown Esmé her
spectacular genetics, her apparently enviable life.

This time Mrs. Stirling hesitates before speaking. "I've never told
this story to a living soul. What daughter would want to hear that
her mother was in love with somebody other than her father?"

And then she tells of a chance meeting, years later, the glorious
shock of discovering she was where she was meant to be. "Can you
understand that? I had felt out of place for so long . . . and then Anthony was there. And I had this feeling." She taps her breastbone.
"That I was home. That it was him."

"Yes," says Ellie. She's perched on the edge of the sofa. Jennifer Stirling's face is illuminated. Suddenly Ellie can see the young girl she had been. "I know that feeling."

"The awful thing was, of course, that having found him again, I wasn't free to go with him. Divorce was a very different matter in those days, Ellie. Awful. One's name was dragged through the mud. I knew my husband would destroy me if I tried to go. And I couldn't leave Esmé. He—Anthony—had left his own child behind, and I don't think he ever really recovered from it."

"So you never actually left your husband?" Ellie feels a sinking disappointment.

"I did, thanks to that file you found. He had this funny old secretary, Miss Thing." She grimaces. "I never could remember her name. I suspect she was in love with him. And then, for some reason, she handed me the means to destroy him. He knew he couldn't touch me once I had those files."

She describes the meeting with the unnamed secretary, her husband's shock when she revealed what she knew at his office.

"The asbestos files." They had seemed so innocuous in Ellie's flat, their power dimmed by age and hindsight.

"Of course nobody knew about asbestos then. We thought it was wonderful stuff. It was a terrible shock to discover that Laurence's company had destroyed so many lives. That was why I set up the foundation when he died. To help the victims. Here." She reaches into a bureau and pulls out a pamphlet. It details a legal-help scheme for those suffering work-related mesothelioma. "There's not much money left in the fund now, but we do still offer legal help. I have friends in the profession who provide their services for free, here and abroad."

"You still got your husband's money?"

"Yes. That was our arrangement. I kept his name and became one of those rather reclusive wives who never accompanied their husbands to anything. Everyone assumed I'd dropped out of society to bring up Esmé. It wasn't unusual in those days, you see. He simply took his mistress to all the social events." She laughs, shaking her head. "There was the most astonishing double standard back then."

Ellie pictures herself on John's arm at some book launch. He has always been careful not to touch her in public, not to give any indication of their relationship. She has secretly hoped that they will be caught kissing, or that their passion will be so apparent they become the subject of damaging gossip.

She looks up to find Jennifer Stirling's eyes on her. "Would you like more coffee, Ellie? I'm assuming you're not in a hurry to be anywhere."

"No. That would be lovely. I want to know what happened."

Her expression changes. The smile fades. There is a short silence.

"He returned to the Congo," she says. "He used to travel to the most awfully dangerous places. Bad things were happening to white people out there at the time, and he wasn't terribly well . . ." She no longer seems to be directing her words at Ellie. "Men are often a lot more fragile than they seem, aren't they?"

Ellie digests this, trying not to feel the bitter disappointment this information seems to induce. This is not your life, she tells herself firmly. This does not have to be your tragedy. "Why did he sign his name as 'B.'?"

"I called him 'Boot.' That was our little joke. Have you read Evelyn Waugh? His real name was Anthony O'Hare. Actually, it's strange, telling it all to you after all this time. He was the love of my life, yet I have no photographs of him, few memories. If it wasn't for my letters, I might have thought I'd imagined the whole thing. That's why your bringing them back to me is such a gift."

A lump rises to Ellie's throat.

The telephone rings, jolting them from their thoughts.

"Do excuse me," Jennifer says. She walks out into the hallway, picks up a telephone, and Ellie hears her answer, her voice immediately calm, imbued with professional distance. "Yes," she is saying. "Yes, we still do. When were you diagnosed? . . . I'm so sorry . . ."

Ellie scribbles the name on her notepad and slips it back into her bag. She checks that her tape recorder has been running, that the microphone is still in position. Satisfied, she sits there for a few minutes longer, gazing at the family pictures, grasping that Jennifer will be a while. It doesn't seem fair to hurry someone who's evidently in the clutches of lung disease. She rips a page from her pad, scribbles a note, and picks up her coat. She goes over to the window. Outside, the weather has cleared and the puddles on the pavement gleam bright blue. Then she moves to the door and stands there with the note.

"Do excuse me for one moment." Jennifer holds her hand over the receiver. "I'm so sorry," she says. "I'm likely to be some time." Her voice suggests that their conversation will not be continued today. "Someone needs to apply for compensation."

"Can we talk again?" Ellie holds out the piece of paper. "My details are there. I really want to know . . ."

Jennifer nods, half her attention on her caller. "Yes. Of course. It's the least I can do. And thank you again, Ellie."

Ellie turns to leave, her coat over her arm. Then, as Jennifer is lifting the receiver to her ear, she turns back. "Just tell me one thing—just quickly? When he left again—Anthony—what did you do?"

Jennifer Stirling lowers the receiver, her eyes clear and calm. "I followed him."

Chapter 21

NOVEMBER 1964

"Madam? Would you like a drink?"

Jennifer opened her eyes. She had been holding the armrests of her seat for almost an hour as the BOAC airplane bucked its way toward Kenya. She had never been a very good flyer, but the relentless turbulence had ratcheted up the tension in the Comet so that even the old Africa hands were clenching their jaws with every bump. She winced as her bottom lifted from the seat, and there was a wail of dismay from the rear of the plane. The smell of hastily lit cigarettes had created a fug of smoke in the cabin.

"Yes," she said. "Please."

"I'll give you a double," the air hostess said, winking. "It's going to be a bumpy ride in."

She drank half of it in one gulp. Her eyes were gritty after a journey that had now stretched to almost forty-eight hours. Before leaving she had lain awake for several nights in London, chasing her thoughts, contradicting herself as to whether what she was attempting was madness, as everyone else seemed to think.

"Would you like one of these?" The businessman beside her held out a tin, its lid cocked toward her. His hands were huge, the fingers like dry-cured sausages.

"Thank you. What are they? Mints?" she said.

He smiled beneath his thick white mustache. "Oh, no." His accent was thick, Afrikaans. "They're to calm your nerves. You might be glad of them later."

She withdrew her hand. "I won't, thanks. Someone once told me that turbulence is nothing to be afraid of."

"He's right. It's the turbulence on the ground you want to be careful of."

When she didn't laugh, he peered at her for a moment. "Where are you headed? Safari?"

"No. I need to catch a connecting flight to Stanleyville. I was told I couldn't get one direct from London."

"Congo? What do you want to go there for, lady?"

"I'm trying to find a friend."

His voice was incredulous. "Congo?"

"Yes."

He was looking at her as if she was mad. She straightened in her seat a little, temporarily loosening her grip on the armrests.

"You don't read the newspapers?"

"A little, but not for a few days. I've been . . . very busy."

"Very busy, huh? Little lady, you might want to turn around and go straight back to England." He gave a low chuckle. "I'm pretty sure you're not going to get to Congo."

She turned away from him to stare out of the airplane window at the clouds, the distant snow-capped mountains beneath her, and wondered, briefly, if there was the faintest chance that, right at this moment, he was there ten thousand feet below her. *You have no idea how far I've come already,* she responded silently.

Two weeks previously Jennifer Stirling had stumbled out of the offices of the *Nation,* stood on the steps, with her daughter's small, chubby hand in her own, and realized she had no idea what to do next. A brisk wind had picked up, sending leaves scurrying after one another along the gutters, their aimless trajectory mirroring her own. How could Anthony have disappeared? Why had he left her no message? She recalled his anguish in the hotel lobby and feared she knew the answer. The fat newspaperman's words swam in her head. The world seemed to sway, and for a moment she thought she might faint.

Then Esmé had complained that she needed to go to the loo. The more immediate demands of a small child had hauled her out of her thoughts and into practicality.

She had booked into the Regent, where he had stayed, as if some small part of her believed it might be easier for him to find her there if he chose to return. She had to believe he would want to find her, would want to know that she was free at last.

The only available room was a suite on the fourth floor, and she had agreed to it easily. Laurence wouldn't dare quibble about money. And as Esmé sat happily in front of the large television, occasionally breaking off to bounce on the huge bed, she spent the rest of the evening pacing, thinking furiously, trying to work out how best to get a message to a man who was somewhere in the vast expanse of central Africa.

Finally, as Esmé slept, curled under the hotel quilt beside her, her thumb in her mouth, Jennifer lay watching her in the hotel bed, listening to the sounds of the city, fighting tears of impotence, and wondering whether, if she thought hard enough, she might somehow send a message to him telepathically. *Boot. Please hear me. I need you to come back for me. I can't do this by myself.*

On the second and third days she spent most of the daylight hours focused on Esmé, taking her to the Natural History Museum, to tea at Fortnum & Mason. They shopped on Regent Street for clothes—she hadn't been organized enough to send what they had with them to the hotel laundry—and had roast-chicken sandwiches from room service for supper, sent up on a silver salver. Occasionally Esmé would ask where Mrs. Cordoza or Daddy was, and Jennifer reassured her that they would see them very soon. She was grateful for her daughter's stream of small, mostly achievable requests, the routines imposed by tea, bath, and bed. But once the little girl had fallen asleep, she would close the bedroom door and be filled with a kind of black fear. What had she done? With each hour that passed, the enormity—and futility—of her actions crept further in on her. She had thrown away her life, moved her daughter into a hotel room—and for what?

She called the *Nation* twice more. She had spoken to the gruff man with the large stomach; now she recognized his voice, his abrupt manner of speaking. He told her, Yes, he would pass on the message as soon as O'Hare called in. The second time she had the distinct impression he wasn't telling the truth.

"But he must be there by now, surely. Aren't all the journalists in the same place? Can't someone get a message to him?"

"I'm not a social secretary. I told you I'll pass on your message, and I will, but it's a war zone out there. I'd imagine he's got other things to think about."

And she would be cut off.

The suite became an insular bubble, her only visitors the daily maid and the bellboy from room service. She dared not ring anybody, her parents, her friends, not yet knowing how to explain herself. She struggled to eat, could barely sleep. As her confidence dissipated, her anxiety grew.

She became increasingly filled with the conviction that she could not remain alone. How would she survive? She had never done anything by herself. Laurence would make sure she was isolated. Her parents would disown her. She fought the urge to order an alcoholic drink that might dull her growing sense of catastrophe. And with every day that passed, the little voice that echoed in her head grew more distinct: *You could always return to Laurence.* For a woman like her, whose only skill was to be decorative, what other option was there? In such fits and starts, in a surreal facsimile of ordinary life, the days went by. On day six she telephoned her house, guessing that Laurence would be at work. Mrs. Cordoza answered on the second ring, and she was humbled by the woman's obvious distress.

"Where are you, Mrs. Stirling? Let me bring you your things. Let me see Esmé. I've been so worried."

Something in Jennifer sagged with relief.

The housekeeper had come to the hotel with a suitcase of her belongings within the hour. Mr. Stirling, Mrs. Cordoza told her, had said nothing except that she should not expect anyone in the house for a few days. "He asked me to clear up the study. And when I looked in there"—her hand lifted briefly to her face—"I didn't know what to think."

"It's all fine. Really." Jennifer couldn't bring herself to explain what had happened.

"I'd be happy to help you in any way I can," Mrs. Cordoza went on, "but I don't think he—"

Jennifer placed a hand on her arm. "It's quite all right, Mrs. Cordoza. Believe me, we'd love to have you with us. But I think that may be difficult. And Esmé will have to go home to visit her father quite soon, once everything has calmed down a little, so perhaps it will be better for everyone if she has you there to look after her."

Esmé showed Mrs. Cordoza her new things and climbed onto her lap for a cuddle. Jennifer ordered tea, and the two women smiled awkwardly as she poured it for her housekeeper in a reversal of their former roles.

"Thank you so much for coming," Jennifer said, when Mrs. Cordoza stood to leave. She felt a sense of loss at her imminent departure.

"Just let me know what you decide to do." Mrs. Cordoza replied as she pulled on her coat. She looked steadily at Jennifer, her mouth compressed into a line of anxiety, and Jennifer, on impulse, stepped forward and hugged her. Mrs. Cordoza's arms reached round her and held her tightly, as if she was trying to imbue Jennifer with strength, and had understood how much she had needed to feel that from someone. They stood like that in the middle of the room for several moments. Then, perhaps a little embarrassed, the housekeeper disengaged herself. Her nose was pink.

"I'm not going back," Jennifer said, hearing her words hit the still air with unexpected force. "I'll find somewhere for us to live. But I'm not going back."

The older woman nodded.

"I'll ring you tomorrow." She scribbled a note on a piece of hotel writing paper. "You can tell him where we are. It's probably best that he knows."

That night, after she had put Esmé to bed, she rang all the news-papers in Fleet Street to ask if she could send messages to their cor-respondents on the off chance that they might run into Anthony in central Africa. She telephoned an uncle who, she remembered, had once worked out there, and asked if he could recall the names of any hotels. She had placed calls with the international operator to two hotels, one in Brazzaville, the other in Stanleyville, and left messages with receptionists, one of whom told her mournfully, "Madam, we have no white people here. There is trouble in our city."

"Please," she said, "just remember his name. Anthony O'Hare. Tell him 'Boot.' He'll know what it means."

She had sent another letter to the newspaper to be forwarded to him:

I'm sorry. Please come back to me. I'm free, and I'm waiting for you.

She had handed it over at Reception, telling herself as she did so that once it was gone, it was gone. She mustn't think about its prog-ress, mustn't imagine over the next days or weeks where it lay. She had done what she could, and now it was time to focus on building a new life, ready for when one of the many messages reached him.

The estate agent was grinning again. It seemed a reflexive, rictus thing, and she tried to ignore it. It was the eleventh day.

"If you could just put your signature there"—Mr. Grosvenor pointed with a beautifully manicured finger—"and there. Then, of course, we'll need your husband's signature here." He smiled again, his lips wavering a little.

"Oh, you'll need to send them to him directly," she said. Around them, the tearoom of the Regent Hotel was filled with women, retired gentlemen, anyone diverted from shopping by a wet Wednesday af-ternoon.

"I beg your pardon?"

"I no longer live with my husband. We communicate by letter."

That floored him. The grin disappeared, and he snatched at the papers on his lap, as if he was trying to regroup his thoughts.

"I believe I have already given you his home address. There." She pointed to one of the letters in the folder. "And we'll be able to move in next Monday, will we? My daughter and I are wearying of hotel living."

Outside, somewhere, Mrs. Cordoza was taking Esmé to the swings. She came daily now, during the hours that Laurence was at his office: "There's so little to do in that house without you," she had said. Jennifer had seen the older woman's face light up when she held Esmé, and sensed that she far preferred being with them in the hotel than in the empty house on the square.

Mr. Grosvenor's brow knitted. "Ah, Mrs. Stirling, may I just establish . . . Are you saying you will not be living in the property with Mr. Stirling? It's just that the landlord is a respectable gentleman. He was under the impression that he would be letting to a family."

"He is letting to a family."

"But you just said—"

"Mr. Grosvenor, we will be paying twenty-four pounds a week for this short let. I am a married woman. I'm sure a gentleman like you would agree that how often, and indeed whether, my husband resides there with me is nobody's business but our own."

His raised palm was conciliatory, a flush staining the skin around his collar. He began to stutter an apology: "It's just—"

He was interrupted by a woman calling her name urgently. Jennifer shifted in her chair to see Yvonne Moncrieff stalking across the crowded tearoom, her wet umbrella already thrust at an unsuspecting waiter. "So you're here!"

"Yvonne, I—"

"Where have you been? I've had absolutely no idea what was going on. I got out of hospital last week, and your ruddy housekeeper wouldn't tell me a damned thing. And then Francis says—" She stopped, having realized how far her voice had carried. The tearoom had hushed, and the faces around them were agog.

"Will you excuse us, Mr. Grosvenor? I do believe we've finished," Jennifer said.

He was already standing, had gathered his briefcase, and now snapped it shut emphatically. "I'll get those papers to Mr. Stirling this afternoon. And I'll be in touch." He made his way toward the lobby.

When he had gone, Jennifer put a hand on her friend's arm. "I'm sorry," she said. "There's an awful lot to explain. Have you got time to come upstairs?"

Yvonne Moncrieff had spent four weeks in hospital: two weeks before and two weeks after the birth of baby Alice. She had been so poleaxed by exhaustion when she'd returned home that it had taken her a further week to work out how long it had been since she had seen Jennifer. She had called twice next door, to be told only that Mrs. Stirling was not there at present. A week later she had decided to find out what was going on. "Your housekeeper just kept shaking her head at me, telling me I had to speak to Larry."

"I suppose he'll have told her not to say anything."

"About what?" Yvonne threw her coat onto the bed, and sat down on one of the upholstered chairs. "Why on earth are you staying here? Have you and Larry had a row?"

There were mauve shadows under Yvonne's eyes, but her hair was immaculate still. She already seemed strangely distant, a relic from another life, Jennifer thought. "I've left him," she said.

Yvonne's large eyes traveled over her face. "Larry got drunk at ours the night before last. Very drunk. I assumed it was business and went up to bed with the baby, leaving the men to it. When Francis came up I was half asleep, but I heard him say that Larry had told him you have a lover, and that you'd taken leave of your senses. I thought I must have dreamed it."

"Well," she said slowly, "part of that is true."

Yvonne's hand flew to her mouth. "Oh, Lord."

Jennifer shook her head, raised a smile. "Yvonne, I've missed you awfully. I so wanted to talk to you . . ." She told her friend the story, bypassing some of the details but allowing most of the truth to come out. It was Yvonne, after all. The simple words, echoing in the still room, seemed to belie the enormity of what she had gone through over the past weeks. Everything had changed; everything. She finished with a flourish: "I'll find him again. I know I will. I just have to explain."

Yvonne had been listening intently, and Jennifer was struck by how much she had missed her acerbic, straight-talking presence.

Finally Yvonne smiled tentatively. "I'm sure he'd forgive you," she said.

"What?"

"Larry. I'm sure he'd forgive you."

"*Larry?*" Jennifer sat back.

"Yes."

"But I don't want to be forgiven."

"You can't do this, Jenny."

"He has a mistress."

"Oh, you can get rid of her! She's just his secretary, for goodness' sake. Tell him you want to make a fresh start. Tell him that's what he has to do, too."

Jennifer almost stumbled over the words. "But I don't want him, Yvonne. I don't want to be married to him."

"You'd rather wait for some penniless playboy reporter who might not even come back?"

"Yes. I would."

Yvonne reached into her handbag, lit a cigarette, and blew a long plume of smoke into the center of the room.

"What about Esmé?"

"What *about* Esmé?"

"How is she going to cope, growing up with no father?"

"She will have a father. She'll see him all the time. In fact, she's going to stay there this weekend. I wrote to him, and he has written back, confirming it."

"You know the children of divorced parents get terribly teased at school. The Allsop girl is in an awful state."

"We're not getting divorced. None of her school friends need to know anything."

Yvonne was still pulling determinedly at her cigarette.

Jennifer's voice softened. "Please try to understand. There's no reason why Laurence and I shouldn't live apart. Society is changing. We don't have to be trapped in something that . . . I'm sure Laurence will be far happier without me. And it doesn't have to affect anything. Not really. You and I can stay the same. In fact, I was thinking perhaps we could get the children together this week. Perhaps take them to Madame Tussaud's. I know Esmé's desperate to see Dottie . . ."

"Madame Tussaud's?"

"Or Kew Gardens. It's just that the weather—"

"Stop." Yvonne raised an elegant hand. "Just stop. I can't listen to another word. My goodness. You really are the most extraordinarily selfish woman I've ever met."

She stubbed out her cigarette, stood up, and reached for her coat. "What do you think life is, Jennifer? Some kind of fairy tale? You think we don't all get fed up with our husbands? Why should you behave like that and expect us just to carry on around you while you gad about as if—as if you weren't even married? If you want to live in a state of moral degeneracy, that's fine. But you have a child. A husband and a child. And you can't expect the rest of us to condone your behavior."

Jennifer's mouth opened.

Yvonne turned away, as if she couldn't even look at her. "And I won't be the only one who feels like this. I suggest you think very carefully about what you do next." She tucked her coat over her arm and left.

Three hours later, Jennifer had made her decision.

At midday the Embakasi airport was a mêlée of activity. Having picked up her suitcase from the stuttering conveyor belt, Jennifer fought her way to the lavatory, splashed cold water over her face, and changed into a clean blouse. She pinned back her hair, the heat already moistening her neck. When she emerged, her blouse was stuck to her back within seconds.

The airport was teeming with people who stood in unruly queues or in groups, shouting at one another in place of conversation. She was briefly paralyzed, watching brightly clad African women jostle with suitcases and huge laundry bags, bound with rope, balanced on their heads. Nigerian businessmen smoked in the corners, their skin shining, while small children ran in and out of those seated on the floor. A woman with a small barrow pushed her way through, selling drinks. The departure boards revealed that several flights were delayed and gave no clue as to when that might be rectified.

In contrast to the noise in the airport building, it was peaceful outside. The last of the bad weather had cleared, the heat burning off any remaining damp so that Jennifer could see the purple mountains in the distance. The runway was empty, except for the plane she had arrived on; beneath it, a solitary man was sweeping meditatively. On the other side of the gleaming modernistic building somebody had built a small rock garden, dotted with cacti and succulents. She admired the carefully arranged boulders, and wondered that someone should have taken so much trouble in such a chaotic place.

The BOAC and East African Airways desks were shut, so she fought her way back through the crowd, ordered a cup of coffee at the bar, grabbed a table, and sat down, hemmed in by other people's suitcases, woven baskets, and a baleful cockerel, its wings bound to its body with a school tie.

What would she say to him? She pictured him in some foreign correspondents' club, perhaps miles from the real action, where journalists gathered to drink and discuss the day's events. Would he be drinking? It was a tight little world, he had told her. Once she got to Stanleyville someone would know him. Someone would be able to tell her where he was. She pictured herself arriving, exhausted, at the club, a recurring image that had kept her going for the last few days. She could see him so clearly, standing under a whirring fan, perhaps chatting to a colleague, and then his amazement at the sight of her. She understood his expression: for the last forty-eight hours she had barely been able to recognize herself.

Nothing in her life had prepared her for what she had done; nothing had suggested she might even be capable of it. And yet, from the moment she had climbed aboard the aircraft, for all her fear, she had felt curiously elated, as if this might be it: this might be the business of living. And if only for that moment of intense feeling she felt a curious kinship with Anthony O'Hare.

She would find him. She had taken charge of events, rather than allowing herself to be buffeted along by them. She would decide her own future. She banished thoughts of Esmé, telling herself that this will have been worthwhile when she'd be able to introduce Anthony to her.

Eventually a young man in a smart burgundy uniform took a seat at the BOAC counter. She left her coffee where it was and half ran across the concourse to the counter.

"I need a ticket to Stanleyville," she said, scrabbling in her handbag for money. "The next flight out. Do you need my passport?"

The young man stared at her. "No, madam," he said, his head moving briskly from side to side. "No flying to Stanleyville."

"But I was told you ran a direct route."

"I'm very sorry. All flights to Stanleyville are suspended."

She gazed at him in mute frustration until he repeated himself, then dragged her suitcase across to the EAA desk. The girl there had the same answer. "No, ma'am. There are no flights out because of the troubles." She rolled every r. "Only flights coming in."

"Well, when are they going to start up again? I need to get to Congo urgently."

The two staff members exchanged a silent look. "No flights to Congo," they repeated.

She hadn't come this far for blank looks and refusals. *I cannot give up on him now.*

Outside, the man continued up and down the runway with his threadbare broom.

It was then that she saw a white man with the upright posture of the civil service walking briskly through the terminal, carrying a leather folder. Sweat had colored a deep triangle on the back of his cream linen jacket.

He saw her as she saw him. He changed direction and strode toward her. "Mrs. Ramsey?" He held out a hand. "I'm Alexander Frobisher, from the consulate. Where are your children?"

"No. My name is Jennifer Stirling."

He closed his mouth and seemed to be trying to gauge whether she had made a mistake. His face was puffy, perhaps adding years to his true age.

"I do need your help, Mr. Frobisher," she continued. "I have to get to Congo. Do you know if there's a train I can catch? I'm told there are no flights. Actually, nobody will tell me very much at all." She was conscious that her own face was glowing with heat, that her hair had already started to come down.

When he spoke, it was as if he was trying to explain something to the unhinged. "Mrs. . . ."

"Stirling."

"Mrs. Stirling, nobody is going into Congo. Don't you know there's—"

"Yes, I do know there's been some trouble there. But I have to find someone, a journalist, who came out perhaps two weeks ago. It's terrifically important. His name is—"

"Madam, there are no journalists left in Congo." He removed his glasses and steered her to the window. "Do you have any idea what has happened?"

"A little. Well, no, I've been traveling from England. I had to take a rather tortuous route."

"The war has now dragged in the U.S. as well as our and other governments. Until three days ago we were in crisis, with three hundred and fifty white hostages, including women and children, facing execution by the Simba rebels. We have Belgian troops fighting it out with them in the streets of Stanleyville. Up to a hundred civilians are already reported dead."

She barely heard him. "But I can pay—and I'll pay whatever it takes. I have to get there."

He took her arm. "Mrs. Stirling, I'm telling you that you will not make it to Congo. There are no trains, no flights, no roads in. The troops were airlifted. Even if there was transport, I could not sanction a British citizen—a British woman—entering a war zone." He scribbled in his notebook. "I'll find you somewhere to wait and help you book your return flight. Africa is no place for a white woman on her own." He sighed wearily, as she had just doubled his burden.

Jennifer was thinking. "How many are dead?"

"We don't know."

"Have you their names?"

"I only have the most rudimentary list at the moment. It's far from comprehensive."

"Please." Her heart had almost stopped. "Please let me see. I need to know if he's . . ."

He pulled a tattered piece of typed paper from his folder.

She scanned it, her eyes so tired that the names, in alphabetical order, blurred. Harper. Hambro. O'Keefe. Lewis. His was not there.

His was not there.

She glanced up at Frobisher. "Do you have the names of those taken hostage?"

"Mrs. Stirling, we have no idea how many British citizens were even in the city. Look." He produced another piece of paper and handed it to her, swatting with his free hand at a mosquito that had landed on the back of his neck. "This is the latest communiqué sent to Lord Walston."

She started to read, phrases leaping out at her:

> *Five thousand dead in Stanleyville alone . . . We believe that there remain in rebel-held territory twenty-seven United Kingdom citizens . . . We can give no indication as to when the areas where British subjects are, even if we knew them with any degree of exactness, will be reached.*

"There are Belgian and U.S. troops in the city. They are taking back Stanleyville. And we have a Beverley aircraft standing by to rescue those who want to be rescued."

"How can I make sure that he's on it?"

He scratched his head. "You can't. Some people don't seem to want to be rescued. Some prefer to stay in Congo. They may have their reasons."

She thought suddenly of the fat news editor. *Who knows? Perhaps he wanted to get away.*

"If your friend wants to get out, he will get out," he said. He wiped his face with a handkerchief. "If he wants to stay, it's perfectly possible that he'll disappear—easily done in Congo."

She was about to speak but was cut off by a low murmur that rippled through the airport as, through the arrival gates, a family emerged. First came two small children, mute, with bandaged arms, heads, their faces prematurely aged. A blond woman, clutching a baby, was wild-eyed, her hair unwashed and her face etched with strain. At the sight of them a much older woman broke free of her husband's restraining arm and burst through the barrier, wailing, and pulled them to her. The family barely stirred. Then the young mother, crumpling to her knees, began to cry, her mouth a great O of pain, her head sagging onto the older woman's plump shoulder.

Frobisher stuffed his papers back into his folder. "The Ramseys. Excuse me. I must look after them."

"Were they there?" she said, watching the grandfather hoist the little girl onto his shoulders. "At the massacre?" The children's faces, immobilized by some unknown shock, had turned her blood to ice water.

He gave her a firm look. "Mrs. Stirling, please, you must go now. There's an East African Airways flight out this evening. Unless you have well-connected friends in this city, I cannot urge you more strongly to be on it."

It took her two days to get home. And from that point her new life began. Yvonne was true to her word. She did not contact her again, and on the one occasion Jennifer bumped into Violet, the other woman was so plainly filled with discomfort that it seemed unfair to pursue her. She minded less than she might have expected: they belonged to an old life, which she hardly recognized as her own.

Most days Mrs. Cordoza came to the new flat, finding excuses to spend time with Esmé, or help with a few household tasks, and Jennifer found she relied more on her former housekeeper's company than she had on that of her old friends. One wet afternoon, while Esmé slept, she told Mrs. Cordoza about Anthony, and Mrs. Cordoza confided a little more about her husband. Then, with a blush, she talked about a nice man who had sent her flowers from the restaurant two streets along. "I wasn't going to encourage him," she said softly, into her ironing, "but since everything . . ."

Laurence communicated in notes, using Mrs. Cordoza as an emissary.

I would like to take Esmé to my cousin's wedding in Winchester this coming Saturday. I will make sure she is back by 7 p.m.

They were distant, formal, measured. Occasionally Jennifer would read them and wonder that she could have been married to this man.

Every week she walked to the post office on Langley Street to find out whether there was anything in the PO box. Every week she returned home trying not to feel flattened by the postmistress's "No."

She moved into the rented flat, and when Esmé started school, she took an unpaid job at the local Citizens' Advice Bureau, the only organization that seemed unworried by her lack of experience. She would learn on the job, the supervisor said. "And, believe me, you'll learn rather quickly." Less than a year later, she was offered a paid position in the same office. She advised people on practical matters, such as how to manage money, how to handle rent disputes—there were too many bad landlords—how to cope with family breakdown.

At first she had been exhausted by the never-ending litany of problems, the sheer wall of human misery that traipsed through the office, but gradually, as she grew more confident, she saw that she was not alone in making a mess of her life. She reassessed herself and found that she was grateful for where she was, where she had ended up, and felt a certain pride when someone returned to tell her that she had helped.

Two years later she and Esmé moved again, to the two-bedroom flat in St. John's Wood, bought with money provided by Laurence and Jennifer's inheritance from an aunt. As the weeks became months, and then years, she came to accept that Anthony O'Hare would not return. He would not answer her messages. She was overcome only once, when the newspapers reported some details of the massacre at Stanleyville's Victoria Hotel. Then she had stopped reading newspapers altogether.

She had rung the *Nation* just once more. A secretary had answered, and when she gave her name, briefly hopeful that Anthony might, this time, happen to be there, she heard, "Is it that Stirling woman?"

And the answer: "Isn't she the one he didn't want to speak to?"

She had replaced the receiver.

It was seven years before she saw her husband again. Esmé was to start at boarding school, a sprawling, red-brick place in Hampshire, with the shambolic air of a well-loved country house. Jennifer had taken the afternoon off work to drive her, and they had traveled in her new Mini. She was wearing a wine-colored suit and had half expected Laurence to make an unpleasant comment about it—he never had liked her in that color. Please don't do it in front of Esmé, she willed him. Please let's keep this civil.

But the man sitting in the lobby was nothing like the Laurence she remembered. In fact, at first she didn't recognize him. His skin was gray, his cheeks hollow; he seemed to have aged twenty years.

"Hello, Daddy." Esmé hugged him.

He nodded to Jennifer, but did not stretch out a hand. "Jennifer," he said.

"Laurence." She was trying to cover her shock.

The meeting was brief. The headmistress, a young woman possessed of a quietly assessing gaze, made no reference to the fact that they lived at separate addresses. Perhaps more people did now, Jennifer thought. That week she had seen four women in the bureau who were seeking to leave their husbands.

"Well, we'll do everything in our power to make sure Esmé's time here is happy," Mrs. Browning said. She had kind eyes, Jennifer thought. "It does help if the girls have chosen to come to boarding school, and I understand she already has friends here, so I'm sure she'll settle in quickly."

"She reads rather a lot of Enid Blyton," Jennifer said. "I suspect she thinks it's all midnight feasts."

"Oh, we have a few of those. The tuck shop is open on Friday afternoons pretty much for that sole purpose. We tend to turn a blind eye, provided it doesn't get too lively. We like the girls to feel there are some advantages to boarding."

Jennifer relaxed. Laurence had chosen the school, and her fears seemed unfounded. The next few weeks would be hard, but she had grown used to Esmé's periodic absences when she was staying with Laurence, and she had her work to occupy her.

The headmistress got to her feet and held out a hand. "Thank you. We'll telephone, of course, if there are any problems."

As the door closed behind them, Laurence began to cough, a harsh, hacking sound that made Jennifer's jaw clench. She made to say something, but he lifted a hand as if to tell her not to. They made their way slowly down the stairs side by side, as if they were not estranged. She could have walked at twice the speed, but it seemed cruel to do so, given his labored breathing and evident discomfort. Finally, unable to bear it, she stopped a passing girl and asked if she would mind fetching a glass of water. Within minutes the girl returned, and Laurence sat down heavily on a mahogany chair in the paneled corridor to sip it.

Jennifer was now brave enough to let her eyes rest on him. "Is it . . . ?" she said.

"No." He took a long, painful breath. "It's the cigars, apparently. I'm well aware of the irony."

She took the seat beside him.

"You should know I've ensured that you will both be taken care of."

She glanced sideways at him, but he appeared to be thinking.

"We raised a good child," he said eventually.

Out of the window, they could see Esmé chatting to two other girls on the lawn. As if at some unheard signal, the three ran across the grass, their skirts flying.

"I'm sorry," she said, turning back to him. "For everything."

He placed the glass at his side, and hauled himself out of the chair. He stood for a minute, with his back to her, focusing on the girls outside the window, then turned toward her and, without meeting her eye, gave a small nod.

She watched him walk stiffly out of the main door across the lawns to where his lady friend was waiting in the car, his daughter skipping beside him. She waved enthusiastically as the chauffeur-driven Daimler made its way back down the drive.

Two months later Laurence was dead.

Chapter 22

OCTOBER 2003

It has not stopped raining all evening, the dark gray clouds scudding across the city skyline until they're swallowed by night. The relentless downpour confines people to their homes, blanketing the street so that all that is audible outside is the occasional swish of tires on a wet road, or the gurgle of swollen drains, or the brisk footsteps of someone trying to get home.

There are no messages on her answering machine, no winking envelopes suggesting a text message on her mobile. Her e-mails are confined to work, advertisements for generic Viagra, and one from her mother detailing the dog's further recovery from its hip replacement. Ellie sits cross-legged on the sofa, sipping her third glass of red wine and rereading the photocopies of the letters she has returned. It is four hours since she left Jennifer Stirling's apartment, but her mind is still humming. She sees the unknown Boot, reckless and heartbroken, in Congo at a time when white Europeans were being slain. "I read the reports of the murders, of a whole hotel of victims in Stanleyville," Jennifer had said, "and I cried with fear." She pictures her walking to the post office week after week on a vain quest for a letter that never arrives. A tear plops onto her sleeve, and she sniffs as she wipes it away.

Theirs, she thinks, was a love affair that meant something. He was a man who cracked himself open in front of the woman he loved; he sought to understand her and tried to protect her, even from herself. When he couldn't have her, he removed himself to the other side of the world and, quite likely, sacrificed himself. And she mourned him for forty years. What did Ellie have? Great sex, perhaps once every ten days, and a host of noncommittal e-mails. She is thirty-two years old, her career is collapsing around her, her friends know she is heading full pelt down an emotional dead end, and every day it is getting harder to convince herself that this is a life she would have chosen.

It's a quarter past nine. She knows she shouldn't drink any more, but she feels angry, mournful, nihilistic. She pours another glass, cries, and rereads the last letter again. Like Jennifer, she now feels she knows these words by heart. They have an awful resonance.

Being without you—thousands of miles from you—offers no relief at all. The fact that I am no longer tormented by your presence, or presented with daily evidence of my inability to have the one thing I truly desire, has not healed me. It has made things worse. My future feels like a bleak, empty road.

She is half in love with this man herself. She pictures John, hears him saying the words, and alcohol makes the two blur into each other. How does one lift one's own life out of the mundane and into something epic? Surely one should be brave enough to love? She pulls her mobile phone from her bag, something dark and bold creeping under her skin. She flips it open and sends a text, her fingers clumsy on the keys:

Please call. Just once. Need to hear from you. X

She presses send, already knowing what a colossal error she has made. He'll be furious. Or he won't respond. She's not sure which is worse. Ellie's head sinks into her hands, and she weeps for the unknown Boot, for Jennifer, for chances missed and a life wasted. She cries for herself, because nobody will ever love her like he loved Jennifer, and because she suspects that she is spoiling what might have been a perfectly good, if ordinary, life. She cries because she is drunk and in her flat and there are few advantages to living on your own except being able to sob uninhibitedly at will.

She starts when she hears the door buzzer, lifting her head and remaining immobile until it sounds again. For a brief, insane moment, she wonders if it's John, in response to her message. Suddenly galvanized, she rushes to the hall mirror, wiping frantically at the red blotches on her face, and picks up the entry phone. "Hello?"

"Okay, smarty-pants. How do you spell 'uninvited random caller'?"

She blinks. "Rory."

"Nope, that's not it."

She bites her lip and leans against the wall. There is a brief silence.

"Are you busy? I was just passing." He sounds merry, exuberant. "Okay . . . I was on the right Tube line."

"Come up." She hangs up the phone and splashes her face with cold water, trying not to feel disappointed when it so obviously couldn't have been John.

She hears him taking the steps two at a time, then pushing at the door she has left ajar.

"I've come to drag you out for a drink. Oh!" He's eyeing the empty wine bottle, and then, for a fraction longer, her face. "Ah. Too late."

She manages an unconvincing smile. "Not been a great evening."

"Ah."

"It's fine if you want to go." He's wearing a gray scarf. It looks like cashmere. She has never owned a cashmere jumper. How has she reached the age of thirty-two and never owned a cashmere jumper? "Actually, I'm probably not great company right now."

He takes another look at the wine bottle. "Well, Haworth," he says, unwinding the scarf from his neck, "it's never stopped me before. How about I stick the kettle on?"

He makes tea, fumbling to locate tea bags, milk, spoons, in her tiny kitchen. She thinks of John, who just last week had done the same thing, and her eyes fill again with tears. Then Rory sits and places the mug in front of her, and as she drinks it he talks uncharacteristically volubly about his day, the friend he has just met for a drink who suggested some oblique route across Patagonia. The friend—he has known him since childhood—has become something of a competitive traveler. "You know the type. You say you're headed for Peru. He says, 'Oh, forget the Machu Picchu trail, I spent three nights with the pygmies of Atacanta jungle. They fed me one of their relatives when we ran out of baboon meat.' "

"Nice." She's curled up on the sofa, cradling her mug.

"I love the guy, but I'm just not sure I can take six months of him."

"That's how long you're going for?"

"Hopefully."

She's buffeted by another groundswell of misery. Granted, Rory isn't John, but it has been some compensation to have a man to call on for the odd evening out.

"So, what's up?" he says.

"Oh . . . I had a weird day."

"It's Saturday. I assumed girls like you went out gossiping over brunch and shopping for shoes."

"No stereotypes there, then. I went to see Jennifer Stirling."

"Who?"

"The letter lady."

She sees his surprise. He leans forward. "Wow. She actually called you. What happened?"

Suddenly she begins to cry again, tears pouring. "I'm sorry," she mutters, scrambling for tissues. "I'm sorry. I don't know why I'm being so ridiculous."

She feels his hand on her shoulder, an arm around her. He smells of the pub, deodorant, clean hair, and the outside. "Hey," he's saying softly, "hey . . . this isn't like you."

How would you know? she thinks. Nobody knows what is like me. I'm not even sure I know. "She told me everything. The whole love affair. Oh, Rory, it's heartbreaking. They loved each other so much, and they kept missing each other until he died in Africa and she

never saw him again." She's crying so hard her words are nearly unin-
telligible.

He's hugging her, his head dipping to catch the words. "Talking
to an old lady made you this sad? A failed love affair from forty
years ago?"

"You had to be there. You had to hear what she said." She tells
him a little of the story and wipes her eyes. "She's so beautiful and
graceful and sad . . ."

"You're beautiful and graceful and sad. Okay, perhaps not graceful."

She rests her head against his shoulder.

"I never thought you were . . . Don't take this the wrong way, Ellie,
but you've surprised me. I never would have thought you could be that
affected by those letters."

"It's not just the letters." She sniffs.

He waits. He's leaning back on the sofa now, but his hand is still
resting lightly on her neck. She realizes she doesn't want it to move.
"Then . . . ?" His voice is soft, inquisitive.

"I'm afraid . . ."

"Of?"

Her voice drops to a whisper: "I'm afraid nobody will ever love me
like that."

Drunkenness has made her reckless. His eyes have softened, his
mouth turns down a little, as if in sympathy. He watches her, and she
dabs feebly at her eyes. For a moment she thinks he's going to kiss her,
but instead he picks up a letter and reads aloud:

> On my way home this evening, I got caught in a row that spilled out
> of a public house. Two men were scrapping, egged on by drunken sup-
> porters, and suddenly I was caught up in their noise and chaos, the curs-
> ing and flying bottles. A police siren sounded in the distance. Men were
> flying off in all directions, cars screeching across the road to avoid the fight.
> And all I could think about was the way the corner of your mouth curves
> into itself when you smile. And I had this remarkable sensation that, at
> that precise moment, you were thinking about me, too.
>
> Perhaps this sounds fanciful; perhaps you were thinking about the

theater, or the crisis in the economy, or whether to buy new curtains. But I realized suddenly, in the midst of that little tableau of insanity, that to have someone out there who understands you, who desires you, who sees you as a better version of yourself, is the most astonishing gift. Even if we are not together, to know that, for you, I am that man is a source of sustenance to me.

She has closed her eyes to listen to Rory's voice, softly reciting the words. She imagines how Jennifer must have felt to be loved, adored, wanted.

I'm not sure how I earned the right. I don't feel entirely confident of it even now. But even the chance to think upon your beautiful face, your smile, and know that some part of it might belong to me is probably the single greatest thing that has happened to me in my life.

The words have stopped. She opens her eyes to find Rory's a few inches away. "For a smart woman," he says, "you're remarkably dim." He reaches out a hand, wipes away a tear with his thumb.

"You don't know . . . ," she begins. "You don't understand . . ."

"I think I know enough." Before she can speak again, he kisses her. She stalls for just a moment, and that freckled hand is there again, tormenting her. *Why should I feel loyalty to someone who's probably having wild holiday sex right at this very minute?*

And then Rory's mouth is on hers, his hands cradling her face, and she's kissing him back, her mind determinedly blank, her body simply grateful for the arms that enfold her, his lips upon hers. *Blank it all out,* she begs him silently. *Rewrite this page.* She shifts, feeling vague surprise that for all her desperate longing, she can want this man very much. And then she's unable to think of anything at all.

She wakes up gazing at a set of dark eyelashes. What very dark eyelashes, she thinks, in the few seconds before consciousness properly seeps in; John's are a caramel color. He has one white lash, toward the outer edge of his left eye, which she is pretty sure no one but her has ever noticed.

Birds are singing. A car is revving insistently outside. There is an arm across her naked hip. It's surprisingly heavy, and when she shifts, a hand tightens momentarily on her bottom, as if reflexively unwilling to let her go. She stares at the eyelashes, remembering the events of the previous evening. She and Rory on the floor in front of her sofa. Him fetching the duvet when he noticed she was cold. His hair, rich and soft in her hands, his body, surprisingly broad, above hers, her bed, his head, disappearing under the duvet. She feels a vague thrill of knowledge and cannot yet quite determine how she feels about this.

John.

A text message.

Coffee, she thinks, grasping for safety. Coffee and croissants. She eases herself out of his hold, her eyes still fixed on his sleeping face. She lifts his arm, lays it gently on the sheet. He wakes, and she freezes. She sees her own confusion momentarily mirrored in his eyes.

"Hey," he says, his voice hoarse with lack of sleep. What time had they finally slept? Four? Five? She remembers them giggling because it was growing light outside. He rubs his face, shifts heavily onto one elbow. His hair is sticking up at one side, his chin shadowed and rough. "What time is it?"

"Almost nine. I'm going to nip out for some proper coffee." She backs to the door, conscious of her nakedness in the too bright morning.

"You sure?" he calls, as she disappears. "You don't want me to go?"

"No, no." She's hopping into the jeans she discovers outside the living-room door. "I'm fine."

"Black for me, please." She hears him sink back against the pillows, muttering something about his head.

Her knickers are half under the DVD player. She picks them up hastily, stuffs them into a pocket. She hauls a T-shirt over her head, wraps herself in her jacket, and without pausing to see what she looks like, heads down the stairs. She walks briskly toward the local coffee shop, already dialing a number into her mobile phone.

Wake up. Pick up the phone.

By now she's standing in the queue. Nicky picks up on the third ring.

"Ellie?"

"Oh, God, Nicky. I've done something awful." She lowers her voice, shielding it from the family that has walked in behind her. The father is silent, the mother trying to shepherd two small children to a table. Their pale, shadowed faces speak of a night of lost sleep.

"Hang on. I'm at the gym. Let me take this outside."

The gym? At nine o'clock on a Sunday morning? She hears Nicky's voice against the traffic of some distant street. "Awful as in what? Murder? Rape of a minor? You didn't call up thingy's wife and tell her you were his mistress?"

"I slept with that bloke from work."

A brief pause. She looks up to find the barista staring at her, eyebrows raised. She places her hand over her phone. "Oh. Two tall Americanos, please, one with milk, and croissants. Two—no, three."

"Library Man?"

"Yes. He turned up last night and I was drunk and feeling really crap and he read out one of those love letters and . . . I don't know . . ."

"So?"

"So I slept with someone else!"

"Was it awful?"

Rory's eyes, crinkled with amusement. His head bent over her breasts. Kisses. Endless, endless kisses.

"No. It was . . . quite good. Really good."

"And your problem is?"

"I'm meant to be sleeping with John."

The barista girl is exchanging looks with Exhausted Father. She realizes they are both silently agog. "Six pounds sixty-three," the girl says, with a small smile.

She reaches into her pocket for change and finds herself holding

out last night's knickers. Exhausted Father coughs—or it might have
been a splutter of laughter. She apologizes, her face burning, hands
over the money, and moves to the end of the counter, waiting for her
coffee with her head down.

"Nicky . . ."

"Oh, for God's sake, Ellie. You've been sleeping with a married
man who is almost definitely still sleeping with his wife. He makes
you no promises, hardly takes you anywhere, isn't planning on leaving
her—"

"You don't know that."

"I do know that. I'm sorry, sweetie, but I'd put my too-small expensively mortgaged house on it. And if you're telling me you've just
had great sex with a nice bloke who's single and likes you and seems
to want to spend time with you, I'm not going to start begging for
Prozac. Okay?"

"Okay," she says quietly.

"Now, go back to your flat, wake him up and have mad hot mon-
key sex with him, then meet me and Corinne tomorrow morning at
the café and tell us everything."

She smiles. How nice to celebrate being with someone, instead of
having perpetually to justify them.

She thinks of Rory lying in her bed. Rory of the very long eyelashes and soft kisses. Would it be so very bad to spend the morning
with him? She picks up the coffee and walks back to her flat, surprised by how quickly her legs are working.

"Don't move!" she calls, as she comes up the stairs, kicking off her
shoes. "I'm bringing you breakfast in bed." She dumps the coffee on
the floor outside the bathroom and dives in, wipes the mascara from
under her eyes and splashes her face with cold water, then spritzes
herself with perfume. As an afterthought she flips the lid off the
toothpaste and bites off a pea-sized lump, swilling it around her
mouth.

"This is so you can no longer think of me as a heartless, selfish abuser of men. And also so you owe me coffee at work. I will, of course, return to my heartless, self-centerd self tomorrow."

She leaves the bathroom, stoops to pick up the coffee, and, smiling, steps into her bedroom. The bed is empty, the duvet turned back. He can't be in the bathroom—she's just been in there. "Rory?" she says, into the silence.

"Here."

His voice comes from the living room. She pads down the hall. "You were meant to stay in bed," she admonishes him. "It's hardly breakfast in bed if you—"

He's standing in the center of the room, pulling on his jacket. He's dressed, shoes on, hair no longer sticking up.

She stops in the doorway. He doesn't look at her.

"What are you doing?" She holds out the coffee. "I thought we were going to have breakfast."

"Yes. Well, I think I'd better go."

She feels something cold creeping across her. Something's wrong here.

"Why?" she says, trying to smile. "I've hardly been gone fifteen minutes. Do you really have an appointment at twenty past nine on a Sunday morning?"

He stares at his feet, apparently checking in his pockets for his keys. He finds them and turns them over in his hand. When he finally looks up at her, his face is blank. "You had a phone call when you were out. He left a message. I didn't mean to eavesdrop, but it's pretty hard not to in a small flat."

Ellie feels something cold and hard settle in the pit of her stomach. "Rory, I—"

He holds up a hand. "I told you once I didn't do complicated. That would—um—include sleeping with someone who's sleeping with someone else." He steps past her, ignoring the coffee she's holding. "I'll see you around, Ellie."

She hears his footsteps fading down the stairs. He doesn't slam the door, but there's an uncomfortable air of finality in the way it closes. She feels numb. She places the coffee carefully on the table, and then, after a minute, steps over to the answering machine and presses play.

John's voice, low and mellifluous, fills the room. "Ellie, I can't talk for long. Just wanted to check you're okay. Not sure what you meant last night. I miss you, too. I miss us. But look . . . please don't text. It's . . ." A short sigh. "Look. I'll message you as soon as we . . . as soon as I get home." The sound of the receiver clicking down.

Ellie lets his words reverberate in the silent flat, then sinks onto the sofa and remains perfectly still, while the coffee grows cold beside her.

Chapter 23

FAO: Phillip O'Hare, phillipohare@thetimes.co.uk
From: Ellie Haworth, elliehaworth@thenation.co.uk

Excuse me for contacting you like this, but I'm hoping that as a fellow journalist you will understand. I am trying to trace an Anthony O'Hare who I guess would be the same age as your father, and in a *Times* column of last May you happened to mention that you had a father of the same name.

This Anthony O'Hare would have spent some time in London during the early 1960s, and a lot of time abroad, especially in central Africa, where he may have died. I know very little about him other than he had a son with the same name as you.

If you are he, or know what became of him, would you please e-mail me? There is a mutual acquaintance who knew him many years ago and would dearly like to find out what became of him. I appreciate this is a long shot, as it is not an uncommon name, but I need all the help I can get.

All best

Ellie Haworth

The new building is set in a part of the city Ellie has not seen since it was a random collection of shabby warehouses, strung together with unlovely takeaway shops she would have starved rather than eaten from. Everything that was in that square mile has been razed, swept away, the congested streets replaced with vast, immaculately clad squares, metal bollards, the odd gleaming office block, many still bearing the scaffold cauls of their nascence.

They are there for an organized tour to familiarize themselves with their new desks and the new computers and telephone systems before Monday's final move. Ellie follows the Features party through the various departments while the young man with the clipboard and a badge marked "Transfer Coordinator" tells them about production areas, information hubs, and lavatories. As each new space is explained to them, Ellie watches the varying responses of her team, the excitement of some of the younger ones, who like the sleek, modernistic lines of the office. Melissa, who has clearly been there several times before, interjects occasionally with information she feels the man has left out.

"There's nowhere to hide!" jokes Rupert as he surveys the vast, clutter-free space. She can hear the ring of truth in it. Melissa's office, on the southeastern corner, is entirely glass, and overlooks the whole Features "hub." Nobody else in the department has their own office, a decision that has apparently rankled several of her colleagues.

"And this is where you'll be sitting." All the writers are on one desk, a huge oval shape, the center spewing wires that lead umbilically to a series of flat-screen computer monitors.

"Who's where?" says one of the columnists. Melissa consults her list. "I've been working on this. Some of it's still fluid. But Rupert, you're here. Arianna, there. Tim, by the chair, there. Edwina—" She points at a space. It reminds Ellie of netball at school; the relief when one was picked from the throng and allotted to one team or the other. Except nearly all of the seats are taken, and she is still standing.

"Um . . . Melissa?" she ventures. "Where am I supposed to be sitting?"

Melissa glances at another desk. "A few people will have to hot-desk. It doesn't make sense for everyone to be allocated a workstation full-time." She doesn't look at Ellie as she speaks.

Ellie feels her toes clenching in her shoes. "Are you saying I don't get my own desk area?"

"No, I'm saying some people will share a workstation."

"But I'm in every day. I don't understand how that will work." She should take Melissa to one side, ask her in private why Arianna, who has been there barely a month, should get a desk over her. She should expel the slight anguish from her voice. She should shut up. "I don't understand why I'm the only feature writer not to—"

"As I said, Ellie, things are very fluid still. There will always be a seat for you to work from. Right. Let's go on to News. They'll be moving, of course, on the same day that we do . . ." And the conversation is closed. Ellie sees that her stock has fallen far lower than even she had thought. She catches Arianna's eye, sees the new girl look away quickly, and pretends to check her phone for more nonexistent messages.

The library is no longer belowground. The new "information resource center" is two floors up, set in an atrium around a collection of oversize and suspiciously exotic potted plants. There is an island in the middle, behind which she recognizes the grumpy chief librarian, who is talking quietly with a much younger man. She stares at the shelves, which are neatly divided into digital and hard-copy areas. All the signage in the new offices is in lower case, which she suspects has given the chief subeditor an ulcer. It couldn't be more different from the dusty confines of the old archive, with its musty newspaper smell and blind corners, and she feels suddenly nostalgic.

She's not entirely sure why she has come here, except that she feels a magnetic pull to Rory, perhaps to find out if she's at least partly forgiven, or to talk to him about Melissa's desk decision. He is, she realizes, one of the few people she can discuss this with. The librarian spots her.

"Sorry," she says, holding up a hand. "Just looking around."

"If you want Rory," he says, "he's at the old building." His voice is not unfriendly.

"Thank you," she says, trying to convey something of an apology. It seems important not to alienate anybody else. "It looks great. You've . . . done an amazing job."

"Nearly finished," he says, and smiles. He looks younger when he smiles, less careworn. In his face she can see something she has never noticed before: relief, but also kindness. How wrong you can get people, she thinks.

"Can I help you with anything?"

"No, I—"

He smiles again. "Like I said, he's at the old building."

"Thank you. I'll—I'll leave you to it. I can see you're busy." She walks to a table, picks up a photocopied guide to using the library, and, folding it carefully, puts it into her bag as she leaves.

She sits at her soon-to-be-defunct desk all afternoon, typing Anthony O'Hare's name repeatedly into a search engine. She has done this numerous times, and each time is astonished by the sheer number of Anthony O'Hares that exist, or have existed, in the world. There are teenage Anthony O'Hares on networking sites, long-dead Anthony O'Hares buried in Pennsylvanian graveyards, their lives pored over by amateur genealogists. One is a physicist working in South Africa, another a self-published writer of fantasy fiction, a third the victim of an attack in a pub in Swansea. She pores over each man, checking age and identity, just in case.

Her phone chimes, which tells her of a message. She sees John's name and, confusingly, feels fleeting disappointment that it isn't Rory.

"Meeting."

Melissa's secretary is standing at her desk.

> Sorry couldn't talk much other night. Just wanted you to know
> I am missing you. Can't wait to see you. Jx

"Yes. Sorry," she says. The secretary is still beside her. "Sorry. Just coming."

She reads it again, picking apart each sentence, just to make sure that, for once, she's not pitching a mountain of unspoken meaning onto a molehill. But there it is: *Just wanted you to know I am missing you.*

She gathers up her papers and, cheeks aflame, enters the office, just in front of Rupert. It's important not to be the last in. She doesn't want to be the only writer without a seat in Melissa's office as well as outside it.

She sits in silence while the following days' features are dissected, their progress considered. The humiliations of that morning have receded. Even Arianna's having bagged an interview with a notoriously reclusive actress doesn't faze her. Her mind hums with the words that have fallen unexpectedly into her lap: *Just wanted you to know I am missing you.*

What does this mean? She hardly dares hope that what she has wished for may have come true. The suntanned wife in a bikini has effectively vanished. The phantom freckled hand with its massaging fingers is now replaced by knuckles, whitened with frustration. She now pictures John and his wife arguing their way through a holiday they have privately billed as a last-ditch attempt to save their marriage. She sees him exhausted, furious, secretly pleased to get her message even as he has to warn her against sending another.

Don't get your hopes up, she warns herself. This might be a little fillip. Everyone's sick of their partner by the end of a holiday. Perhaps he just wants to ensure he still has her loyalty. But even as she counsels herself, she knows which version she wants to believe.

"And Ellie? The love-letters story?"

Oh, Christ.

She shuffles the papers on her lap, adopts a confident tone. "Well, I've got a lot more information. I met the woman. There's definitely enough for a story."

"Good." Melissa's eyebrows lift elegantly, as if Ellie's surprised her.

"But"—Ellie swallows—"I'm not sure how much we should use. It does seem . . . a bit sensitive."

"Are they both alive?"

"No. He's dead. Or she believes he is."

"Then change the woman's name. I don't see the problem. You're using letters that she'd presumably forgotten."

"Oh, I don't think she had." Ellie tries to pick her words carefully. "In fact, she seems to remember an awful lot about them. I was thinking it would be better if I used them as a peg to examine the language of love. You know, how love letters have changed over the years."

"Without including the actual letters."

"Yes." As she answers, Ellie feels hugely relieved. She doesn't want Jennifer's letters made public. She sees her now, perched on her sofa, her face alive as she tells the story she has kept to herself for decades. She doesn't want to add to her sense of loss. "I mean, maybe I could find some other examples."

"By Tuesday."

"Well, there must be books, compilations . . ."

"You want us to publish already published material?"

The room has fallen silent around them. It is as if she and Melissa Buckingham exist in a toxic bubble. She is conscious that nothing she does will satisfy this woman anymore.

"You've been working on this for the time it takes most writers to knock out three two-thousand-word features." Melissa taps the end of her pen on her desk. "Just write the piece, Ellie." Her voice is icily weary. "Just write it up, keep it anonymous, and your contact will probably never know whose letters you're discussing. And I'm assuming, given the sheer amount of time you've now spent on this, that it's going to be something extraordinary."

Her smile, bestowed on the rest of the room, is glittering. "Right. Let's move on. I haven't had a list from Health. Has anyone got one?"

She sees him as she's leaving the building. He shares a joke with Ronald, the security guard, treads lightly down the steps, and walks away. It's raining, and he carries a small backpack, his head down against the cold.

"Hey." She jogs until she's beside him.

He glances at her. "Hey," he says neutrally. He's headed for the Tube station and doesn't slow his pace as he reaches the steps down into it.

"I wondered . . . do you fancy a quick drink?"

"I'm busy."

"Where are you off to?" She has to lift her voice to be heard against the thunderous noise of feet, the Victorian acoustics of the underground system.

"The new building."

They're surrounded by commuters. Her feet are almost lifting off the ground as she's borne down the stairs among the sea of people. "Wow. That must be some overtime."

"No. Just helping the boss with a few final things so that he doesn't wear himself out completely."

"I saw him today."

When Rory doesn't reply, she adds, "He was nice to me."

"Yeah. Well. He's a nice man."

She manages to walk alongside him until they reach the ticket barrier. He steps to one side to allow others to pass through.

"Silly, really," she says. "You pass people every day without having a clue—"

"Look, Ellie, what do you want?"

She bites her lip. Around them the commuters separate like water, earphones on, some tutting audibly at the human obstacles in their path. She rubs at her hair, which is now damp. "I just wanted to say I'm sorry. About the other morning."

"It's cool."

"No, it's not. But it's . . . Look, what happened, it's nothing to do with you, and I really like you. It's just this is something that—"

"You know what? I'm not interested. It's fine, Ellie. Let's leave it at that." He goes through the ticket barrier. She follows. She caught a glimpse of his expression before he turned, and it was horrible. She feels horrible.

She positions herself behind him on the escalator. Little pearls of water are dotted across his gray scarf, and she fights the urge to sweep them off. "Rory, I'm really sorry."

He's staring at his shoes. He glances at her, his eyes cold. "Married, huh?"

"What?"

"Your . . . friend. It was pretty obvious from what he said."

"Don't look at me like that."

"Like what?"

"I didn't mean to fall in love."

He lets out a short, unpleasant laugh. They have reached the bottom of the escalator. He picks up his pace, and she's forced to run a little to keep up. The tunnel smells of stale air and burned rubber.

"I didn't."

"Rubbish—you make a choice. Everyone makes a choice."

"So you've never been transported by something, never felt that pull?"

He faces her. "Of course I have. But if acting on it meant I was going to hurt someone else, I took a step back."

Her face flames. "Well, aren't *you* wonderful?"

"No. But you're hardly a victim of circumstance. Presumably you knew he was married and chose to go along with it anyway. You had the choice to say no."

"It didn't feel like that."

His voice lifts sarcastically. "'It was bigger than both of us.' I think you've been more affected by those love letters than you think."

"Oh, well, good for you, Mr. Practical. Bully for you that you can turn your emotions on and off like taps. Yes, I let myself fall into it—okay? Immoral, yes. Ill-advised? Well, judging by your response, obviously. But I felt something magical for a bit and—and don't worry, I've been paying for it ever since."

"But you're not the only one, are you? Every act has a consequence, Ellie. In my view the world divides into people who can see that, and make a decision accordingly, and those who just go for what feels good at the time."

"Oh, Christ! Have you any idea how bloody pompous you sound?" She's shouting now, barely conscious of the curious commuters who file past, fed into the tunnels of the District and Circle lines.

"Yes."

"And no one in your world is allowed to make a mistake?"

"Once," he says. "You can make a mistake once."

He stares off into the distance, his jaw set, as if working out how much to say. Then he turns to face her. "I was on the other side, okay, Ellie? I loved someone who found someone else that she couldn't resist. Something that was 'bigger than both of them.' Until, of course, he dumped her. And I let her back into my life, and she burned me a second time. So, yes, I do have an opinion on it."

She's rooted to the spot. There's a rush of noise, a blast of hot, disturbed air as a train approaches.

Passengers surge forward.

"You know something?" he says, his voice lifting over the din. "I'm not judging you for falling in love with this man. Who knows? Perhaps he's the love of your life. Perhaps his wife really would be better off without him. Perhaps the two of you really were *meant to be*. But you could have said no to me." Suddenly she sees something unexpected, something raw and exposed, in his face. "That's what I'm having trouble getting my head round. You could have said no to me. That would have been the right thing to do."

He hops lightly into the packed carriage just as the doors close. It pulls away, with a deafening whine.

She watches his departing back in the illuminated window until it disappears. *The right thing for who?*

Hey, babe,

*Thought of you all weekend. How is uni? Barry says all birds who go
to uni eventually find someone else, but I told him he was talking out of
his backside. He's just jealous. He went out with that girl from the estate
agent's on Tuesday and she blew him out after the main course. Just said
she was going to the ladies' and went!!! He said he sat there twenty minutes
before he realized. We were all killing ourselves down at the Feathers . . .*

*Wish you were here, babe. Nights seem long without you. Write to me
soon.*

Clive XX

Ellie sits in the middle of her bed, a dusty cardboard box on her
lap, the correspondence of her teenage years spread out around her.
She is in bed at nine thirty, trying desperately to think of some way
of salvaging the love-letters feature for Melissa without exposing Jennifer to public view. She thinks of Clive, her first love, a tree surgeon's
son who had gone to the same secondary school. They had agonized
over whether she should go to university, sworn that it wouldn't affect
their relationship. They lasted about three months after she went to
Bristol. She remembers how the appearance of his battered Mini in
the car park outside her halls of residence morphed frighteningly
swiftly from being glorious, a signal for her to spray on perfume and
belt down the corridor, to a sinking feeling of dismay when she knew
she no longer felt anything for him, except a sensation of being pulled
back into a life she no longer wanted.

Dear Clive,

*I have spent much of the night trying to work out how to do this in a
way that is going to cause each of us as little pain as possible. But there is
no easy way to.*

Dear Clive,

*This is a really difficult letter to write. But I have to come out and
say that I*

Dear Clive,
  I'm really sorry but I don't want you to come down anymore. Thanks
for the good times. I hope we can still be mates.
  Ellie

She fingers her crossed-out versions, folded in a neat pile among other correspondence. After he had received the final letter, he had driven 212 miles just to call her a bitch in person. She remembers being curiously untouched by it, perhaps because she had already moved on. At university, she had scented a new life far from the small town of her youth, far from the Clives, the Barrys, the Saturday nights at the pub, and a life where everyone not only knew you but what you'd done at school, what your parents did, the time you sang in the choir concert and your skirt fell down. You could only truly reinvent yourself far from home. On trips to see her parents, she still feels a little stifled by all that communal history.

She finishes her tea and wonders what Clive is doing now. He'll be married, she thinks, probably happily; he was an easygoing sort. He'll have a couple of children, and the high point of his weekend will still be Saturday nights at the pub with the lads he has known since school.

Now, of course, the Clives of this world won't be writing letters. They'd text her. All right babe? She wonders whether she would have ended the relationship by mobile phone.

She sits very still. Looks around her at the empty bed, the old letters strewn across the duvet. She hasn't read any of Jennifer's since her night with Rory; they are somehow uncomfortably linked to his voice. She thinks of his face as he stood in the Tube tunnel. *You could have said no to me.* She remembers Melissa's face, and tries not to think about the possibility of having to return to her old life. She could fail. She really could. She feels as if she's balanced on a precipice. Change is coming.

And then she hears her phone chime. Almost relieved, she stretches across the bed for it, her knee sinking into the pile of pastel paper.

No reply?

She reads it again and types:

Sorry. Thought you didn't want me to text you.

Things have changed. Say whatever you want now.

She murmurs the words aloud into the silence of the little room, hardly able to believe what she's seeing. Is this what actually happens outside romantic comedies? Can these situations, the ones everyone counsels against, really work out? She pictures herself in the café on some unspecified future date, telling Nicky and Corrine: *Yes, of course he'll be moving in here. Just till we can find somewhere bigger. We'll have the children on alternate weekends.* She pictures him returning in the evenings, dropping his bag, kissing her lengthily in the hallway. It's such an unlikely scenario that her mind spins. Is this what she wants? She scolds herself for her moment of doubt. Of course it is. She couldn't have felt like this for so long if it isn't.

Say whatever you want now.

Keep your cool, she tells herself. It may not be in the bag yet. And he's disappointed you so many times.

Her hand drops to the little keys, hovers over them, undecided. She types,

Will do, but not like this. I'm happy that we will get to talk.

Then adds:

Finding this all a little hard to get my head round. But I missed you too. Call me as soon as you get back. E xx

She's about to put her phone on her bedside table when it chimes again.

Still love me?

Her breath stops briefly in her throat.

Yes.

She sends it almost before she's thought about it. She waits a couple of minutes, but there's no response. And, not sure whether she's glad or sorry, Ellie lies back against her pillows and gazes, for a long time, out of her window into the empty black sky, watching the airplanes wink silently through the darkness toward unknown destinations.

Chapter 24

Rory feels a hand on his shoulder and pulls out one of his earphones.

"Tea."

He nods, turns off the music, and shoves his MP3 player into his pocket. The lorries have finished now; only the newspaper's own small delivery vans remain, scurrying backward and forward with forgotten boxes, small loads of things vital to the newspaper's survival. It's Thursday. On Sunday the last of the boxes will have been packed away, the last mugs and teacups transported. On Monday the *Nation* will start its new life in its new offices, and this building will be stripped for demolition. This time next year some shimmering glass and metal construction will be in its place.

Rory takes a seat at the back of the van beside his boss, who is contemplating the old black marble frontage of the building. The metal insignia of the newspaper, a carrier pigeon, is being dismantled from its plinth at the top of the steps.

"Strange sight, isn't it?"

Rory blows on his tea. "Bit weird for you? After all this time?"

"Not really. Everything comes to an end eventually. There's a bit of me that's quite looking forward to doing something different."

Rory takes a sip.

"It's a strange thing, to spend your days among other people's stories. I feel as if my own has been on hold."

It's like hearing a picture speak. So unlikely. So utterly compelling. Rory puts down his tea and listens. "Not tempted to write something yourself?"

"No." His boss's tone is dismissive. "I'm not a writer."

"What will you do?"

"I don't know. Travel, perhaps—maybe I'll go backpacking like you."

They both smile at the idea. They have worked together in near silence for months, rarely mentioning anything beyond the practical needs of the day. Now the fast-approaching end of their task has made them garrulous.

"My son thinks I should."

He can't hide the surprise in his voice. "I didn't know you had a son."

"And a daughter-in-law. And three very badly behaved grand-children."

Rory finds himself having to reassess his boss. He's one of those people who gives off a solitary air, and it's an effort to reposition him in his imagination as a family man.

"And your wife?"

"She died a long time ago."

He says it without discomfort, but Rory still feels awkward, as if he has overstepped some mark. If Ellie was here, Rory thinks, she'd ask him straight out what happened to her.

If Ellie was here, Rory would have slunk off into a distant part of the library rather than talk to her. He dismisses her. He won't think about her. He won't think about her hair, her laughter, the way she frowns when she's concentrating. The way she felt under his hands: uncharacteristically yielding. Uncharacteristically vulnerable.

"So, when are you going off on your travels?"

Rory hauls himself back from his thoughts and is handed a book, then another. This library's like the Tardis: things keep turning up out of nowhere. "Gave notice yesterday. Just got to look up the flights."

"Will you miss your girl?"

"She's not my girl."

"Just doing a good impression, eh? I thought you liked her."

"I did."

"I thought you two had a kind of shorthand."

"Me too."

"So what's the problem?"

"She's . . . more complicated than she looks."

The older man smiles wryly. "I've never met a woman who wasn't."

"Yes . . . Well. I don't like complications."

"There's no such thing as a life free of complications, Rory. We all end up making compromises in the end."

"Not me."

The librarian raises an eyebrow. There's a small smile on his face.

"What?" Rory says. "*What?* You're not going to give me some Waltons-family lecture about missed opportunities and how you wish you'd done things differently, are you?" His voice is louder, snappier, than he intended, but he can't help himself. He starts to move boxes from one side of the van to the other. "It would have been pointless, anyway. I'm going away. I don't need complications."

"No."

Rory shoots him a sideways look, registers the creeping smile. "Don't go getting sentimental on me now. I need to remember you as a miserable old bugger."

The miserable old bugger chuckles. "I wouldn't dare. Come on. Let's go and do a last check of the microfiche area and load up the tea stuff. Then I'll buy you lunch. And then you can not tell me all about what happened between you and this girl you patently couldn't care less about."

The pavement outside Jennifer Stirling's block is bleached a barnacle gray under the winter sun. A street sweeper is working his way along the curb, deftly picking up pieces of rubbish with a pair of pincers. Ellie wonders when she last saw a street sweeper in her part of London. Perhaps it's considered too Sisyphean a task: her high street is a riot of takeaways and cheap bakeries, their red-and-white-striped paper bags floating merrily around the neighborhood, telling of yet another lunchtime orgy of saturated fat and sugar.

"It's Ellie. Ellie Haworth," she shouts into the entry phone, when Jennifer answers. "I left you a message. I hope it's okay if I—"

"Ellie." Her voice is welcoming. "I was just coming down."

As the lift makes its unhurried way down the stories, she thinks about Melissa. Unable to sleep, Ellie had arrived at the *Nation*'s offices shortly after seven thirty. She needed to work out how to salvage the love-letters feature; rereading Clive's communications to her has made her realize there's no way she can return to her old life. She'll make this feature work. She'll get the rest of the information from Jennifer Stirling and somehow turn it around. She's her old self; focused, determined. It helps her not think about how utterly confusing her personal life has become.

She had been shocked to discover Melissa already in the office. Features was otherwise empty, but for a silent cleaner, listlessly pushing a vacuum cleaner between the remaining desks, and Melissa's door was propped open.

"I know, poppet, but Nina's going to take you." She had lifted a hand to her hair and was twisting a shining strand restlessly. The hair wove through her slim fingers, illuminated by the low winter sun, pulled, twisted, released.

"No, I told you on Sunday night. Do you remember? Nina's going to take you there and pick you up afterward. . . . I know. . . . I know . . . but Mummy has to go to work. You know I have to work, sweetie—" She sat down, briefly rested her head in her hand so that Ellie struggled to hear.

"I know, I know. And I will come to the next one. But do you remember I told you we were moving our offices? And it's very important? And Mummy can't—"

There was a long silence.

"Daisy, darling, can you put Nina on? . . . I know. Just put Nina on for a minute. . . . Yes, I'll speak to you afterward. Just put—" She glanced up, saw Ellie outside the office. Ellie turned away quickly, embarrassed to have been caught eavesdropping, and picked up her own phone, as if involved in some equally important call. When she looked up again, Melissa's office door was closed. It was hard to tell, from that distance, but she might have been crying.

"Well, this is a nice surprise." Jennifer Stirling is wearing a crisp linen shirt and a pair of indigo jeans.

I want to wear jeans when I'm sixty-something, Ellie thinks. "You said I could come back."

"You certainly can. I must admit, it was a guilty pleasure unburdening myself last week. You remind me a little of my daughter, too, which is rather a treat for me. I do miss having her around."

Ellie feels a ridiculous thrill of pleasure at being compared with the Calvin Klein woman in the photograph. She tries not to think about why she's there. "As long as I'm not bothering you . . ."

"Not at all. As long as you're not horribly bored by the ramblings of an old woman. I was going for a walk on Primrose Hill. Care to join me?" They walk, talk a little about the area, the places each has lived, Ellie's shoes, which Mrs. Stirling professes to admire. "My feet are awful," she says. "When I was your age we used to cram them into high heels every day. Your generation must be so much more comfortable."

"Yes, but my generation never looked like you did." She's thinking of the picture of Jennifer as a new mother, the makeup and perfect hair.

"Oh, we didn't really have a choice. It was a terrible tyranny. My husband wouldn't have let me have my picture taken unless I was shipshape." She seems lighter today, less bowed by the dredging of memories. She walks briskly, like someone much younger, and occasionally Ellie has to jog a little to keep up. "I'll tell you something. A few weeks ago I went to the station to get a newspaper, and a girl was standing there in what were plainly her pajama bottoms and those enormous sheepskin boots. What do you call them?"

"Uggs."

Jennifer's voice is merry. "That's it. Atrocious-looking things. And I watched her buy a pint of milk, her hair standing up at the back, and I was so horribly envious of her freedom. I stood there staring at her like an absolute madwoman." She laughs at the memory. "Danushka, who runs the kiosk, asked me what on earth the poor girl had done to me. . . . I suppose, looking back, it was a terribly hemmed-in existence."

"Can I ask you something?"

Jennifer's mouth lifts slightly at the corners. "I suspect you're going to."

"Do you ever feel bad about what happened? Having an affair, I mean."

"Are you asking if I regret hurting my husband?"

"I suppose so."

"And is this . . . curiosity? Or absolution?"

"I don't know. Probably both." Ellie chews a fingernail. "I think my . . . John . . . may be about to leave his wife."

There is a short silence. They are at the gates of Primrose Hill and Jennifer stops there. "Children?"

Ellie does not look up. "Yes."

"That's a great responsibility."

"I know."

"And you're a little frightened."

Ellie finds the words she hasn't been able to say to anyone else. "I'd like to be sure I'm doing the right thing. That it's going to be worth all the pain I'm about to cause."

What is it about this woman that makes it impossible to keep back any truth? She feels Jennifer's eyes on her, and wants, indeed, to be absolved. She remembers Boot's words: *You make me want to be a better man.* She wants to be a better person. She doesn't want to be walking here with half her mind wondering which bits of this conversation she's likely to plunder and publish in a newspaper.

Years of listening to other people's problems seem to have given Jennifer an air of wise neutrality. When she speaks, finally, Ellie senses she has chosen her words carefully. "I'm sure you'll work it out between you. You just need to talk honestly. Painfully honestly. And you may not always get the answers you want. That was the thing I was reminded of when I reread Anthony's letters after you left last week. There were no games. I never met anyone—before or afterward—that I could be quite so honest with."

She sighs, beckons Ellie through the gates. They begin to walk up the path that will lead them to the top of the hill. "But there is no absolution for people like us, Ellie. You may well find that guilt plays a much larger part in your future life than you would like. They say passion burns for a reason, and when it comes to affairs, it's not only the protagonists who are hurt. For my part, I do still feel guilty for the pain I caused Laurence. . . . I justified it to myself at the time, but I can see that what happened . . . hurt all of us. But . . . the person I have always felt most bad about is Anthony."

"You were going to tell me the rest of the story."

Jennifer's smile is fading. "Well, Ellie, it's not a happy ending." She tells of an abortive trip to Africa, a lengthy search, conspicuous silence from the man who had previously never stopped telling her how he felt, and the eventual forging of a new life in London, alone.

"And that's it?"

"In a nutshell."

"And in all that time you never . . . there was never anyone else?"

Jennifer Stirling smiles again. "Not quite. I am human. But I will say that I never became emotionally involved with anyone. After Boot, I—I didn't really want to be close to anyone else. There had been only him, for me. I could see that very clearly. And, besides, I had Esmé." Her smile broadens. "A child really is a wonderful consolation."

They have reached the top. The whole of north London stretches beneath them. They breathe deeply, scanning the distant skyline, hearing the traffic; the cries of dog walkers and errant children recede beneath them.

"Can I ask why you kept the PO box open for so long?"

Jennifer leans against the cast-iron bench, thinks before replying. "I suppose it must seem rather silly to you, but we had missed each other twice, you see, both times by a matter of hours. I felt it was my obligation to give it every chance. I suppose shutting down that box would have been admitting it was finally over."

She shrugs ruefully. "Every year I've told myself it's time to stop. The years crept by without my noticing how long it had been. But somehow I never have. I suppose I told myself it was a rather harmless indulgence."

"So that was actually it? His last letter?" Ellie gestures somewhere in the direction of St. John's Wood. "Did you really never hear from him again? How could you bear not knowing what happened to him?"

"The way I saw it, there were two possibilities. Either he had died in Congo, which was, at the time, too unbearable to contemplate. Or, as I suspect, he was very hurt by me. He believed I was never going to leave my husband, perhaps even that I was careless with his feelings, and I think it cost him dearly to get close to me a second time. Unfortunately I didn't realize how dearly until it was too late."

"You never tried to have him traced? A private investigator? Newspaper advertisements?"

"Oh, I wouldn't do that. He would have known where I was. I had made my feelings plain. And I had to respect his." She regards Ellie gravely. "You know, you can't make someone love you again. No matter how much you might want it. Sometimes, unfortunately, the timing is simply . . . off."

The wind is brisk up there: it forces itself into the gap between collar and neck, exploits any hint of exposure. Ellie thrusts her hands into her pockets. "What do you think would have happened to you if he had found you again?"

For the first time, Jennifer Stirling's eyes fill with tears. She stares at the skyline, gives a tiny shake of her head. "The young don't have a monopoly on broken hearts, you know." She begins to walk slowly back down the path so that her face is no longer visible. The silence before she speaks again causes a small tear in Ellie's heart. "I learned a long time ago, Ellie, that 'if only' is a very dangerous game indeed."

Meet me—Jx

We're using mobiles? X

I have a lot to tell you. I just need to see you. Les Percivals on
Derry Street. Tomorrow 1 pm x

Percivals?!? Not your usual thing

Ah. I'm all surprises these days Jx

She sits at the linen-clad table, flicking through the notes she has
scribbled on the Tube, and knows in her heart that she can't run this
story, and that if she doesn't, her career at the *Nation* is over. Twice she
has thought of running back to the apartment in St. John's Wood and
throwing herself on the older woman's mercy, explaining herself, begging her to let her reproduce her doomed love affair in print. But
whenever she does, she sees Jennifer Stirling's face, hears her voice: *The
young don't have a monopoly on broken hearts, you know.*

She stares at the glossy olives in the white ceramic dish on the
table. She has no appetite. If she doesn't write this story, Melissa will
move her. If she does write it, she's not sure she'll ever feel quite the
same about what she does or who she is. She wishes, again, that she
could talk to Rory. He would know what she should do. She has an
uncomfortable feeling that it might not be what she wants to do, but
she knows he would be right. Her thoughts chase each other in cir-
cles, argument and counterargument. *Jennifer Stirling probably doesn't even
read the* Nation. *She might never know what you did. Melissa is looking for an
excuse to elbow you out. You really don't have a choice.*

And then Rory's voice, sardonic: *Are you kidding me?*

Her stomach tightens. She can't remember the last time it wasn't
tied in knots. A thought occurs: surely if she can find out what happened to Anthony O'Hare, Jennifer will have to forgive her? She
might be upset for a while, but surely, ultimately, she will see that
Ellie has given her a gift? The answer has dropped into her lap. She'll

find him. If it takes her ten years, she'll find out what happened to him. It's the flimsiest of straws, but it makes her feel a little better.

Five minutes away. Are you there? Jx

Yes. Table on ground floor. Chilled glass waiting. Ex

She lifts a hand unconsciously to her hair. She still hasn't been able to work out why John doesn't want to go straight to her flat. The old John always preferred to go directly there. It was as if he couldn't speak to her properly, see her even, until he had got all that pent-up tension out of the way first. In the early months of their relationship, she had found it flattering, and later a little irritating. Now some small part of her wonders whether this restaurant meeting is to do with them finally going public. Everything seems to have changed so dramatically that it isn't beyond the new John to want to make some kind of public declaration. She notices the expensively dressed people at the neighboring tables, and her toes curl at the thought.

"What are you so fidgety about?" Nicky had said that morning. "This means you've got what you wanted, doesn't it?"

"It's just . . ."

"You're not sure you want him anymore."

"No!" She had scowled at the phone. "Of course I want him! It's just that everything's changed so swiftly I haven't had a chance to get my head around it."

"You'd better get your head around it. It's entirely possible that he's going to turn up to lunch with two suitcases and a couple of screaming kids in tow." For some reason this idea had amused Nicky hugely, and she had giggled until it had become a little annoying.

Ellie had the feeling that Nicky still hadn't forgiven her for "messing things up," as she put it, with Rory. Rory had sounded nice, she said repeatedly. "Someone I'd be happy to go to the pub with." The subtext: Nicky would never want to go to the pub with John. She would never forgive him for being the kind of man who could cheat on his wife.

She glances at her watch, then signals to the waiter for a second glass of wine. He's now twenty minutes late. On any other occasion she would have been mutely furious, but she's so nervous now that a small part of her wonders whether she might throw up at the mere sight of him. Yes, that's always a good welcome. And then she glances up to find a woman standing at the other side of her table.

Ellie's first thought is that she's a waitress, and then she wonders why she isn't holding the glass of wine. Then she realizes that not only is the woman wearing a navy coat, rather than a waitress's uniform, but she is staring at her, a little too intently, like someone about to start singing to themselves on the bus.

"Hello, Ellie."

Ellie blinks. "I'm sorry," she says, after her mind has flicked through a mental Rolodex of recent contacts and turned up nothing. "Do we know each other?"

"Oh, I think so. I'm Jessica."

Jessica. Her mind is blank. Nicely cut hair. Good legs. Perhaps a little tired. Suntan. And then it explodes onto her consciousness. Jessica. *Jess.*

The woman registers her shock. "Yes, I thought you might recognize my name. You probably didn't want to put a face to it, did you? Didn't want to think too much about me. I suppose John's having a wife was a bit of an inconvenience to you."

Ellie can't speak. She's dimly aware of the other diners as they glance her way, having picked up on some strange vibration emanating from table 15.

Jessica Armor is going through text messages on a familiar mobile phone. Her voice lifts a little as she reads them out: "'Feeling very wicked today. Get away. Don't care how you do it, but get away. Will make it worth your while.' Hmm, and here's a good one. 'Should be writing up interview with MP's wife, but mind keeps drifting back to last Tues. Bad boy!' Oh, and my personal favorite. 'Have been to Agent Provocateur. Photo attached . . .'" When she looks at Ellie again, her voice is shaking with barely suppressed rage. "It's pretty hard to compete with that when you're nursing two sick children and coping with the builders. But, yes, Tuesday the twelfth. I do remember that day. He brought me a bunch of flowers to apologize for being so late."

Ellie's mouth has opened but no words come out. Her skin is prickling.

"I went through his phone on holiday. I'd wondered who he was ringing from the bar, and then I found your message. 'Please call. Just once. Need to hear from you. X.'" She laughs mirthlessly. "How very touching. He thinks it's been stolen."

Ellie wants to crawl under the table. She wants to shrink to nothing, to evaporate.

"I'd like to hope you end up a miserable, lonely woman. But actually, I hope you have children one day, Ellie Haworth. Then you'll know how it feels to be vulnerable. And to have to fight, to be constantly vigilant, just to make sure your children get to grow up with a father. Think about that the next time you're purchasing see-through lingerie to entertain my husband, won't you?"

Jessica Armor walks away through the tables and out into the sunshine. There may have been a hush in the restaurant; it's impossible for Ellie to tell over the ringing in her ears. Eventually, cheeks flaming, hands trembling, she motions to a waiter for the bill.

As he approaches, she mutters something about having to leave unexpectedly. She isn't sure what she's saying: her voice no longer seems to belong to her. "The bill?" she says.

He gestures toward the door. His smile is sympathetic. "No need, madam. The lady paid for you."

Ellie walks back to the office, impervious to traffic, to jostling commuters on pavements, to the rebuking eyes of the *Big Issue* sellers. She wants to be in her little flat with the door shut, but her precarious position at work means that's impossible. She walks through the newspaper office, conscious of the eyes of other people, convinced deep down that everyone must see her shame, see what Jessica Armor saw, as if it were drawn upon her, like a scarlet letter.

"You okay, Ellie? You're awfully pale." Rupert leans around from behind his monitor. Someone has fixed an "incinerate" sticker to the back of his screen.

"Headache." Her voice sticks in the back of her throat.

"Terri's got pills—she has pills for everything, that girl," he muses, and disappears behind his monitor again.

She sits at her desk and turns on her computer, scanning the e-mails. There it is.

> Have lost phone. Picking up new one lunchtime. Will e-mail
> you new number. Jx

She checks the time. It had arrived in her in-box while she was interviewing Jennifer Stirling. She closes her eyes, seeing again the image that has swum in front of them for the past hour: Jessica Armor's set jaw, the terrifying eyes, the way her hair moved around her face while she spoke, as if it was electrified by her anger, her hurt. Some tiny part of her had recognized that in different circumstances she would have liked the look of this woman, might have wanted to go for a drink with her. When she opens her eyes again, she doesn't want to see John's words, doesn't want to see this version of herself reflected in them. It's as if she's woken from a particularly vivid dream, one that has lasted a year. She knows the extent of her mistake. She deletes his message.

"Here." Rupert places a cup of tea on her desk. "Might make you feel better."

Rupert never makes anyone tea. The other feature writers have run books in the past on how long it will take him to head to the canteen, and he's always been a racing certainty. She doesn't know whether to be touched by this rare act of sympathy or afraid of why he feels she's in need of it.

"Thanks," she says, and takes it.

It's as he sits down that she spies a familiar name on a different e-mail: Phillip O'Hare. Her heart stops, the humiliations of the last hour temporarily forgotten. She clicks on it, and sees that it is from the Phillip O'Hare who works for the *Times*.

Hi—A little confused by your message. Can you call me?

She wipes her eyes. Work, she tells herself, is the answer to every-thing. Work is now the only thing. She'll find out what happened to Jennifer's lover, and Jennifer will forgive her for what she's about to do. She'll have to.

She dials the direct line at the bottom of the e-mail. A man an-swers on the second ring. She can hear the familiar hum of a news-room in the background. "Hi," she says, her voice tentative. "It's Ellie Haworth. You sent me an e-mail?"

"Ah. Yes. Ellie Haworth. Hold on." He has the voice of someone in his fifties. He sounds a little like John. She blocks this thought as she hears a hand placed across the receiver, his voice, muffled, and then he's back. "Sorry. Yes. Deadlines. Look, thanks for calling me back. . . . I just wanted to check something. Where was it you said you worked? The *Nation*?"

"Yes." Her mouth has gone dry. She begins to babble. "But I do want to assure you that his name is not necessarily going to get used in what I'm writing about. I just really want to find out what hap-pened to him for a friend of his who—

"The *Nation*?"

"Yes."

There's a short silence.

"And you say you want to find out about my father?"

"Yes." Her voice is draining away.

"And you're a journalist?"

"I'm sorry," she says. "I don't understand what you're getting at. Yes, a journalist. Like you. Are you saying you're uncomfortable giv-ing any information to a rival newspaper? I've told you that—"

"My father is Anthony O'Hare."

"Yes. That's who I'm—"

The man at the other end of the line is laughing. "You're not in the investigative unit, by any chance?"

"No."

It takes him a moment to gather himself. "Miss Haworth, my father works for the *Nation*. Your newspaper. He has done for more than forty years."

Ellie sits very still. She asks him to repeat what he has just said.

"I don't understand," she says, standing up at her desk. "I did a byline search. I did lots of searches. Nothing came up. Only your name at the *Times*."

"That's because he doesn't write."

"Then what does—"

"My father works in the library. He has done since . . . oh . . . 1964."

Chapter 25

OCTOBER 1964

"And give him this. He'll know what it means." Jennifer Stirling scribbled a note, ripped it from her diary, and thrust it into the top of the folder. She placed it on the subeditor's desk.

"Sure," Don said.

She reached over to him, took hold of his arm. "You will make sure he gets it? It's really important. Desperately important."

"I understand. Now, if you'll excuse me, I need to get on. This is our busiest time of day. We're all on deadlines here." Don wanted her out of the office. He wanted the child out of the office.

Her face crumpled. "I'm sorry. Please just make sure he gets it. Please."

God, he wished she'd just leave. He couldn't look at her.

"I'm—I'm sorry to have bothered you." She appeared suddenly self-conscious, as if she was aware of the spectacle she had created. She reached for her daughter's hand and, almost reluctantly, walked away. The few people gathered around the sub's desk watched her go in silence.

"Congo," said Cheryl, after a beat.

"We need to get page four off stone." Don stared fixedly at the desk. "Let's go with the dancing priest."

Cheryl was still sawing at him. "Why did you tell her he'd gone to Congo?"

"You want me to tell her the truth? That he drank himself into a bloody coma?"

Cheryl twisted the pen in her mouth, her eyes drifting across to the swinging office door. "But she looked so sad."

"She should look bloody sad. She's the one who's caused him all the trouble."

"But you can't—"

Don's voice exploded into the newsroom. "The last thing that boy needs is her stirring things up again. Do you understand? I'm doing him a favor." He tore the note from the folder and hurled it into the bin.

Cheryl stuck her pen behind her ear, gave her boss a hard look, and sashayed back to her desk.

Don took a deep breath. "Right, can we get off O'Hare's bloody love life and on with this bloody dancing-priest story? Someone? Shove some copy over sharpish or we're going to be sending the paperboys out with a load of blank pages tomorrow."

In the next bed a man was coughing. It went on and on, a polite, staccato tattoo, as if something was caught at the back of his throat. He did it even in his sleep. Anthony O'Hare let the sound recede to some distant recess of his consciousness, just like everything else. He knew the tricks now. How to make things disappear.

"You have a visitor, Mr. O'Hare."

The sound of curtains being pulled back, light flooding in. Pretty Scottish nurse. Cool hands. Every word she said to him was spoken in the tone of someone about to bestow a gift. *I'm just going to give you a little injection, Mr. O'Hare. Shall I get someone to help you to the lavatory, Mr. O'Hare? You have a visitor, Mr. O'Hare.*

Visitor? For a moment hope floated, and then he heard Don's voice through the curtains and remembered where he was.

"Don't mind me, sweetheart."

"I certainly won't," she said primly.

"Lie-in, is it?" A moon-sized ruddy face somewhere by his feet.

"Funny." He spoke into his pillow, pushing himself upright. His whole body ached. He blinked. "I need to get out of here."

His vision cleared. Don was standing at the end of his bed, arms folded, resting on his stomach. "You're not going anywhere, sonny Jim."

"I can't stay here." His voice seemed to come straight from his chest. It croaked and squeaked like a wooden wheel in a rut.

"You're not well. They want to check your liver function before you go anywhere. You gave us all a fright."

"What happened?" He could remember nothing.

Don hesitated, perhaps trying to judge how much to say. "You didn't turn up at Marjorie Spackman's office for the big meeting. When nobody had heard from you by six p.m. I got a bad feeling, left Michaels in charge, and shot over to your hotel. Found you on the floor, not too pretty. You looked worse than you do now, and that's saying something."

Flashback. The bar at the Regent. The wary eyes of the barman. Pain. Raised voices. An endless careening journey back to his room, clutching at walls, swaying upstairs. The sound of things crashing. Then nothing.

"I hurt all over."

"So you should. God knows what they did to you. You looked like a pincushion when I saw you last night."

Needles. Urgent voices. The pain. Oh, Jesus, the pain.

"What the hell is going on, O'Hare?"

In the next bed, the man had started coughing again.

"Was it that woman? She turn you down?" Don was physically uncomfortable discussing feelings. This manifested itself in a jiggling leg, in the way his hand ran backward and forward over his balding head.

Don't mention her. Don't make me think about her face. "Not as simple as that."

"Then what the hell is all this about? No woman's worth . . . this." Don's hand waved distractedly above the bed.

"I—I just wanted to forget."

"So go and sling your leg over someone else. Someone you can have. You'll get over it." Perhaps saying it would make it true.

Anthony's silence lasted just long enough to contradict him.

"Some women are trouble," Don added.

Forgive me. I just had to know.

"Moths to a flame. We've all been there."

Forgive me.

Anthony shook his head. "No, Don. Not like this."

"It's always 'not like this' when it's your own—"

"She can't leave him because he won't let her take the child." Anthony's voice, suddenly clear, cut through the curtained area. Just briefly, the man in the next bed stopped coughing. Anthony watched his boss grasp the implication of the sentence, the creeping frown of sympathy.

"Ah. Tough."

"Yes."

Don's leg had begun to jiggle again. "Doesn't mean you had to try and kill yourself with drink. You know what they said? The yellow fever screwed your liver. Screwed it, O'Hare. One more drinking session like that, and you . . ."

Anthony felt infinitely weary. He turned away on his pillow. "Don't worry. It won't happen again."

For half an hour after he'd returned from the hospital, Don sat at his desk, thinking. Around him the newsroom was waking slowly, as it did every day, a sleeping giant spurred into reluctant life: journalists chatting on telephones, stories rising and falling on the newslists, pages formed and planned, the first being mocked up on the production desk.

He rubbed his hand across his jaw, called over his shoulder toward the secretary's desk.

"Blondie. Get me the number of thingy Stirling. The asbestos man."

Cheryl listened in silence. Minutes later, she handed him the number she had scribbled down from the office *Who's Who.* "How is he?"

"How'd you think?" He stubbed his pen on the desk a few times, still deep in thought. Then, as she walked back to her desk, he picked up the phone and asked the switchboard to put him through to Fitzroy 2286.

He coughed a little before he spoke, like someone uncomfortable with using the telephone. "I'd like to speak to Jennifer Stirling, please."

He could feel Cheryl watching him.

"Can I leave a message? . . . What? She doesn't? Oh. I see." A pause. "No, it doesn't matter. I'm sorry to have troubled you." He put the phone down.

"What happened?" Cheryl was standing over him. She was taller than him in her new heels. "Don?"

"Nothing." He straightened up. "Forget I said anything. Go and get me a bacon sandwich, will you? And don't forget the ketchup. I can't eat it without."

He screwed the scribbled number into a ball and threw it into the wastepaper basket at his feet.

The grief was worse than if someone had died; at night it came in waves, relentless and astonishing in their power, hollowing him out. He saw her every time he closed his eyes, her sleepy-lidded pleasure, her expression of guilt and helplessness as she had caught sight of him in the hotel lobby. Her face told him they were lost, and that she already knew what she had done by telling him so.

And she was right. He had felt anger, at first, that she should raise his hopes without telling him the truth of her situation. That she should force her way back into his heart so ruthlessly when there was no chance for them. What was the saying? *It was the hope that would kill you.*

His feelings swung wildly. He forgave her. There was nothing to forgive. She'd done it because, like himself, she couldn't have not done it. And because it was the only bit of him she could reasonably hope to have. *I hope the memory of it keeps you going, Jennifer, because it has destroyed me.*

He fought the knowledge that, this time, there really was nothing left for him. He felt physically weakened, left frail by his own disastrous behavior. His sharp mind had been hijacked, its lucid parts shredded, just the steady pulse of loss beating through it, the same relentless beat he had heard back in Léopoldville.

She would never be his. They had come so close, and she would never be his. How was he supposed to live with that knowledge?

In the small hours, he worked through a thousand solutions. He would demand that Jennifer get a divorce. He would do everything he could to make her happy without her child through the sheer strength of his will. He would hire the best lawyer. He would give her more children. He would confront Laurence—in his wilder dreams, he went for his throat.

But Anthony had been for years a man's man, and even then some distant male part of him could not but feel what it must be like for Laurence: to know that his wife loved someone else. And then to have to hand over his child to the man who had stolen her. It had crippled Anthony, and he had never loved Clarissa like he loved Jennifer. He thought of his sad, silent son, his own constant ache of guilt, and knew that if he imposed that on another family, any happiness they gained would lie over a dark current of grief. He had destroyed one family; he could not be responsible for destroying another.

He rang the girlfriend in New York and told her he wouldn't be returning. He listened to her astonishment and barely disguised tears with only a distant sense of guilt. He couldn't return there. He couldn't sink into the steady urban rhythms of life in New York, the days measured by journeys backward and forward to the UN building, because now they would be tainted by Jennifer. Everything would be tainted by Jennifer: her scent, her taste, that she would be out there, living, breathing, without him. It was worse, somehow, to know that she had wanted him as much as he had wanted her. He couldn't employ the necessary anger against her to propel himself away from thoughts of her.

Forgive me. I just had to know.

He needed to be in a place where he couldn't think. To survive, he had to be somewhere where survival was the only thing he could think about.

Don picked him up two days later, on the afternoon that the hospital had agreed to discharge him, with appropriate liver-function results and dire threats of what would happen to him if he dared to drink again.

"Where are we headed?" He watched Don load his small suitcase into the boot of his car and felt like a refugee.

"You're coming to mine."

"What?"

"Viv says so." He didn't meet Anthony's eye. "She thinks you need some home comforts."

You think I can't be left alone. "I don't think I—"

"It's not up for discussion," Don said, and climbed into the driver's seat. "But don't blame me for the food. My wife knows a hundred and one ways to incinerate a cow, and as far as I can tell she's still experimenting."

It was always disconcerting to see one's workmates in a domestic setting. Over the years, although he had met Viv—red-haired and as vivacious as Don was dour—at various work functions, Anthony had somehow seen Don, more than anyone, as someone who physically inhabited the *Nation*. He was always there. That office, with its towering piles of paper, its scribbled notes and maps pinned haphazardly to walls, was his natural habitat. Don in his house with velvet slippers, his feet up on an overstuffed sofa, Don straightening ornaments or fetching pints of milk, went against the rules of nature.

That said, there was something restful about being in his house. A mock-Tudor semi in the commuter belt, it was large enough that he didn't feel under anybody's feet. The children were grown and gone, and aside from framed photographs, there were no constant reminders of his own failure as a parent.

Viv greeted him with kisses on both cheeks, and made no reference to where he had been. "I thought you boys might like to play golf this afternoon," she said.

They did. Don was so hopeless at it that Anthony realized afterward it must have been the only thing his hosts could think of that the two men might do together that didn't involve drinking. Don didn't mention Jennifer. He was worried still, Anthony could tell. He made frequent references to Anthony being all right, to the resumption of normality, whatever that was supposed to be. There was no wine at lunch or supper.

"So, what's the plan?" He was sitting on one of the sofas. In the distance they could hear Viv washing up, singing along to the wireless in the kitchen.

"Back to work tomorrow," Don said. He was rubbing his stomach.

Work. Part of him wanted to ask what that might be. But he didn't dare. He had failed the *Nation* once, was afraid to have it confirmed that this time he had done so conclusively.

I've been talking to Spackman."

Oh, Christ. Here it comes.

"Tony, she doesn't know. Nobody upstairs knows."

Anthony blinked.

"It's just us on the desk. Me, Blondie, a couple of the subs. I had to ring them to tell them I wasn't coming back to work when we got you to hospital. They'll keep their mouths shut."

"I don't know what to say."

"That's a bloody change. Anyway." Don lit a cigarette, and blew a long plume of smoke. His eyes met Anthony's almost guiltily. "She agrees with me that we should send you back out."

It took Anthony a beat to register what he was saying.

"To Congo?"

"You're the best man for the job."

Congo.

"But I need to know . . ." Don tapped his cigarette on an ashtray.

"It's fine."

"Let me finish. I need to know you're going to look after yourself. I can't be worrying."

"No drinking. Nothing reckless. I just . . . I need to do the job."

"That's what I thought." But Don didn't believe him—Anthony could see it in the sideways look. A short pause. "I would feel responsible."

"I know."

Clever man, Don. But Anthony couldn't reassure him. How could he? He wasn't sure how he was going to get through the next half an hour, let alone how he'd feel in the heart of Africa.

Don's voice broke in again before the answer became overwhelming. He stubbed out his cigarette. "Football's on in a minute. Chelsea versus Arsenal. Fancy it?" He climbed heavily out of his chair and flicked on the mahogany-clad box in the corner. "I'll tell you one bit of good news. You can't get that bastard yellow fever again. When you've been as sick as you were, apparently you're immune."

Anthony stared unseeing at the black-and-white screen. *How do I make the rest of me immune?*

They were in the foreign editor's office. Paul de Saint, a tall, patrician man with swept-back hair and the air of a Romantic poet, was studying a map on the desk. "The big story's in Stanleyville. There are at least eight hundred non-Congolese being held hostage there, many in the Victoria Hotel, and perhaps a thousand more in the surrounding area. Diplomatic efforts to save them have so far failed. There's so much infighting between the rebels that the situation is changing by the hour, so it's near impossible to get an accurate picture. It's pretty woolly out there, O'Hare. Until maybe six months ago, I would have said the safety of any white man was guaranteed, whatever was going on with the natives. Now, I'm afraid, they seem to be targeting *les colons*. There are some fairly horrific stories coming out. Nothing we can put in the paper." He paused. "Rape is only the half of it."

"How do I get in?"

"There's our starting problem. I've been talking to Nicholls, and the best way is going to be via Rhodesia—or Zambia, as they're now calling the northern half. Our man there is trying to work out a land route for you, but many of the roads have been destroyed, and it'll take days."

As he talked travel logistics with Don, Anthony let the conversation drift away from him and saw, with some gratitude, that not only had a whole half hour gone by in which he hadn't thought of her but that the story was pulling him in. He could feel nervous anticipation germinating in his belly, and was drawn to the challenge of getting across the hostile terrain. He felt no fear. How could he? What worse things could happen?

He leafed through the files that de Saint's deputy handed him. The political background; the Communist aid to the rebels that had so enraged the Americans; the execution of the American missionary, Paul Carlson. He read the ground-level reports of what the rebels had done, and his jaw tightened. They took him back to 1960 and the turmoil of Lumumba's brief rule. He read them as if at a distance. He felt as if the man who had been out there before—the man so shattered by what he had seen—was someone he no longer recognized.

"So, we'll book flights to Kenya tomorrow, yes? We've got a man on the inside at Sabena who'll let us know if there are any internal flights to Congo. Otherwise it's drop at Salisbury airport and make your way across the Rhodesian border. Yes?"

"Do we know which correspondents have made it there?"

"There's not an awful lot coming out. I suspect communications are difficult. But Oliver has a piece in the *Mail* today, and I've heard the *Telegraph* is running big tomorrow."

The door opened. Cheryl's face was anxious.

"We're in the middle of something, Cheryl." Don sounded irritated.

"Sorry," she said, "but your boy is here."

It took Anthony several seconds to grasp that she was looking at him. "My boy?"

"I've put him in Don's office."

Anthony stood up, barely able to digest what he had heard. "Excuse me a moment," he said, and followed Cheryl out across the newsroom.

There it was: the jolt he experienced on the few occasions he got to see Phillip, a kind of visceral shock at how much he had changed since the last visit, his growth a constant rebuke to his father's absence.

In six months his son's frame had elongated by inches, tipped its way into adolescence, but not yet filled out. Hunched over himself, he resembled a question mark. He looked up as Anthony entered the room, and his face was blanched, his eyes red-rimmed.

Anthony stood there, trying to work out the cause of the grief etched across his son's pale face, and some distant part of him wondered, Is it me again? Did he find out what I did to myself? Am I such a failure in his eyes?

"It's Mother," Phillip said. He blinked furiously and wiped his nose with his hand.

Anthony took a step closer. The boy unfurled and threw himself with unexpected force into his father's arms. Anthony felt himself gripped, Phillip's hands clutching at his shirt as if he would never let him go, and he allowed his own hand to fall gently onto his boy's head as sobs racked the thin body.

The rain was so loud on the roof of Don's car that it almost drowned thought. Almost, but not quite. In the twenty minutes it had taken them to edge through the traffic on Kensington High Street, the two men had sat in silence, the only other sound Don's fervent drags on his cigarette.

"Accident," Don said, staring at the snaking red taillights in front of him. "Must have been a big one. We should ring the newsroom." He made no effort to pull over by the telephone boxes.

When Anthony said nothing, Don leaned over and fiddled with the radio until static defeated him. He examined the end of his cigarette, blew on it, making it glow. "De Saint says we have till tomorrow. Any later than that, and we have to wait four days for the next scheduled flight." He spoke as if there was a decision to be made. "You could go, and we'll pull you off if she deteriorates."

"She's already deteriorated." Clarissa's cancer had been shocking in its swiftness. "She's not expected to last the fortnight."

"Bloody bus. Look at it, taking up twice the road." Don wound down his window and threw his cigarette into the soaked street. He brushed the raindrops off his sleeve as he closed it again. "What's the husband like, anyhow? No good?"

"Only met him once."

I can't stay with him. Please, Dad, don't make me stay with him.

Phillip had gripped his belt like someone hanging on to a life raft. When Anthony had finally taken him back to the house in Parsons Green, he had felt the weight of those fingers long after he had handed him over.

"I'm very sorry," he had said to Edgar. The curtain merchant, older than he had expected, had eyed him suspiciously, as if some insult had lain in what he'd said.

"I can't go." The words were out there. It was almost a relief to say them. Like finally being given the death sentence after years of possible reprieves.

Don sighed. It might have been melancholy or relief. "He's your son."

"He's my son." He had promised: *Yes, of course you can stay with me. Of course you can. It's going to be all right.* Even as he said the words, he had not fully understood what he was giving away.

The traffic had begun to move again, at first a slow crawl and then walking speed.

They were at Chiswick before Don spoke again. "You know, O'Hare, this might work. It might be a bit of a gift. God knows what could have happened to you out there."

Don glanced sideways.

"And who knows? Let the boy settle down a bit . . . you can still go off into the field. Maybe we'll have him to stay. Let Viv look after him. He'd like it at ours. God knows, she misses having children around the place. Christ." A thought occurred. "You're going to have to find yourself a bloody house. No more living out of hotel rooms."

He let Don ramble on, laying before him this mythical new life, like stories on a page, promising, soothing, the fellow family man emerging to make him feel better, to hide what he had lost, to quell the drum still beating somewhere in the darker regions of his soul.

He had been given two weeks' compassionate leave to find himself somewhere to live and to shepherd his son through his mother's death and the dour formality of her funeral. Phillip had not wept in front of him again. He had expressed polite pleasure at the small terraced house in southwest London—close to his school, and to Don and Viv, who had thrown herself into her role as prospective auntie with relish. He sat now with his pitiful suitcase, as if awaiting some future instruction. Edgar did not telephone to see how he was.

It was like living with a stranger. Phillip was anxious to please, as if afraid he would be sent away. Anthony was at pains to tell him how pleased he was that they were living together, although he felt secretly as though he had cheated someone, been given something he didn't deserve. He felt horribly inadequate to deal with the boy's overwhelming grief, and struggled to function in the face of his own.

He embarked upon a crash course in practical skills. He took their clothes to the launderette, sat beside Phillip at the barber. He didn't know how to cook much more than a boiled egg, so they went each night to a café at the end of the street, huge, hearty meals of steak and kidney pie and overboiled vegetables, steamed puddings swimming in pale custard. They pushed the food listlessly around their plates, and every evening Phillip would announce that it had been "delicious, thank you," as if going there had been a great treat. Back at the house, Anthony would stand outside his boy's bedroom door, wondering whether to go in or if acknowledging his sadness would only make it worse.

On Sundays they were invited to Don's house, where Viv would serve a roast dinner with all the trimmings, then insist that they play board games after she had cleared up. Watching the boy smile at her teasing, her bullish insistence that he join in, her enfolding of him into this strange extended family, made Anthony's heart ache.

As they climbed into the car, he saw that even as Phillip waved at Viv, blowing kisses from the front window, a solitary tear rolled down his cheek. He grasped the steering wheel, paralyzed by such responsibility. He couldn't work out what to say. What did he have to offer Phillip when he still wondered hourly whether it wouldn't have been better if Clarissa had been the one to survive?

That night he sat in front of the fire, watching the first television pictures of the freed Stanleyville hostages. Their blurred shapes emerged from army aircraft and huddled in shocked groups on the tarmac. *"Crack Belgian troops took a matter of hours to secure the city. It is still too early to count the casualties with any accuracy, but early reports suggest at least a hundred Europeans died in the crisis. There are many more still unaccounted for."*

He turned off the television, mesmerized by the screen long after the white dot had disappeared. Finally he went upstairs, hesitating outside his son's door, listening to the unmistakable sound of muffled sobbing. It was a quarter past ten.

Anthony closed his eyes briefly, opened them, and pushed open the door. His son started and shoved something under the bedspread.

Anthony turned on the light. "Son?"

Silence.

"What's the matter?"

"Nothing." The boy composed himself, wiping his face. "I'm fine."

"What was that?" He kept his voice soft, sat down on the side of the bed. Phillip was hot and damp. He must have been crying for hours. Anthony felt crushed by his own parental inadequacy.

"Nothing."

"Here. Let me see." He peeled back the cover gently. It was a small, silver-framed picture of Clarissa, her hands resting proudly on her son's shoulders. She was smiling broadly.

The boy shuddered. Anthony laid a hand on the photograph and smoothed the tears from the glass with his thumb. *I hope Edgar made you smile like that,* he told her silently. "It's a lovely photograph. Would you like us to put it downstairs? On the mantelpiece, perhaps? Somewhere you can look at it whenever you like?"

He could feel Phillip's eyes searching his face. Perhaps he was preparing himself for some barbed comment, some residual charge of ill feeling, but Anthony's eyes were locked on the woman in the picture, her beaming smile. He couldn't see her. He saw Jennifer. He saw her everywhere. He would always see her everywhere.

Get a grip, O'Hare.

He handed the picture back to his son. "You know . . . it's fine to be sad. Really. You're allowed to be sad about losing someone you love." It was so important that he get this right.

His voice had cracked, something rising from deep within him, and his chest hurt with the effort of not letting it overwhelm him. "Actually, I'm sad, too," he said. "Terribly sad. Losing someone you love is . . . it's actually unbearable. I do understand that."

He drew his son to him, his voice lowering to a murmur: "But I'm so very glad you're here now, because I think . . . I think you and I just might get through this together. What do you think?"

Phillip's head rested against his chest, and a thin arm crept around his middle. He felt the easing of his son's breathing and held him close as they sat, shrouded in silence, lost in their thoughts in the near dark.

He had failed to grasp that the week he was due to return to work was half-term. Viv said without hesitation that she would have Phillip for the latter part, but she was due to go to her sister's until Wednesday, so for the first two days Anthony would have to make alternative arrangements.

"He can come with us to the office," said Don. "Make himself useful with a teapot." Knowing how Don felt about family life interfering with the *Nation*, Anthony was grateful. He had been desperate to work again, to restore some semblance of normal life. Phillip was touchingly eager to accompany them.

Anthony sat down at his new desk and surveyed the morning's newspapers. There had been no vacant posts in Home News, so he had become reporter-at-large, the honorific title designed to reassure him, he suspected, that he would, once more, be so. He took a sip of the office coffee and winced at the familiar awfulness. Phillip was going from desk to desk, asking if anybody would like tea, the shirt Anthony had pressed for him that morning crisp on his skinny back. He felt suddenly—gratefully—at home. This was where his new life started. It was going to be fine. They would be fine. He refused to look at the foreign desk. He didn't want to know just yet who they had sent to Stanleyville in his place.

"Here." Don threw a copy of the *Times* at him, a story circled in red. "Do us a quick rewrite on the U.S. space launch. You're not going to get any fresh quotes from the States at this hour, but it'll make a short column on page eight."

"How many words?"

"Two fifty." Don's voice was apologetic. "I'll have something better for you later."

"It's fine." It was fine. His son was smiling, bearing a loaded tray with almost excessive caution. He glanced toward his father, and Anthony nodded approval. He was proud of the boy, proud of his bravery. It was indeed a gift to have someone to love.

Anthony pulled his typewriter toward him, fed carbons between the sheets of paper. One for the editor, one for the subs, one for his records. The routine had a kind of seductive pleasure. He typed his name at the top of the page, hearing the satisfying snap of the steel letters as they hit the paper.

He read and reread the *Times* story and made a few notes on his pad. He nipped downstairs to the newspaper library and pulled up the file on space missions, flicking through the most recent cuttings. He made some more notes. Then he placed his fingers on the typewriter keys.

Nothing.

It was as if his hands wouldn't work.

He typed a sentence. It was flat. He ripped out the papers, rethreaded them into the cylinder.

He typed another sentence. It was flat. He typed another. He'd shape it up. But the words resolutely refused to go where he wanted them. It was a sentence, yes, but nothing that would work in a national newspaper. He reminded himself of the pyramid rule of journalism: most important information in the first sentence, fanning out in lesser significance as you went on. Few people read to the end of a story.

It wouldn't come.

At a quarter past twelve Don appeared at his side. "You slung that piece over yet?"

Anthony was sitting back in his chair, his hands on his jaw, a small mountain of balled-up paper on the floor.

"O'Hare? You ready?"

"I can't do it, Don." His voice was hoarse with disbelief.

"What?"

"I can't do it. I can't write. I've lost it."

"Don't be ridiculous. What is this? Writer's block? Who do you think you are—F. Scott Fitzgerald?" He picked up a crumpled sheet and smoothed it out on the desk. He picked up another, read it, re-read it. "You've been through a lot," he said finally. "You probably need a holiday." He spoke without conviction. Anthony had just had a holiday. "It'll come back," he said. "Just don't say anything. Take it easy. I'll get Smith to rewrite it. Take it easy for today. It'll come back."

Anthony gazed at his son, who was sharpening pencils for Obits. For the first time in his life he had responsibilities. For the first time in his life it was vital that he could provide. He felt Don's hand on his shoulder like a great weight. "What the hell am I going to do if it doesn't?"

Chapter 26

Ellie stays awake until four o'clock in the morning. It's not a trial: for the first time in months everything is clear to her. She spends the early evening solidly on the phone, cradling the receiver between neck and shoulder as she watches her computer screen. She sends messages, calls in favors. She wheedles, cajoles, won't take no for an answer. When she has what she needs, she sits at her desk in her pajamas, pins up her hair, and begins. She types swiftly, the words spilling easily from her fingers. For once she knows exactly what she has to say. She reworks each sentence until she's happy; she shuffles information until it works in the way that has the most impact. Once, rereading it, she cries, and several times she laughs out loud. She recognizes something in herself, perhaps someone she had lost for a while. When she has finished, she prints out two copies and sleeps the sleep of the dead.

For two hours. She is up and in the office by seven thirty. She wants to catch Melissa before anyone else is there. She showers away her tiredness, drinks two double espressos, makes sure she has blow-dried her hair. She is brimming with energy; her blood fizzes in her veins. She is at her desk when Melissa, expensive handbag slung over her shoulder, unlocks her office door. As her boss sits down, Ellie sees the barely disguised double take when she notices she has company.

Ellie finishes her coffee. She nips into the ladies' to check she has nothing on her teeth. She's wearing a crisp white blouse, her best trousers, and high heels, and looks, as her friends would say jokingly, like a grown-up. "Melissa?"

"Ellie." The surprise in her tone manages to carry with it a mild rebuke.

Ellie ignores it. "Can I have a word?"

Melissa consults her watch. "A quick one. I'm meant to be talking to the China bureau in five minutes."

Ellie sits opposite. Melissa's office is now empty of everything except the few files she needs to make that day's edition work. Only the photograph of her daughter remains. "It's about this feature."

"You're not going to tell me you can't do it."

"Yes, I am."

It's as if she's primed for this, already teetering on the burst of bad temper. "Well, Ellie, that's really not what I wanted to hear. We have the busiest weekend of the newspaper's life ahead of us, and you've had weeks to get this thing sorted. You really aren't helping your own case by coming to me at this stage and—"

"Melissa—please. I found out the man's identity."

"And?" Melissa's eyebrows arch as only the professionally threaded can.

"And he works here. We can't use it because he works for us."

The cleaner propels the Hoover past Melissa's office door, its dull roar briefly drowning the conversation.

"I don't understand," Melissa says, as the drone fades.

"The man who wrote the love letters is Anthony O'Hare."

Melissa looks blank. Ellie realizes, with shame, that the features editor has no idea who he is either.

"The chief librarian. He works downstairs. Used to."

"The one with the gray hair?"

"Yes."

"Oh." She's so taken aback that she briefly forgets to be annoyed with Ellie. "Wow," she says, after a minute. "Who'd have thought?"

"I know."

They mull this over in almost companionable silence until Melissa, perhaps remembering herself, shuffles papers on her desk. "Fascinating as that may be, though, Ellie, it doesn't get us past a very big problem. Which is that we now have a commemorative issue, which needs to go to print this evening, with a great big two-thousand-word hole where the lead feature should be."

"No," says Ellie. "There's not."

"Not your thing about the language of love. I'm not having a recycled-books piece in our—"

"No," says Ellie, again. "I've done it. Two thousand wholly original words, on the last letters of people's love affairs. Here. Let me know if you think it needs rejigging. Are you okay if I pop out for an hour?" She has begged them from her friends, relatives, friends of relatives, from the problem pages of her own newspaper. They are funny, sad, and in two particular cases, heartbreaking. It is a heartfelt paean to the lost art of letter writing, and to lost love.

She's stumped Melissa. She hands over the pages, watches the editor scan the first, her eyes lighting as they do when she reads something that interests her. "What? Yes. Fine. Whatever. Make sure you're back for conference."

Ellie fights the urge to punch the air as she walks out of the office. It's not that hard: she finds it almost impossible to move her arms emphatically while balancing on high heels.

She had e-mailed him the previous evening, and he had agreed without demur. It's not his kind of place; he's all gastropub and smart, discreet restaurant. Giorgio's, across the road from the *Nation*, does egg, chips, and bacon of unknown provenance for £2.99.

When she arrives, he is already sitting at a table, oddly out of place among the construction workers in his Paul Smith jacket and soft, pale shirt. "I'm sorry," he says, even before she sits down. "I'm so sorry. She had my phone. I thought I'd lost it. She got hold of a couple of e-mails I hadn't deleted and found your name . . . the rest . . ."

"She'd have made a good journalist."

He looks briefly distracted, waves the waitress over, and orders another coffee. His thoughts are elsewhere. "Yes. Yes, I suppose she would."

She sits and allows herself to examine the man opposite, a man who has haunted her dreams. His suntan doesn't hide the mauve shadows under his eyes. She wonders absently what had happened the previous evening.

"Ellie, I think it would be a good idea if we lay low. Just for a couple of months."

"No."

"What?"

"That's it, John."

He's not as surprised as she'd thought he'd be.

He considers her words before he replies. Then, "You want . . . are you saying you want to end this?"

"Well, let's face it, we're not some great love story, are we?" Despite herself, she's dismayed at his failure to protest.

"I do care about you, Ellie."

"But not enough. You're not interested in me, in my life. In our lives. I don't think you know anything about me."

"I know everything I need to—"

"What was the name of my first pet?"

"What?"

"Alf. Alf was my hamster. Where did I grow up?"

"I don't know why you're asking me this."

"What have you ever wanted from me, other than sex?"

He looks around. The builders at the table behind them have gone suspiciously quiet.

"Who was my first boyfriend? What's my favorite food?"

"This is ridiculous." He compresses his lips in an expression she has never seen before.

"No. You have no interest in me, apart from how quickly I can get my clothes off."

"Is that what you think?"

"Have you ever cared about anything I've felt? What I've been through?"

His hands lift in exasperation. "Jesus Christ, Ellie, don't paint yourself as some kind of victim here. Don't act as if I'm some villainous seducer," he says. "When did you ever talk to me about feelings? When did you ever tell me this wasn't what you wanted? You made out you were some kind of modern woman. Sex on demand. Career first. You were"—he fumbles for the right word—"impenetrable."

The word is strangely hurtful. "I was protecting myself."

"And I'm supposed to know that by osmosis? How is that being truthful?" He appears genuinely shocked.

"I just wanted to be with you."

"But you wanted more—a relationship."

"Yes."

He studies her, as if he's seeing her for the first time. "You were hoping I'd leave my wife."

"Of course I was. Eventually. I thought if I told you how I really felt, you'd—you'd leave me."

Behind them, the builders begin to talk again. She can see from the surreptitious glances that they are the topic of conversation.

He runs a hand through his sandy hair. "Ellie," he says, "I'm sorry. If I'd thought you couldn't handle this, I would never have got into it in the first place."

And there's the truth of it. The thing she has hidden from herself for a whole year.

"That's just it, isn't it?" She gets up to go. The world has fallen in, and, weirdly, she's stepping out of the rubble. Still upright. Unbloodied. "You and I," she says. "It's ironic, given what we do for a living, but we never actually told each other anything at all."

She stands outside the café, feeling the cold air tighten her skin, the smells of the city in her nostrils, and pulls her mobile phone from her bag. She types a question, sends it, and without waiting for a reply, sets off across the road. She doesn't look back.

Melissa passes her in the lobby, her heels clicking neatly on the polished marble. She's talking to the executive editor but breaks off as she passes Ellie. She nods, hair bouncing around her shoulders. "I liked it."

Ellie releases a breath she hadn't known she was holding.

"Yes. I liked it a lot. Cover front, Sunday for Monday. More, please." And then she's in the lift, back in conversation, the doors closing behind her.

The library is empty. She pushes the swing door to find that only a few dusty shelves are left standing. No periodicals, no magazines, no battered volumes of *Hansard*. She listens to the ticking of the boiler pipes that run along the ceiling, then climbs over the counter, leaving her bag on the floor.

The first chamber, the one that had held almost a century's worth of bound copies of the *Nation*, is entirely empty, aside from two cardboard boxes in the corner. It feels cavernous. Her feet echo on the tiled floor as she makes her way toward the center.

Cuttings Room A to M is empty, too, except for the shelving units. The windows, set six feet above the floor, send glittering dust motes swirling around her as she moves. Although there are no newspapers here now, the air is suffused with the biscuity smell of old paper. She thinks, fancifully, that she can almost hear the echoes of past stories hanging in the air, a hundred thousand voices, no longer heard. Lives moved, lost, twisted by fate. Hidden within files that may remain unseen for another hundred years. She wonders which other Anthonys and Jennifers are buried in those pages, their lives waiting to be swung by some accident or coincidence. A padded swivel chair in the corner is labeled "Digital Archive," and she walks over to it, swinging it one way and then the other.

She is suddenly, ridiculously tired, as if the adrenaline that had fueled her for the last few hours has drained away. She sits down heavily in the warmth and the silence, and for the first time she can remember, Ellie is still. Everything inside her is still. She lets out a long breath.

She doesn't know how long she has been asleep when she hears the door click.

Anthony O'Hare is holding up her bag. "Is this yours?"

She pushes herself upright, disoriented and a little giddy. For a moment she can't work out where she is. "God. Sorry." She rubs her face.

"You won't find much here," he says, handing it to her. He takes in her rumpled air, her sleep-shrunk eyes. "It's all in the new building now. I've just come back to collect the last of the tea things. And that chair."

"Yes . . . comfy. Too good to leave . . . Oh, God, what's the time?"

"Quarter to eleven."

"Conference is at eleven. I'm fine. Conference is at eleven." She's babbling, casting around her for nonexistent belongings. Then remembers why she's there. She tries to gather her thoughts, but she doesn't know how to say what she must to this man. She glances surreptitiously at him, seeing someone else behind the gray hair, the melancholy eyes. She sees him through his words now.

She gathers her bag to her. "Um . . . is Rory around?"

Rory will know. Rory will know what to do.

His smile is a mute apology, an acknowledgment of what they both know. "I'm afraid he's not in today. He's probably at home preparing."

"Preparing?"

"For his grand tour? You did know he's going away?"

"I'd kind of hoped he wouldn't. Not just yet." She reaches into her bag and scribbles a note. "I don't suppose . . . you have his address?"

"If you want to step into what remains of my office, I'll dig it out for you. I don't think he leaves for a week or so."

As he turns away, her breath catches in her throat. "Actually, Mr. O'Hare, it's not just Rory I wanted to see."

"Oh?" She can see his surprise at her use of his name.

She pulls the folder from her bag and holds it toward him. "I found something of yours. A few weeks ago. I would have given them back earlier, but I just . . . I didn't know they were yours until last night." She watches as he opens copies of the letters. His face alters as he recognizes his own handwriting.

"Where did you get these?" he says.

"They were here," she says tentatively, afraid of what this information will do to him.

"Here?"

"Buried. In your library."

He glances around him, as if these empty shelves can provide some clue to what she's saying.

"I'm sorry. I know they're . . . personal."

"How did you know they were mine?"

"It's a long story." Her heart is beating rapidly. "But you need to know something. Jennifer Stirling left her husband the day after she saw you in 1964. She came here, to the newspaper offices, and they told her you'd gone to Africa."

He is so still. Every part of him is focused on her words. He is almost vibrating, so intently is he listening.

"She tried to find you. She tried to tell you that she was . . . she was free." She's a little frightened by the effect this information seems to have on Anthony. The color has drained from his face. He sits down on the chair, his breath coming hard. But she can't stop now.

"This is all . . . ," he begins, his expression troubled, so different from Jennifer's barely disguised delight. "This is all from so long ago."

"I haven't finished," she says. "Please."

He waits.

"These are copies. That's because I had to return the originals. I had to give them back." She holds out the PO box number, her hand trembling, either from nervousness or excitement.

She had received a text message two minutes before she went down to the library:

No he isn't married. What kind of question is that?

"I don't know what your situation is. I don't know if I'm being horribly intrusive. Perhaps I'm making the most awful mistake. But this is the address, Mr. O'Hare," she says. He takes it from her. "This is where you write to."

Chapter 27

Dear Jennifer?
    *Is this really you? Forgive me. I have tried to write this a dozen times
and I don't know what to say.*

    Anthony O'Hare

Ellie tidies the notes on her desk, turns off her screen, and, closing her
bag, makes her way out of Features, mouthing a silent good-bye at
Rupert. He is hunched over an interview with an author who, he has
complained all afternoon, is as dull as ditchwater. She has filed the
story about surrogate mothers, and tomorrow she will travel to Paris
to interview a Chinese charity worker who is not allowed to return to
her home country because of controversial comments she made in a
British documentary. As she wedges herself into the crowded bus
home, her mind is on the background information she has gathered
for the piece, already organizing it into paragraphs. It feels good to be
thinking this way again.

On Saturday she will meet Corinne and Nicky at a restaurant none
of them can really afford. They will not talk about John, Ellie has
decided; it is the first relationship she has ever ended that she does not
feel the urge to dissect for hours afterward.

"I see his latest book got a terrible review," Corinne says when Ellie answers her phone. Corinne rings her most evenings. Ellie knows it's just to make sure she's okay. She doesn't know how to make her friends believe her when she says she's fine.

"I hadn't noticed."

She tidies her flat as she talks, the receiver wedged between chin and shoulder. She has decided to redecorate. She has been emptying her home of clutter, driving to and from the dump with the detritus of several years stuffed into cardboard boxes. She is unsentimental about what she throws away.

Corinne sniffs. "'Unconvincing dialogue,' apparently. Personally I always found his stuff very derivative."

Ellie empties a drawer into a black garbage bag as Corinne talks. She has specifically asked not to write for Books just now.

Dear Anthony,

Yes, it is me. Whatever me is, compared to the girl you knew. I'm guessing you know our journalist friend has spoken to me by now. I'm still struggling to comprehend what she has told me.

But in the Post Office box this morning, there was your letter. With the sight of your handwriting, forty years fell away. Does that make sense? The time that has passed shrank to nothing. I can barely believe I'm holding what you wrote two days ago, can hardly believe what it means.

She has told me a little about you. I sat and wondered, and hardly dared think that I may get the chance to sit and talk to you.

I pray that you are happy.

Jennifer

It's the upside of newspapers: your writing stock can rise stratospherically, twice as quickly as it fell. Two good stories and you can be the talk of the newsroom, the center of chatter and admiration. Your story will be reproduced on the Internet, syndicated to other publications in New York, Australia, South Africa. They liked the letters piece, Syndication told her. Exactly the kind of thing they can find a market for. Within forty-eight hours she has had e-mails and a few handwritten letters from readers, confiding their own stories. Within a week, a literary agent has rung, wondering if she has enough of the letters to turn into a book. They have penciled in a date for lunch.

Melissa wants a follow-up feature, using the new material. It is, she says, the perfect example of connecting with your readers. She uses the words "interactivity" and "added value." As far as Melissa's concerned, Ellie is back in the game. She suggests Ellie's name in conference when someone mentions an idea that needs a good thousand words. Twice, this week, her short features have crossed to the front page. It's the newspaper staffer's equivalent of winning the lottery. Her increased visibility means she's more in demand. She sees stories everywhere. She's magnetic: contacts, features, fly to her. She's at her desk by nine, works till late in the evening. This time, she knows not to waste it.

Her space on the great oval desk is gleaming and white, and on it sits a seventeen-inch nongloss high-resolution screen, and a telephone with her name, clearly marked, on the extension number.

Rupert no longer offers to make her tea.

Dear Jennifer,

I apologize for this tardy reply. Please excuse what may seem to you like reticence. I have not put pen to paper for many years, except to pay bills or record some complaint. I don't think I know what to say. For decades now I have lived only through other people's words; I reorder them, archive them, duplicate and rank them. I keep them safe. I suspect I have long forgotten my own. The author of those letters seems like a stranger to me.

You sound so different from the girl I saw at the Regent Hotel. And yet, in all the best ways, you are so evidently the same. I am glad you are well. I am glad I have had the chance to tell you this. I would ask to meet

you, but I am afraid you would find me much removed from the man
you remember. I don't know.

Forgive me.

Anthony

Several days previously Ellie had heard her name shouted a little
breathlessly as she made her way down the stairs of the old building
for the last time. She had turned to find Anthony O'Hare at the top.
He was holding out a piece of paper bearing a scribbled address.

She had skipped up again, to save him further effort.

"I was thinking, Ellie Haworth," he said, and his voice was full of
joy, trepidation, and regret, "don't send a letter. It's probably better if
you just, you know, go and see him. In person."

Dearest, dearest Boot,

My voice has exploded in me! I feel I have lived half a century not
being able to speak. All has been damage limitation, an attempt to carve
out what was good from what felt destroyed, ruined. My own silent
penitence for what I had done. And now . . . now? I have talked poor
Ellie Haworth's ear off until she stares at me in stunned silence and I can
see her thinking: Where is the dignity in this old woman? How can she
sound so like a fourteen-year-old? I want to talk to you, Anthony. I
want to talk to you until our voices croak and we can barely speak. I have
forty years of talking to do.

How can you say you don't know? It cannot be fear. How could I
be disappointed in you? After all that has happened, how could I feel
anything other than acute joy at simply being able to see you again? My
hair is silver, not blond. The lines on my face are emphatic, determined
things. I ache, I rattle with supplements, and my grandchildren cannot
believe I have ever been anything but prehistoric.

We are old, Anthony. Yes. And we do not have another forty years.
If you are still in there, if you are prepared to allow me to paint over the

vision you might hold of the girl you once knew, I will happily do the same
for you.

Jennifer X

Jennifer Stirling is standing in the middle of the room, wearing a dressing gown, her hair standing up on one side. "Look at me," she says despairingly. "What a fright. What an absolute fright. I couldn't sleep last night, and then I finally dropped off some time after five and I slept right through my alarm and missed my hair appointment."

Ellie is staring at her. She has never seen her look like this. Anxiety radiates from her. Without makeup her skin looks childlike, her face vulnerable. "You—you look fine."

"I rang my daughter last night, you know, and I told her a little of it. Not all. I told her I was due to meet a man I had once loved and hadn't seen since I was a girl. Was that a terrible lie?"

"No," says Ellie.

"You know what she e-mailed me this morning? This." She thrusts a printed sheet, a facsimile from an American newspaper, about a couple from New Jersey who married after a fifty-year gap in their relationship. "What am I supposed to do with that? Have you ever seen anything so ridiculous?" Her voice crackles with nerves.

"What time are you meeting him?"

"Midday. I'll never be ready. I should cancel."

Ellie gets up and puts the kettle on. "Go and get dressed. You've got forty minutes. I'll drive you," she says.

"You think I'm ridiculous, don't you?" It's the first time she has seen Jennifer Stirling look anything other than the most composed woman in the entire universe. "A ridiculous old woman. Like a teenager on her first date."

"No," says Ellie.

"It was fine when it was just letters," Jennifer says, barely hearing her. "I could be myself. I could be this person he remembered. I was so calm and reassuring. And now . . . The one consolation I have had in all of this was knowing there was this man out there who loved me, who saw the best in me. Even through the awfulness of our last meeting I've known that in me he saw something he wanted more than anything else in the world. What if he looks at me and is disappointed? It'll be worse than if we'd never met again. *Worse*."

"Show me the letter," Ellie says.

"I can't do this. Don't you think that sometimes it's better not to do something?"

"The letter, Jennifer."

Jennifer picks it up from the sideboard, holds it for a moment, then offers it to her.

> *Dearest Jennifer,*
>
> *Are old men supposed to cry? I sit here reading and rereading the letter you sent, and I struggle to believe that my life has taken such an unexpected, joyous turn. Things like this are not meant to happen to us. I had learned to feel gratitude for the most mundane gifts: my son, his children, a good life, if quietly lived. Survival. Oh, yes, always survival.*
>
> *And now you. Your words, your emotions, have induced a greed in me. Can we ask for so much? Do I dare see you again? The Fates have been so unforgiving, some part of me believes that we cannot meet. I'll be felled by illness, hit by a bus, swallowed whole by the Thames's first sea monster. (Yes, I still see life in headlines.)*
>
> *The last two nights I have heard your words in my sleep. I hear your voice, and it makes me want to sing. I remember things I'd thought I'd forgotten. I smile at inopportune moments, frightening my family and sending them running for the dementia diagnosis.*
>
> *The girl I saw last was so broken; to know that you made such a life for yourself has challenged my own view of the world. It must be a benevolent place. It has taken care of you and your daughter. You cannot imagine the joy that has given me. Vicariously. I cannot write more. So I venture, with trepidation: Postman's Park. Thursday. Midday?*
>
> *Your Boot X*

Ellie's eyes have filled with tears. "You know what?" she says. "I really don't think you need to worry."

Anthony O'Hare sits on a bench in a park he hasn't visited for almost forty-four years with a newspaper he won't read and realizes, with surprise, that he can recall the details of every commemorative tile.

> Mary Rogers, stewardess of the *Stella*, self-sacrificed by
> giving up her life-belt and voluntarily going down in
> the sinking ship.

> William Drake lost his life in averting a serious accident
> to a lady in Hyde Park whose horses were unmanageable
> through the breaking of the carriage pole.

> Joseph Andrew Ford, saved six persons from a fire in
> Grays Inn Road but in his last heroic act he was
> scorched to death.

He has been sitting here since eleven forty. It is now seven minutes past twelve.

He lifts his watch to his ear and shakes it. Deep in his heart he didn't believe this could happen. How could it? If you spend long enough in a newspaper archive, you see that the same stories repeated themselves over and over again: wars, famines, financial crises, loves lost, families divided. Death. Heartbreak. There are few happy endings. Everything I have had has been a bonus, he tells himself firmly, as the minutes creep past. It is a phrase that, over the years, has become achingly familiar to him.

The rain is heavier and the little park has emptied. Only he is sitting in the shelter. In the distance he sees the main road, the cars sluicing their way along, sending sprays of water across the unwary.

It is a quarter past twelve.

Anthony O'Hare reminds himself of all the reasons he should feel grateful. His doctor is amazed he is alive at all. Anthony suspects he has long sought to use him as a cautionary tale to other patients with liver damage. His rude health is a rebuke to the doctor's authority, to medical science. He wonders, briefly, whether he might indeed travel. He doesn't want to revisit Congo, but South Africa would be interesting. Maybe Kenya. He will go home and make plans. He will give himself something to think about.

He hears the screeching brakes of a bus, the shout of an angry bicycle courier. It's enough to know that she had loved him. That she was happy. That had to be enough, didn't it? Surely one of the gifts of old age was meant to be the ability to put things in perspective. He had once loved a woman who turned out to have loved him more than he'd known. There. That should be enough for him.

It is twenty-one minutes past twelve.

And then, as he is about to stand up, fold his newspaper under his arm, and head for home, he sees that a small car has stopped near the gates of the park. He waits, shielded from view by the gloom of the little shelter.

There is a slight delay. Then the door opens and an umbrella shoots open with an audible whoosh. It is up, and he can see a pair of legs beneath it, a dark mackintosh. As he watches, the figure ducks to say something to the driver, and the legs walk into the park and along the narrow pathway, making straight for the shelter.

Anthony O'Hare finds he's standing up, straightening his jacket and smoothing his hair. He can't take his eyes off those shoes, the distinctive upright walk, visible despite the umbrella. He takes a step forward, not sure what he'll say, what he'll do. His heart has lodged somewhere near his mouth. There is singing in his ears. The feet, clad in dark tights, stop in front of him. The umbrella lifts slowly. And there she is, still the same, startlingly, ridiculously the same, a smile playing at the corners of her lips as her eyes meet his. He cannot speak. He can only stare, as her name rings in his ears.

Jennifer.

"Hello, Boot," she says.

Ellie sits in the car and wipes the steam from the passenger window with her sleeve. She's parked on a red route, no doubt drawing down the wrath of the parking gods, but she doesn't care. She can't move.

She watches Jennifer's steady progress down the path, sees the slight hesitation in her step that tells of her fears. Twice the older woman had insisted they return home, that they were too late, that all was lost, useless. Ellie had pretended to be deaf. Sang *lalalalalalala* until Jennifer Stirling told her, with uncharacteristic crossness, that she was an "interminable, ridiculous" girl.

She watches Jennifer moving forward under her umbrella and is afraid that she'll turn and run away. This thing has shown her that age is no protection against the hazards of love. She has listened to Jennifer's words, spinning wildly between triumph and disaster, and heard her own endless analyses of John's words, her own desperate need for something that was so transparently wrong to be right. Her own conjuring of outcomes, emotions, from words whose meanings she could only guess at.

But Anthony O'Hare is a different creature.

She wipes the window again and sees Jennifer slow, then stop. And he is stepping out of the shadows, taller somehow than he had appeared before, stooping slightly at the shelter's entrance before he stands squarely before her. They face each other, the slim woman in the mackintosh and the librarian. Even from this distance Ellie can see they are now oblivious to the rain, to the neat little park, to the curious eyes of observers. Their eyes have locked, and they stand as if they could stand there for a thousand years. Jennifer lets her umbrella fall, dips her head to one side, such a small movement, and lifts her hand tenderly to his face. As Ellie watches, Anthony's own hand lifts and presses her palm against his skin.

Ellie Haworth watches a moment longer, then moves away from the window, lets the steam obscure the view. She shuffles over to the driving seat, blows her nose, and starts the engine. The best journalists know when to bow out of a story.

The house is in a Victorian terraced street, its windows and doorways iced in white masonry, the mismatched selection of blinds and curtains telling of the varied ownership within. She turns off the ignition, climbs out of the car, and walks up to the front door, gazing at the names on the two bells. It is only his name on the ground floor. She's a little surprised; she had assumed he wouldn't own a flat outright. But then, what does she know of his life before the newspaper? Nothing at all.

The article is in a large brown envelope, with his name on the front. She pushes it through the door, letting the letterbox clap loudly. She walks back to the front gate, climbs up, and sits on the brick pillar that supports it, her scarf pulled up around her face. She has become very good at sitting. She has discovered there is joy in letting the world move around her. It does so in the most unexpected ways.

"You spelled my name wrong. It's R-u-a-r-i-d-h."

She glances behind her, and he's propped against the door frame, the newspaper in his hand. "I got a lot of things wrong."

He is wearing the same long-sleeved T-shirt he had on the first time they spoke, soft from years of use. She remembers she liked the way he wasn't fussy about his clothes. She knows how that T-shirt feels under her fingers.

"Nice piece," he says, holding the newspaper up. "'Dear John: Fifty Years of Love's Last Letters.' I see you're the golden girl of Features again."

"For now. Actually," she says, "there's one in there that I wrote myself. It's something I would have said. Had I had the chance."

It's as if he hasn't heard her. "And Jennifer let you use that Paddington letter."

"Anonymously. Yes. She was great. I told her the whole thing, and she was great." His face is even, untroubled.

Did you hear what I said? she asks him silently. "I think she was a little shocked, admittedly, but after everything that had happened, I don't think she cared what I did."

She stands there as he gazes at the article in his hands. "'I was once told by someone wise that writing is perilous, as you can't always guarantee your words will be read in the spirit in which they were written. So I'm going to be straightforward. I'm sorry. Forgive me. If there is any way I can change your opinion of me, please let me know.'" They had been the easiest words to write in the whole piece.

He folds the newspaper. "Anthony came here yesterday. He's like a different man. I don't know why he came. I think he just wanted to talk to someone." He nods to himself, remembering. "He was wearing a new shirt and tie. And he'd had a haircut."

The thought makes her smile, despite herself.

In the silence, Rory stretches on the step, his hands linked above his head. "It's a nice thing you did."

"I hope so," she says. "It would be nice to think that someone got a happy ending."

An old man walks past with a cane, the tip of his nose the color of red grapes, and all three murmur a greeting. When she looks up, Rory is looking at his feet. She watches him, wondering if this is the last time she will see him. *I'm sorry*, she tells him silently.

"I'd invite you in," he says, "but I'm packing. Got a lot to do." He places the folded newspaper under his arm.

She lifts a hand, trying not to let her disappointment show. She climbs down off the pillar, the fabric of her trousers catching slightly on the rough surface, and hoists her bag onto her shoulder. She can't feel her feet.

"So . . . was there something you wanted? Other than to, you know, play papergirl?"

It's turning cold. She shoves her hands into her pockets. He's looking at her expectantly. She's afraid to speak. If he says no, she's afraid of how crushed she'll feel. It's why it's taken her days to come here. But what does she have to lose? She's never going to see him again.

She takes a deep breath. "I wanted to know . . . if you might write to me."

"*Write* to you?"

"While you're away. Look, I screwed up. I can't ask anything of you, but I miss you. I really miss you. I'd—I'd just like to think that this wasn't it. That we might"—she fidgets, rubs her nose—"write."

"Write."

"Just . . . stuff. What you're doing. How it's all going. Where you are." The words sound feeble to her ears.

He has wedged his hands into his pockets and peers down the street. He doesn't answer. The silence is as long as the street. "It's freezing," he says eventually.

Something large and heavy has settled in the pit of her stomach. Their story is over. He doesn't have anything left to say to her. He glances behind him apologetically. "I'm letting all the heat out of the house."

She can't speak. She shrugs, as if in agreement, engineers a smile that she suspects looks like more of a grimace. As she turns away, she hears his voice again.

"I suppose you could come in and make me a coffee. While I'm sorting my socks. Actually, you owe me a coffee, if I remember rightly."

When she turns back, his face has thawed. Actual warmth is still some degrees away, but it's definitely there. "Perhaps you could run your eye over my Peruvian visa while you're at it. Check I've spelled it all correctly."

She lets her eyes rest on him now, on his socked feet, his too-long-to-be-tidy brown hair. "You wouldn't want to confuse your Patallacta with your Phuyupatamarca," she says.

He raises his eyes to the heavens, slowly shaking his head. And, trying to hide her beaming smile, Ellie steps in behind him.